Enc
WHEN MOI

MW00615166

If you are a fan of Kurt Vonnegut's novels, there is good news for you all. Jon Sorensen will likely be hailed universally as the new Vonnegut with the appearance of his debut novel, "When Mommy Was A Commie." Full of colorful characters, wacky situations and make-you-laugh-out-loud writing, this is a book that will keep you reading for "just another page" and then "just another chapter." It will all be over much too quickly.

MARC HUMBERT, NEW YORK STATE CHIEF POLITICAL WRITER
FOR *THE ASSOCIATED PRESS* FOR 25 YEARS (RETIRED)

. . . .

Jon Sorensen has set us up for a joyride of reading, taking us into a Schenectady, New York of commies and come-ons, where the men have big hair and the women have big plans for America. Who knew that the Electric City was such a live wire and hotbed of subversive activity and who knew it could all be so much damn fun?

MARION ROACH SMITH, AUTHOR,
*THE MEMOIR PROJECT, A THOROUGHLY
NON-STANDARDIZED TEXT FOR WRITING & LIFE*

. . . .

Jon Sorensen's novel accurately captures both the pervasive fear and absurdity of an America struggling to grapple with Communism. He tells the story with a sense of humor and the knowledge that the world his characters live in is not too far removed from our present moment. This hilarious trip through Cold War Schenectady serves as a cautionary tale for those who would be King.

JACOB HOUSER, AUTHOR,
WHEN THE WORLD SEEMED NEW: UE LOCAL 301
AND THE DECLINE OF THE AMERICAN LABOR MOVEMENT

WHEN MOMMY WAS A COMMIE

WAS A COMMIE

novel by
JON SORENSEN

COVER ARTWORK BY Alex Hughes | alexdrawsyou@gmail.com
BOOK DESIGN BY Meradith Kill | The Troy Book Makers

Excerpts from *Witness* by Whitaker Chambers are reprinted with permission from Regnery Publishing.

An excerpt from *Security, Loyalty, and Science* by Walter Gellhorn is reprinted with permission from Cornell University Press.

Excerpts from *Joe McCarthy and the Press* by Edwin Bayley are reprinted with permission from The University of Wisconsin Press.

Printed in the United States of America

The Troy Book Makers • Troy, New York • thetroybookmakers.com

To order additional copies of this title,
contact your favorite local bookstore
or visit www.shoptbmbooks.com

ISBN: 978-1-61468-743-6

FOR CATE TULLY,
MY WIFE, MY LOVE

Not a day goes by ...

"While I cannot take the time to name all of the men in the State Department who have been named as members of the Communist Party and members of a spy ring, I have in my hand here a list of 205 that were known to the Secretary of State as being members of the Communist Party and who, nevertheless, are still working and shaping the policy in the State Department."

        SENATOR JOSEPH MCCARTHY ✳ *WHEELING, WEST VIRGINIA* ✳ *FEB. 9, 1950*

FOUR ✳ The number of "Communists" McCarthy could identify just 48 hours after claiming to have a list of 205. Of those four, one never worked for the State Department, while two others had retired.

C H A P T E R   O N E

SCHENECTADY NOIR, 1954:
the End of Joe McCarthy

He never thought it would get this big: the daily newspaper headlines and nightly news cameras, civic awards and testimonial dinners. There were envelopes stuffed with cash. Phone numbers scribbled onto perfumed pieces of paper, slipped into his pocket "from your biggest fan!" Gold Star Mothers were baking him cookies, cakes, and pies. People even named their kids after him – years after they were born!

Then somebody nailed a rat to his door.

The final surprise was a few nights later when a fat revolver came swinging toward his face. Closing his eyes, he braced for a slug to the nose until the gun stopped in mid-air. He slowly opened one eye and there, glistening in the moonlight, was the muzzle of stainless steel, stained with somebody else's blood.

For no good reason, he stepped toward the gun. Maybe he could scare 'em off – act like the tough guy – when all he wanted to do was run. Now the cold, hard barrel was pressed between his bloodshot eyeballs.

Shot and bloody: this was no way to die. Not for somebody like him.

But he was a big talker, he always had something to say. It had gotten him in and out of trouble before. So why not this time – big mouth versus big gun?

This time was different. He was cornered at the hot end of a loaded gun. It was too close, too sudden.

Too late.

Just a squeeze of the trigger and there would be no time left for another speech, no more autographs or sweaty handshakes at the Fourth of July barbeque. His days of kissing babies were through. He just didn't know it yet. Nerve pulses were still racing from synapse to synapse, straining to shout something – *do anything* – before the bullet smashed a hole through that thick skull.

Did he want to ask … why?

No, he wasn't stupid. He already knew why.

Everybody wanted him dead.

Only the cops had questions now. They were far off the road, searching for clues, when they heard the muffled thud of a car door slamming shut.

"Finally!" groused one of the patrolmen, shivering from the cold. "Meat wagon's here!"

Seconds later, the sound of footsteps came out of the darkness. Squishing through the mud and snow, they moved quickly toward the two detectives, the four patrolmen, and the one dead body gathered on the south shore of the Mohawk River.

A couple of yards off the road, where the hillside gets steeper, the footsteps started moving faster – and then faster – until the noise stopped and the ground shook as something heavy came sliding through the snow. The cops smiled at each other as filthy obscenities drifted over their heads and down toward the ice cold river. The patrolmen turned their flashlights toward the noise, the beams bobbing unsteadily through the dark, catching glimpses of two shiny black boots, a red silk shirt, and then a tall, furry hat moving in and out of the light. Finally, the cops were able to fix their lights on a single spot – the red, scowling face of Connor McGuire, Schenectady's Chief of Police.

"Get those goddamned lights outta my eyes!" the Chief hollered. The officers quickly lowered their flashlights as the big-bottomed cop struggled out of the chest-high cattails. Chief McGuire was breathing hard from his trek through the snow, but also from panic. He had raced out from police headquarters overwhelmed by a single thought: Was this the body of Joe McCarthy?

The Chief frantically pushed the patrolmen aside. "Get outta my way! Let me see him, goddammit!" McGuire grabbed a flashlight and found what he was looking for.

"Oh thank you Jesus," the Chief exhaled and quickly blessed himself. This wasn't Joe McCarthy after all – just an unlucky stiff with a bald head and a bullet hole gouged through his face.

McGuire's relief did not last long. Senator Joseph R. McCarthy, the most famous and most hated politician in America, was still missing. No one had seen him for the past six hours. Meanwhile, half the city of Schenectady was looking like a complete madhouse, still in the midst of its "Red Scare Days."

Now this – a dead body by the river. What the hell is next, McGuire fumed, and where the hell is McCarthy?

As the Chief stood up, his tall Cossack hat was the first thing to emerge from the circle of cops, like a fuzzy missile slowly rising out of the ground. McGuire heard the cops snickering and he knew instantly that this had been a mistake. He should have changed his clothes, or at least put on a coat, before he rushed out of the station. Now he was standing before his men dressed as a Russian security officer – puffy riding breeches, a Red Star medal pinned to his chest, and the fireplug hat to top it off. He looked and felt ridiculous.

The mayor had begged him to wear the Commissar costume and after weeks of pestering McGuire finally agreed – but only for "Commietown," the day when every idiot in Schenectady would be dressed up like a Communist. The Chief tugged at the velvet sash tied around his gut when one of the cops asked, "Should we call Moscow, Chief?" McGuire pretended not to hear the wisecrack as Detective Flanagan leaned in close and whispered, "You've got something on your face."

McGuire reached up and felt the fake mustache turned awkwardly on his upper lip. He grimaced and ripped away the phony whiskers, bringing more laughter from his men.

"All right, knock it off," the Chief growled. "Anybody thinks a dead body is funny can spend the rest of the night searchin' the river!"

"Inspector Volk is down there now, Chief," one of the patrolmen offered.

McGuire wasn't listening. He tilted his head to one side examining the small man stretched out in the blood-drenched snow, his arms spread like wings and his eyes staring past the stars. The patrolmen took a step back as McGuire circled the body.

"How long has he been here?" the Chief snapped.

Detective Flanagan tried to lift one of the dead man's arms. "At least a day, Chief. The body is getting – "

"VOLK?!" McGuire shouted into the air. "Where the hell is Volk?"

Wotan Volk was Schenectady's Chief of Detectives. (Chief *Inspector* Volk, he always insisted.) McGuire knew how much he depended on Volk, especially on a case like this one. Volk knew it too.

The Chief looked helplessly into the night. There was no sense calling his name. Volk would come when he was damn good and ready.

"Never mind him," McGuire snarled. "What else we got?"

Flanagan tipped his flashlight toward the disfigured face of the dead man. "He was plugged once – to the face, obviously. The shooter was pretty close. There are some signs of a struggle so it might have been an ambush or maybe this guy knew the shooter."

"What the hell are they doin' down here?" McGuire said, lifting his head toward the sound of the river lapping the shore. This was a remote corner of General Electric's manufacturing plant – so remote there was not even a fence around it.

McGuire sighed. "So that's all we got? No gun, no wallet? Keys?"

"Nothing yet," Flanagan said. "We'll have better luck in the daylight."

"Christ, of all the nights. Of all the goddamned nights!" The Chief took off his hat and rubbed the sweat from his bald dome. "Look, I gotta get back to this crap downtown. When you see Volk, tell him to meet me at City Hall – right away! Until then, we keep this quiet, understand? I don't want nobody talkin' about a murder until I find out where McCar … Never mind. Just keep quiet – and tell Volk to hurry it up!"

The cops smiled at each other again. Who was stupid enough to tell Wotan Volk to "hurry it up?" Inspector Volk stood six foot four and weighed nearly 300 pounds. The Chief called him "a Frigidaire with a head," but never to his face. Volk was touchy that way.

As McGuire turned to leave, he felt the moist night air on his head.

"You dropped your hat, Chief," a patrolman said. The "Commissar" snatched it up, muttering to himself as he struggled up the hill.

"Hey Chief!" another patrolman called. The cop had seen something familiar about the dead man: on the right side of his head, there was a small ball of twisted flesh where his ear should have been. "I know this guy! It's Arthur Klingman. He writes that Commie newspaper for the union!"

The Chief did not turn around. He just waved his flashlight and kept on walking.

Great, McGuire sighed. A union guy murdered on the night everybody is chasing Commie lunatics like Arthur Klingman.

At the top of the hill, McGuire leaned against his squad car, struggling to catch his breath. He looked back down the hill, knowing he should stay and search for the killer, but there wasn't time for that, not on this night.

McGuire pulled off the Cossack hat and slumped behind the wheel. He wanted to sleep, needed to sleep, but something else was nagging at him. Something was missing and it wasn't just McCarthy.

There it was.

Reaching for his keys, McGuire felt the sticky strip of mustache hair stuck deep inside his pocket. He pulled himself up to the mirror and pressed the bushy, black mustache into place.

"Should we call Moscow, Chief?" McGuire said mockingly into the mirror. With a last look of disgust, he shoved the mirror aside and started the car.

Pulling away from the river, the Chief tried to organize a list of likely suspects. It would be a short list because this was a highly unlikely murder. A typical killing in Schenectady was impetuous and unplanned, emotional, messy. The killers were easy to find. The last one happened on the West Side, a 4-19: husband found up to his chest inside an oven with a meat thermometer jammed in his butt. The wife claimed she was "too busy cooking the bastard's dinner" to notice anything unusual.

This killing by the river – a single bullet fired at close range – looked professional. There were only a couple of mugs capable of a tidy hit like this one and they probably had a good reason for doing it. Bad guys shooting bad guys hardly seemed like a crime. As far as McGuire was concerned, it was more like a public service.

If it had been McCarthy, God forbid, there would have been too many suspects to count. Of the thousands of Reds and their fellow travelers – stretching from Maine to California – every one of them was eager to destroy the man who was so utterly dedicated to destroying them. McCarthy would badger them: "Are you now or have you ever been a member of the Communist Party?" The question had ruined more lives than "Will you marry me?"

Joe McCarthy may have been the biggest and most celebrated of the Red Hunters, but he was hardly alone. By 1954, the Red Scare had become a thriving cottage industry. Pundits, politicians, and patriotic vigilantes were doggedly pursuing the Reds no matter where they were hiding. The Commie Hunters, like political entomologists, had compiled exhaustive, unverified lists of every genus and species of Communist: Suspected Communists, Friends of Suspected Communists, Suspected Friends of Suspected Communists, and so on.

In Schenectady, you didn't need a list. The Reds were everywhere, and proud of it.

Everywhere, McGuire sighed. He looked down at his costume again – the puffy pants, the red sash, the silk shirt. The stupid mustache. This time it was turned sideways, a hairy propeller tilted above the Chief's clenched teeth. Tossing it out the window, McGuire slammed a muddy boot on the gas.

He had to get back to Commietown.

"The ordinary American has no idea of the alien world which exists right here in our own country, as exemplified by the Communist Party. Here is a walled-in community, in the midst of free America, whose leadership works secretly in the shadows and is not infrequently dictated to by the secret police or other agents of a foreign government and even threatened on occasion with removal by such police."

EX-COMMUNIST LOUIS BUDENZ ✶ *This is My Story, 1947*

CHAPTER TWO

ONE YEAR EARLIER

It was Thursday night: League Bowling night at The Capri.

Beau Duffy was tying on his bowling shoes when one brown, square-toed boot and then another stepped in front of him, blocking the light and spoiling his good mood.

It was the Morale Coordinator, Helen Gamble.

"*Comrade Doff-fee*," Helen said, clipping her consonants in that strange accent of hers. Strange because this was Schenectady, New York and Helen had lived there her entire life. She had never been farther east than Pittsfield, but now she was talking like a cross between Greta Garbo and Bela Lugosi.

"Go away Helen," Beau said. Helen's big shoes did not move. Beau kept his head down, pretending that the only thing he wanted to strangle were the laces on his bowling shoes.

Helen bent over, hissing in Beau's ear, "*Eet ees time, Comrade Doff-fee. But here you are zitting – always zit, zit, zit!*"

"In a minute, *comrade!*" snapped Beau, snapping a shoelace.

They had known each other since they were kids, back when Beau thought Helen might be his first … kiss? His first girlfriend? Something like that. She was tall and blonde with bright green eyes and a turned-up nose. Even as a kid, Helen was more than just pretty. Twenty years later, she was even more beautiful, except now there was something foreign, even a little sinister, about the girl next door.

She used to be so quiet, always willing to listen to whatever Beau had to say. Now Helen Gamble was just so goddamned pushy, constantly telling people what to do and how to think. Worst of all, she had to do it on League Bowling night!

Helen was wearing another of those shapeless, blue-gray dresses she was always wearing and her hair was bunched underneath a red kerchief. Sliding down her nose was a pair of thick, black-rimmed glasses. She looked like she was ready to milk a goat.

Long gone were those days of puppy love and sweaty palms, holding hands in their secret hiding spot underneath the porch at Beau's house.

First girlfriend – ha! First nut job was more like it. Look at her with that flour-bag dress and those Mister Peepers glasses! And what's with that Russian accent – all those v's and z's popping out of her mouth? The glasses were probably as fake as her accent. What's next? A hairy mole on her upper lip?

Helen made him so mad lately that all Beau wanted to do was punch a hole in something – because all he could think about was Helen Gamble.

Beau Duffy went back to tying his bowling shoes as Helen continued to lurk over him, impatiently tapping one of her clunky shoe-boots.

"*Comrade,*" Helen sighed, "*vee don't have all night, do vee?*"

Beau gritted his teeth. Pressing his fists against his knees, he pushed himself up and out of Helen's shadow, stopping just inches from that perfect face – close enough to smell her, to kiss her lips, to pick her up and carry her away with him. But this was no dream. Beau tried to see beyond his reflection in Helen's Coke-bottle glasses, struggling not to blink, until he found her big, green eyes glaring back at him.

Be cool, Beau reminded himself. You're Beau Duffy. This is your town, not hers.

He reached for a cigarette from the pack he kept rolled in his sleeve. Flipping a Chesterfield into his mouth, Beau casually drew a match across the bottom of his shoe. Then he furrowed his brow like John Garfield would, narrowing his eyes and pressing his lips together for a long, cool drag.

"Listen Princess, I'm not your '*comrade*,' you got that?" Beau flicked some butt ash over her shoulder. Still, Helen would not leave. She was not impressed.

"*I am no Prinz-sess*," Helen sprayed back at him. John Garfield would have slugged her, but all Beau Duffy could do was stand there as the blood came rushing to his face. Their standoff was starting to draw a crowd. Feeling everyone's eyes on him, Beau's mind was getting cloudy, unable to plot an escape. Finally, desperately, he blew a mouthful of smoke into her eyes. Helen tried not to flinch until she had to turn her head away.

"*Hell to you!*" Helen cursed.

"Commie lunatic," Beau shot back.

It was like this every Thursday night. All they did was fight – ever since that summer when Helen went away on "*zee-kret union beez-ness.*" She came back with that stupid accent, the phony glasses, and a new job: Morale Coordinator and Director of the Social Awareness Committee for Local 1389. Everything else was a mystery – where she had been, what she had been doing. All she would say was "*I cannot tuck about eet.*" But all she ever did was *tuck, tuck, tuck.*

She was forever talking about the oppression of the working class, the rights of the workers and the greed of the corporate elite, spreading her Commie bullshit all over town – even on League Bowling night, the one night when Beau and the guys could relax and get away from everything!

And here she was again: creepy Comrade Helen, the great Communist cheerleader. There was no escaping her. She was the Iron Curtain of bowling.

Beau sat back down – disgusted, trapped – just like every other Thursday night. He hung his head and took another drag on his cigarette. When the smoke cleared, his eyes fell upon the cloth patch sewn onto his ruby red bowling shirt – the patch with the cartoon picture of Joseph Stalin shaking hands with Uncle Sam. Uncle Sam looked frail and sickly next to the Russian leader who was radiating vigor and muscular strength. Beau took hold of the shirt and rubbed his chest with the itchy fabric. He hated those damn, Commie bowling shirts.

"*Hurry along zen,*" Helen pestered. "*Ev'ry-vun ees vaiting for you!*"

"Vell!" said Beau, throwing up his hands in mock surprise. "Zen I von't keep zem vaiting, vill I!"

Grinding his cigarette into the floor, Beau casually shuffled to the back of the bar. He was a large man and when he walked Beau lurched from side to side, slowly placing one enormous foot in front of the other. Everyone made room for Big Beau Duffy. But even Beau jumped – just a little – when Helen bellowed across the bowling alley: "*Comrades – PLACES!*"

From one end of The Capri to the other, the members of Local 1389 quickly bunched together like bowling pins at the head of each lane. Beau couldn't watch. These were the toughest guys he knew, but just one word from Helen Gamble and they scattered like frightened mice.

Why are we afraid of this little Commie girl? What the hell has happened to us?

Beau knew it all too well: Comrade Helen is what happened.

He lifted the lid of the record player and dropped the needle onto a well-worn 78. The speakers hissed and popped as somber, military drums slowly rolled out across The Capri. Next came a distant fanfare of trumpets, trombones, and tubas. The music was building, the drums pounding louder, until cymbals crashed and a chorus began to sing:

Arise, you prisoners of starvation!
Arise, you wretched of the earth!
For justice thunders condemnation: A better world's in birth!"

It was "The Internationale," the worldwide anthem of the International Communist Party. Every Thursday night, before the first bowling ball knocked over the first pin, the members of Local 1389 of the Amalgamated Electrical Workers of America stood at attention for the Glorious Anthem of the Workers Revolution.

"We want no condescending saviors to rule us from their judgment hall.
We workers ask not for their favors.
Let us consult for all!"

Helen shouted out the lyrics as Beau and the other bowlers mumbled along. Standing at the top of the stairs, her arms pinwheeling in the air, Helen exhorted the men to *"SINK! Sink louder!"* Most of the guys simply hung their heads in shame, fidgeting with their hands and muttering a few words whenever Helen looked their way. Even when they could remember the words, none of them made any sense.

"Make the thief disgorge his booty to free the spirit from its cell?" What the hell are they talking about? It was typical of the Communists. They were always speaking a language only they could understand, handing out impenetrable pamphlets and strutting around with their posters and banners in countless, pointless parades, shouting clumsy slogans of revolution and workers' rights.

"Decay the imperialists, the war instigators and their base agents!"

"Raise up the toiling masses with Marxian dialectical materialism, internationalism and the general ethics of the new Socialist society!"

All of it was over the bowlers' heads – literally. A huge banner hung from the rafters of The Capri: "Bowlers of the World Unite: You Have Nothing to Lose but Your Lanes!" Helen thought it was funny, but nobody else understood what it meant. Some of the guys even worried that it might be some kind of threat.

If we don't do what she says, would Helen take away our bowling night?

Nobody was willing to find out, so they never raised a beef with the Queen Communist of Schenectady. If Helen wanted them to "unite," then that's what they would do.

"'Tis the final conflict,
Let each stand in his place.

The international soviet
Shall be the human race!"

Yes, on Thursday nights, they would obey. They would stand and sing the Communist anthem. They would wear their itchy bowling shirts and keep score with the cheap Russian pencils that were always breaking at the point. They would eat the stale, briny pretzels that Helen served – the ones that were twisted into the shape of a hammer and sickle – and they would roll their red bowling balls at pins painted with the face of Leon Trotsky.

Leon who? Bowling pins painted with glasses and a goatee?

It was just another Commie mystery. No one complained about that either – not in front of Helen at least.

If the Reds want us to knock the little creep over, then who's going to care? Keep the Commies happy, the bowlers agreed, because the Reds were buying the beer, the pretzels, and the free bowling. Like everything else with the union, the Communists were in charge.

Silence and conformity – those were the keys to getting along with the Reds in the AEWA.

The Communists were not only buying the beer, they were brewing it. The Social Awareness Committee had started the Red Star Beer Collective two years earlier and now it was all over town, advertised on billboards with the picture of a big-bellied Russian smiling at a foaming mug of Red Star – "The Beer That Makes the World Go 'Round!"

A foaming mug, my ass, Beau Duffy sneered. Red Star beer was so flat it could barely bubble. It was just another Communist lie.

Billboards weren't the only things getting plastered in Schenectady. Red Star beer tasted thin and oily, but it was always cheap and extremely potent. After two or three bottles of Red Star, nobody cared if it was brewed by the Reds of Schenectady or little red men from Mars.

Nobody except Beau. Beau Duffy cared a lot.

He despised it all – the lousy beer, the stale pretzels, the big-shot Communists and their street-corner baloney: Rise up, you workers, and unite! Feed the hungry masses! Feed yourself: take what is rightfully yours!

Yes, please, take it, Beau silently pleaded. Take it all and just leave us alone!

Beau took another swig of Red Star, puckering his face as if he were drinking lighter fluid. He scowled at the label on the bottle: "This Date in Russian History: April 19, 1934 – Cabbage production reaches all-time high."

Beau winced as he took another sip. Christ, cabbage soup would taste better than this crap! But what choice did he have? What choice did any of them have? They all belonged to the union and Local 1389 made the beer. So Beau drank the beer, swallowing his pride along with the bile taste of this Commie swill.

As Beau tossed the empty bottle over his shoulder, he spotted Helen Gamble watching him from the top of the stairs.

I'll show her, Beau promised himself.

He picked up his bowling ball, weighing it carefully in his giant hands before slowly raising it to his eyes. He took in a deep breath, leveling his gaze at the ten tiny Trotskys standing 60 feet away.

You're going down, little man.

The ancient game of bowling can be traced back to the Stone Age and Man's earliest fascination with rocks: holding them, stacking them, throwing them. Many anthropologists believe Stonehenge may have been the world's first bowling alley, although further analysis suggests that it was actually the first snack bar at the first bowling alley. By the 20th Century, the game of bowling had developed into a true art form, elegant and mathematical – a virtual proof of physics in which an 18-pound sphere is propelled at a precise speed and a particular rotation, spinning to the very edge of the lane where it clings to the gutter's edge before snapping back across the alley and smashing into the pocket.

There was nothing elegant or mathematical when Beau Duffy threw a bowling ball. No matter the score or the number of pins he was facing, Beau simply heaved the ball as hard and as far as he could. When it was launched from those huge, hairy hands, the ball would sail halfway down the alley, sucking the air up behind it before disappearing into a blur of flying bowling pins, echoing with the percussive explosion of wood and metal. Beau loved that sound. He loved the carnage. Bowling was just another chance to destroy something.

Like a bowling Zeus, Beau stared down the alley at the fallen Trotskys, daring the pie-eyed lumber to stand up again. Sometimes, even his bowling ball would not return. With a confident smirk on his face, Beau turned back toward Helen – but she was gone. Beau felt a crimson heat spread across his face.

You goddamned idiot! Why are you showing off for her? Why should you care what she thinks? Why do you care what anybody thinks around here?

Beau looked at the other bowlers, all of them drinking their Commie beers, eating their twisted pretzels, and having a grand old time. None of them had a clue. They couldn't see what was happening all around them. In every corner of the city, the Communists were spreading their revolutionary bushwa. They had been at it for decades. Now, with Helen's help, things were worse than ever.

Just two blocks from The Capri, the downtown shops were full of happy customers. Thanks to Helen and her Social Awareness Committee, the best deals in town were available in stores and restaurants that displayed a Red Fist in the window. The Communist emblem told customers that this was a place friendly to members of Local 1389. When someone showed their Party membership card – or their Fellow Travelers Coupon Book – they not only got a discounted price, they also got a little more food on their plate. The service was faster and friendlier. There could be an extra scoop of ice cream at the soda fountain or free medical care at the union's new clinic. Kids enjoyed games and prizes on "Young Communist Nights" at the YMCA and their mothers took free cooking classes from the Red Sash Society. The Communists set up a consignment shop, a credit union, and they even gave out turkeys at Christmas.

It's enough to make you sick, Beau muttered to himself. But not enough to turn down a free turkey and Beau would never say 'no' to an extra scoop of mashed potatoes. Of course, he always drank his share of Red Star beer. But he did not have to like it – not any of it!

Who the hell is paying for all of this? Beau wanted to know. The same question was going around the Local and nobody was getting any answers. Communists don't like questions.

But the thing that really tore at Beau was the secret that no one else knew: there was only one man responsible for all of this chaos. Only one man was allowing Helen to spread her Bolshevik bullshit, ruining Bowling Night with those cartoon bowling pins and her Commie sing-alongs. It was the same guy who had promised over and over that someday – *someday!* – he was going to get rid of these lousy Reds and set the Local free.

That liar: the little son of a bitch, Milo Milwaukee.

> "After all, the chief business of the American people is business … So long as wealth is made the means and not the end, we need not greatly fear it."
>
> **PRESIDENT CALVIN COOLIDGE** *speaking to newspaper editors four years before the Great Depression*

> "Why should the Russians have all the fun of remaking a world?"
>
> **ECONOMIST STUART CHASE** *mistaking the horrors of Soviet Russia for 'fun' in Chase's 1932 book, A New Deal – the phrase later borrowed by FDR*

CHAPTER THREE

MILO

The good times, for Communists at least, should have started with the Great Depression – a decade of massive unemployment with the destruction of billions of dollars in personal wealth; families devastated by homelessness, suicide, and despair. Capitalism had fallen like a stockbroker off the 25th floor.

This was supposed to be Communism's Big Bang – the protogenetic spark to a worldwide revolution – just as Karl Marx had prophesied a century before. But it never happened. The perfect catastrophe ended without the Glorious Revolution. How could capitalism go so wrong and still end up all right?

It was the question Karl Heinrich Marx had wrestled with his entire life, a life spent indignantly indigent. "The Deadbeat of Düsseldorf" was constantly out of work, forever scheming for a place to sleep or sponging a free meal off his friends. Everyone called him "der Mooch."

Marx always had more opinions than money. According to his Robin Hood theory of economics, Communism would eventually rise out of Capitalism's ashes to create a "dictatorship of the proletariat," transforming workers into bosses and bosses into workers. It was a dreamy, potent vision and very attractive to people like Marx who had dead-end jobs or no job at all.

They all wanted more. What others had, they wanted a share. "From each according to his ability, to each according to his need."

The entire nation was in need during the Great Depression. As the bread lines and shanty towns grew larger, poverty and despair drew thousands of Americans toward the Communist Party. Eventually, the misery gave way to hope and new opportunities. The banks reopened and people went back to work. The Depression ended without a life-altering bang, without the Reds marching down Wall Street. In America, the best known Marx was still Groucho.

Twenty years later, Communists in America were still clinging to their dream, still meticulously plotting their secret Revolution – "*Forward to October!*" But an American revolution in 1950 was far more difficult than it might have been in 1930. Despair was in shorter supply as Americans were enjoying the greatest economic boom in modern history. The Depression and the Dust Bowl were nearly forgotten and it seemed happy days were here again.

Despite its newfound prosperity, America was still on edge. It had been more than a decade since the attack on Pearl Harbor and eight years had passed since V-E day and still the country felt as if it were slipping toward a third world war. This time, the enemy was Communism.

This was an anxious, suspicious time. Watch your neighbors! Beware of your co-workers! "Who knows what evil lurks in the hearts of men – "

People began fighting shadows, shooting blindly into the dark. Everyone had to take cover because the old rules, even the Bill of Rights, did not seem to matter much anymore. Freedom was no longer so free, especially if you were a Communist.

In Indiana, the state adopted a three-year prison sentence for "un-American activities." The law did not specify what those activities might be and, if you had to ask, then you were probably a Red yourself. Tennessee went even further, enacting a death penalty for "unlawful advocacy." Anti-subversive laws were popping up around the country, making it illegal to run for office – or even hold a public job – if you were a Communist. You could get into trouble for simply knowing a Communist or belonging to a group that included Communist members. Several states outlawed the Communist Party altogether.

Lists were compiled as names and organizations were lined up before political firing squads. Thoughts, as much as actions, were now considered criminal. Using a list created by the Justice Department, the State of Maryland decided that members of "subversive" groups could be jailed for up to five years. When this blacklist was thrown out, others picked it out of the trash and more names were added to it.

Where was the proof? The list was the proof!

In New York, the state government reacted to the Red hysteria by enacting a "Security Risk Law" in which any government worker, including janitors and even elevator operators, could be fired for "doubtful trust and reliability." In New York City, the purge of Communist and left-leaning teachers was entering its fourth year. It didn't matter if you were actually a Communist or not, bad things could still happen to you.

Being different was the difference. It was safer to keep your head down and conform.

In all this paranoia, Schenectady seemed a world away – a little Red island where Communists were not denounced as international spies or feared as subversive traitors. Here, the Reds were welcomed as friends and neighbors because that is who they were.

They could be members of your own family or maybe a coworker or someone who lived on your block. There was Mrs. Tataro the nurse, Bob Hughes the postman, or the German butcher, Boris Schicksal. They were the sons and daughters of the Communists who in 1927 created Local 1389 of the Amalgamated Electrical Workers of America, back when American industries greeted labor organizers with Pinkerton guards and blood-stained nightsticks. Behind these early unions were the Communists. They were in Schenectady before the Bolsheviks toppled the Czar. For a while, the Communist Party was even listed in the Schenectady phone book.

Decades earlier, when the Reds were taking over Russia, Schenectady was electing a Socialist mayor, Stennison Gaynor. The new mayor quickly expanded the size and scope of the city government and soon city workers were organizing their own labor unions. First were the city's Mattress Tag Inspectors. Next came the Triplicate Form Filers and Paper Stackers Local 517. They were followed by the New York Association of Highway Flag Wavers, Cone Handlers, and Clock Watchers. For Mayor Gaynor, it was a chicken in every pot and a union for every job.

The mayor's Socialist plans looked good on paper – until that paper was left on a heap of stinking garbage. The garbage collectors preferred to stay in their office, putting up their feet instead of picking up the trash. Nobody, least of all the mayor, was able to stop them. Seniority work rules, featherbedding, overtime pay, and a book full of union regulations prevented anything from getting done. The public soon tired of Mayor Gaynor's brand of "Civic Socialism."

Just as the voters were ready to throw Gaynor out of office, fate intervened with a gaggle of hungry ducks.

It was less than a week before the election and the Mayor was out for a stroll, spreading bread crumbs along the Mohawk, when he spied a discarded newspaper floating on the water. An ardent champion of the environment, Gaynor could not stomach any kind of trash in the river – especially *The Ledger*. Schenectady's daily newspaper had always despised the mayor and his Socialist agenda.

The Ledger was tired of Gaynor's social goody-goodiness and civic pomposity, the constant overextending of the city's reach through superfluous government services and make-busy programs. Under the Socialist mayor, Schenectady government had added Staircase Safety Inspectors and

Mortuary Monitors, Swimming Pool Temperature Testers, Street Cleaning Technologists, and Crosswalk Protection Specialists. The editors of *The Ledger* were sick of it all. Mostly, they were sick of Stennison Gaynor.

Their wish was granted that day by the river. As the mayor tried to pull the newspaper out of the water, he fell in headfirst and drowned beneath a circling whirlpool of bread crumbs and quacking ducks. The newspaper editors could not contain their glee. Within a few hours, a special edition hit the streets with a front page photograph of the mayor's empty hat sitting on the water and a banner headline mocking the mayor's demise:

CRUMBS ALONG THE MOHAWK
Halfwit Gaynor Suffers Fatal Half Gainer - Ducks and City Will Survive

The newspaper article briefly mentioned another survivor of this tragedy, the mayor's young son, Charlie. The memory of Stennison Gaynor and his radical politics would haunt the boy for his entire life, leaving him with a hatred for Communists, ducks, bread crumbs, and everything else that Charlie blamed for his father's unexpected demise. Decades later, this enmity for Communism would make Charlie Gaynor more famous than his father ever was. Back then, however, very little changed with the death of Stennison Gaynor.

It certainly did not stem the growth of unionism in Schenectady. Over the next decades, labor unions would thrive as Socialists continued to emigrate from Europe. They understood the power of collective action and from this tradition was born the Amalgamated Electrical Workers of America.

By 1950, the AEWA was among the largest and strongest labor unions in the country – and also the most-fervently Red. The union had half a million members across the United States and its largest Local was in Schenectady. Here, it represented nearly all of the craftsmen, mechanics and engineers, along with assembly line workers and semiskilled laborers – 40,000 workers in all – inside the sprawling industrial works of the General Electric Corporation.

Known throughout the region as "The G.E.," the company was born from the genius of Thomas Alva Edison, inventor of the lightbulb and then later, the quicker-burning, replaceable lightbulb. By 1946, the modern-day G.E. was one of the giants of American industry, feeding America's postwar hunger for household gadgets and electronic conveniences: wood-paneled television sets, frost-free refrigerators, multiple-slice toasters, electric can openers, time-saving dishwashers, spoon-chewing garbage disposals, and dozens of other gizmos that people never knew they needed until they rolled off the assembly lines at The G.E.

From the Schenectady plant, the company also designed and manufactured hundreds of the world's most-sophisticated weapons – secret military hardware like advanced missile guidance systems and cameras equipped for high-altitude spy planes. All of them were shipped out of the same industrial works that made toasters and transistor radios. While household goods were big business for G.E., defense contracts were even bigger – an arsenal as deadly as it was spectacularly profitable.

Were these military secrets also important to the Communists? Were you born yesterday? screamed *The Ledger*.

"Why do the Reds control Local 1389? To get inside General Electric, that's why!" howled the newspaper's editorial page. "Do they want to take over the world with G.E. can openers and color television sets? NO! The Commies have burrowed deep inside General Electric so they can steal our nation's military secrets! Wake up Schenectady! The Red Scourge is all around us and Local 1389 is a tremendous threat to our national security! Throw out the Reds before Uncle Sam takes his business somewhere else – somewhere safer! Get rid of them now before the Russians drop the A-bomb on us all!"

It was not such a fantastic notion. At that moment, Julius and Ethel Rosenberg were waiting for the electric chair, convicted of helping the Russians create their own atomic bomb. Russian spy rings had also been uncovered in Canada and Great Britain. People were starting to wonder: was Schenectady next on the Soviets' list?

To the members of Local 1389, this was all nonsense. Newspapers, like the factories, were all controlled by the rich. Money-grubbing businessmen would oppose anything that helped the little guy whether it was unions, the New Deal, even bottled beer. An attack on Communism was simply an attack against their union.

It was the Local, after all, that had brought a better life to 40,000 Schenectady families, boosting their wages to the highest they had ever been. Those families now earned enough to buy a house and to put a coat of white paint on that house. People used to worry about putting shoes on their kids' feet; now they could put their kids through college! They could buy a car, a television set, or vacation out of state *and* waiting for them in retirement was a comfortable pension. All of it thanks to their union.

Not only was the pay better, but the holidays were longer and the factory was safer than ever before. This, too, was due to the union. The AEWA and Local 1389 made sure that you could get a job without having to bribe the foreman or submit to sex with some low-life manager. When the company tried to speed up the assembly line or change the piece rate, the union would step in just as fast. And if you asked any one of those GE workers who was responsible for all of these improvements, every man and woman in Local 1389 would give the same answer: it was the "Little Giant," Milo Milwaukee.

They called him the Little Giant because Milo was a little guy who accomplished big things. He had worked his way up the line and then off the factory floor before he was elected Business Agent and the undisputed boss of Local 1389. The pay raises, the longer holidays, and the safer working conditions – all of it came from Milo's hard-nosed negotiating on behalf of those coil winders, box cleaners, and the other skilled and semiskilled laborers inside General Electric.

Even the company liked Milo. There were occasional strikes and walkouts by the union, but the G.E. brass knew they could eventually make a deal with Milo. He might be a Red, but at least Milo saw things the way the company did: Milo always kept his eye on the bottom line. The Little Giant made sure everybody made money – the workers, the company, and especially Milo himself.

As popular as he was among the members of Local 1389, no one loved Milo Milwaukee more than Beauregard J. L. Duffy.

Beau Duffy owed everything to Milo, from frequent bail bonds to the quick dismissal of so many criminal charges. Milo made sure Big Beau was happy with ready access to spending money, plenty of booze, and fast cars. Beau was especially grateful for the letter Milo's doctor wrote to the Schenectady County Draft Board in 1942, revealing a previously undiagnosed heart condition in Milo's friend, Beau. With this deferment from military service, Beau was given a different uniform: Milo chose Beau to lead the "Flying Squadron." This was the goon squad of Local 1389, ten powerful men in motorcycle boots and heavy leather jackets emblazoned with a picture of a wild-eyed eagle, its talons stretching out to attack.

Everyone in the union was afraid of the Fliers – which was just what Milo Milwaukee wanted.

Beau and his men were always together and on Thursday nights they bowled as a team, always on Lane 38, the alley closest to the bar. From that end of The Capri, Beau could see everyone and everyone could see Beau.

Between the bowling and the beer, all eyes were locked on Beau Duffy. Everyone knew that after bowling that night, Beau and the Flying Squadron would be out on the streets giving someone the "nerve treatment." It was a reminder for everyone to stay in line: Milo Milwaukee was in charge of Local 1389.

As The Capri echoed with the sound of 38 bowling balls rolling and crashing into the pins, the men laughing, shouting, and horsing around, a single, silent gesture sent a shudder across the bowling alley. Beau slowly turned his head down the length of The Capri, his jaw slack and his eyes glaring like an angry bull. Everyone stopped bowling and the place went quiet.

Like an ocean wave barreling toward shore, every head in The Capri turned to follow Beau's malevolent gaze. Row by row, in a cascade of wide-eyed stares, bowler after bowler looked over their shoulders in search of the unlucky bastard who was standing in the middle of Beau Duffy's bullseye. All eyes stopped on Lane 3 – it was Wally Speerman.

Beau took a long slug of his beer and glared at Wally – stupid, stupid Wally. Wally Speerman who would never take "shut up" for an answer. For weeks, Speerman had been pestering Milo about the union dues that were collected by the Local and nagging him about where the money was spent.

"Why won't you open the books, Milo?" Speerman asked. "You collect millions of dollars from us every year – where does all that money go?"

This was not the first time someone had challenged Milo's leadership. Although he was loved and admired by thousands of his followers, there was always someone ready to complain, especially those scheming to take over the Local. Enemies, like questions, were unavoidable. Both could be tolerated – up to a point – and that point sat on the knuckles of Beau Duffy's fists.

After this night, Wally Speerman would not be asking so many questions about the financial management of Local 1389.

Beau grabbed somebody's beer and chugged it down. Glaring at Wally, Beau wondered how some people could be so thick.

Smart ass Wally – always asking questions and always the *wrong* questions! He should be asking about the Communists and how they were paying for the free bowling and all the rest of their civic-minded hogwash – the soup kitchen, free turkeys, the free medical clinic! Why doesn't Wally ask about this piss-poor beer or the itchy bowling shirts? And why does everyone bow down to Helen Gamble, the great Queen Communist – her royal Pain in the Ass?

Beau needed to punch something. He grabbed another Red Star, drained the bottle and smashed it against the floor. Beau could feel the frightened stares of the other bowlers, but Beau didn't care. No one would dare ask Beau Duffy to clean up his mess. They knew a bigger mess was on its way.

Beau did not want to, but he would do his job that night: Wally Speerman would get the nerve treatment and then some. As Beau slammed his massive fists into Wally's rib cage – once, twice, *three* times – the questions kept nagging at Beau: What the hell am I doing? Who am I protecting? Is this for Milo or the goddamned Communists?

The Threat of Red Sabotage: Sardine Cans Used to Import Communist Manuals of Destruction
HEADLINE FOR "THE FIRST OF A SERIES OF 10 SENSATIONAL ARTICLES"
on Communism in the New York Herald Tribune, 1950

CHAPTER FOUR

MARTHA

While most people assumed that Milo was a Communist, there was never any doubt about his wife, Martha.

Every May Day, Martha would parade down Fifth Avenue atop the Communist Party float, as it carried a human tableau of dusty migrants and stalwart ironworkers. Martha stood above them, dressed like Lady Liberty in a shimmering silver gown, a bloody pitchfork in one hand and, in the other, an oversized copy of the Communist Manifesto. A cheer went up every few blocks as Martha would raise the pitchfork over her head and "sever" the head of a banker, a landlord or some other Enemy of the People. The ketchup flowed freely that day as a light breeze ruffled the banner flying overhead: "The Communist Party – Getting Even Since 1917."

A few months later, Martha would ignite a near riot inside Madison Square Garden. It was her famous "Lincoln was a Communist" speech.

"You all know Abraham Lincoln – the Great Emancipator – the man who freed the slaves!" Martha shouted over the heads of 18,000 union members. "But Lincoln was much more than that. He WANTED more than that! He wanted all of us to be free – to be cast out of the bondage and tyranny of capitalist slavery! My brothers and sisters, this is a fact: Abraham Lincoln once said that when the people 'grow weary of the existing government, they can exercise their Constitutional right to amend it or their *revolutionary right to dismember and overthrow it!*'"

The crowd went silent for a moment, trying to absorb the idea that Honest Abe might have been a Red. Martha just smiled and waited.

"Well grab your ax, Mr. Lincoln, because it's time to *GET TO WORK!*"

The place went nuts. Martha spread her arms out wide, drawing the frantic crowd toward her.

"And Lincoln was not alone, my brothers and sisters! It was Vladimir Lenin who declared, 'The proletarian revolution is impossible without the forcible destruction of the bourgeois state machine!' That, my friends, is the machine that has been holding you down! Lenin was a Communist! Abraham Lincoln was a Communist! I AM A COMMUNIST! What about you? Where do YOU stand?"

A beastly howl rose out of the audience as Martha kept shouting until her words were swallowed by the noise of the crowd.

"Do you want to be free? We all want to be free! So tell me: Will you use your two strong hands to tear down the capitalist machine? Who is with me? LET ME HEAR YOU!"

Martha said it again, but no one was listening. Chairs were tossed into the air, the metal clanging against the Garden floor, as the room echoed with a jungle roar. Stoked by Martha's battle cry, the union men behaved like knuckle-dragging barbarians, hungry for something or someone to throttle! The cops slowly backed toward the exits, hands poised over their guns in case anyone might charge. The only thing that prevented a full-on riot was when Martha grabbed the microphone and started singing "God Bless America." The next day's tabloids dubbed her the "Red Flame of New York."

Martha was suddenly a bona fide star of the American labor movement and soon she was crisscrossing the nation stirring up union rallies (and their mostly male audiences) with speeches that were as hot and overstuffed as the tight, red dresses she wore on stage. Her sudden fame led to a first for women: Martha was elected to the executive council of the Amalgamated Electrical Workers of America – the first woman ever voted to serve on the board of an International.

Martha was a firecracker, all right.

Back then.

Look at me now, Martha whimpered, as she slouched against the kitchen table. Ten thirty in the morning and she was still dressed in a ratty housecoat and thin cotton slippers. Martha stared mournfully at her reflection on the side of a G.E. toaster, struggling to comprehend the twisted mess that her life had become. Once she had traveled the world, unleashing thunder and lightning in the glorious struggle to bring peace and prosperity to the entire world. Now her greatest struggle was to get out of bed.

What the hell happened to me?

She could not even look at herself. The toaster was more like a funhouse mirror. Martha shoved the toaster aside, revealing the dirty dishes heaped in the sink. The soap bubbles were all gone, floated away like the crowds that once cheered her every word. Who are they cheering now? Martha wondered.

Madison Square Garden is a long way from Schenectady, N.Y. It is even farther from the manicured shores of Lake Winnanonga, the tony town in east New Hampshire where Martha grew up – the town where the Scandal of Martha Appleton Mossbaum Milwaukee still lives on.

Martha was the girl that the other girls were warned about. Her parents, John and Doris Appleton, had always been the popular, fashionable couple of their wealthy enclave – until Martha came along. To this day, a "tsk, tsk" will follow any mention of their trouble-making daughter. (Martha, it was whispered, might very well have been adopted – a rumor secretly started by her father.)

She had always been different from everyone else in Lake Winnanonga, or at least Martha wanted to be seen that way. Dancing on the front lawn naked in the moonlight. Smoking cigarettes outside of church. She even wore a red dress to the country club cotillion and she made no secret of her interest in human anatomy with the able assistance of Tommy Haines, the butler's son! Things changed after boarding school. Martha seemingly renounced her rebellious ways. She went off to college where she became the Vassar Golden Girl – pretty, popular, and athletic. That didn't last long.

During the fall of Martha's junior year, a cream-colored envelope arrived at her parents' home. Inside was a hand-engraved note announcing the marriage of Martha Appleton Mossbaum.

Their little girl had eloped!

Martha had run away with Harold Mossbaum, the "recruitment director" for the international union of laundry workers, the United Hangers and Folders of America.

" – and we'll be getting free dry cleaning!" Martha gushed in her letter back home. What she could not tell her parents was that Harold Mossbaum was actually a Soviet spy, one of hundreds of Russian agents cleverly planted inside American labor unions, universities, government agencies, and top research centers. Wherever there was an opportunity for disinformation or influence, the Kremlin placed one of their agents, helping the Soviets to worm their way into America's apple pie.

The Russians did not stop there. They also placed agents among the working people, assigning Russian spies to supermarkets and candy stores, others to newspaper offices, book shops and movie houses. Quietly, slowly, the Reds infiltrated every corner of American society – from garden clubs to bird watchers, the Kiwanis to the Lions Club.

Clueless America was an easy target. No one seemed to notice when a Communist resolution was quietly proposed or a letter sympathetic to Russia was submitted to the local newspaper. The Mont Pleasant Stamp Club was, unexpectedly, endorsing the Russian annexation of Poland. The Rotterdam Bird Watchers were officially opposed to the Marshall Plan and The Ladies Book Club of Schenectady was thoroughly confused and disappointed after reading "Ten Days That Shook the World."

Ten days? Ha! The ladies would have settled for just a few pages of romance, but they could not find anything the least bit titillating in that book, certainly nothing that would "shake the world."

Then the Communists came to Vassar College. Harold Mossbaum's job was to recruit impressionable college students for the People's Revolution, but he spent most of his time seducing the co-eds. If he could get them into bed with the Russians, maybe he could lure them into his own bed first.

It was on the Vassar campus where Mossbaum spotted Martha walking into a lecture on Relative Positivism by the Socialist academic Edvar Provence. When the French philosopher asked the audience if they were ready to fight for the betterment of mankind, Martha stood up and shouted, "Take me!"

"With pleasure," Mossbaum sneered from the back of the auditorium.

Martha was not much more than a kid, barely 20 years old, when Mossbaum introduced her to Communism and then to the facts of life, romancing Martha in the back seat of his '37 Packard, their bodies writhing and crunching on stacks of Communist propaganda.

"What are you studying?" Mossbaum whispered anxiously, pulling her lips to his.

"Post Modern Humanism and Liberal Sociology," Martha replied through passionate breaths.

"Perfect," Mossbaum responded, reaching for her enormous breasts.

"Yes," Martha panted. "I'm a double major."

"You certainly are, my dear."

Martha fell in love with Mossbaum and the Soviet agent was pleased to have found such a beautiful and enthusiastic pupil. With Harold, Martha thought she had found the truth: Russia was offering peace, love, and brotherhood, while Capitalist America was trying to drag the world back to war! Through the Communist Party and Mother Russia, a new world could begin and Martha was ready to join the Revolution.

They soon ran off to Niagara Falls to become Mr. and Mrs. Harold Mossbaum. For their one-month anniversary, Mossbaum gave his bride a shortwave radio. At first, she didn't know what to do with it.

"We always used a telephone in our house," Martha offered innocently.

"Yes," Mossbaum replied, "but this will help us reach your new family from very far away." Soon Martha was learning how to tap out Morse code, to decode secret messages, and how to hide encrypted packages inside knot holes – skills not normally acquired by the society girls of Lake Winnanonga.

Quitting school and "marrying that Bolshevik" became a terrible scandal back home. The only thing worse was when Harold fled to Russia two years later.

Martha came home from a speech in Pittsburgh to find the FBI waiting at her door. Harold had jumped over the back fence, leaving behind his pants, his mustache pomade and the shortwave radio hidden under the bassinette of their baby boy, Michael. The child grew up never knowing his father and Martha was determined that he never would.

Even though Martha was through with Harold, she was not ready to turn her back on the Communist Party. Her son was going to be raised Red, Martha vowed. A young soldier in the New Vanguard!

Michael became a true "Red Diaper" baby. Tiny hammers and sickles twirled on the mobile above his crib as Martha read him tales of the People's Revolution, stories like *Little Red Riding Hood* and the *Little Red Lighthouse*. Michael was still teething when Martha finally got the news about Harold.

On the back page of the *Daily Worker,* a blurry picture of Mossbaum appeared under the headline, "Russia Welcomes Union Leader from America." It was Harold all right, right down to his beady eyes and that junior high school mustache. Surrounded by Russian generals, Mossbaum could be seen holding a small sign with the number '19' on it. That was their signal: 19 meant "Everything is okay. It is safe for you to join me."

"Bastard," hissed Martha as she threw the newspaper into the trash.

Everybody had expected Martha to follow Harold to Russia. Certainly, the FBI did. They watched her constantly, hoping she would lead them to Mossbaum or some other Soviet agent. They even tailed her home on those infrequent visits back to Lake Winnanonga.

"They seem nice," said Martha's mother, pulling aside the curtains. Doris would smile and wave at the stern FBI agents leaning against their cars at the end of the Appleton's driveway. "Should we invite them in for a snack? Perhaps you could introduce us?"

When it came to her Communist daughter, Doris Appleton was always looking for a silver lining. Martha was constantly under surveillance or testifying before Congressional investigators so Doris could only hope that one day her daughter would meet a forgiving congressman or a lonely FBI agent – anyone who could rescue her little girl from the Reds.

"Because you know, dear," Doris would say, "no one looks good in red."

"They'll give you a striped outfit in prison!" Martha's father would mutter from his easy chair.

Martha never listened to them. Her parents were so bourgeois, mindlessly loyal to their country club and the Republican Party. "Would it hurt you to smile once in a while?" Doris pleaded after Martha was called before another Congressional hearing. "And why can't you be more cooperative? Young ladies don't plead the Fifth, dear. It's not attractive."

No one in Congress seemed to care if Martha took the Fifth, the Sixth, or the Seventh. They were thrilled just as long as she showed up – all six feet of her voluptuous, Communist loveliness. With those pillow-plump lips and her seductive eyes, Martha could have read the Moscow phone book and congressmen would still elbow each other for a better view.

"Are you now or have you ever been a member of the Communist Party?" they would begin. In a husky, baby-doll voice, Martha would purr, "Senator – while I appreciate your question – I feel … yes, I really, really feel that I must invoke my right to plead …"

And then she would pause as the whole room was pulled toward those luscious, red lips. Senators, congressmen, pages, security guards, and reporters would all lean forward, drawn like helpless moths toward the Red Flame of New York. Martha would toss back her long, flowing hair, giving it a shake, as she closed her eyes and exhaled, " … the Fifth!"

It was what they all had been waiting for. Congressmen would ask her the same question over and over just to see her waive her right to self-incrimination. Nobody could waive it like Martha. Sometimes, she would make them beg for it.

"That's such a good question, Senator Hostings," Martha would tease. "But I must be firm with you, Senator. And you too, Senator Bitwell ... and you, Senator Mullweed." Down the table she would go, calling each senator by name and pointing her finger at them as she went along, making each name sound sexier than the last. The congressmen would close their eyes and dream that marvelous Martha was calling them to her bed.

She was just getting started.

"I'm feeling so ...*frustrated*, Senator," Martha pouted. "I really wish I could answer your question. I really do. Because I would love – REALLY love – to cooperate with *you*."

The members were sitting up straight now, anticipating those next delicious words.

"But I must ... I really, really *must* – " She tossed her hair again, fingers moving across her mouth and down her slightly-buttoned blouse. The salivating solons were draped across the conference table, beckoned by her siren call.

" – invoke my privilege and plead – "

"THE FIFTH!" exclaimed Senator Bitwell. Realizing what he had just done, the Senator's eyes bugged out of his head. Bitwell jumped from his seat, clutching papers to his lap as he waddled out of the hearing room.

Senators would swoon and congressmen coo, but Martha's mother would never get her wish: no politician was going to marry the Commie Queen of Lake Winnanonga. Martha didn't care. She was a star and would always be a star, at least to people in the American labor movement and, of course, to the stalwarts of the Communist Party USA. Among her most-fervent admirers was a pint-sized union leader from Schenectady, New York.

Milo Milwaukee was in the crowd when Martha brought old Communists to tears and the entire audience to its feet inside the Syracuse War

Memorial. From Seat 27, Row G, Milo Milwaukee fell in love with the Red Flame of New York.

For Martha, however, Cupid's arrow was not as sharp.

She first saw Milo in the pages of *Watts News,* the electrical workers' weekly newsletter. There was Milo, in a photo with other members of Local 1389, smiling through the bars of the Schenectady City Jail. Little Milo Milwaukee – he barely stood five feet tall – was beaming at the camera with a busted lip, a swollen right eye, and two missing teeth, clubbed out by Pinkerton guards. "Feisty Schenectady Steward Pummels Pinkertons" was the headline above the photo.

"Look in the sky – is it a bird? Is it a plane? No, it's Shop Steward Milo Milwaukee, the Birdman of Local 1389! See young Milo hurl his body onto a pack of Pinkerton thugs as they try to stop our AEWA brothers and sisters from staging a lawful protest outside the General Electric works in Schenectady. Congratulations to Milo Milwaukee – Our Man of Steel! He lost a couple of teeth, but not his pride! Way to go Milo!"

Even with all his teeth, Milo did not present an especially handsome face. The first thing people noticed was his pyramidal hair. To make up for his lack of height, Milo would pile his hair high in the front, sweeping it back and then up again in a great, pointed pompadour. But Milo and his pointy hairdo were quickly forgotten by the future Mrs. Milwaukee. It would take the Communist Party to bring Martha and Milo together.

It happened one beautiful, spring day when Milo came calling to Martha's apartment building in New York. The Party had told Martha to expect "a great admirer" at her door and she was ready with a new dress, new shoes, and a lipstick called Devil's Desire. The rest would be a surprise. Martha certainly was.

When she opened the door, there was tiny Milo in a crumpled seersucker suit, two sizes too big. Milo, meanwhile, was transfixed by this radiant vixen standing above him. Like a sad, silent clown, Milo reached up to offer Martha a wilting bouquet of red petunias. Nothing was spoken as an electric spark shot between them. Martha dropped the flowers at the doorstep and hoisted the little man up to her bedroom.

They made love that entire afternoon. Awkward and unsure, Milo tried his best to keep up with this Amazonian beauty as Martha tossed Milo back and forth across her bed. When she was through with him, Milo lay against Martha, exhausted and supremely happy, his head bobbing on top of her heavenly breasts. Suddenly, Martha lifted her nose in the air.

What was that smell? She was sniffing a powerful aroma that was both familiar and totally unexpected. "Milo? Do you smell ... bacon?"

Milo blushed. It was true, he said. Whenever he got excited, Milo would cast off a strong odor that resembled fried bacon. This was the first time he had ever told anyone.

"Well," Martha purred, "I just love the smell of bacon."

A few months later, they were married.

"Then she married another one!" Martha's father would thunder years later. "Another goddamned Communist! You'd think she got a list from Joe McCarthy! 'I hold in my hand all the Communists that Martha Appleton should marry!'"

Martha could not believe it either. She could never have imagined this fate: her life in New York was over. No more traveling around the country, exhorting the adoring masses, teasing congressmen with her pleas for the Fifth, foiling the FBI and her mother's dream of a respectable marriage. All of that was over, even more than she could have imagined. She had moved to Schenectady, New York – only a few miles from the Canadian border!

To live with a man who smelled like breakfast meat!

But she was a good Party member. She would follow orders. She married Milo and, after carrying him across the threshold, Martha did not object when Milo told her – firmly – that she must leave the Communist Party.

"I have to protect you now," Milo told her with great affection, "for our new life and our new family."

Yes, Martha promised. Her days as a Red were over.

"That's my girl," said Milo, giving her a hug and pretending to believe her. Milo knew she was lying. In his baggy suits and pointy hair, Milo Milwaukee may have looked foolish, but he was nobody's fool – especially when it came to Communists.

"When planning your new house, remember atom bombs, recommends Howard W. Blakeslee, Associated Press science editor, in this ninth of a series of 12 suggestions. Keep to a minimum the ornamental fixtures and ornamental plaster or other interior treatments. The concussion of an atom bomb can knock all these down, and make them dangerous missiles. Even when buildings stand up under an atomic blast, the concussion comes in through the windows and may wreck the interior except where it is solidly constructed. Your house does not need to be a prison cell, but it does need some of the cell's simple solidarity."

"WHAT TO DO IF A-BOMBS COME" ✶ *A weekly science series by the Associated Press, 1950*

"Hiroshima, Nagasaki
We must choose between —
The brotherhood of man or smithereens
The people of the world must pick out a thesis:
Peace in the world, or the world in pieces!"

"OLD MAN ATOM," *a record pulled off shelves in 1950 because of "Communist 'peace' agitation"*

CHAPTER FIVE

MICHAEL

MILWAUKEE, MICHAEL
SCHENECTADY ELEMENTARY SCHOOL
Grade: 4   April 1950

Michael stared at the rectangular piece of tin hanging from the chain around his neck.

"Keep these tags with you at all times!" Miss Warburton scolded the class. "You must wear these in case – in case!" She turned away from the class again, her face red and puffy. The teacher had been crying for most of the morning.

Michael looked around the classroom. None of the kids seemed upset. Why was Miss Warburton crying?

Now I'm crying too!

Michael jumped out of his seat and ran to the playground. He hid under the slide and would not come out until someone called his father. By then, school was over and the building was nearly empty.

"Dog tags?" Milo asked. "Who gave you dog tags?"

Michael pointed toward Miss Warburton's classroom.

"Teacher did," Michael sniffed.

"All you kids got them?"

"For when we get burned up."

"Burned up?"

"From the comic bomb."

Milo was more confused.

"The comic bomb? Michael – what are you talking about?"

"Miss Warburton said some bad country hates us and they're going to drop a comic bomb on us."

The words echoed in Michael's head until he looked up at his father and started bawling again. The boy wrapped his arms around Milo's legs and held on tight.

What the hell is going on? Milo wondered. Then he saw the comic book sticking out of Michael's back pocket, "Earth Destroyed!!" On the gruesome cover, bloodied bodies were spread across smoking rubble and the American flag, torn and muddied, lay mangled under the boot of an enormous Russian soldier. The giant Soviet was shaking his fist in the air and gloating, "Take that America! Now WE have your atomic bomb!"

"Did the teacher give you this comic book?" Milo asked. Michael nodded, his head still wedged between Milo's legs.

Milo took the boy by the hand. "Come on, son. We're going to see about this!"

They could hear Miss Warburton weeping and moaning as soon as they entered the school. Her wailing, miserable and ghostly, echoed through the darkened hallways.

"Miss Warburton!" Milo snapped. "What's the idea of you giving my son – " Milo took one step into the classroom before he wheeled around and pushed Michael back into the hall.

"Stay here," Milo said firmly.

Cautiously, Milo went back in, shocked at the sight of Michael's teacher crawling across the floor and disappearing behind her desk. Milo stepped carefully forward as Miss Warburton's shoes churned against the linoleum floor, straining to squeeze her hips under the desk.

"Miss Warburton? It's Milo Milwaukee, Michael's father. Could you please come out of there? I need to speak with you."

Struggling to catch her breath, Miss Warburton backed out and flopped against the wall. Tears were pouring down her cheeks as she tried to steady herself, clutching the chalk tray above her head. Then her glassy eyes began to darken and a furious scowl crossed over her face. Milo stepped back as Miss Warburton grabbed a dusty eraser and with a ferocious grunt, she ripped the eraser in two. Realizing what she had done, Miss Warburton threw back her head and wailed even louder.

"Ihh – Ihh – IT'S JUST TOO MUCH!" she cried. "Just *TOO MUCH!*"

Milo turned back toward Michael who was peeking around the doorway. He waved at the boy to go back into the hallway, but Michael could only stand there, gaping at his teacher sprawled on the classroom floor.

Milo reached a hand toward Miss Warburton's shoulder, but she was already back on her hands and knees, pushing herself under the desk again.

"Miss Warburton – WAIT! What's too much? Have the children been misbehaving?"

"Noooooo!!" Miss Warburton cried, her voice reverberating inside the metal desk. "It's not the children. They're fine! THEY'RE going to be perfectly safe! But not me! NOT MEEEEEE!"

Miss Warburton suddenly reached up and yanked Milo down on the floor, squeezing his face against her watery cheeks.

"Help me, Mr. Milwaukee. HELP ME, please! I don't want to die!"

Milo struggled to break free. "Die? Who said anything about dying?"

"Well look at me!" Miss Warburton cried. Milo did not understand. He looked over at Michael hoping for an answer. Michael pointed toward Miss Warburton's desk.

"She can't fit," Michael said.

"It's true!" Miss Warburton said. "Can't you see that?" She grabbed Milo's tie and with each word she shook him back and forth: "I – JUST – DON'T – FIT!"

Miss Warburton headed back for the desk, muttering to herself, "All I need is a BIGGER DESK! But the school won't give me one! And the union doesn't care. All I get is, 'You should stay in the classroom, Wanda. Stay with the children, Wanda. Make sure the children are lined up in front of their lockers, WANDA!' Meanwhile, all those cowards will be running for the bomb shelter!"

"This school has a BOMB SHELTER?" Milo exclaimed.

"Not yet, but I heard them talking about it! It will be right under the teachers' lounge. How lucky for them! But not for me – not for Wanda! When they drop the bomb on us, Mr. Milwaukee, where will I go? WHERE CAN I HIDE?"

Milo took a worried glance toward Michael.

"Miss Warburton, please! I'm sure the school will keep everyone safe – the students and teachers!"

"Oh no they won't! Not me! Not me!"

"Why not you?"

"BECAUSE I DON'T HAVE TENURE, THAT'S WHY NOT!"

As a union man, Milo could understand her situation. There was no way you could get around tenure, even in the face of a nuclear attack.

Miss Warburton slid back onto her stomach, her cries echoing against the floor. Her tantrum only grew louder as Milo pulled Michael out of the classroom.

"They make you kids go under your desks?" Milo asked as they ran to the car.

"With a sheet."

"A sheet?"

"From my bed."

"A bed sheet?" Milo asked. "You crawl under your desk with a bed sheet and that's going to protect you from an atomic bomb?"

"That's – what – they say-ay," Michael sang as he jumped into the front seat. He was feeling better now that he could not hear Miss Warburton sobbing.

Milo stared back at the school, still shaken by what he had seen.

"It's going to be okay," Michael said soothingly. "Miss Warburton can use my sheet if she wants to." Milo smiled at the little boy's generosity.

"Sure, sport. You're right. Everything's going to be okay."

But Milo knew the truth – everything was not okay. Dog tags and bed sheets? School teachers hiding under their desks? Comic books about the atomic bomb?

In the spring of 1950, it felt like the whole world was going nuts.

"There exists a world Communist movement which, in its origins, its development, and its present practice, is a world-wide revolutionary movement whose purpose it is, by treachery, deceit, infiltration into other groups (governmental and otherwise), espionage, sabotage, terrorism, and any other means deemed necessary, to establish a Communist totalitarian dictatorship in the countries throughout the world through the medium of a world-wide Communist organization."

PREAMBLE TO THE MCCARREN INTERNAL SECURITY ACT *requiring the registration of Communists, as well as the arrest and detention of "probable" spies and saboteurs*

"The idea of requiring communist organizations to divulge information about themselves is a simple and attractive one. But it is about as practical as requiring thieves to register with the sheriff. Obviously, no such organization as the Communist Party is likely to register voluntarily."

PRESIDENT TRUMAN'S VETO MESSAGE OF THE MCCARREN ACT *a veto overridden by Congress in bipartisan votes the very next day, Sept. 23, 1950*

CHAPTER SIX

MILO MILWAUKEE'S OFFICE,
July 1950

America came back from the war exalted, but exhausted. After six years and more than 70 million lives lost, Hitler and the Third Reich were finally vanquished. Fighting in the Pacific would continue for another six months until 100,000 people would die in Hiroshima and three days later

50,000 people would perish in Nagasaki. In the face of America's "most cruel bomb," Emperor Hirohito was forced to lower the Japanese sword.

"Should we continue to fight," the Emperor told his people, "not only would it result in an ultimate collapse and obliteration of the Japanese nation, but also it would lead to the total extinction of human civilization."

Still the conflicts continued.

When American soldiers returned from Europe, the Soviets stayed behind. The Russians quickly seized cities, farms, and factories, along with the freedom of Poles, Hungarians, Czechs, and millions more. Eastern Europe was swallowed up just as the Nazis had done only a few years earlier.

Being the consummate bureaucrats, the Soviets required their soldiers to officially record everything they plundered: people, furniture, animals, houses. Even the firing squads had to catalog the number of bullets they had shot, as well as the bullets they recovered. The Russians would have pushed farther west if there had not been so much paperwork.

America was also tired. It was ready to withdraw from the world, confident that the United States was too powerful to worry about anyone else's army. America alone possessed that "most cruel bomb" and peace seemed assured as long as the United States – and only the United States – controlled the world's most powerful weapon.

But all that changed in 1949 when Russia exploded its own atomic bomb. Thanks to American Communists collaborating with Russian spies, America's secret weapon was no longer a secret. It meant that America was no longer supreme. For Americans, the world was no longer safe.

In his office at Local 1389, Milo Milwaukee stretched a stubby arm across his desk, reaching for a newspaper with the headline blaring across the front page: 'Marxist Sympathizer, Julius Rosenberg, Arrested As Atom Spy.' With his round glasses and perplexed expression, Julius Rosenberg did not look like an international saboteur. He seemed more like a small-time electrical engineer, which, in fact, he was. It did not take the FBI long to catch him – not after they squeezed his brother-in-law, David Greenglass. Greenglass even turned in his sister, Ethel Rosenberg.

Milo shook his head. You loan your brother-in-law a lawnmower or a hammer, but you don't trust him with a conspiracy to commit treason.

"Communists," Milo sighed, tossing the newspaper onto the floor. But Milo's disdain could not mask his fear, the Red Scare was taking over America. Communism in America was no longer a political sideshow. The prosecution of Communists – and the persecution of liberal sympathizers – was real and with it a new kind of warfare had broken out between the United States and Russia: a surreptitious war – a Cold War – without bullets, guns or bombs.

The Red Menace seemed to be everywhere. First, Eastern Europe and then China fell to the Communists and now America was in the shadow of a Russian A-bomb. Are we strong enough to stop a Communist invasion of Iowa? Manhattan? Were the Communists already in place and ready for war, disguised as grocery clerks, defense analysts, and Kiwanis Club members? Clearly, Milo knew, this was a bad time to be working for a union run by Communists.

He looked around his office. On the wall, Joseph Stalin's photograph sneered placidly between portraits of George Washington and Abraham Lincoln. The bookshelves were filled with how-to books on Communism, Five-Year planning guides, and an assortment of Moscow propaganda. In the wastebasket was that day's edition of *The Daily Proletariat*, the Communist newspaper of Local 1389. The paper was written, printed, and delivered around the entire G.E. complex by just one man – Arthur Klingman – arguably the most ardent Communist in a town filled with fervent Reds.

Every day, *The Daily Proletariat* railed against the Rockefellers, the Vanderbilts and the terrible persecution of the Working Man. Never once would Klingman deviate from the Party line – even in his advice column for lovelorn Communists.

QUESTION: "My boyfriend won't tell me any of his secrets! How can I trust someone who won't confide in me?"

ANSWER: "Party members must be extremely careful. The authorities are always watching us. Still, if you think your boyfriend is up to something, have him followed."

Such things Milo could ignore. But he could not avoid the envelope that was sitting on his desk – another "urgent resolution" from the Local's Communist Information Committee.

What the hell is it this time? Milo sighed.

The Communists were obsessive about their Great Struggle – their not so cryptic war to stamp out Capitalism and bring Communism to the entire world. American Communists proudly thought of themselves as the vanguard of a new world – a world without prejudice or discrimination, a place where everyone's needs are fulfilled and all are happy. This was already happening in Russia, the Communists insisted, and with their help the rest of the world could also be free.

To make it more palatable to the average American, the Reds called Communism "20th Century Americanism." Their brand of Communism was modern, progressive, and seemingly free to do whatever it wanted to do (so long as the Kremlin approved). In their telling, Russia was America without the imperfections – the greed, the racial prejudice, self-interest, poverty, sickness, or crime that infected the Western world. These aspirations naturally suited the idealistic people drawn to Communism and its promise of a better world.

Idealistic, Milo harrumphed. Gullible is more like it.

For rank and file Communists, Party doctrine was unshakeable, infallible – at least until Stalin changed his mind and then new directives were issued from the Communist International. If Moscow said it was true, then it must be so. When Moscow said it was no longer true, then it never happened in the first place. Such flexibility left the Communists with a unique ability to follow the Party line no matter how often or how quickly it changed. One day's policy was the next day's forgotten contradiction.

Before World War II, the Communists were among the first to recognize the evils of the Third Reich, largely because the fascists in Nazi Germany posed the greatest threat to the Russian homeland. Because of this threat, American labor unions demanded American action: U.S. troops and machines must be sent overseas to stop Hitler from invading Russia! Resolutions were drafted, speeches delivered, and donations collected – all to protect Mother Russia.

That was the official Communist policy until the day that Molotov had a cocktail with Ribbentrop and suddenly a peace pact was announced between the Soviets and their former foes, the Germans. The Nazis immediately captured eastern Europe, but that didn't matter so much to Joseph Stalin. The Soviet leader had purchased peace from his new friend, Adolph Hitler. New orders were soon dispatched from Moscow: America must stay home! Communists must oppose the war in Europe because now there was peace between Russia and the Third Reich!

For a while anyway.

American Reds were still at the mimeograph when the Hitler-Stalin romance ended and Nazi Panzers began rolling toward Moscow. Like bears in a carnival arcade, American Communists wheeled back around and marched the opposite way – *to war*! The Schenectady Reds raced back to Milo with the latest orders from Moscow.

"Milo, we need a new resolution! Hitler must be stopped! America must go to war and save the Soviet Socialist Republic!"

"Why are we changing our minds – again?" Milo asked when the Communists delivered their new, "make war" resolution. The Reds had no answer for that. They looked at Milo as if he had two heads. Only Milo could see the irony: two heads were standard equipment on the 1939 model Communist.

Without another word, Milo reached inside his desk and took out the original "Go to War" resolution. He simply changed the date and the Reds went away happy.

How puny, Milo scoffed. These Communists and all their public hoo-haw, scribbling away at useless resolutions, waving them in the air as if they were something to be feared.

"Ideas are the bullets that can be fired every day!" That was the favorite saying of Ira Glabberson, the local Communist leader and Deputy Program Supervisor for Local 1389.

Paper bullets, jeered Milo. Where is Glabberson now? No doubt hiding in his office, typing out more pointless resolutions, conducting endless meetings to discuss his intricate strategies with his not-so-trusted inner circle. (The Communists always met in a circle, never trusting their backs to any of their comrades.) It would be easy to call them stupid, but Milo saw the Reds as more clueless than brainless.

Their obedience to Moscow – their slavish devotion to the Revolution – was more like a reflex than a conscious decision. Did they really understand what they were talking about? Milo wondered. Were they actually prepared to violently overthrow the American government? Could one of them shoot a cop or blow up a school? Set fire to a movie theater? How far were they willing to go? It was like the Cold War itself: it's safer when the guns aren't loaded and battle plans are nothing more than wishes on paper.

Milo was glad that Glabberson and the Reds kept to themselves, out of sight and out of their minds. Except for these resolutions! Now here was another one sitting on his desk like an unexploded bomb!

Milo looked sadly at the bulky envelope, stamped URGENT and wrapped tightly in a yard of Scotch tape. Milo was too exhausted to saw through it. It was just another sign that the Cold War was closing in on him. It was even waiting for him at home.

Despite Martha's promise to forsake her Communist past, Milo was still finding Soviet propaganda stashed in their house on Tuckahoe Row. The week before, she brought home a dog and named it Red. On the refrigerator door was a list of secret "drops" that Martha had designated around the neighborhood for microfilm and other spy matter. Then Milo found the radio transmitter that Martha had stashed in the basement, a gift from her first husband, Harold. Martha could never make the damn thing work – Milo had made sure of that. Still, Martha would not give up.

This was a daily struggle and Milo tried to keep his cool – until the day he found a copy of the *Daily Worker* in the upstairs bathroom. He could not believe the name printed on the subscription label:

Michael Milwaukee
2943 Tuckahoe Row
Schenectady, N.Y.

Milo hollered, "Dammit Martha! I asked you to leave the boy alone! He doesn't need any of this Communist crap!"

"Milo, lower your voice!" Martha hissed back. "And don't you tell me what's crap! I've been to Russia – at least, I've met Russians – and I know what Communism means to the children over there! It turns them into great leaders."

"Well in this country it turns them over to the FBI! What the hell were you thinking – a subscription to the *Daily Worker?* Why don't you put a hammer and sickle on his lunchbox?"

Martha stomped her foot. "The boy needs something important in his life – something to be proud of! Something to belong to!"

"Michael's got plenty to be proud of. How about me, for instance – the boss of the biggest union in town? And he's got the Little League – and the Boy Scouts!"

"Let me tell you about those Boy Scouts with all their creepy finger signals, wrapping themselves in that Masonic voodoo. It's horrible how they vandalize the ancestry of the noble American Indian! What lessons are we teaching these children: just hand over a few beads and now you own Manhattan? I want Michael to respect people – people of all kinds – and I want him to make a name for himself!"

"By getting his name on a government list? Let's just paint him red and hang a sign around his neck: My mother is a Commie loon!"

Milo had gone too far. Martha stood there in silence, her arms clenched against her chest and her face growing red. First came a tiny whimper and then a geyser of tears ran down her face.

"That's not fair!" Martha bawled. "That's not fair at all! You know I left the Party when I married you and I have kept that promise! The Party is all in the past now. But we've got Michael's future to think about. We've got the future of the whole world to think about!"

Now Martha had gone too far.

"Oh give me a break, Martha – the future of the world! Who do you think you're talking to? I have to listen to that nonsense every day from Glabberson and his band of living room revolutionaries! I've had enough of it!"

As usual, Michael had been listening by the back door. He had heard this argument many times before. The boy hated to hear his parents fight so he never told Milo about the other "Party activities" that were happening when Milo was away, about the strangers who would come to the house (always through the back door) and how they would argue late into the night, shouting about things that Michael could not understand – the proletariat, capitalist oppression, and counter-revolutionaries.

Still, Milo could tell something was up. After one of Martha's secret meetings, Milo would patrol the entire house, his nose in the air, peering into rooms and checking behind cushions, certain that something strange had occurred the night before. Michael never knew it, but his father could literally smell trouble and that included Communists.

The envelope on Milo's desk had just such an aroma. Picking it up with outstretched arms, Milo peeled back the elaborate seal, his face curdled in disgust as if a rotten egg were about to fall out. Instead, it was several typewritten pages, the letters stamped dark by the furious fingers of Ira Glabberson: "July 14, 1950, PROPOSED RESOLUTION FOR AEWA LOCAL 1389: OPPOSING AMERICA'S WAR WITH NORTH KOREA."

Not Korea, Milo cringed. Not now!

"This is not the war for America!" Glabberson's resolution screamed. "Let the Koreans fight the Koreans! We have no business in Korea or anywhere else in Indochina! America must leave Korea before it is too late!"

Only a few weeks earlier, America had gone back to war to protect South Korea from the Communists of North Korea. American boys – boys from Schenectady – were now dying at the hands of Communists. And what does Schenectady's largest union want to do about it? Cheer for the Communists!

Milo put his head on the desk. He wanted to cry.

Is this it? Milo wondered. Is this the end?

Was it time to finally tell the truth?

For years, Milo had only been pretending to be a Red, helping him move up the union's leadership ladder in a union controlled by Communists. Now Milo's charade was growing dangerous. Working for the nation's largest Communist union was not going to win him any medals. Avoiding trouble meant you belonged to the Kiwanis, not the AEWA. Leading a Communist union could even land you in prison.

One of the new anti-Communist laws was the Hatch Act, requiring Milo and other union leaders to sign an affidavit affirming that they were not members of the Communist Party. As Al Capone once discovered, a government form can put you in prison as easily as robbing a bank. Sign a piece of paper and you are just one step away from a perjury conviction.

Milo thought about the comfortable life he had given his family, about their big house on Tuckahoe Row – right alongside the homes of G.E. executives – the big, blue Continental parked in the driveway, the new G.E. appliances, and all the other perks that came with being a union boss. What will happen to all of these nice things if I'm carted away with the Commies?

Mostly he worried about Michael. The Red Scare had been swirling around the country for decades, but it had never touched down in Schenectady. But for how much longer? How long before Michael starts hearing rumors about his parents – those dirty Commies living down the block?

Milo glanced at the newspaper lying on the floor. There was Joe McCarthy again. "Tailgunner Joe Vows New Red Spy Disclosures," the headline blared. Every day there was more news about this senator from Wisconsin, the latest and loudest of the Red Hunters. How long before McCarthy turns his sights on Schenectady and Local 1389?

On *ME,* Milo worried.

Milo jumped at the knock on his door. A young woman, Helen Gamble, walked in. She was the secretary for Ira Glabberson and the Communist Central Committee of Local 1389.

"Mr. Milwaukee? Deputy Glabberson and the Committee would like to know if you received their latest resolution?"

Milo frowned. "He's right down the hall, isn't he?"

"Mr. Glabberson? Well … yes."

"And he can't walk down the hall and talk to me?"

Helen shrugged, an apologetic smile on her face.

Milo carefully placed the "Surrender Korea" resolution onto his desk, firmly pressing the pages smooth. If Helen had not been there, Milo might have tried to eat the pages.

"Can't we just praise the Russian wheat harvest? Who doesn't like wheat?"

"Wheat?" Helen smiled with a puzzled look on her face. Milo realized that he had been talking out loud. He cleared his throat, adjusted his pointy hair, and straightened himself in his chair as he pretended to study Glabberson's resolution, hoping it might somehow burst into flame.

"Should I tell Mr. Glabberson about the wheat harvest?" Helen asked.

"No, no. I'll talk to him about that … later." Milo looked up at Helen and, as she smiled, thoughts of North Korea, Joe McCarthy, and every other worry suddenly disappeared. Helen Gamble had that effect on people. There was something compelling about this young woman. In the spring of 1950, Helen did not yet have a Russian accent and she was not annoying anyone about the virtues of Communism. She was just Helen Gamble, sweet and beautiful.

"I wouldn't worry about it," she said.

"Worry?" Milo said in surprise.

"Nobody really cares about these resolutions – except for Mr. Glabberson, of course."

She was right. The members of Local 1389 seldom paid attention to the Communists. The union membership had no time for the Reds and their stuffy basement meetings, endlessly debating the Marshall Plan and Marxian philosophy. But their disinterest was helping the Communists maintain control of the union.

It was always the Reds who volunteered for the thankless jobs, the necessary work that kept the union running. They organized the Local's meetings, settled grievances with the company, kept everybody fed and clothed during a strike. The Communists of Local 1389 were always the first to arrive and the last to leave. The dirtier the job, the more the Reds seemed to enjoy it.

In return for all this work, the Reds were given all of the paid positions inside the union's leadership. They also controlled the voting, the dues, and almost everything else about the union. The only thing they didn't control was Milo. The Reds thought they did and Milo did everything to make them think so. When Milo wasn't pretending to be a Communist, he was devising strategies to get rid of them.

"*Nobody really cares.*" Helen's words echoed like a bell inside Milo's head. *Nobody cares.* How can anything change if nobody cares about what the Communists are doing?

If he was ever going to free the Local from the Communists – and save himself in the process – Milo needed something to wake up the membership, to make them see how dangerous the Reds had become. Make them care! The members needed to get angry! How could he get them as irritated as he was?

The Communists, of course! Helen jumped as Milo's tiny fist struck the desk. What's more annoying than Communism? Milo was astonished at the thought: he would use Communism to get rid of the Communists!

Helen wasn't sure what to make of the odd smile that spread across Milo's face. She took a step back toward the door as Milo offered her a chair. Cautiously, Helen sat down, a beautiful bird perched on the crocodile's nose.

"Helen," Milo said earnestly, "it's clear to me that our membership needs a new direction. The members of Local 1389, even its leaders, are losing touch with our roots – the union's origins, our foundation, the birthplace of our great struggles! We've forgotten about the hard-working men and women who fought to make this union great!"

"You mean the Party – here in Schenectady?"

"Precisely. Brick by brick, they built this city by building a great union. Your father was one of those pioneers, wasn't he? He and all the other Party members are an important part of our past, but we've allowed that past to be forgotten. We must recapture it now – as a bridge to our future, for the Local, and for young people like you. It's the future I'm talking about!"

Milo was circling his desk, not completely sure where he was headed.

"A future of peace and prosperity for everyone in the world! Peace for all mankind! And then we can make this union even bigger and stronger than it is already! Can I count on your help, Helen?"

Helen nodded enthusiastically even as she searched Milo's face, unsure of what he was asking her to do. Without another word, Milo grabbed his hat by the door and turned off the lights, leaving Helen sitting in the dark. Behind him, a single lightbulb hung in the hallway, swaying like a noose.

"Come now, Helen. It's time for us to go!"

Helen looked for Milo's face in the shadows. "Go where, Mr. Milwaukee?"

"Your training! I'm sending you to Camp Unity where you can learn all of the skills to become a great union leader!"

"A leader? Oh my gosh, Mr. Milwaukee. What are you saying?"

Milo kneeled next to Helen. "I'm saying this union needs someone like you, Helen Gamble – a fresh-faced cheerleader – a morale booster! Someone with a big heart who can pump up our Red … blood cells and help us conquer the world!"

"A cheerleader!" Helen gulped, falling back against the chair. She had always wanted to be a cheerleader.

Milo got back on his feet and took Helen by the hand. "A few minutes ago, I was asking myself, 'Milo, what are you waiting for?' And then look what happens: you walked in the door!"

"But why me?"

Milo looked at the newspaper tossed on the floor, the photo of Joe McCarthy and his gonna-getcha grin leering back at him. Pressing his shoe over McCarthy's face, Milo smiled down at Helen.

"You're asking, 'Why me?' This is Schenectady, kid. I ask myself that question every day."

"They spoke about ex-party members who had been tortured in the so-called capitalist dungeons and how ... to act under duress, under torture, and under questioning. We were given a thorough schooling in that respect."
WITNESS DESCRIBING TRAINING AT THE LENIN SCHOOL *during HUAC*
hearings on "Communism in Labor Unions in the United States"

C H A P T E R   S E V E N

ON THE ROAD TO CAMP UNITY

The Blue Bonnet bus squealed as it heaved off the road, shuddering to a stop next to weedy farmland. The sudden lurch woke Helen. She had been dozing since the bus passed Kingston and now they were ninety miles south of Schenectady. It was the farthest Helen had been from home since her family's vacation to Niagara Falls and, before this trip to Camp Unity, the Falls had been the greatest adventure of her life. That trip to Canada came to Helen's mind as she looked out the window as dust swirled in the air like the mist above "Ongniaahra," the Iroquois name for Thunder of the Waters.

"One of the Seven Thunders of the World!" Helen's father joked as he nudged his seven-year-old daughter closer to the railing above Horseshoe Falls. Helen tried to resist, her little shoes dragging against the wet pavement and years later she could still feel that thrilling tremble of terror as she moved closer – step by step, inch by inch – toward the wild, rushing water at the edge of the Falls.

It hardly seemed real, standing so close to something that ferocious. When her father handed Helen a crumpled ball of paper, she tossed it over the railing thinking it would float down the river and then over the Falls. She drew back in horror as the paper ball was sucked into the current as if it were consumed by some invisible menace. Helen did not go near the Falls again, certain that she would be eaten next.

Helen looked around the empty bus, now sunk into the sand along the deserted roadway. Sunshine streaked across the dirty windows, obscuring the fat elm trees that flanked a long dirt road adjoining the turnpike. No one was there to meet her.

"Excuse me," Helen called to the old man driving the bus, "is this Camp Unity?"

The skinny driver, tan as old leather, did not answer Helen. Still gripping the steering wheel, he slowly leaned over his left arm and from out of his mouth dropped a long string of tobacco juice that stretched into a coffee can wedged against the floor. The driver pulled himself out of his seat and without a glance toward Helen, he said, "Yup. This here is Camp Commie." The tiny man ambled down the stairs as Helen hurried to catch up.

By the time she got off the bus Helen's suitcase, now covered in dust, was thrown to the side of the road. Seeing Helen's distress, the bus driver smiled mischievously as he turned his head aside and lobbed another gob of spit into the air. The brown sluice landed close to Helen's suitcase.

Helen shouted, "Hey now! Be careful, please!"

"Sorry there, Commie girl," the driver laughed under his breath. He stared at Helen as if he were inspecting a bug or something dead along the road. Putting a finger to one side of his nose, the driver blew the snot out of his nostril. Helen tried to look away, but it was too late. Her grimace made the driver chuckle again.

"You sure don't look like a Commie," he said, squinting into the mid-morning sun. He pushed another wad of Red Man into his jaw. Helen crooked her head to one side, taking in the driver's hard stare.

"And what's a Communist supposed to look like?"

The driver clucked his tongue impatiently. "What I mean is, you look like a nice girl. But here you are itchin' to get down to that Commie camp." He wiped his mouth on his sleeve. "I guess looks can be deceivin'."

"Camp Unity is a school for labor organizers," Helen said firmly. "It's one of the best labor schools in the country and my union has sent me here to attend classes to become – "

"A smarter Commie," the driver finished her sentence. "So you think you're goin' to school, do ya? With neat little books and a shiny red apple for the teacher? Ha! Only thing they'll be teachin' you is how to be a god-damned Red. Hell – what am I talking to you for? Perfect waste of a sunny day. I shoulda dropped you off in Russia."

"Whose side do you think I'm on?"

The driver pointed down the unmarked road. "Well you must be for them Ruskies if you're goin' down there! I don't suppose you'll be singin' 'God Bless America' around the campfire, now will ya?"

"And why not?" Helen raised her chin defiantly. She picked up her suitcase and shook the dirt off. "We're all on the same side, you know!"

"Oh yeah? And what side is that, you figger?"

"The side that's for the working people – people like you and me! That's why I came here. I want to help people in their everyday struggles – people just like you!"

Putting his hands against his bony hips, the driver let out a croaking laugh. "I ain't got no struggles, little girl!" He bent over with a heavy cough before spitting out more tobacco juice. "I don't need any of your help and I sure as hell don't want *their* help neither!"

The driver looked down the road toward Camp Unity and then he eyed Helen's overstuffed suitcase. "Looks like the only person with a struggle is gonna be you draggin' that big bag down the road. How come none of yer Commie friends are here to help ya? Well, go ahead now. You go struggle all you want."

The old man snickered to himself as he shuffled back to the bus. Helen looked at her heavy suitcase and then over to the long dirt road. She clenched her fists and stuck out her tongue at the driver. Spying her reflection in the window, the driver let out another ragged laugh.

"Is that the best you got?" he asked.

"What?" said Helen, pretending not to know.

"Listen here, kid. You gotta learn how to do things right in this world and there are some things they ain't gonna teach ya in school – even in Commie school."

The driver walked over to Helen. "Don't be stickin' out your tongue like some snot-nosed brat. If you wanna tell somebody to go jump in the lake, then you gotta give 'em one of these!" He took hold of Helen's right hand and pulled up her middle finger. "There. Now turn your hand around like this and stick it up in the air like so. That's how you do it," the old man squawked with delight. "You give 'em the bird!"

He climbed back onto the bus and was about to close the folding doors when he shouted, "Now go back to Russia, you dirty Commie!" – flipping his middle finger at Helen. Helen smiled and shot him "the bird" right back.

"Ha ha, atta girl!" the driver hooted, slapping the steering wheel. "You'll do okay yet!" He turned over the motor and pushed the bus back into gear, rocking onto the asphalt and down the road to Poughkeepsie. As the bus pulled away, another cloud of dust swirled in the air, stinging Helen's eyes. When she could open them again, a message suddenly appeared above her. Stretched between two elm trees, arbor vines had been woven into an archway of crudely-shaped letters: "**Come Forth and Learn**."

Helen marveled at the ingenuity.

How clever – creating a message out of vines and tree branches! A message of hope, shaped by nature, welcoming her to Camp Unity. It made her smile as she set off on the twisting, rocky road.

Yes, she decided, this would be a place where she could learn. Exactly what they would teach her, Helen had no idea, but her excitement and anticipation kept building with every turn in the road – each step closer to Helen becoming a "cheerleader" for Local 1389!

Half an hour later, the road was still twisting, but not ending. Helen put down her suitcase and stopped to rest under an enormous oak tree. She had been sitting for only a few seconds when she spotted a burly man out of the corner of her eye. Stout and hairy, he was sitting in a Jeep parked on the other side of the tree. Helen was so startled, she fell off her suitcase and onto the road.

"*Goodness me, Miss!*" the man shouted in a Russian accent. "*I did not mean to frighten you!*"

He looked like a character from a story book. His beard and ragged hair were spread across thick shoulders and a powerful chest. He jumped off the Jeep and pulled Helen to her feet. The man suddenly looked up in surprise as Helen towered over him.

"*Women of Schenectady are so tall! Please – do not step on little Petrov!*" With one hand, Petrov swung Helen's suitcase onto the Jeep. "*Hop on now. I bring you to Camp Unity!*"

Helen tried to smile even as her arms and legs ached from the long walk. She wondered to herself: Why did he park so far from the bus stop? Petrov sensed her aggravation.

"*I am sorry to have you walk so far. But we must be careful out there. Sometimes there is trouble by the road. Nothing Petrov cannot handle, let me tell you. But now you are here and this day is too beautiful to think of such things! Now we are off!*"

Helen had barely sat down when Petrov hit the gas, the tires spraying dust and stones behind them. Before she could catch her breath, Petrov whipped the Jeep around and tore down the narrow path. Helen grabbed her seat with one hand and squeezed the windshield with the other as trees along the roadside disappeared into a blur of green with bursts of sunlight flashing past Helen's eyes.

"*American workers – good union workers – they make this Jeep! Fast car, yes?*" Petrov bellowed over the noise. Helen wasn't listening. She was trying to open her eyes as the wind pressed against her face. "*I love fast car!*"

"No kidding!" Helen shouted, locking her feet against the dashboard as the Jeep rocked and bumped down the road. Petrov casually leaned back in his seat, one enormous hand gripping the steering wheel while his other hand pushed the clutch.

"You have met Harold the bus driver, yes? Such an ignorant man, Harold – no sense of the world and how it works – the class conflicts and oppression of the proletariat. Another tool for the Wall Street machine, would you agree? Someday he will understand. Someday, he will be thanking us – thanking you, Helen."

The Jeep jumped over a rise, offering a glimpse of something huge and brilliantly white that was far back in the forest and high above the trees. They raced around another curve and Helen saw it again – a face or a gigantic head? – somewhere deep in the woods. Climbing another hill, Helen could see a small lake below and, at the far end of the water, there stood an enormous statue of Jesus Christ, a replica of the giant Redeemer statue in Rio de Janeiro.

"What in the world?" Helen gushed.

"Something, yes? That side is for the Catholics, the priests. They teach their own school down there. We call it Our Lady of Needless Suffering," Petrov laughed as he gunned the Jeep over another rise.

"Whooo-hooo!" he shouted. *"Fast car! Hang on!"*

They were heading downhill now, increasing in speed and gaining on a collection of wooden buildings set along the lakeside. At last, Helen had found Camp Unity.

Petrov skidded to a stop as Helen pulled the hair from her face and staggered out on wobbly legs. They were parked next to a long, wooden cabin where a young woman, pale and very thin, was standing near the door. Petrov nodded at Helen to walk over.

The young woman was reading a list posted on the wall:

CLASS SCHEDULE FOR WEEK OF JULY 24, 1950:

It Was Yours, Now It's Mine: Confiscating personal property with tips on how to keep your plunder well-organized.

Power to the People: Introductory course in Marxism, reducing complicated concepts into easy-to-remember slogans.

What About Me? The Life of Friedrich Engels, Communism's Second Fiddle. Socialist visionary or petulant bore?

Helen was confused. Where were the classes on labor organization, union rallies, parade organizing, and morale boosting? She turned to another list on the bulletin board. This one was labeled "CLUBS AND ACTIVITIES."

CRAFTS THAT CAN KILL. *Learn how to make* a comb case, lanyard or ceramic ashtray that is both attractive and lethal.

SONG AND DANCE. *You can't change a thing if you ain't got that swing!* Learn toe-tapping songs of the People's Revolution as you explore artistic styles from the Bolshoi to Gdansk.

GOURD YOUR SECRETS. *Discover the many hiding places Mother Nature has to offer.* Instruction in how to safeguard your secrets inside pumpkins, squash, and other produce.

"What classes would you recommend?" Helen asked.

Without answering Helen, the young woman lowered her head before glancing once to left and then to the right.

"All of these classes are worthwhile, Comrade," the girl mumbled quickly.

"Why are you whispering?" Helen laughed, thinking it was some kind of joke. The young woman was incredulous, shocked by Helen's laughter. She scurried away without another word.

Petrov came up behind Helen. "*That is Patrice. Very unhappy. She lost a friend just now.*"

"That's terrible. What happened?"

"*A misfortunate young man. He criticized the food he was served – a very counter-revolutionary remark, you would say.*"

"And now her friend is – ?" Helen asked, horrified at the thought.

"*What are you thinking? This young man was only punished – scolded really. He will be re-educated after working in kitchen for six months. Then he will be dead.*"

"They're actually going to kill him?"

"*No, no, no. Dead because he will be thrown out of Party.*"

For criticizing the food? Helen could not believe what she was hearing.

"*Come now!*" Petrov called. "*Let us find you a bed!*"

Petrov led Helen past several dormitories, each one bearing the name of a Communist icon. There was the Paul Robeson, the Joe Hill, the Karl Marx, and then, finally, the Bella Dodd Dormitory for Women. Workmen were up on ladders, tearing down the 'Bella Dodd' sign. Helen was about to ask why, but then she stopped herself. She now realized that some questions should not be asked.

Helen and Petrov walked into the dormitory where rows of metal beds were jammed against each other. At the far end of the room, Patrice was sitting on her cot, straining to play a guitar. Again, Petrov nodded Helen toward her. She took a seat on the cot opposite Patrice.

"What are you playing?" Helen asked.

Patrice looked up without returning Helen's smile and then turned back to the guitar.

"It's a Russian folk song. Comrade Petrov showed it to me."

"What is it called?"

"I can't remember. Something in Russian," Patrice sighed, pushing the guitar away. "I can't do it!"

"Is that yours?"

"The guitar? No, it belongs to the camp. I mean, everybody – it belongs to everybody!" Patrice stammered. "Anyone can play it. Except me, I guess." Patrice looked at the guitar as if it were about to agree with her. She turned back to Helen, her face expressionless except for her large, sad eyes. "What's your name?"

"Helen Gamble."

"How long do you have to stay here?"

"For a while, I guess. I suppose they'll tell me when it's time to go home."

"Maybe," Patrice said, glancing over her shoulder again.

"And what's your name?" Helen asked brightly.

"Patrice – as in Say the Least." She looked up at Helen, hoping she liked the joke.

"Don't like to talk much, huh?" Helen laughed, coaxing a grin from Patrice. It made Helen relax too.

"I only talk when I'm comfortable. Otherwise, I just clam up." Patrice suddenly jumped off her cot and grabbed Helen by the hand. "Come, Comrade! Let me show you around."

They stepped out of the dormitory, past the smell of mothballs and disinfectant and out into the fresh, forest air. Helen's eyes were immediately captured by the dazzling white statue at the far end of the lake, its arms stretched out above the trees. The enormous statue of Jesus seemed to glow in the sunlight.

"That is something!" Helen marveled. "Can we see it up close?"

"We're not supposed to go over there," Patrice said, looking around to see who might be listening. "Say – do you know what time it is?"

"Almost noon," Helen answered.

"Oh my gosh! Come quick – we're late for Dialectical Materialism!"

Patrice grabbed Helen's hand and went running toward a bright red building with a steeple on top. Passing the flagpole in the center of the courtyard, Patrice skidded to a stop. She snapped to attention and gave a quick, hard salute to the Russian flag flying overhead. Helen also stopped and saluted as Patrice sprinted ahead toward the schoolhouse.

Inside were nearly fifty students seated at small desks crammed into eight neat rows. As Helen and Patrice took seats in the back, a bell rang and the classroom door slowly opened. Every student jumped to their feet, their eyes locked in attention to the front of the room. Helen kept watching the door: it had been open for several seconds and still no one had walked through. Then she heard the sound of footsteps plodding slowly toward them. With each heavy step there followed a quick "thump-thump," another loud step and then another "thump-thump." From around the corner, a frail little woman, well into her sixties, crept toward them. Helen could feel the students stiffen as the old woman entered the classroom.

Dressed in a high-buttoned collar and long woolen skirt, she looked as withered and brittle as the hairless cat that lay in the crook of her arm. Everything about the old woman seemed pointy and dangerous, especially the big cat. In her other hand, she carried a ping-pong paddle. The miserable scowl on her face made it clear that she was not interested in playing a game.

"That's Madame!" Patrice whispered from the seat behind Helen.

Madame placed the wrinkled cat on the desk before writing a single word on the blackboard: V I G I L A N C E. The chalk was hardly off the board when – THWACK! – a sharp crack from the ping-pong paddle made Helen jump.

Madame paced slowly between the rows of students, her limp echoing with a thump-thump and another THWACK as Madame struck the paddle against one of her pencil-thin thighs.

"Yes, comrades. Vigilance." Her voice was thin and sour. "Now tell me: What does vigilance mean to you?" A hand shot up in the front row.

"Vigilance means that each comrade must be aware of his surroundings," the young man offered.

"What else?" Madame demanded. Across the room, an older woman raised her hand.

"And we must warn the Party whenever we see or hear something suspicious."

"Better – " Madame muttered. The old woman scanned the classroom for more volunteers. Finding none, Madame cried out, "Then why, comrades? WHY?"

The students sank into their chairs, unsure of what to say. Madame repeated the question over and over as she snaked her way toward Helen and Patrice. The hairless cat arched its back, hissing at the ignorant students as Madame shouted, "WHY THEN? WHY, WHY, *WHY?*"

Patrice and Helen anxiously eyed one another as Madame slithered up to Helen's desk. The class drew in a breath as Madame thrust her ping-pong paddle straight at Helen's face.

"I say HALT! Who is this woman and WHY is she here?"

Helen was about to explain when Madame tottered back to the front of the class, aiming her paddle at a young man in the far corner of the room. "Did YOU know she was there?"

"NO!" the young man shouted. Madame took her paddle and whacked him on the side of the head. The young man turned to the woman behind him and he too demanded, "Did YOU know she was there?" When the woman said no, the young man slapped her hard across the face. Around the room, the question was passed from student to student, each one slapping the next, as Madame followed behind, smiling in approval.

Helen turned around to Patrice, wondering what she should do.

"It's okay," Patrice whispered. "Just do it. She doesn't care if you can take it. She wants to see if you can GIVE it."

"HALT!" Madame shouted when the question came to Helen. "Comrades, vigilance means that we must always be thinking about our enemies! Vigilance is our only protection. But for now, you may relax. There is no cause for alarm. The security of Camp Unity has not been breached. Comrades, I want you all to welcome Comrade Helen Gamble. She has come to us from the AEWA, the electrical workers union in Schenectady, where, I am informed, Comrade Gamble will soon accept the title of Morale Coordinator for Local 1389. Congratulations, Comrade!"

"Thank you, Comrade Madame," Helen said enthusiastically. Patrice rolled her eyes to the ceiling: no one ever addressed their leader as 'Comrade Madame.' Worse still, Helen was extending her hand toward Madame – offering to shake hands! Patrice let out an audible moan.

"Very well then," Madame said stiffly, ignoring Helen's hand. "You may continue."

"Continue?" asked Helen. With a flick of her paddle, Madame motioned toward Patrice. Slowly, Helen turned around.

"Did you know?" Helen said meekly.

"LOUDER!" Madame shouted.

"Did you … DID YOU KNOW?" Helen shouted at Patrice.

Patrice did not know what to say. She did know, of course, but everyone else had said no, so what else could she say? In the Communist Party, conformity was nearly as important as vigilance. Patrice looked to Madame for the answer, but the old woman only smiled in anticipation.

"No!" Patrice finally shouted, shutting her eyes tightly. Helen was reaching back to slap Patrice when her arm was stopped by Madame's paddle.

"That is enough for now," Madame purred as she returned to the front of the classroom.

"Comrades, I have told you why Comrade Gamble is here. I want to know why the rest of you are here. Are you here for the scenery? Is Camp Unity a relaxing holiday for you?"

"No, Madame!" the class responded in unison.

"Do you know who you are fighting? In America today, only the strong survive! Only the zealots can win!"

"We are ready!" the students shouted.

"And have you dedicated yourselves – with all your heart and soul – to leading our Glorious Revolution?"

"Yes! Yes!"

"Then tell me: What must you learn?" Madame pointed her paddle at a woman in the front row.

"How to blow up a factory!" the woman shouted.

"And you?"

"Sabotage a train!"

Helen was shocked. She turned to Patrice in wide-eyed amazement. What were these people talking about? All Helen could think about was the next Labor Day parade! As Helen turned around to the front of the class, Madame was now pointing at her!

"I, uh … me?" Helen stammered. "I want to learn how to decorate a float – for our next parade, I mean." Madame's paddle fell limply to her side and the classroom suddenly went quiet. Patrice dropped her head into her hands.

"Very good, comrades! Very good!" A tall woman, much younger than Madame, was at the front door clapping her hands enthusiastically. "Those were very good answers everyone! It will be time for lunch soon. Let us make preparations for this beautiful day. Forward to October!"

"Forward to October!" the class called back.

"What's happening in October?" Helen asked Patrice.

"I'll tell you later – " Patrice muttered as she scurried toward the door. Confused, Helen ran after her.

At the doorway, the tall woman was congratulating each student as they left the room. She held out her hand to Helen. "Welcome to Camp Unity, Comrade Gamble! I am Comrade Tilson, Anna Tilson." Helen returned her smile, instantly admiring this woman's elegance and poise.

"I know you will do a great job lifting the spirits of our union brothers and sisters! And don't worry about Madame," Comrade Tilson smiled. "She enjoys a good parade as much as anyone."

Helen grimaced, embarrassed that her answer was not more vigilant. She was about to ask where everyone was going in October when Patrice pulled her toward the exit.

"What's the matter?" Helen asked. "Did I say something wrong?"

"Please don't talk about parade floats or things like that. Madame wants us to be more – "

"More what?"

"Prepared!" It was Madame slinking up behind them. Perched on her arm was the bony cat, glaring savagely at Helen and Patrice. Madame ran her fingers between the creases of the cat's wrinkled skin and the cat stretched itself, exposing its enormous claws. Helen turned to Madame, but the old woman returned no expression as she took a menacing step toward Helen.

"Do not worry, Comrade Gamble. We will prepare you fully for the tasks that you must learn before returning home. And just like a cat, you will learn when it is time to use your claws."

Helen reached out to pet the cat when the animal viciously swatted at her! Helen snatched her hand back just in time.

Vigilance! Helen was already learning – even from the cat.

As Madame limped away, the cat glared back at Helen, as if sizing her up for its next meal. Helen scowled back at the awful beast, wondering what would happen if a hairless cat went over Niagara Falls.

Camp Unity was just one of many "labor" schools around the country, all of them modeled on the famous Lenin School in Moscow. As this New Vanguard of the Communist Party was taking shape, another secret army was being formed. Three years earlier, leaders in Washington had devised plans for their own training school as part of a new spy service dedicated exclusively to thwarting the Red Menace.

It began with the remnants of the Office of Strategic Services, the American spy agency created haphazardly in the midst of World War II. This was not a popular decision. Many derided the OSS for being "Oh So Social," a reference to its Ivy League lineage and its free-spirited officers. But under its new and secret reconstitution, the OSS would evolve into America's most far-reaching defense against the Soviet Union and its incursions around the globe.

Straight up or on the rocks, the agents of the new Central Intelligence Agency were quickly trained to fight their nation's Cold War with Russia. American warfare would never be the same again.

"(The) Washington Post has for several years carried on this Communist smear propaganda to try to force Negroes into white schools, playgrounds, swimming pools, and churches of the District of Columbia, for the sole purpose of stirring trouble between the races here in Washington. The better element of the Negroes here in the District of Columbia have appealed to us to help them get segregated places where they can meet and not be bothered by members of other races, especially the ones who are interested in promoting Communism and stirring up racial friction throughout the country."

MISSISSIPPI CONGRESSMAN JOHN E. RANKIN, *in a speech before the House, August 8, 1950*

CHAPTER EIGHT

WASHINGTON, D.C. 1947:
the CIA is Born

Harry Truman was the joy buzzer of American politics.

"Give 'em hell Harry" was always full of surprises, gleefully raising the faulty front page of the *Chicago Tribune* – 'Dewey Beats Truman' – and shocking the political world by winning another four years in office. Truman had only just become President when America dropped the biggest and deadliest surprise of all, unleashing atomic bombs over Hiroshima and then Nagasaki.

"They have been repaid many fold," the White House press release stated primly. "They" were mainly civilians as tens of thousands of men, women, and children perished at 8:15 on a Monday morning in Hiroshima, the target chosen because it was small enough for a single bomb to destroy the entire city. Thousands more would die slowly over the following weeks, suffering the agony of radiation poisoning and third-degree burns. The "Bomb to End All Bombs" had ended the war, but armed conflicts would continue throughout Truman's unexpectedly long stay in the White House.

Another constant of the Truman years was J. Edgar Hoover. While presidents would come and go, Hoover had been the first and only director of the Federal Bureau of Investigation. After a quarter of a century as America's top lawman, Hoover had become an institution in his own right, permanent and unchangeable, the Old Testament of American law enforcement. Rivers of blood and swarms of locusts were child's play in the crime-fighting world of J. Edgar Hoover. The Director had invented the famous list of "Ten Most Wanted" fugitives, leading to the capture of Pretty Boy Floyd, Ma Barker, and other headline-grabbing gangsters of the early 20th century. By the 1950s, however, Hoover's foremost target was the Red Menace.

When it came to punishing "the Commonists," as he called them, John Edgar Hoover had made a sacred vow: there would be no Communist Revolution in America – not under his watch. America's G-Man hated the Communists because Hoover hated change. It was also why Hoover hated Harry Truman. During the next four years, Hoover would discover that this Munchkin from Missouri would change his life as no one had before.

Hoover grew up in The District, back when Washington was considered more southern than northern. It was a segregated hothouse of seemingly gentle manners and sweaty refinement, proudly upholding antebellum values of honor, chivalry, and always knowing one's place in society. Always and forever.

Even as a boy, Hoover realized that one day his legacy – his greatness – would be remembered by a grateful Republic and that the American people would demand a suitable monument to commemorate his many achievements. On his tenth birthday, Hoover began a careful survey of the city, thoughtfully searching for the perfect location for his public memorial. He would consider the light from all angles and how the sun would set against his image – or, rather, how his image would set against the sun. Should it be cast in marble or bronze? Would there be enough shade for people to sit and admire Hoover's monument or would too many trees bring too many birds to poo on Hoover's magnificent marble shoulders? All of these specifications were carefully listed in a velvet-covered notebook that young J. Edgar kept under his pillow.

By all accounts, he was a pompous little shit.

Hoover's favorite landmark, by far, was the White House. If the Colonies had remained in the British Empire, the White House would have been America's Buckingham Palace. Young J. Edgar often played outside the White House gates, imagining what life must be like inside this palace. Stepping into his imagination, Hoover could see the majestic ballroom filled with proper lords and ladies dressed in their finest laces and satins, dancing regally past the throne where Hoover, of course, would be standing beside the King.

This is where the dream had become reality: Hoover truly was the Archduke and Royal Advisor for every president since Calvin Coolidge, always ready with news about the latest intrigue in Washington and the most salacious gossip culled from the FBI's vast files. His primary mission, Hoover believed, was to keep the president focused on Communism. The Reds were the biggest threat to American freedom and Hoover was determined to stop them in every way possible.

Nothing was too severe – or even slightly illegal – in thwarting the "Commonists," including the thousands of dossiers Hoover collected on elected officials, prominent bureaucrats, and the rest of official Washington. These reports brimmed with intimate details – sometimes confirmed, other times not – on a person's job, their family, love life, reading habits, and, most importantly, their political beliefs. Sprinkled with rumors and neighborhood gossip, the FBI files held every possible clue on whether someone might be – or ever was – a member of the Communist Party. There was even a file on Harry Truman as there was for every other president, vice president and cabinet member during the reign of J. Edgar Hoover.

Once the FBI opened a file on someone, it was like a pebble dropped in the water with an ever-widening circle of investigations of friends and acquaintances. No tidbit was too small to throw away as the FBI spread its net ever wider, capturing secrets on thousands of people with less-important jobs in less-important cities than Washington. These dossiers became Hoover's Terracotta Army: row upon row of overstuffed file cabinets – heavy enough that they nearly collapsed the fifth floor of the FBI's headquarters. It was a compilation so vast that everyone in Washington was asking the same question: What does Hoover have on me?

Information is power, but misinformation is often more powerful. Hoover traded in both, quickly becoming the most-feared man in Washington. He made sure every President knew about these "secret" files, delivering truckloads of new reports to the White House every month. He gave the President just enough information to conclude that Communists – homegrown or foreign – were the single greatest threat to America.

But Harry Truman was a farm boy and far too impatient for that much reading. Unlike his predecessors, President Truman showed very little interest in the FBI files. "Wouldn't need that much paper if I sat on the crapper for the rest of my life," Truman scoffed. (Truman's barnyard humor was one of the items frequently noted in his FBI file.)

Soon after his surprising defeat of Thomas Dewey, Truman dropped another bombshell. He was closing the White House.

"We used to have mice in here," the President quipped. "But this place is such a dump, all the mice have moved out!" Truman ordered a complete renovation of the 150-year-old mansion. The Trumans would move across the street to Blair House and for the next four years the White House would be closed, even for the galas that Hoover loved. When the shocking news broke, it was one of the saddest days in the life of J. Edgar Hoover. America's Sheriff – this tough-as-nails lawman – was inconsolable. He was losing his palace, his playhouse! It was just another reason to despise Harry Truman.

Back and forth, Hoover would drive along the White House gates until his heart could no longer bear the separation. His limousine would pull to the curb and Hoover would drag himself to the White House gates, pressing his fleshy cheeks against the bars, a prisoner locked away from his freedom, returning there only in his dreams.

Night after night, Hoover would escape to this dreamland, floating through the elegant parlors of America's First Ladies and the ornate halls of its Great Leaders. Under the baroque chandeliers of the Green Room, Hoover would be enraptured with the regal beauty of its chamois-colored wallpaper burnished with imprints of swans and nymphs on golden medallions. Drifting into the East Room, he would run his fingers along the elegant glassware and gilt-edged tableware (slipping the occasional dessert spoon into his pocket) and then on to the Violet Room where Hoover admired the glistening mahogany tables and carved-oak cabinetry. But for all of this splendor, nothing could surpass the grandeur of the Blue Room.

Here were the French Neoclassics, collected by the original – the genuine – presidents and their sophisticated wives: the James Monroe bergère, the Dolly Madison armoire, the Millard Fillmore spittoon, each surrounded by thick satin draperies of majestic blue. Watching over the magnificent Blue Room was Hannibal, the noble warrior of Carthage. The gilt-bronze statuette stood in the center of an ornate French clock decorated with scenes from the Battle of Cannae.

Poor Hannibal, Hoover sniffed. What will happen to you once the Blue Room is redecorated by Hayseed Harry, this Midwestern clodhopper? Will he paint it all Barnyard Red? Add corn stalks and milk cans next to straw-wicker rockers and antique butter churns? It was too much to even think about! Like Hannibal on the mantel clock, Hoover could only count the minutes (*four more years!*) before Harry Truman and "mah wife" Bess would hitch a mule to their wagon and "git on back to Missourah."

Tears flowed down the iron-gate creases of J. Edgar Hoover's face.

Just before the White House refurbishment was to begin, Truman invited Hoover to a State Dinner honoring the Bolivian ambassador.

Hoover wasn't sure if he could bring himself to visit the White House again – the palace was no longer regal. It had once been the domain of kings, but now it was occupied by the village smithy! He half expected to find a horseshoe nailed to the front door and the roof decorated with a rooster weathervane.

The President's invitation did not mention that the nation's leading trade unionists would also be attending. Hoover was shocked to find himself surrounded by these Reds and their filthy fellow travelers. There was Adrian Flornoy, president of the American Association of Nail Holders and Thumb Whackers, Daniel Flanagan of the Cement Mixers and Mortuary Helpers United, and Barney Loguidice of the International Ladder Holders – all of them Commonists!

Hoover was disgusted. The file on Harry Truman grew with each hand Hoover refused to shake.

As the guests took their seats for dinner, the FBI director and two of his agents quietly slipped out of the dining room. Hoover led the agents over to the William Howard Taft Reinforced Staircase.

"Okay you two, which one of you has done any 'black bag' work?"

The younger agent, Bradley Thompson, stared blankly at the FBI director.

"Black … bag?" he asked, choking on the thought of breaking the law.

"I'll take care of it," said Special Agent Walter Thurston. "What do you need, Director?"

Hoover smiled at the senior agent. "Here's what I need you to do, Thurston. Upstairs, second door on the left, you'll find Mrs. Truman's dressing room. Get in there and bring me any bedroom attire that you can find. Not everything, of course – just a few pieces. The softer the better, but nothing frilly."

Agent Thurston's face remained impassive and, with practiced determination, his eyes did not blink as the words "bedroom attire" ricocheted through his brain. Like other senior agents, Walter Thurston was well aware of the rumors surrounding The Boss. There had long been talk of Hoover's interest in unconventional social gatherings and unusual manners of dress. But Thurston maintained his composure and nodded sharply to the Director, "You can count on me, sir."

"Excellent. When you're done, meet me in the Green Room."

Thurston silently raced up the carpeted stairs, trying to imagine what he would find in Bess Truman's wardrobe and trying NOT to think about what he would find later in the Green Room. It took Agent Thurston less than five minutes to find Mrs. Truman's trousseau and then make his escape downstairs. He found the Director sitting alone in the Green Room, a look of great expectation on his face.

"Let me see what you've got!" Hoover exclaimed, bouncing in his chair. From underneath his coat, Thurston pulled out a pinkish nightgown and a pair of furry slippers. Hoover wrinkled his nose.

"Oh my goodness! Can you believe this?" He held the nightgown up to the light. Agent Thurston tried to look away as Hoover clucked his disapproval. "My, my goodness. This is hideous. All the taste and elegance you would expect to find in Kansas City."

"And no wonder," Hoover chortled as he checked the label. "Sears and Roebuck – 100 percent Rayon."

"I'd better be getting back to the dining room, sir," Thurston said, moving toward the door.

"Thank you, Agent Thurston, that will do. And I must say, I am quite impressed – with you, not with this! You did what I ordered you to do and you did it well. And don't think I don't notice this sort of thing. I always keep my eye out for men like you."

Thurston tried to smile at the Director's compliment, but a worried grimace was all he could manage. Closing the door behind him, Thurston turned to see the FBI Director standing before a mirror, measuring the nightgown against himself. A bracing chill cut through Thurston's body. He had seen crime scenes less frightening than this.

By the time Hoover exited the Green Room, the other guests had left the White House and the President was sitting alone in the Blue Room, smoking one of his favorite "Wet Willy" cigars.

"Mr. President, may I have a word?" Hoover said gravely.

"You can have a word. You can also have the supper you didn't eat!"

Hoover smiled stiffly. Then his eyes grew wide as he realized that the President was lying on the Martha Washington sofa – *with his shoes on*! Hoover suddenly felt very hot. He needed to sit down.

Get yourself together, J. Edgar! He looked around the room wondering if the President might take out his corncob pipe.

"Mr. President," Hoover grimaced, "I want to discuss a matter of great importance, sir – the greatest importance!"

"Well, do tell," Truman said as he reached down and pulled off his shoes – and then his socks! Hoover tried to focus on the ceiling.

"Yes sir, indeed. It concerns the fate of our nation and its security, both here and abroad! I want to convince you, Mr. President, that America must have only one agency to confront the Commonist threat. Only one agency can gather the necessary intelligence and carry out the vital counter-intelligence needed to protect ourselves from the Reds. That agency, I'm proud to say, is the Federal Bureau of Investigation and not this so-called Central Intelligence Agency – a ragtag mob of Ivy League Nancy-boys, shooting first and asking questions later. America already has a central intelligence agency, sir, and it's called the FBI!"

Truman smiled patiently as he examined his feet, tugging at his toes as Hoover searched the room for somewhere to retch.

"Well, Mr. Director," the President said quietly. "I am well aware of your concerns regarding the Communists and I know you're not happy with the idea of a new intelligence agency. But you have been telling me for years that there are what – a million? – Communists living in the United States today. And each one of those Reds is potentially an agent of espionage for the Soviet Union, dedicated to the violent overthrow of our glorious Republic. Isn't that what you've said?"

Truman paused as he brought a naked foot up to the light, examining each toe carefully.

"Now is that what I understand you to be telling me, Mr. Director?" the

President said as he started peeling back a hangnail. Clutching his stomach, Hoover quickly swiveled his head toward Hannibal on the mantelpiece.

"Yes, the numbers are truly frightening," Hoover said, gripping the mantel with both hands as the room began to spin. "The Commonists are a dangerous army within our gates."

"Well then, how in the world can just one agency – even your vaunted FBI boys – keep track of that many Communists? It's just not possible, Mr. Director. I know it and you know it!"

Hoover could kick himself. In his speeches, radio broadcasts, and official reports, Hoover had been inflating the true number of Communists for years. The Party's actual membership was far less, thanks in no small part to the FBI's crackdown on the Reds. The FBI had been so successful in sabotaging the American Communist Party that there were often three informants for every true member of any single Communist organization. Frequently, those informants were filing reports on each other.

Hoover had also been keeping the Communists afloat by secretly funneling FBI funds to the Communist Party USA and its affiliates. Without Hoover's cash, the CPUSA would have folded years ago. But Hoover needed the Communists, just as any country needs a Great Enemy to make itself stronger. Without the Reds, Hoover would have seen his own power diminish. If there was no need for political dossiers and secret files, then who would need J. Edgar Hoover?

"It's precisely because of our enemies that I think we need a CIA," the President said emphatically. Truman sat up and started scratching his bare foot against the leg of the Abigail Adams loveseat. The room started to spin again as Hoover fell against the Mary Todd rocker.

"I am now in the process of assembling the most-extensive loyalty program this country has ever had – although I'm still not convinced that Communism poses that great a risk here at home. Internationally, yes. The U.S. must not allow the Reds to expand any farther. That goes for Indochina just as it does for Europe as well as the Middle East. But the Truman Doctrine will not succeed unless we convince the American people that a Red menace – or at least the possibility of one – also lies within our borders. So we will show them that we mean business with these new loyalty boards. Their investigations will flush out the Reds as well as any Congressman can. Besides – why should those Republicans get all the credit? Oh Jesus!"

Hoover turned around in fright. "What's the matter?"

"Will you look at that toe?" Truman held his foot up before Hoover could snap his head away. Putting his socks back on, Truman smiled up at Hoover. "It's like my pappy used to say, 'You can't beat a cow with a chicken,' and we're not gonna contain Stalin's aggression by shooting our way into Moscow. Bombs and bullets are not the answer. That's too dangerous now. No, this has to be a surreptitious war – battles fought with ideas and propaganda. Containment – that's the key! I'm going to build a well-trained cadre of super-secret spies, propaganda agents, and clandestine fighters. The British have offered to help and I'm inclined to accept their offer."

This was getting worse by the minute: CIA spies trained by the British! Hoover had to think fast.

"Everyone knows Stalin is a madman," Hoover protested. "He's more dangerous than Hitler ever was and the Russian spy service is decades old. They're tough and experienced – very deadly. The FBI knows how to handle dangerous thugs. Besides, you can't expect to train and mobilize a competent intelligence agency in just a matter of months. It's just not possible!"

"Well, we're going to try, Mr. Director. To be honest, I have already signed the executive order and at this moment the CIA is preparing specific covert tactics and comprehensive psychological warfare to loosen the Soviet grip on Eastern Europe. It's like my grandpappy always said, 'You can shoot a bear in the ass or you can lure 'em with honey. Either way, you better make it stick.' I'm going to see to it that the CIA makes it stick!"

Hoover couldn't believe what he was hearing. It was like discussing foreign policy with the Farmer's Almanac. Hoover made one final plea.

"Mr. President, as you know, some of the Joint Chiefs are worried about a sneak attack from the Russians. No one wants another Pearl Harbor – missiles falling out of the sky, bombing Manhattan … or even St. Louis! I feel you are about to make another big mistake."

Truman stopped and stared at Hoover. "What do you mean *another* big mistake?"

Hoover gulped. He could not mention his fears about the White House refurbishment. Opening the CIA was one thing, but closing the White House – the most beautiful home in America – that was unthinkable! Hoover wanted to shout, "You bumbling bumpkin! Close the White House just so you and Ma Tucker can ruin everything I hold precious! Hang gingham drapes on the walls and press American eagles all over the furniture! You'll probably want a stuffed bear in the foyer and taxidermy trophies hanging from the walls! It's just what the Blue Room needs, you know – a goddamned moose head over the Thomas Jefferson fireplace!"

Hoover cleared his throat. "Excuse me, Mr. President, I must have misspoken."

Hoover's "last" night in the White House had been a complete disaster, from Bess Truman's nightgown to Harry Truman's big toe. Worst of all was the news about the CIA! Hoover's driver had to help him down the presidential driveway as the FBI director staggered to his limousine. Moments later, as they were driving past the Washington Monument, something stirred inside of Hoover. Hannibal of Carthage was calling to him: "Take up your sword, J. Edgar! You can still fight!" Yes, Hoover realized, it was time to be a warrior!

"Take me to the office!" Hoover barked at his driver.

It was two in the morning when Hoover called his secretary in to work. The FBI Director dictated two secret orders that night. The first directed every employee of the FBI to follow a new mission. When not in pursuit of the Communists, all their efforts must be directed toward a single goal: thwart the CIA.

In his second command, Hoover ordered Junior Agent Bradley Thompson to be reassigned to the FBI field office in northern Maine. At

Thompson's going-away party, the highly agile Walter Thurston presented Thompson with a pair of mukluks and a moose whistle. He never told anyone about that day in the White House Green Room with the Sears and Roebuck nightgown pressed against the director of the FBI.

It was a secret that would be kept forever because that was how long J. Edgar Hoover would be in charge of the FBI.

"The seeds of totalitarian regimes are nurtured by misery and want. They spread and grow in the evil soil of poverty and strife. They reach their full growth when the hope of a people for a better life has died. We must keep that hope alive. The free peoples of the world look to us for support in maintaining their freedoms. If we falter in our leadership, we may endanger the peace of the world — and we shall surely endanger the welfare of this Nation."

PRESIDENT TRUMAN UNVEILS THE "TRUMAN DOCTRINE" *to contain Communist aggression internationally, before a Joint Session of Congress, March 12, 1947*

C H A P T E R   N I N E

ONE YEAR LATER:
Radio Free Berlin is On the Air

"Comrade, are you there?" purred the syrupy voice of Wolfgang Hyvitz.

"Comrade? Yes, I'm talking to you there – in the Red Army barracks. Turn up your radio, Comrade, before they take that from you too! We must play a record – some red hot American jazz, yes?"

In the desecrated and divided city of Berlin, from Steinstücken to the Friedrichstrasse, every radio was tuned to the "Wolfgang Hyvitz Hit Parade," three hours of big-band jazz and boogie woogie blues, courtesy of the CIA. The Germans loved their jazz and, for more than a decade, jazz had been verboten in Hitler's Germany. By order of Der Fürher, only "traditional" music was permitted: the oom-pow-pow of Teutonic tubas and gut-busting arias in Wagnerian opera. Der Fussbudget was determined to keep Germany pure – and terribly boring. (Hitler had other reasons for banning swing music: the leader of the Third Reich had two left feet. If Hitler could not dance, then neither could anyone else!)

Thanks to America's new spy agency, Radio Free Berlin had German toes tapping once more. Wherever there was electricity or a few black market batteries, Germans across the war-beaten Rhineland were tuning to Radio Free Berlin – 50,000 watts of American jazz and CIA propaganda. The radio station was a beacon of hope in cities where people fought for scraps of food and across the countryside where Russian tanks stood like menacing sentinels.

The Germans especially loved the fast "hot" jazz from America. They were also drawn to the pro-American messages of peace and freedom that were broadcast daily to thousands of people trapped behind the Soviet lines. These people would officially become East Germans, and for the next 40 years their country would remain divided between East and West, freedom and imprisonment. Until then, the CIA would try almost anything – even sarcasm – to stop the Russian incursion.

"Comrade – do you know where your girlfriend was last night? She was over at my place and she was a very naughty girl! We were dancing and kissing – kissing and dancing! She got so excited when I turned up the music. Let's try some of that music now, shall we? From America, the Andrews Sisters and the Boogie Woogie Bugle Boy of Company B!"

Out of the radio came the familiar bugle blast and syncopated piano of the Boogie Woogie Bugle Boy, but on Radio Free Berlin the words were changed to tell a different, anti-Communist story:

"There was a Russian soldier boy who spoke his mind one day.
He didn't like the food they slopped upon his tray.
When he refused to clean his plate,
That's when they broke down his door and then they took him away.
He's in Siberia now – that's where he's gonna stay.
He's the boogie woogie Commie boy who tried to complain."

"Ha, ha, ha! Too bad for the Bugle Boy and too bad for you there in the Eastern sector! At least you have me, Wolfgang Hyvitz – your jolly

German announcer – keeping you company on Radio Free Berlin. Thanks to Herr Stalin, you have nothing else now, do you? No food, no blankets, no lovely lady to keep you warm at night. You should come over to our side, Comrade! Do you think they are listening in Moscow? If not, tell them Radio Free Berlin *IS ON THE AIR!*"

It was a page straight out of the Nazi's World War II songbook. During the war, the Germans used black propaganda of many kinds, including radio broadcasts by British traitors such as "Major Haw Haw." On the other side of the world, the Japanese tried to break American morale with sexy messages from "Tokyo Rose." Now it was the CIA's turn with Wolfgang Hyvitz and Radio Free Berlin reminding everyone that life was greener *auf der anderen seite.*

"While you sit there suffering in the East, here in the West we are always out to parties, eating good food, drinking the best wine. And the beer! *Ach der lieber,* German beer is the best in the world! It's too bad you can't have any! What do you Russians drink? Potato vodka, yes? That is not a drink for the ladies, am I right, Comrade? No, vodka is too strong for the beautiful *frauleins!* And those girls are waiting for you over here, Comrade. Why don't you put down your gun and come across the lines tonight? We will save a place for you at the table! Until then, I am looking for caller number 16 for a chance to win a book of petrol coupons! Call now! I will take caller 16. While we are waiting, let's open the door to Mr. Sandman. Hit it boys!"

"Mr. Stalin – please set me free!
And free my country from your tyranny.
There is no food, hot water or blankets.
And we must stand in line for gruel that's rancid!"

Mocking the Soviets was not going to win the Cold War. Song parodies and jazz records did not feed hungry people. But the Americans hoped Radio Free Berlin might offer a sliver of hope to anti-Soviet insurgents hiding somewhere in the Eastern Bloc. Huddled around their radios, anti-Communist brigades might hold out a little longer if they believed what they were hearing on the radio – that they were not fighting alone, that someday the American Army would return and set Europe free once more. And when they came, they would bring more than jazz trumpets and slide trombones. They would bring guns and tanks and the will to fight!

Fat chance, scoffed Henry Brownale.

Henry knew the truth: no one was coming to rescue the Germans, the Poles or the Czechs, no one except Gene Krupa and Count Basie. Radio Free Berlin was such a cruel joke!

Henry kicked at the puddle growing around his shoes. The rain was pounding against the roof over Buchewald Station, echoing across the train platform like conga drums. More drums, lamented Henry. After five months of managing Radio Free Berlin, Henry Brownale had suffered enough syncopation for a lifetime.

Give me a gun, not a baton! Spinning Duke Ellington records was not the reason I joined the CIA! All of it made Henry sick. Still, Radio Free Berlin was a tonic for the Germans. They were never a cheerful crowd, of course, and losing the war did not help their disposition. But with jazz back on the radio, at least they could brood to a livelier beat. Henry, meanwhile, was feeling more German every day.

It was probably the rain. Since his arrival in West Berlin, Henry could not remember a day without rain. Of course, the announcers on Radio Free Berlin would insist that the rain was only falling in the Russian sector. In the West, everything was sunshine!

Well, something is running down my nose, Henry complained to himself. Tell me, Herr Hyvitz, please tell me that it's not raining here like the monsoons of Mumbai. Or tell me another fairy tale – tell me the Americans are coming back to fight the Communists. Better yet, tell me the CIA has any plan at all!

Henry checked his watch: ten minutes before the train would arrive from Stuttgart. Another Nazi creep arriving under the protection of the CIA. This one was code-named "Strudel."

Strudel, Henry muttered under his breath. It had only been a few years since Henry had been shooting at these strudel-eating bastards. Now that the war was over and Hitler was dead, unemployed Nazis were jumping at the chance to work for the CIA.

Welcome to the American side, boys. Leave your brown shirts and jackboots by the door, gentlemen. And please remember the proper way to salute!

The Americans were desperate for help. The Soviets were tougher than the CIA could have imagined and now the Agency was quickly running out of "spies" – luckless refugees who could be launched across the border like human cannonballs. These new American agents were literally being dropped on top of the Russians – hundreds of slightly-trained Czechs, Hungarians, Slavs, Poles, and Germans were parachuted behind the Russian lines where they were slaughtered as soon as they touched the ground! They always knew precisely when and where these hapless American agents would come falling from the sky. The few that survived were sent back across the lines as double agents for Mother Russia. They made sure to inform their Soviet handlers on where and when the next parachutes would be falling.

Instead of rethinking this "strategy," the CIA simply recruited more bodies and the parachutes kept dropping. The supply was limitless. Even the short life of an American spy was better than starving to death in the post-war wasteland. This whole cynical scheme was revolting to Henry Brownale.

When had America ever fought a war that it was not prepared to win? Why should the Cold War be any different? Henry asked himself. Worse, the CIA was now running an employment agency for the Third Reich! How sickening! Why didn't we just bomb them with job applications during the war? It didn't matter what you did in the war. The Cold War had wiped everything clean.

The CIA was holding its nose with one hand and extending greetings with the other, welcoming "retired" Nazis along with the dregs and riff-raff of Europe. The results were predictable: thieves, con men, and worse were lining up for a chance to work for Uncle Sam. Then it was Henry's job to figure out which of these recruits could be trusted. While they were vetted, Henry put them to work at the radio station.

Typists, singers, announcers, trumpet players – there was always plenty of work at a propaganda radio station. Not the sort of jobs that the Nazis were trained for, of course, like rape and torture. The CIA didn't care. America was fighting Communism now.

So where is this next one – Strudel?

The rain was coming down harder, slapping against the hood of Henry's anorak and filling his shoes with oily water. Two steps backward and Henry would have been out of the rain. He didn't care. He wanted to be miserable and he wasn't going to feel any better once Strudel arrived.

Let's see if misery loves company, Henry smirked. Let's have Herr Strudel stand in the rain for a while. Give this Nazi a thorough cleaning before I put him into my car.

What would his father think of all this? His only son, Henry Brownale, a Nazi chauffeur! Henry had to laugh at that one. His father, of course, was the great Conrad Birthright Brownale – or C.B. Brownale as he was better known – the renowned congressman from the Fourth District of Connecticut and one of the most feared men in Washington.

Maybe C.B. Brownale would not think so badly of Henry's new job. As far as Congressman Brownale was concerned, even a stinking Nazi was better than a filthy Communist.

"Kill some Reds, get yourself some medals, and then we'll finish The Plan," C.B. Brownale had told his dutiful son. Henry did not question his father. He never could. So there he was, standing in a German rain puddle, wondering why he had joined the CIA and why he always listened to his father.

On Capitol Hill, everyone listened to C.B. Brownale. They had to because Brownale had discovered the political mother lode – fighting Communism. Congressman Brownale was the most vicious and effective of all the Red Hunters and it helped him win nine terms in Congress, eight of them unopposed.

Brownale's investigations were always great theater, like a matinee at the Coliseum, but instead of lions munching on Christians, Brownale had Communists devouring each other. Slobbery pleas for mercy were all well and good, but Chairman Brownale was not satisfied until a witness betrayed a friend or a relative – even someone they might never have known. Names of Communists were what he wanted and C.B. Brownale wanted them all.

Congressman Brownale especially enjoyed grilling a Communist who came from money. After all, these were *his* people – people of wealth and status who were willing to throw it all away because they suddenly realized that life was unfair, that not everyone was as rich or as lucky as they were! These embryonic radicals were determined to make a change – even if it led to a Communist Revolution! Perhaps then, life would be fair to everyone. C.B. Brownale could not stomach such pious stupidity.

Of course, life was unfair, Brownale thundered. If no one had it bad, how would anyone know they had it good?

As a boy, Henry could recite his father's admonitions word for word: Trust Fund Communists were contemptible traitors and the most contemptible of them all was Franklin Delano Roosevelt, the Red Robin Hood of Washington, leader of these gold-plated Socialists.

Roosevelt was from the oldest of old money and, despite that pedigree and the country needing a steady hand for the commonweal, Roosevelt had run the country up against the rocks, flooding the Ship of State with Social Security, Unemployment Insurance, the PWA, the TVA, and the rest of that alphabet soup of Big Government – all in the name of the Little People.

The Little People! You, Henry, are not one of THEM, the father reminded his son.

What was the use of making money, C.B. demanded, if the government was just going to take it from you and give it to some poor slob you never met? To prove his point, C.B. would take Henry downtown in the days before Christmas. There he would drop washers, nuts, and slugs into the tin cups of the poor.

"Better luck next year," Brownale would chortle.

Thanks to the Red Scare and his personal crusade against the Commies, Congressman Brownale was beloved by his constituents. They were terrified of the Reds, along with immigrants and anyone else they considered un-American.

"Why do the Commies want to take away your guns and put fluoride in our water?" Brownale shouted to the voters. "Why do they want to vaccinate your children? Because it's all part of their plot to poison America! Save your children! Save yourselves! SAVE AMERICA!"

But fear could not get C.B. Brownale into the White House. Henry would be the family's last chance at winning the presidency. Baby Henry was barely crawling when his father started their march toward the 1958 election: newspaper photos showed Henry stretched out on a carpet of stars and stripes with the number '58 written on his diaper bottom.

Drooly, needy, and clueless, baby Henry was ready for political office.

C.B. Brownale gave Henry every advantage in his schooling, starting with the best prep schools, admission to Yale, and then his ticket into Harvard Law. Henry was certainly smart, but he was no genius and he never had his father's gift for "salesmanship" – his ability to exploit a person's deepest fears.

Awkward and shy, Henry was always willing to take turns and forever wanting to please. He was the first to volunteer and the last one to know what he was getting himself into.

After law school, Henry joined the prestigious Manhattan law firm of Perry and Thrust where he volunteered for an assignment in the Trusts and Estates department. This was not part of his father's plan for reaching the White House. Henry needed campaign stories full of valor and bravery: a swashbuckling litigator or hawkeyed prosecutor, grabbing headlines and enthralling courtroom juries – not working as some back-office schmo, fiddling with wills and probate!

Fortunately, World War II came along to rescue Henry from further obscurity.

"This is a great opportunity," C.B. declared. "America loves a war hero, my boy! You should enlist today!"

"Of course I will, Father," Henry declared. His next stop was Camp Lagoon and Army basic training.

"Of course I can," Henry lied when the gunnery sergeant asked if he knew how to shoot a gun. To his amazement, Henry was a crack shot. He had never held a gun before, but once he tried it, Henry could not miss. He easily hit targets from 100, then 200, and finally 300 yards so the Army made him a sniper. This, again, was not part of the plan.

Shooting Nazis from out of a bush was not going to produce heroic tales of valor! A sniper does not charge up a bloody hill, leading his men to victory before he leads voters to the polls! Snipers can only hide in the shrubbery. Snipers are not elected President!

But Henry was very good at being a sniper – a silent, covert killer. With a rifle in his hands, Henry learned how to control every part of his body, lowering his heart rate, slowing his breathing, and freezing every muscle in his body until – POW! – another Nazi would bite the dust. Only then would Henry open his eyes.

Back at the train station, Henry looked down at the puddle swamping his feet. Who is that sad man staring back at me?

Him? Well, he'll never be president, that's for sure. Future presidents don't spend their days playing jazz records on propaganda radio stations and they don't stand in the rain waiting to chauffeur Nazi war criminals to their new jobs! Henry kicked at the man in the puddle. That's when Henry realized that the rain had stopped and the sun was paying a brief visit to bombed-out Berlin.

Can a blood-sucking Nazi survive in the brilliant light of day? Henry wondered. He practiced his greeting: "Herr Strudel, welcome to the CIA! May I carry your bags, sir? Your car is waiting for you over here. If we see any Jews along the way, I'll be sure to run them over for you."

With the sun out, Henry should have been feeling better. The truth was Henry preferred the rain because it reminded him of his last night in New York. That wonderful night when he met Anna Tilson.

What an idiot you are, Henry scolded himself. You knew her for one night. Hardly knew her – you were together for just a few hours! One brief dinner and then she was gone. Gone because of you, Henry, you insufferable idiot. You let her drive away!

All these months later, Henry would sometimes forget her name, but he could never forget that face. A singular beauty, Anna Tilson was Henry's favorite memory of home and always his greatest regret.

"Those who do not believe in the ideology of the United States shall not be allowed to stay in the United States."
ATTORNEY GENERAL AND (LATER) SUPREME COURT JUSTICE THOMAS CLARK
at the Cathedral Club of Brooklyn, Jan. 15, 1948

CHAPTER TEN

HENRY REVISITS HIS LAST NIGHT IN NEW YORK

There was no goodbye party on Henry's final day at the law firm. There were no goodbyes at all. No one even looked up from their desk as Henry walked out that night.

Just as well, Henry told himself. They might have asked about his future plans and Henry could not reveal that he would soon be off to "spy school" at the CIA training academy. He wasn't supposed to tell anyone – not that they were asking, of course. Not that they would have believed him.

Henry walked out with a cardboard box carrying his law school diploma and a few empty sniper shells. Once outside, he dropped the box into a trash can and headed downtown.

Goodbye Perry and Thrust. Henry Brownale is out on the town!

He was almost skipping down the street, imagining himself in a Hollywood movie musical – the handsome, lonely sailor out on leave, dancing down the streets of Manhattan in search of a dame and a couple of laughs. Hell, maybe a laugh and a couple of dames!

With every girl he passed, Henry Brownale was ready to fall in love. And then he found Anna Tilson.

For God's sake Henry, grow up! *Wake* up! That part of your life is over. It was over that night – that *one* night – and now there's nothing else to think about.

Except that face. Anna Tilson's marvelous face. Why didn't I kiss that wonderful face?

Because you're a bonehead, that's why.

Henry looked down the tracks at Buchewald Station, then farther down to where the rails wrapped around the hill and out of sight, stretching farther and farther away.

Where the hell is that train? Where is this "Strudel" character? Henry was getting tired. He wasn't used to the sun being out. As he closed his eyes, he found himself back on the streets of New York – his last night in town, desperate to find a girl.

Maybe the kind of girl who is drawn to folk music – the kind of girl and the kind of music that his father had warned him never to touch. Those girls who wore their hair long and stayed out even longer. They were loose and immoral, smoking cigarettes of who knows what.

And their parents voted for Democrats!

Oh boy, thought Henry. What were the chances that he could meet one of those loose, immoral women? Would they be interested in spending the night with a lonely guy on his last night in town?

What if she discovers that he is a man of mystery, a man with secrets – a silent, solitary man, smoldering with an inner fire like the cigarette clenched between his teeth, knowing he must protect her from those secrets or they both will be dead?

"I'd love to stay here, baby, but trouble is waiting for me around the next corner. You know how I hate to be late."

"No, no!" his girl would plead. "You musn't leave! When will I see you again?"

"Just call my name when night falls, doll."

"Just like I fell for you, ya big lug."

Boy, would that be swell! Henry had to find himself a sensitive, folk music girl and he had to find her quick. Maybe a girl with a guitar – or a 'Wallace for President' button – then maybe this could be his first lucky night in New York.

When he arrived at The Lamplighter, a folk music club in Greenwich Village, Henry was surprised to see so many people crowded on the street. He had never been to a folk music show, but these people looked more like the lawyers at Perry and Thrust. Milling outside the club were large men in tan overcoats, crisp fedoras, and thin black ties. Two of these men were hanging a sign over The Lamplighter's railing: CLOSED BY POLICE ORDER.

"What's going on?" Henry asked one of the overcoats.

"Better move along there, bub," the police officer responded sharply. "This place has been shut down until further notice."

"On whose authority?" Henry demanded.

"Can't you read, mister? This is the Red Squad – now beat it!"

The cop was moving toward Henry when a piercing scream came from inside the basement club. Another detective was climbing up the stairs with a woman draped over his shoulder, her feet thrashing in the air as she beat the cop with both fists.

"Put me down! You can't arrest me! This is a free country, you know! At least it used to beeeeeee!" As soon as her feet hit the pavement, the woman uncorked a roundhouse punch that sailed over the cop's head.

"Try that again, lady, and I'm taking you in!"

"I'd like to see you TRY!" she shouted. "You're already going to arrest me and for what – singing? Well, I know my rights! I can sing if I want to! LAAAAAA!"

She tried to sneak another punch at the cop, but this time Henry grabbed her arm. Anna Tilson glared ferociously at Henry.

"You two better scram," a cop barked.

"That's all right, officer, I'm her attorney," Henry smiled at Anna. She wrenched her arm free and was reaching back with her foot when Henry stepped between her and the cop. The officer took a quick step toward Anna.

"Get wise, lady. You kick me and you're gonna be singing all night in the Tombs."

"Very funny, flatfoot," Anna snarled. She turned back to Henry. "And I don't need a lawyer because all I want are my civil rights! MY - CIVIL - *RIGHTS!*"

"You'd better listen to him, Miss," Henry said firmly, but Anna had turned her back on all of them.

"You sure about this, counselor?" the detective said, observing Henry's expensive suit and Anna's beatnik getup. "She doesn't seem like your kind of client."

Anna snapped around, "What is that supposed to mean?"

Trying to sound confident in front of this beautiful young woman, Henry nodded to the police. "I can take it from here, fellas."

"Well just a minute there – FELLA," Anna said sarcastically, poking Henry in the chest. "You're not taking 'IT' anywhere – have you got that?" Then she turned on her heel and stormed away. Without thinking, Henry ran after her. When they reached the next block, Anna flew back around when she heard Henry approaching.

"Just where do you think you're going?" she demanded. "And what business do you have pretending to be my lawyer?"

"What are you – a cop?!" Henry shouted back, surprising himself as he said it. He smiled and shouted again, "I know my rights! Can't a person just walk down the street without being accosted by some angry woman?! I want my civil rights!"

Then they both laughed.

"So you're looking for your civil rights, huh?" Anna asked. "Better tell it to the judge."

"Well, your Honor, may I buy you dinner?"

Three blocks later, they were at Angelo's Fine Italian, sitting at a small table by the kitchen.

This is smart, Henry thought. I'm starting to think like the CIA. An inconspicuous table in the back of a restaurant – this is just what a spy would choose. An inconspicuous table with a beautiful woman was even better. Incognito.

At this table, however, there was no cognito whatsoever. No one, certainly not the waiters, seemed to notice that Henry and Anna were waiting there. After twenty minutes, they had not seen a menu or ordered a drink. Down to their last breadstick, Henry was running out of things to say.

"It's my fault, really," Henry said a little too loudly. "People say I have a forgettable face. It seems to be working on these waiters."

Anna sighed and glanced toward the door. Sensing her anxiety, Henry continued, "You know, for a lot of people, I'm actually the last person on Earth."

Anna looked at him confused.

"You've heard of a Last Will and Testament, right? Well, I'm the kind of lawyer who writes those up – wills, that is. It's steady work, you know. Like they say – "

" – everyone's gotta die?" Anna offered.

"And they can't take it with them. So I help very rich people prepare for that inevitable day, making sure that the only thing that's taken away is them and not their money. At least that's what I used to do."

"So what are you doing now?"

Henry was not sure what to say. It was the question he was never to answer. "Now? Well, dinner, of course, if we ever find a waiter."

"Well," Anna said, "working as a lawyer – writing wills – that sounds like an important job. You didn't enjoy it?"

"I liked it, I suppose. My father wasn't so keen on it. It's not the kind of law that will make you famous and that's what he's been planning for me. He's found something new for me to do," Henry's voice trailed off again. "Funny thing is, I think I was happiest during the war. To be honest, planning for someone to die is not as much fun as, well – "

"As what?" Anna laughed. "Killing people? That's a little grim, soldier."

"True, but life can be pretty grim. It's more than a little grim when you work day and night plotting and replotting the eventual resting place for millions of dollars, searching for secret places where the government can't tax it or certain relatives won't find it. Before they depart for that great mansion in the sky, my clients spend their last breath worrying about who is in and who is out of their will. Until then, I have to listen to these people carp and complain about their ungrateful children, their lazy siblings, their conniving in-laws. And with each new complaint there is always another change in the will. It gets to a point where I only want to use a pencil."

"Funny and they call it the *Last* Will and Testament?"

"Exactly! It's only the last one when they can't change it anymore!"

Henry poured himself a glass of wine. Anna smiled as Henry, still talking about himself, put the cork back in the bottle without filling her glass.

"And it's always for the most trivial of things – a birthday someone forgot, an invitation that wasn't mailed, the renewal of an old grudge, or the start of a new one. The smaller the cut, the deeper the wound, and the faster they call me to rewrite the will. And let me tell you, no wound goes unpunished. At all hours of the day or night, they are on the phone, hopping mad – unable to sleep! – cackling about something or somebody who has '*finally* crossed the line!' I swear, sometimes I think it's only in their dreams. Real or imaginary, it doesn't matter! They call and I have to jump! It's punishment they're demanding and I was the executioner, stuffing the offending party into this metaphorical cannon and then – Ka-boom! – out of the will they fly! So long sucker!"

Anna laughed, "I've got it! It's not the Last Will and Testament. It's a testament to who will last."

"Verrry good," Henry said, clinking his glass to Anna's. He poured himself some more wine, forgetting to fill hers again.

"Finally," Henry continued, "the big day arrives: Dear Aunt Matilda has passed on and we must now commence with the reading of her will! Since I've come back from the war, I can honestly say that reading the will is the closest thing to actual combat."

"Because someone has died?"

"No, no, no – because the real carnage is about to begin!"

Henry grabbed the salt and pepper shakers and positioned the wine glasses around the tablecloth like soldiers on a battlefield.

"Now here they come – the mourners! Those poor greedy – I mean, grieving – souls! Their only solace – their only prayer – is a bag full of money left to them by their dear Aunt Matilda!" Henry picked up the salt and pepper shakers and danced them across the table. "Here they come, sadly marching into my office, completely unaware of the danger that awaits them!"

"Danger!" Anna exclaimed, throwing her hands up in mock horror.

"Yes, danger!" said Henry. He jumped onto his chair, crouching like a sniper.

"What are you doing?" Anna laughed.

"I'm getting ready to read the will! What does it look like?"

Anna giggled, "Of course – you're a lawyer! What was I thinking?"

"You'd better take cover!" Henry warned. Anna held a napkin up to her eyes.

"Good! Now look – THERE! – the bereaved are standing out in the open, completely unprotected! BANG! POW! Down goes Priscilla, the daughter who dropped out of college and married a jazz drummer."

"Oh no!" Anna cried. "Not Priscilla!"

"Yes! And according to Aunt Matilda's last wishes, Priscilla will be left with some mismatched pieces of old china and a monthly allowance of only fifty bucks!"

"Poor Priscilla!"

"Look now, here comes Robert, the ungrateful nephew who never visited his poor Aunt Matilda. BOOM! Robert is left holding the crummy birthday card he had scribbled as a child – the card that reminded his Dear Aunt that Robert's birthday was coming soon. No more happy birthdays for you, Robert! Ka-BLAM!"

Henry kept on shooting. POW! POW! Ka-BOOM! Buh-BAM! The bodies continued to pile up until –

"There's only one man left standing!" Henry announced.

"Who can it be?"

"No one can believe it, but it's Horace the Gardener – now and forever to be known as the Secret Lover of Frisky Aunt Matilda! Their clandestine romance has finally been revealed! Horace had a key to her bedroom and now this lucky gardener gets the keys to her entire estate – and nearly every penny of Matilda's vast fortune! Horace planted his seeds and now his garden is about to bloom!"

"What a secret!" Anna exclaimed. "So … are you good at keeping secrets?"

"I'd better be – especially now!" Henry said, spilling a little wine onto the table. He moved closer to Anna. "I can't tell you this, but I'm about to leave on a very important mission."

"Is it dangerous?" Anna asked, thinking he was joking again. "Will you be saving the world?"

For the first time that night, Henry had nothing to say as he gazed dreamily at Anna, her face illuminated by candlelight. She was quite possibly the loveliest woman he had ever seen! Everything was so lovely that night – the restaurant, the plates on the table, the waiters by the bar! But this woman, leaning toward him now, was the most beautiful of all.

"Everything!" Henry nearly shouted.

"What?"

"Everything is beautiful!" Henry said, falling back against his chair. He raised his glass for a toast. "Let us drink to beauty, in all its … beauty-ness!" Henry took another drink of wine and gazed lovingly across the table.

"Stop it," Anna blushed. Henry looked over his shoulder and then leaned across the table. He reached for her hands and Anna did not pull them away. He whispered, "I really have to tell you something. I am about to do something really, really important – even a little dangerous – and you're the only person who can tell me about it."

"Right," Anna smiled. "Well, it's a good thing we're alone then."

"But you cannot breathe a word of this to me! I mean, you."

"That's easy. You haven't told me what it is yet!"

Henry waved his hand for Anna to come closer. "They are going to make me a spy!"

Anna threw back her head and laughed. Henry was surprised by this, but then he laughed too. He didn't mind – he loved the sound of her laughter. He loved the sound of her voice. Henry loved her and everybody else that night. And he loved that word – 'spy.' He was going to be a spy! Didn't that sound important? Henry leaned back in his chair, smiling contentedly at Anna's magnificent face, basking in the secret that he was not supposed to tell.

"Then let's drink to that!" Anna laughed, raising her glass. "To spies and secret lovers!"

"Hear hear! To Horace the Gardener and Henry the Spy, good fortune to men who can keep a secret!"

"So it's Henry, is it? I was waiting for you to introduce yourself."

"Yes, indeed! Henry Brownale. Henry the Spy to you, madam! No longer Henry the boring lawyer." Henry the Spy took another, bigger drink.

"Henry?" she said.

"That's me."

"I'm Anna Tilson. I'm very pleased to meet you."

"And I am very pleased to meet me too, Anna Tilton. You know, I have a client who looks just like you. I'm going to get her some civil rights."

Anna laughed again and Henry joined in, laughing at how clever he was. Now that his secret was out, Henry told her everything else: about his plans for the CIA and his bigger plans for when he got back. He was going to be President of the United States! Through the warmth and fuzziness of the wine, Henry tried to ignore the little voice that was calling from inside his brain, shouting at him to shut up about the CIA, about the White House, and every other secret he was giving away. Maybe it was his father's voice shouting, "Stop! She might be a Communist!"

"You know my father wouldn't like you. He hates folk music! He says it's only for 'those filthy Communists!'"

"Well, that's not very nice!" Anna laughed. "Maybe I'm a Republican in folk music clothing."

Henry took another drink. "Oh, I get it! Like a sheep in wolf's clothing. I like sheep. I like you! I'll bet you're soft like a sheep." With a perplexed expression, Henry looked down into the empty wine bottle.

"So what's your father got against Communists?"

"Well, come on now! The Communists are the worst thing since … since New York City cops!"

They both laughed again as Henry ordered more wine. He could not remember much of what happened after that. There was the rain, of course, pouring over the yellow cab as Anna pressed her hand against the window, waving goodbye. Mostly Henry remembered what he had forgotten to do that night: how he should have kissed her and gotten into the cab with her and how he should never have left New York City but simply stayed with Anna Tilson.

Or was it Tilton?

Henry sighed. He did this a lot – and with great commitment – reminding himself that at least one person in the world knew how miserable he was. Why couldn't that one person be Anna?

Does she ever think about me – Henry the Spy, the mysterious man who saved her from the police on that romantic night in New York? Did she tell her folk music friends about the secret agent she met outside The Lamplighter, the one who couldn't stand Communists? He almost wished that she had. It would be nice to think someone in New York remembered him.

From the train station loudspeaker the jolly German announcer, Wolfgang Hyvitz, was reading the weather forecast: "Comrades, tomorrow there will be sunshine and a pleasant temperature here in West Berlin. In the East, I'm afraid there will be nothing but rain. Terrible, terrible rain. Wait now! I am kidding, Comrades! You, too, can expect beautiful weather. You just won't be able to enjoy it!"

Henry checked his watch. Where the hell is this Strudel?

Just then, a whistle blew as a train arrived at the far end of the station. Another hundred yards and Henry could have stepped right in front of it. No more out-of-work Nazis, lonesome memories, and everything else that was wrong in his life. Goodbye cruel world – SQUISH!

Wearily, Henry staggered toward the passengers as they stepped off the train. Then he stopped short because it felt like something was in his eyes. It might have been the rain dripping off his hat or the damn sunshine because Henry was wiping his eyes as if he was waking up from a dream.

Coming out of the train, was that woman ... Anna Tilson?

"Her beauty served a mob of terror whose one mission is to destroy!"
PUBLICITY POSTER FOR "I MARRIED A COMMUNIST" ✳ *Howard Hughes' first anti-Communist motion picture for RKO Pictures, 1949*

C H A P T E R   E L E V E N

KLAUS VILBRICHT

"Surprise!" Anna called as she ran up to Henry. She reached out to hug him, but Henry could not move his arms. His entire body was in shock.

"What's the matter?" Anna laughed. "I never thought I could make YOU speechless. Or have you finally learned how to keep a secret?"

If he could have moved, Henry would have done cartwheels and if he could have spoken, he would have shouted, "Anna, darling, you couldn't stay away from me, could you? You've traveled across the ocean just to be with me – because you're in love with me, because you want to spend your whole life with me!" But the words were all balled up in Henry's throat. Finally, he blurted, "Anna! Fancy meeting you here!"

Fancy? Christ, Henry, you are such an idiot!

"I mean, WHAT are you doing here?"

"I'm your new singer, of course!" Anna announced.

"Yessss … you are." Nothing seemed to be making sense. Anna Tilson was miraculously here – standing next to him on a train platform in West Berlin – and she was going to sing for him?

"My new singer!" he croaked. "Well yes – of course! Welcome to Radio Free Berlin."

As Henry moved to embrace Anna, she suddenly turned and called out, "Wait – here he comes!"

"You are too fast for me!" said the handsome man running toward them. He was tall and muscular too, this giant of a man laughing as he pretended to struggle with three large suitcases. He looked big enough to pick up the entire train! Henry noticed that he was also carrying a trumpet case. Anna threw her arms around this man – a tighter embrace than she had offered Henry!

Anna sang, "Henry, say hello to Herr Vilbricht. He's going to be your – or should I say, *our* – new trumpet player!"

Klaus Vilbricht strode up to Henry and snapped to attention, cracking his heels together. Vilbricht was about to thrust his right arm into the air when he burst out laughing.

"Ha! You thought I was going to do it, didn't you? The Nazi salute, yes?" Vilbricht laughed as he turned to Anna, "He thought I was going to do it! The Heil Hitler, yes?"

Henry forced himself to smile as Vilbricht and Anna started jabbering at each other – in German! – laughing and touching like two people who had shared more than just a train ride. Vilbricht held Anna close with one arm and elbowed Henry with the other.

"Tell me, Herr Henry, why would you come to Germany when there are such beautiful women back in New York?"

"We all know the reason I'm here," Henry snapped in his most officious tone. "I assume you are Strudel?"

"I will be whatever pastry you require of me, Herr Henry!" Vilbricht smiled as he turned to Anna, who laughed a little too hard at Vilbricht's playful expression. Henry glowered at Vilbricht, waiting for him to respond properly to his code name.

"Oh, jah, forgive me, Herr Henry. Let me see: I am supposed to say, 'The strudel is ready. Is the coffee hot?'"

"Yes," Henry bit hard. "Coffee is served."

Anna gushed, "Klaus was just telling me about all of his adventures during the war."

Henry rolled his eyes. He tried not to look at her as he held out his hand for Vilbricht's identification papers. "Ah yes. Adventures during the war," Henry said, forcing a laugh. "So many Jews, so little time, isn't that right, Herr Vilbricht? What do you think, Anna? Do you suppose Herr Vilbricht ever took a shot at me during the war?"

Anna was surprised by the angry look on Henry's face.

"Well, I was never such a good shot, I must say! I play the trumpet much better!" Vilbricht laughed again as he tugged Anna to his side. When Anna did not pull away from him, Henry turned sharply on his heel and headed for the car. He tried to walk a half step ahead of them, revolted by the sight of Anna in the arms of this Nazi swine.

Vilbricht and Anna talked excitedly about Berlin and all the fun they would have "playing together."

Anna laughed, "You mean in the band?"

"That too!" Vilbricht howled and they both fell into hysterics. When the laughter suddenly stopped, Henry turned to see the two of them locked in a passionate kiss. Henry made a mental note to kick himself in the ass.

How could he think Anna would still have feelings for him after just a single night in New York – a night so long ago? Averting his eyes from Anna's, Henry barked, "I'm sorry to say that there won't be much time for you to be … together in Berlin. Not at first, anyway. Herr Vilbricht and I will be very busy discussing his *adventures* during the war – starting tonight, in fact."

"Tonight?" Anna whined. "Oh really Henry, must it be tonight? Klaus said he knows the best little Hofbrau – " and then the two of them began jabbering in German again. Henry broke up this *schnuckelig* nonsense with a sharp whistle to his driver.

Vilbricht smiled and kissed Anna's hand. "Herr Henry is correct, dear Fraulein. Now, my beautiful lady, your chariot awaits!" Vilbricht led Anna to the car and, before Henry could move, Vilbricht slid in next to her. Henry stewed outside of the car, shaking the rain off of his coat. He looked back at the train platform, reliving the heart-beating excitement when Anna first appeared.

Thanks to Klaus Vilbricht, it had all been a mirage.

Through the car window, Henry could see Vilbricht excitedly pawing at Anna. Henry wanted to throw open the door and thrash this lecherous creep. But Henry was more of a sniper than a fighter. He climbed into the front seat, trying not to look into Anna's dark blue eyes. He could not let her see the tears that were gathering in his.

Driving through Berlin, the noise of the city was not loud enough to disguise the rustling of coats and clothes as Anna and Vilbricht playfully ran their fingers across each other. Henry coughed harshly until they got his cue.

"So," Vilbricht said casually. "Anna says you two know each other from New York. But she will not tell me your secret. How did you meet such a fascinating creature in so big a city. Have I perhaps reunited two lost lovers?"

"No!" Anna said a little too quickly, so quickly that Henry nearly turned around to confront her. Instead, Henry just stared out the window, crushed again.

"I didn't know you could sing, Anna," Henry said, calculating all the other things he did not know about her.

"Well enough, I suppose." Anna turned to Vilbricht. "That's how we met. Henry was coming to see me perform at a little club in New York."

This was another surprise for Henry the Clueless Secret Agent. Anna was going to perform that night at The Lamplighter?

How in the world could the CIA hire someone like her – a likely Communist – to work at Radio Free Berlin? Perhaps the better question was how could the CIA have hired a knucklehead like me? Henry wondered if they should turn back to the station. Perhaps it wasn't too late to throw himself under that train.

Vilbricht followed Henry's eyes in the rear view mirror as he gently caressed Anna's face with the back of his hand. "Ah – New York!" Vilbricht cooed. "I have always dreamed of going to New York!"

"So did the Führer," Henry muttered.

"What fun we will have!" Anna said brightly. "Singing and playing together from dawn until who knows when?"

"Who knows when? Ooh-lah-lah!" Vilbricht grinned mischievously. "I think this girl is trouble, Herr Henry. Quick, someone call the politzei!"

Better call the fire department too, Henry fumed. Hose you two down.

Henry whipped around in his seat. "Funny that you should mention the police, Herr Vilbricht. That was how we met, don't you remember, Anna?"

"Oh my goodness, yes," she laughed. "You're right, Henry! I had forgotten all about the police. They wanted to arrest me that night!"

Of course she had forgotten.

Henry said sternly, "From now, you two must not call me 'Henry.' My public name here is Hansel Meinhoff, have you got that?"

Vilbricht bit his lip. "Hansel? I swear to guard your secret, Herr Hansel. I will not even tell Gretel!" Klaus Vilbricht and Anna laughed so hard that they fell against each other crying. Henry straightened himself stiffly, digging a fingernail into his palm.

As they passed through a city park, Henry noticed Anna pointing to an anarchist shouting at the crowd gathered around him. Anna looked seriously at Vilbricht. He stared into Anna's eyes and nodded his approval.

It would be seven months before they would pass this way again.

Through the dark and empty park, Henry would be alone with Anna, driving quickly toward the Russian sector of Berlin. Klaus Vilbricht was on the run and Anna would soon be a fugitive herself. Henry knew he was taking an enormous risk. For both their sakes, he had to get her past the checkpoint and into East Berlin. If she did not escape, Henry could also be arrested.

"Get me to the border," she promised, "and I will take care of the rest. I have contacts there – they will keep me safe." It was more information than Henry wanted to know, more questions that he did not want to ask.

Henry tried not to think about how foolish he had been. His CIA career might now be over thanks to his trust in Anna. Their plan – Vilbricht's and Anna's – had always included Henry. From the beginning, they had counted on Henry to make the wrong move at the right time. He was dependable that way. Stupid, really. Vilbricht knew that Henry was deeply in love with Anna. If he could not be with her then Henry would do anything to protect her. True to his heart, Henry stayed true to Vilbricht's plan.

As they weaved through the back streets of West Berlin, Henry was powerless to stop it. Vilbricht had won. Once they reached East Berlin, Anna disappeared across the border, back into the arms of that trumpet-playing pseudo-Nazi.

Back to Klaus Vilbricht, the Russian spy.

C H A P T E R   T W E L V E

AUGUST 1950:
Helen Continues Her Training at Camp Unity

When chirping for a mate and with the temperature rising at night, the fricative love call of the male cricket becomes more frequent and more fervent. And louder.

A cricket looking for love can be very, very loud.

In the trees above them, owls can be heard for several miles, hooting lustily for feathery companionship. The same is true of tree frogs and katydids – all of them chirping, croaking, hooting, and buzzing for *l'amour* on a hot summer night.

All goddamned night.

Helen sat up in bed, the humidity glistening on her face. She could not sleep in this arboreal hothouse of love. Looking out the bunkhouse window, she dreamily imagined that all of these woodland creatures were wildly humping on the lawn. Everything seemed to be fully awake – and fully in heat – as the horny frogs croaked, "Give-it. Give-it. Give-it."

Helen was also looking for love. What girl doesn't? Camp Unity, however, was not the place to find it. The men here were too single-minded. Their commitment to the Communist cause was too complete to contemplate copulation or cohabitation. She could only imagine how awkwardly they would kiss: lips puckered and their eyes wide open, vigilant as always. It would be like kissing a bulletin board.

The animals seemed to be having more fun. The chirping and heaving and cooing and calling were growing louder as Helen tried covering her head with a pillow. That's when she noticed the cabin down near the water. A dim light flickered against the windows as she heard a different sound coming up the hill. Was someone crying?

The metal cot squeaked as Helen rolled out of bed. The insects and animals went silent as Helen pressed against the screen door. She cringed with every squeak and groan from the door, but Helen was unaware of all the eyes that were following her. Vigilance!

She stood still on the porch, listening for the sound. There it was again – frightened and anxious and coming from somewhere near the lake. It sounded like someone in pain!

Helen stepped onto the moist grass, her heart racing to the tempo of the chirping and croaking as the bugs and animals got back to business. At the water's edge, Helen pushed herself onto a large rock, hoping to see through a window of the cabin. She knew this was wrong, but she felt compelled to look inside.

Unable to see anything from the rock, Helen went up to one of the small windows and there, inside, was the camp's music instructor, Anna Tilson, kneeling on the floor, her arms wrapped in a self-embrace. Helen needed a closer look.

She crept around to the other side of the cabin where her toes brushed against a pile of loose stones. Comrade Tilson called, "Who's there?" Helen froze in place.

Anna opened the door and looked out into the darkness. Ashamed, Helen slowly moved into the light. "Comrade Tilson, it's only me – Helen Gamble."

Anna stood silently in the doorway, her face half in shadow and her eyes looking up toward the moon. Behind her came the sound of a woman – not crying, but singing – with violins playing softly from a record on the phonograph.

"Comrade – ?" Helen whispered.

"Shhhh!" Comrade Tilson smiled, holding a finger to her lips. "Listen now."

The voice on the record became more excited and the orchestra grew louder, surging behind the passionate soprano. Anna Tilson leaned against the cabin door, gazing at the stars, until the music softly receded and the phonograph needle skipped against the end of the record. She smiled at Helen. "Isn't that marvelous?" she said as Helen followed her into the cabin.

"My father always liked the opera," Helen offered shyly.

"Then he must know Madame Butterfly."

"Madame Butterfly?" Helen repeated. "Was that her singing?"

"Yes, that was Cio-Cio-San. She is Madame Butterfly."

"It sounded very nice," Helen said. "To tell you the truth, I thought someone was crying. That's why I came down here. I'm sorry for looking in your window."

"That's all right. In a way, she was crying – tears of joy, anyway."

"What was she saying?"

"She was singing '*Un Bel Di*' – one beautiful day. Cio-Cio-San has been waiting for this beautiful day when finally she will see – " Anna stopped and turned her head away. She walked over to the kitchen where a vase of red and white verbena sat on the table.

"She finally sees what?" Helen asked. Anna did not respond, her head was bowed as she pretended to arrange the flowers. Next to the phonograph, a picture and a letter were lying on the floor, and both were spotted with tears. It was Anna who had been crying.

Comrade Tilson cleared her throat and wiped her face. "Cio-Cio-San is a proud peasant girl and like millions of other people she waits for that one beautiful day when Communism will set them free – when no one will be poor and there will be peace everywhere. The good life that everyone deserves."

"Someone wrote an opera about Communism? My father never told me," Helen said.

Anna sat next to Helen and told her the story of Madame Butterfly – but not the tale of the young geisha who falls in love with an American sailor. In Anna's telling, Cio-Cio-San was a virtuous young Communist, a leader of her village who is offered great riches if she agrees to marry a wealthy prince. Cio-Cio-San accepts his offer, but with one condition: he must share his fortune with the people to aid their struggle for a better world.

"That world will come one beautiful day," Anna said. "Until then, Cio-Cio-San will wait." She put the needle back on the record.

"I stay upon the brow of the hillock
And wait there
And wait for a long time
But never weary of the long waiting."

Helen leaned closer to Anna. "Is she also waiting … for a man?" Helen whispered.

Comrade Tilson smiled. "There might also be a man." Anna closed her eyes again, falling deeper inside the music.

"From out the crowded city
There is coming a man
A little speck in the distance
Climbing the hillock
Can you guess who it is?
And when he's reached the summit
Can you guess what he'll say?
He will call, 'Butterfly' from the distance."

Helen reached for the photograph on the floor. It was a picture of Anna standing between two men.

"He will call, he will call
'Dear baby wife of mine,
Dear little orange blossom'
The names he used to call me when he came here."

"Listen to the orchestra," Anna said softly. "The music … so powerful. It can't be stopped. It lifts up Cio-Cio-San, up to the top of the hill where she can see everything down below her. She vows to hold back her fears."

Then Comrade Tilson began to sing, "All this will happen, I promise you this. Never fear. I will wait for you."

Pressing her trembling lips together, Anna lifted up her face, drawing back her tears, pulling back the memories. She quickly wiped her eyes and smiled bravely at Helen.

"Are you okay?" Helen asked.

"Silly, isn't it? It's only music, but it gets me every time." Anna stood up and walked over to the sink again, dabbing her eyes with a cloth.

Helen turned the photograph over. It read, "To my ignorant Americans – Love, Klaus."

"Which one is the spy?" Helen asked, holding the photograph up to Anna.

Anna whipped around. "What did you say?" She snatched the photograph out of Helen's hands. "Who said anything about a spy?"

Helen was embarrassed again. "Patrice," Helen said meekly. "Patrice told me. She said you had once outfoxed an American spy and that's why you're here now at Camp Unity."

"Oh really? And what other stories does Patrice have to tell?"

"Don't be mad at her – please. She's very fond of you. She admires you – and your singing. She said you were once a great singer on Broadway. Is that true? You sang on Broadway? How exciting!"

"I was a singer once, but never on Broadway. We were folk singers. Our little group never aspired for Broadway. Our audiences were the common people."

"Oh, I would love the idea of being on Broadway," Helen said. "I can't even imagine such a place!"

Helen noticed Anna studying the photograph. She looked happy in the picture – smiling as she stood arm and arm between two men – but this picture, it seemed, was not a happy memory. Anna slid the photograph under the couch.

"So … was one of those men a spy?" Helen asked again, a sly smile on her face.

"You are such a pill!" Anna scolded. "It's too late to tell you that story. You must get to bed now, Comrade. Madame will be very angry if she finds you wandering outside at night. Back to bed with you!"

"Wait!" Helen laughed as Anna gently nudged her toward the door. "You can't expect me to sleep now – not after you tell me something as romantic as Madame Butterfly! What about those two men? And the spy! Does he come back for Madame Butterfly?"

"You've got your stories mixed up," Anna said, forcing a laugh. She was surprised by Helen's intuition. She playfully shoved the girl out the door. "Come on now – out! Back to bed. Forward to October!"

Pressing it shut, Anna bowed her head against the door. Another tear fell to the floor as the latch clicked shut. Outside the cabin, Helen continued to protest.

"This isn't fair!" Helen whispered through the door. "You can't start a love story and then not finish it!"

"Of course you can," Anna said, choking back her tears. "It happens all the time."

Helen clambered back up the hill. The watchful eyes in the dormitory were still alert as Helen climbed back onto her cot.

There would be four reports on Madame's desk the next morning, each of them reporting Helen's late-night excursion to Comrade Tilson's cabin.

Vigilance!

Madame noticed, however, that one report was missing: there was nothing reported by Anna Tilson. Madame frowned as she opened Anna Tilson's file. Her lack of vigilance would be noted.

"In the United States, the working class are Democrats. The middle class are Republicans. The upper class are Communists."

ANOTHER EX-COMMUNIST, WHITAKER CHAMBERS * *Witness, 1952*

CHAPTER THIRTEEN

ONE WEEK LATER

"*Comrades, your attention!*" The students quickly took their places as Petrov called for order.

"*Today we have special guest! A labor organizer, inspirational speaker and loyal Party member, she has inspired workers around the world! Please give big Camp Unity welcome to Mrs. Martha Mil-vaukee!*"

Ready for her cue, Martha waltzed through the classroom door, her arms outstretched to gather the adoration that always poured over her. With a graceful turn she paused, angling her feet just so, and then, turning once more, she came to an elegant repose: hands clasped in front of her fashionable suit, shoulders back, chin high – ladies and gentlemen, look who's back!

Nearly a decade of waiting and finally this day was here! Martha was standing before an audience once again! It wasn't Madison Square Garden, but that did not matter. There were faces raised up to hers, eyes and ears giving her what she needed most: undivided attention! If only Michael were here to see his mother perform! Without telling Milo, Martha had left the boy in the care of Rhonda Glabberson and then borrowed the Glabberson's car for the two hour drive to Camp Unity. (Martha did not have a license to drive, but she wasn't going to let the DMV or anyone else try to stop her – not today! Nothing was going to stand between her and applause!)

With her most radiant and beneficent smile, Martha gazed about the room, inspecting each student's face like Mother Nature greeting the sprouts of a new Spring.

Here they are, Martha marveled. Here is the next generation, the New Vanguard! Look at these fresh, young minds waiting to be cultivated by the Red Flame of New York!

Now watch carefully, kids. Let me show you how it's done.

"Comrades!" Martha began, "I would like to tell you the story of a young girl who grew up in a lavish cocoon of wealth and privilege. This innocent child never realized that the real world was full of suffering, that it was rife with hunger and injustice. Little did she know that beyond those ivy-covered walls, the world was wracked in pain from the oppression of capitalist greed – pain inflicted by her own father – a Wall Street *banker*!"

Martha stood motionless, her finger pointed skyward, waiting for the students to react to her father's evil profession. It always brought exclamations of horror from every other audience. This time, there was not a single gasp.

Martha lowered her finger and pressed on.

"As she grew up, protected from reality, the little rich girl soon realized that she was not expected to be anything more than what her mother had become: a liberal arts graduate who forgoes a career for the sake of her inevitable marriage. And for what? Her only real function is to provide a ready incubator for more sons and daughters of the perpetual aristocracy! Another Republican bun in the oven!"

Martha looked around the room again. Still no reaction. Someone in the back of the room started to yawn until Madame raised her ping-pong paddle in warning. Martha smiled stiffly at Madame and continued her speech.

"As you may have guessed, I was that daughter of wealth and privilege and I might have stayed that way if not for one courageous woman – a genuine martyr to the Revolution – my sixth grade teacher, Mrs. Margaret Hanrahaty."

An elementary school teacher – a martyr to the Revolution? This got the students' attention.

As Martha told it, Mrs. Hanrahaty had been the most nurturing influence in young Martha's life and Martha was her prized pupil. As her teacher's pet, Martha obeyed her every lesson and yielded to each command – everything except the Pledge of Allegiance. Martha refused to say the words. When the other children would stand and salute the flag, Martha stayed in her seat, convinced that America was not worthy of anyone's adoration.

Guilty about her family's substantial wealth, Martha was obsessed with the inequality in the world. Why was there so much starvation and desperation? Someone must be responsible! This question was all Martha could think about. Her parents would shrug, explaining that "some people just aren't that lucky." So Martha turned to Mrs. Hanrahaty for the answer.

Every day, she pestered her teacher, demanding to know who was to blame for all this suffering. But Mrs. Hanrahaty could never explain it, not to a child at least.

"Martha – please!" said her teacher. "You're much too young to understand. It's just the way it is, dear. It's how the country is – for now anyway."

The country! That was the answer.

So Martha blamed America. She began her sit-down the very next morning.

As the other students recited the Pledge, Martha plugged her fingers into her ears. Soon she was humming and then stamping her feet until the class stopped the recitation. When the rest of the class joined her protest, Martha's parents had to meet with the principal.

"The attention grew so large that it prompted an official investigation!" Martha told the Camp Unity students. Government investigations are always interesting to Communists. They trade these stories like some people gossip about bad medical news. The students were so enthralled by Martha's story that she decided to lay it on a little thicker.

"Suffice to say that I learned more than reading, writing and arithmetic from this brave woman. And when they discovered the guns, the bombs and the cash hidden in Mrs. Hanrahaty's basement, the authorities realized that even in Lake Winnanonga, there are people who are willing to do whatever is necessary to bring justice to the world. So that was the start of my journey – a journey that has brought me here today. That was the day I realized who I was – the day that I became … a Communist!"

Martha was pointing to the ceiling again, waiting for the applause that always followed her passionate speeches. The lingering silence was finally broken by Helen Gamble, whose enthusiastic clapping continued even as the class got up to leave.

"Oh, Mrs. Milwaukee! Thank you so much for coming!" Helen gushed. "You are so inspiring and, of course, I've heard so much about you back home! I can't believe that I am meeting you face to face!"

"Well thank you, my dear," Martha said regally. "And where is 'back home'?"

"Schenectady, of course! I'm Helen Gamble – your husband, Milo, sent me here!"

Martha's mouth fell open. "Milo? You say Milo sent you here?"

"He sure did! Your husband is such a great man, Mrs. Milwaukee. Truly an inspiration to the Party!" Helen was still shaking Martha's hand as Martha tried to disguise her shock.

"What did you mean when you said, Milo 'sent' you here? He gave you directions from Schenectady?"

"Oh no! He paid my way here! He's appointed me Morale Coordinator for Local 1389! I am so lucky and grateful to him and I have been working hard every day, learning how to raise the morale of our members and reignite their Communist zeal. That's just what your husband said. He said, 'We must reignite their zeal!'"

Martha's mind was racing. How could this be? Milo talking about Communist zeal? The same man who ordered Martha to walk away from Communism was paying for this young woman to attend a Communist labor school?

Any time Martha uttered the word 'Communist,' Milo was ready to call out the National Guard!

Now this? Now her?

As the shock wore off, Martha started to feel something she had not felt in years. Something was stirring deep inside her, a tingling excitement she had not experienced since she left New York City! And it was all because of Milo – her man, Milo!

That dear, sweet man!

Milo is not the enemy, Martha realized. He is one of us – a Communist! That clever, clever man! My husband, my hero! All of his hectoring about Communism had just been for show. Obviously, he was trying to protect her and Michael from a world filled with hate – a world not yet ready to embrace the Communist Revolution. Martha now realized that there was one man, one truly brave man, who was willing to save the world – and save his marriage – through Communism!

Milo has been working on a secret plan all along! A plan to bring new life to the union! To restore its Communist zeal and move it forward! Forward to October! And Martha never suspected a thing!

But why didn't he tell me? Martha wondered. This troubled her, but she pushed that thought aside.

Milo must have his reasons for not telling me. How and why it had happened were not important now. Finally, this was her chance to escape the drudgery of being a Schenectady housewife. This was her moment! With Milo standing behind her, Martha could recapture the magic she had known in Buffalo, in St. Paul, and Ypsilanti, Michigan! Already, she could feel the warmth of the spotlight caressing her face.

Martha had to calm herself.

If Milo can be that secretive, then so can I. There must be a reason why he hasn't told me anything, Martha decided. There are bigger things afoot than simply the training of this young woman. I must remain silent and wait until Milo brings me into this fight!

And this young woman! How can she possibly know what to do? I will have to guide her and help her, just as I will guide Milo!

Sliding an arm around Helen, Martha said, "My dear, you and I can help each other – as comrades, yes? I want you to look me up as soon as you return to Schenectady. I'm usually at home with our little boy, Michael, so you can find me there at almost any time of the day. It's 2943 Tuckahoe Row. But please remember one thing: Milo does not like to mix his union work with his home life so make sure you don't mention our little talk, all right? Honestly, my dear, I am so pleased for you! I'm so pleased for the both of us! It's all very exciting and we'll have so much to discuss once you return! There are people I want you to meet – so many people who can help us – help *you* – for the sake of the Party and all the little people of Schenectady! I just know you are going to be a great success!"

Helen looked at Martha in profound gratitude. "Mrs. Milwaukee, you are truly – truly – inspirational."

Nearby, Petrov was listening. He was not convinced that Helen was there on behalf of her union. No one at the Local seemed to know anything about a new "Morale Coordinator." So Petrov was suspicious. He knew there were spies everywhere. Even someone as young and beautiful as Helen Gamble could be an agent for the American FBI. Vigilance! With Martha Milwaukee's help, Petrov would keep track of Helen once she returned to Schenectady.

If this was a trap – and Helen was actually a spy – then Petrov would bring her back to Camp Unity and she would never leave there again.

On September 18, 1950, the City Council of New Rochelle, N. Y. approved an ordinance requiring police registration for every member of the Communist party or any other "subversive" organization, who lived, worked, conducted business in, or "regularly traveled through" the city. After a businessman filed a complaint about the new law, the mayor explained that registration was required for Communists, not commuters.

TESTIMONY BEFORE THE UNITED STATES SENATE
SUBCOMMITTEE ON CONSTITUTIONAL RIGHTS

CHAPTER FOURTEEN

MARTHA RETURNS HOME WITH MILO'S "SECRET"

Racing back from Camp Unity, Martha burst through the Glabberson's door as if the house was on fire.

"Misha! Misha!" Martha yelled. "Come quick, darling! Quickly!"

Rolling his eyes, Michael pulled himself off the floor. It was the most exercise he had gotten all day after sitting in front of the television with Morris, the Glabbersons' immovable son.

Martha called, "Rhonda! I'm sorry, dear, but I'll bring the car back tomorrow! Bye! See you then!" The front door slammed shut just as Rhonda Glabberson came into the living room.

"Morris, was that Mrs. Milwaukee? Morris? Morris!" she repeated. "Did Michael leave with his mother?"

Morris turned slowly from the green-gray glow of the television, peering through his glasses like a deep sea diver surfacing for air. After an entire day in front of the enormous Philco television, Morris mumbled, "It's not over yet."

"Never mind, dear," said Mrs. Glabberson, wiping Morris' glasses on her apron. "You go back to your show. And remember – if you're having trouble seeing the screen, just move closer."

Martha was already several blocks away, rocketing back to Tuckahoe Row before Milo would arrive home from work. She would need a story to explain why she was driving the Glabbersons' car. But it really didn't matter: Martha was too excited from her trip to Camp Unity!

"What a day, Misha! WHAT - A - DAY!" Martha shouted, slamming her palms against the steering wheel. 'Misha' was one of her Russian pet names for Michael. Whenever Milo wasn't around, Martha would indulge her Russian fantasies and most of them involved Michael: Misha, Mikhail, Mika.

Michael hated them all.

It had been this way for as long as the boy could remember. He was barely four years old when Michael had the terrible realization that his mother – *his own mother*! – had apparently forgotten his name. It was always Misha-this or Mikhail-that. One day, he shouted, "I'm Michael, Mommy! Michael, Michael, Michael!"

There were so many other things about his mother that Michael could never understand, so many reasons why "Misha" never let his friends come over to the house. It wasn't even safe outside the house. Martha would call Michael in for dinner, shouting 'Mikhail!' out the front door, loud enough for the whole neighborhood to hear.

"Did your mother just say, Sieg Heil?" asked Tommy Wasserman. The other boys stared at Michael, waiting for an answer. What could he say? The neighborhood kids already knew that Martha was strange. Their parents had told them so.

But why was his mother so different, Michael worried. Why was she always talking about things that none of the other boys heard from their mothers? At bedtime, Martha would tell stories of brave Bolsheviks lopping off the heads of the evil Romanovs. After so much carnage, Michael would not fall asleep for hours.

"You are a very special child, Mikhail, and Momma loves you very much. You are the son of two countries and one day you will help bring these countries together for peace and brotherhood!"

"And remember, Michael," Martha would constantly remind him, "we are the Vanguards of a new world order!"

The Vanguards? WHO are the Vanguards?! I thought we were the Milwaukees! She can't remember my first OR my last name!

There were so many other Mother Mysteries for Michael. He had no idea what Martha was doing around the house. She never seemed to care about cleaning or cooking. She spent more time in the basement talking to herself.

"Is anyone out there? Come in, comrades. This is the Red Flame – can you hear me?" Michael could hear his mother speaking urgently into the shortwave radio. She could never get the thing to work, never realizing that Milo had unplugged it. Every time Martha tried to fiddle with it, she would end up crying in her room until Milo got home.

Martha never said anything about this to Milo, so Michael knew that her time in the basement was another secret to keep from his father.

Next came the scarves: ridiculous, red scarves that Martha tied tight enough to asphyxiate the kid. Made of scratchy wool with stiff, pointy ends, these neck-clutching nooses were always flapping in Michael's face and slapping him in the eye when he ran. He tried to tug them off but the knots only got tighter until Michael was left gasping for air. Sometimes they got so tight, Martha had to cut them off with a knife. A knife!

That was an image Michael would never forget – his mother stumbling toward him, squinting through the cigarette smoke that curled around her face, as she raised the knife to Michael's throat! "Now don't … move … a muscle – !"

The scarves were only the start of it. It was just before Michael's ninth birthday when the mailman delivered a package covered with strange looking stamps. Michael was about to join the neighborhood kids for a game of baseball when Martha called him back to the kitchen. Clutching the brown paper package, Martha was beaming from ear to ear.

"I've got a present for you, Mikhail!" Now Michael was excited, imagining an early birthday present.

"It's your new uniform – just arrived from Stalingrad!" Martha gushed. "All the way from Russia!"

A baseball uniform – from Russia?

"They play baseball in Russia?" Michael asked.

"No, silly – not baseball! It's your uniform for the Young Pioneers!"

Michael's mind went blank, his body numb as Martha unbuttoned his shirt and pulled down his pants. From out of the package she removed an assortment of brown shirts, shorts, and pants, along with a red cap and more scarves. Powerless to stop her, Michael was pushed in front of the mirror on the closet door.

He could not recognize himself. Who was that sad little boy dressed in the starchy brown shirt, matching shorts, and clunky brown shoes? He looked like some kind of Halloween turd. Martha, meanwhile, was beaming as if it were May Day.

"Oh – wait, wait, wait, wait, wait!" she shouted, running back to the kitchen. "I forgot your kerchief!"

The dreaded red noose! Michael knew there would be no baseball that day.

"Come darling – let's get in the car!" Martha announced, pulling Michael out the door. He stopped her at the doorway, slowly peering one way and then the other. If his friends saw him dressed this way, his life would be over. When the coast was clear, Michael sprinted to the car, throwing the field cap – and himself – underneath the dashboard.

Michael wanted to die. Maybe he would be sucked into the engine and ground up into little brown chunks.

"It's time for you to meet the other Pioneers!" Martha said gaily.

Holy cow! Michael suddenly remembered. The Pioneers were the boys and girls on the Howdy Doody Show! Of course, Buffalo Bob's Pioneers! She's taking me to see Buffalo Bob! Well, this isn't so bad after all!

Michael jumped onto the front seat next to his mom. He didn't care who saw him now. He was going to see Buffalo Bob!

I'm going to be a Pioneer!

Michael had never seen his mother act so nervous and giddy before. And no wonder: Buffalo Bob was the most important man on television! Everybody knew Buffalo Bob and Howdy Doody!

Martha smiled as she spied Michael carefully arranging the kerchief around his neck, pressing it neatly across his shoulder and smoothing out the creases. Michael wanted to look sharp for Buffalo Bob. Young Pioneers have to make a good first impression!

"Here we are darling!" Martha sang as they pulled in front of a small house, jammed tightly against other tiny houses. Michael didn't recognize this neighborhood. This place was much older than his house and not as clean as the houses on his block.

Was this Doodyville?

Outside the car, Martha kneeled next to Michael, straightening his kerchief and field cap. "Take my hand, darling, and remember what I taught you: 'A Pioneer stands straight and true. Fighting oppression and tyranny too!'"

Michael followed his mother, repeating the Pioneer pledge: "A Pioneer stands for peace and justice – "

" – opposing the evil forces against us!" they chanted together.

"Very good, darling!" Martha smiled as she led Michael up a decrepit set of stairs. The paint was peeling on the house and everything smelled like cats. Martha rapped on the door and out came a woman who Michael recognized from school.

"Well, hello there!" the big woman bellowed. "And don't you look handsome in your new uniform!"

Martha pushed Michael inside. "Michael, you know Mrs. Glabberson, don't you?"

Rhonda Glabberson was one of the lunch ladies in the school cafeteria. Without her hair net and white uniform, Michael did not recognize her until he smelled the cabbage boiling on the stove. At school, you could not escape that smell – or forget the oddly-shaped foods that were served by Mrs. Glabberson.

Rhonda was a loyal Party member and she considered herself the chief provocateur of the school cafeteria. When the Soviets marched into Eastern Europe, the students would find their mashed potatoes served in the shape of Poland, their meatloaf resembling Czechoslovakia, and their bread sliced into whichever country Stalin was slicing up that week.

Seeing her outside of school was strange to Michael. How does the lunch lady know Buffalo Bob? Sensing his confusion, Martha said, "Your father and Mr. Glabberson work together for the union, Mikhail."

"Mikhail – what a beautiful name!" Mrs. Glabberson exclaimed. "So much nicer than Michael!" Michael glared at Mrs. Glabberson until Martha grabbed him by the ear and pulled him to the other side of the room.

"What's with that face, mister?" Martha demanded.

"My name is Michael!"

"You stop that right now! She's only trying to be nice! Now take that scowl off your face. The Young Pioneers are waiting for us."

Michael's mood brightened – but only for a moment – as he followed his mother into the next room. This must be where Buffalo Bob does his show, Michael figured.

They walked into a room that was very dark. There appeared to be five other boys, all crammed together on a small couch. They too were dressed like Halloween turds.

Michael looked around in wide-eyed panic. Wait a minute – this is no television studio! There is no Howdy Doody! This is just a living room! I've been had – by my own mother! Before Michael could escape, Mrs. Glabberson was standing over him, pushing him toward the couch.

"You know all these boys, don't you Mikhail?" A row of sad little faces turned toward Michael. He recognized most of these boys from school.

They were the quiet kids in class and some of them spoke with accents. They came from families that had only recently moved to Schenectady, lured by their relatives to good-paying jobs at G.E.

Michael's attention turned to two large pictures on the opposite wall. They were the same photographs that Martha would hang on the walls at their house as soon as his father left for work. One pictured a large man with a smug expression, his face dominated by a large mustache and heavy eyebrows. The other man looked like a mad scientist, his eyes staring intensely into the distance.

"Do you know who these men are, Mikhail?" asked Mrs. Glabberson. "This is our Supreme Leader, Joseph Stalin. Stalin means 'Man of Steel' and isn't he just that – a man of steel! This other man is Vladimir Lenin, the progenitor of modern Communism. These are two very important men, indeed – men who have changed the course of history! I'll be telling you more about them in our next meeting."

Michael shot up. "What meeting?" he asked Mrs. Glabberson.

"Why Michael – didn't your mother tell you? This is your first meeting of the Young Pioneers! We'll be meeting here every Saturday!"

The other little turds looked at Michael as if HE was the idiot. Michael closed his eyes and threw his head back against the crunchy sofa. Nine months later, Michael's nightmare was continuing.

On the day his mother travelled to Camp Unity, Michael had been stuck listening to Morris Glabberson crunch cups of ice in front of the television set. Driving home now, Michael expected the usual litany of complaints about whatever was irritating his mother that day. Instead, Michael was surprised to see how happy she was – perhaps a little too happy – as Martha frantically zigzagged the car across town.

"Your father, Misha! Your father is the most brilliant man in the world! He has got a plan, Misha – a marvelous plan! A plan that is going to change this whole city and with my help, we are going to change the whole WORLD!"

As usual, "Misha" had no idea what his mother was talking about. He was too busy trying to stay in his seat as the DeSoto ripped around street corners, jumping up on two wheels, until the car came shrieking to a sudden stop and Michael flew under the dashboard.

"Oh, Misha, I'm so sorry. Are you okay?"

"I guess so," Michael said, rubbing his head as he climbed back onto the seat. "What's the matter?"

"A squirrel ran out in front of the car. I nearly ran the poor thing over."

"Is that against the law?"

"No dear, it's just something I try not to do. Squirrels are like some people, scurrying around, lost and confused, so it's important for people like us – the New Vanguard – to protect them. To lead them."

"Like a pet squirrel?"

"In a way, yes," Martha said, pleased with her analogy. She hit the gas again, whipping around another corner. "So did you have fun with Morris today?"

"MOM!"

Martha slammed on the brakes again, stopping only a few feet away from a little girl standing in the crosswalk. Michael could not believe it! Below the DeSoto's curved hood, Michael could see a familiar head of blonde hair. He stood up on the front seat and there, glaring back at him, was Sandra Pepper – the most beautiful girl in the entire fourth grade! Michael slowly sank behind the dashboard.

"Misha? Is that Frankie Pepper's little girl?"

"Yes," muttered Michael, hiding from the awesome power that pretty girls hold over insignificant boys. Martha muttered, "Frankie Pepper, that traitor." Racing the car's engine, Martha and Sandra stared each other down, neither one willing to move.

Michael knew Frankie Pepper's name the way Romeo knew the Capulets. Sandra Pepper's father was the leader of a rival union – a union that Frankie Pepper created after he abandoned the AEWA, destroying his great friendship with Milo. No one on Tuckahoe Row ever spoke a kind word about the Peppers. But Michael had no need for words. Harps and violins would play during his many dreams about the lovely Sandra Pepper.

Martha gave a half-hearted smile and waved Sandra Pepper along, but the little girl would not move, still scowling at Martha and blocking the DeSoto. Sandra Pepper knew all about the Milwaukees, "those damn Reds" as her father would curse them. She learned a lot of new words whenever her father mentioned the name of Milo Milwaukee.

Finally, Sandra turned away and Martha hit the gas before the little girl could reach the other side of the street. Michael crawled out from under the dash and looked cautiously out the back window, hoping to catch one more glimpse of the fair-haired Sandra.

Maybe she didn't see me, Michael hoped.

Maybe he could change schools.

Maybe he was adopted.

"Made it!" Martha exclaimed as the car careened into the driveway on Tuckahoe Row. Milo was still not home. "Got to start dinner!" she called over her shoulder.

Dinner? Michael could only imagine what his mother would be burning that night. Fried bologna and toast were about the best she could manage. So Michael stayed in the car, thinking of the perfect Sandra Pepper: Her blonde hair, so long and soft, it practically shimmered in the playground sunshine. She always smelled so good on those lucky days when Michael stood next to her in the lunch line or when he would walk past her desk and she would sneer at him. Sandra Pepper sneered at all the boys.

What if I had different parents – or at least a normal mother? Michael wondered. Maybe then, Sandra Pepper would sneer only at me.

"The Party has recognized that many people do have a liking and love for folk music and square dancing. (The Communist Party also) started a 'Record of the Month Club,' records for children between the ages of 3 and 12 … (reaching) into homes with subtle indoctrination."

"One of these songs is called 'Banks of Marble.' The last line goes, 'And the vaults are stuffed with silver that we sweated for. The banks are made of marble with a guard at every door. We will own those banks of marble with a guard at every door and we will share the vaults of silver that the people sweated for.'"

EX-COMMUNIST HARVEY MATUSOW *testifying before investigators of the Ohio State Legislature*

CHAPTER FIFTEEN

CAVALCADE FOR PEACE AND JUSTICE

Simple, authentic, universal: Folk music is music of the people. Just folks.

Anybody could sing it. Almost anyone could play it. Singers call and the people respond like two spoons slapping together.

In the 1940s and '50s, folk music was the personal anthem of the liberals and radicals who came together in America's Popular Front. It was the musical rendition of their lives: like-minded people fighting against social injustice and inequality. Tap your toes, bob your head, and change the world. At least it felt that way as folk music attracted young people, working people, caring people – the disenfranchised and the disenchanted.

This was not the crowd at the opera or the symphony. Folk music came to them. All they needed was a guitar, a washboard bass, and the rest of the world to sing along. This was church without the collection plate.

For the American Communist Party, folk music was used like a political duck call. When the Communists went looking for members – and they were always looking for new recruits – folk music was a sure way to draw a crowd. In between songs about love and family, neighbor helping neighbor, there were the protest songs – songs to get people fired up and motivated to do what needed to be done. Something noble, something courageous. If we had a hammer.

All of this was a mystery to the CIA, the FBI, and the other Red Hunters. They did not understand folk music's allure to the Communists and other "progressives." As with every other riddle involving the Communists, investigators suspected that there must be more to this music than simply singing and clapping. Researchers were brought in to examine the syncopation of various folk tunes, while linguists analyzed the lyrics and symbolism in popular folk songs. ("Good Night Irene" was one of the most vexing: who was this woman Irene and why was someone trying to get her into bed?) When the answers were not forthcoming, the CIA decided to go inside the folk music world and learn its secrets firsthand. For this undercover assignment, the Agency chose a little-known country and western singer named Orley Post.

As leader of The Cowpies, Orley Post had played every honky-tonk, cathouse and dirtbag saloon in West Central Texas. Most days started with a bottle of beer and a pull of beef jerky, but as low-down as he was, Orley knew there had to be more to life than lonesome songs about heartbreak and hound dogs. When the CIA offered him a job, Orley grabbed this unexpected escape. Soon, Orley and his wife Darlene were riding out of Texas on the "Cavalcade for Peace and Justice," playing folk songs of brotherhood, love, and anything else that would attract Communists and their fellow travelers.

Play your music, sing your songs, but keep your ear to the ground, the CIA instructed Orley. Get the Communists to start talking and we will do the rest.

The Cavalcade began with a tour of Europe where the Agency hoped to lure the usual assortment of radicals and free-thinkers, anyone who could provide some glimpse into life behind the Iron Curtain. When the Cavalcade arrived in East Berlin, Orley was approached by a man with a shaggy beard and two woeful eyes searching warily from underneath a dirty fisherman's cap. He called himself "Volga the Boatman" and he offered a croaking, off-key rendition of that old Communist standard "Your Land Will Be My Land." It was the worst thing Darlene Post had ever heard, but Orley hired him on the spot.

"Don't matter if he can sing or not," Orley said, "Folks back home are gonna melt when they see a genuine Ruskie on the bill."

What Orley could not tell his wife was that Volga the Boatman was neither genuine nor Russian. He was Henry Brownale, the CIA's former station chief in West Berlin. The Agency was giving Henry one more chance.

Only the son of Congressman C.B. Brownale would get this many chances, the Agency reminded "Volga." You're a lucky man, they said.

Some luck, Henry sniffed. One day I'm working for a white-shoe law firm on Wall Street and now look at me: Volga the Joke Man. A beard, a guitar and one last chance to prove that I can be an undercover agent for the CIA. One more chance to forget West Berlin, to forget Anna Tilson and maybe, finally, to forgive her.

The next stop for Volga and the rest of Orley's Cavalcade was a tour of the northeastern United States, including a stop at a farm field outside of Poughkeepsie. It didn't take long for the news to reach Camp Unity.

"There's going to be a hootenanny!" Patrice shouted as she ran around the camp, spreading the good news.

"Can you believe it?! Orley Post! The Parson Pipers! The Love Bucket Boys! Al Abama With the Banjo on His Knee! They're all coming to a farm just down the road!"

Helen could only nod her head as Patrice joyfully bounced around the bunkhouse. The Fiddle Sticks? Happy Trails? Volga the Boatman? Helen had no idea what all the fuss was about and, like everyone else at Camp Unity, she could not foresee the terror that was heading toward them.

"And he will be a wild ass of a man; his hand will be against
every man, and every man's hand against him."
GENESIS 16: 7-16

CHAPTER SIXTEEN

AUGUST 4, 1950:
a Farm Field Outside Poughkeepsie

They stood in a ring at the edge of the concert grounds, a dozen deputy sheriffs gazing vacantly over the audience with the practiced countenance of the armed and fully loaded. Behind them, another line was forming. Large men in coveralls and dirty work boots, the good ole boys of the Poughkeepsie countryside, truck farmers, and third-generation tenants were climbing out of their trucks and looking downright disgusted. They stood together in small circles with their heads bowed like scavenging crows, looking for new places to spit.

These men were as out of place as the rocks and rotting vegetables that were hidden in their trucks. The audience, however, was typical for a hootenanny. Helen Gamble, Anna Tilson, and lonely Patrice were there and like everyone else in the crowd they were looking forward to singing along with Orley Post and his Cavalcade for Peace and Justice.

No one was being vigilant. They did not notice when the exits were blocked by the farm boys and their trucks and nobody asked why the cops were quietly walking away.

On the other side of the stage, hidden in the woods, another group of men stood waiting. They had driven down from Schenectady and each one was dressed in the distinctive white robe and triangular hood of the Ku Klux Klan. One of those pointy hoods stood more than a foot above the rest.

What he was doing in a farm field outside of Poughkeepsie, Beau Duffy could not say. But there he was, covered in a bed sheet and waiting for the signal to attack.

Beau could hear the crowd on the other side of the stage – much larger than he had expected – clapping and cheering as Orley and Darlene Post finished another song. He squeezed the baseball bat that was resting against his shoulder as the morning sun moved closer to the edge of the woods.

"How many y'all come here for a good time?" Orley hollered. "Well come on then – LET'S GO!" The crowd responded with a loud hillbilly "Whooooop!" as Orley and the band charged into a wild, bluegrass romp. Everyone was on their feet, clapping, dancing, and stomping to the music, making the crowd sound three times larger than it did a minute ago. All of it was making Beau hot underneath his KKK uniform. He could feel the sweat running down his neck as the thump-thump-thump of the band beat against his chest. Or was it Beau's heart that was pounding?

He looked nervously to his right, checking on the rest of the Flying Squadron. They were also disguised in hoods and robes, but they weren't acting like menacing Klansmen. Darrell Johnston was swinging his hips to the music – the bottom of his KKK robe swishing from side to side. Farther down the tree line, Dooley Wilson had his arms spread wide, twisting his shoulders back and forth like a big white bird. In a half-whisper, Beau shouted, "Hey you guys – knock it off! We're not here to dance, goddammit! Get ready now!"

The Fliers snapped to attention.

Beau turned back toward the music, trying to calculate the distance he had to cover and the time it would take him to reach the stage. The ground was still wet and running in this Klan robe was going to slow him down.

But a bigger question kept pestering him: What the hell will I do once I get there?

Beau could see women and children in the crowd. Nobody had said anything about women and children! Beau yanked off the Klan hood, struggling to catch his breath.

Women and children? Beau thought of his mother and sister back home. Being home would be good right about now, Beau realized.

A few days earlier, Beau had gone looking for Helen because someone said she had gone away "on union business." But no one, not even Milo, seemed to know where she was. Instead of finding Helen, Beau ran into an old friend, Robbie Reynolds.

Had Beau heard about the trouble coming to Poughkeepsie, Robbie asked. "We're goin' down there to bust a few skulls," Robbie laughed. "What do you say, Beau? You wanna come along and kick some Commie ass?"

The next thing he knew, Beau and the rest of the Flying Squadron were heading south to Poughkeepsie with baseball bats, bicycle chains, and no sense of the trouble they were about to cause.

Beau had listened quietly as the Klansmen laid out the plan: everyone would wait in the woods until the truck horns sounded and then they would all "meet in the middle." Everybody was fair game, the Klansmen said, and the cops would make sure that everyone stayed for the show. Beau nodded his head as if he understood.

"Meet in the middle" and then what? Pop some stranger in the nose – right in front of his wife and kids?

I'm no Klansman, Beau fretted. I am not an Anything. Beau had never been a joiner, but now he was going to follow the KKK into a crowd of women and children? How will I tell which ones are the Communists?

Working for Milo meant Beau never had to think about such things. Milo always picked the targets. All Beau had to do was choose which hand to use and what body part to punch!

As he waited for the signal, Beau tried to relax in the only way he knew how – he reached back with the baseball bat and slammed it against a tree. Instantly the lumber snapped back against his face, slamming the bridge of his nose. Tears filled his eyes and then the rage flooded through his body. Suddenly Beau wasn't worried about women and children. He just wanted to smash something and he didn't care who would get hurt.

"Come on, Beau!" Dooley Wilson called over his shoulder. Beau had missed the signal. He was alone in the woods as Dooley and the other Fliers were racing toward the crowd while the Poughkeepsie farm boys attacked from the other side. Musicians dove off the plywood stage as it echoed with the sound of rocks and vegetables falling from the sky. The only thing louder were the screams of women and children scrambling for somewhere to hide.

Beau was running as hard as he could, swinging the baseball bat high above his head, but his legs were getting tangled in the Klan robe. He tried lifting it up like a skirt, but that made him run even slower. Worse, Beau could not see where he was going. Being so tall, he had cut two extra eye holes into his Klan hood, but even with two eyes on top and two below, Beau was struggling to make sense of what was happening up ahead of him.

Dooley Wilson suddenly stopped running and then his body went limp as he spun around and fell face-first into the field. Right behind Dooley, another member of the Flying Squadron went down and then another. Beau pulled the Klan hood away to get a better view and that's when he saw the man in a fisherman's cap running straight at him. It was Volga the Boatman, brandishing a busted guitar and his CIA training to crush the Klansmen. His next target was this big, four-eyed Klansmen running back to the woods.

The distance between Henry and Beau was shrinking rapidly as the heavy Klan robe pulled against Beau's legs. Desperately, he heaved the baseball bat over his shoulder, but it flew far over Henry's head. Now gasping for breath and struggling to reach the woods, Beau searched for safety in the dizzying kaleidoscope of sunlight and shadow that was spinning inside the Klan hood. Beau knew he was losing this race and he would soon have to fight his way out. Leaping over a huge log, Beau went flying through the air and landed headfirst into a small ravine.

Tough as he was, Beau knew his pursuer might be tougher so he decided to stay down. He lay still, pretending to be unconscious, as Henry stood on the ridge above him, triumphantly clenching the remains of his shattered guitar. Henry was about to head back to the melee around the stage when he heard a familiar voice coming into the woods.

Was that … Anna Tilson?

Anna was calling, "Helen! Where are you? Helen!"

In a panic, "Volga" threw himself behind a tree.

This can't be happening! From West Berlin to a cow pasture in Poughkeepsie, how in the world did she find me? Hasn't Anna punished me enough?

Anna was the reason Henry was in this mess – traveling the countryside as a folk music minstrel, pretending he could sing and play the guitar when everybody at the CIA knew he could do no such thing. What could he do now?

He could be a man, Henry decided. He could use his skills as a highly-trained secret agent!

Henry dove into a cluster of ferns, covering his face with dirt and mud as he burrowed underneath the dense vegetation. From his CIA training, Henry knew he could breathe underground for at least fifteen minutes, possibly longer.

How deep would he have to go before Anna Tilson could no longer find him? How much deeper before Henry could escape the love of his life?

> Comrade Jenny: I needn't have to remind you that one of the greatest threats to Communism is internal – from within the party itself: Diversionists, traitors, opportunists, social patriots, reformers. You'll make every effort to discover these traitors and report them to me. And if you fail to report them I'll be forced to conclude that you are one of them yourself.
>
> "I LED THREE LIVES," 1953 ✳ *A television show based on the*
> *true story of FBI undercover agent Herbert Philbrick*

CHAPTER SEVENTEEN

"I NEED ROCK"

Beau's heart was still racing as he pressed himself against a moss-covered log. He had not played possum like this since he was a kid, playing in the woods behind his house. He recalled the soothing sensation of the soft grass – or was it that sound? That was another memory from years ago: a particular cry of pain. It sounded like Helen crying!

Beau slowly raised his head up, straining to peek through one of the four eyeholes in his hood. Over the rise, there was a woman down on her knees, crying into her hands, her body shaking with deep, frightened breaths. Beau slid back behind the log.

"Holy Christ!" Beau said to himself. "What if Helen sees me?"

Helen looked up as she heard Beau frantically pulling off his Klan robe and stuffing it inside the rotting log.

"*Patrice?*" Helen called. When no one answered, she pushed herself up and scanned the forest floor. "*Who ees there?*"

That can't be Helen, Beau realized. This woman is speaking with a Russian accent!

Then a shadow fell over Beau. When he looked up, his heart sank: Helen Gamble was standing on the ridge above him.

Christ, thought Beau. How am I going to explain this?

But Helen was not asking any questions. There were no accusations. The shock and terror on her face melted into relief as soon as she saw her old friend.

Helen jumped into Beau's arms and pressed her head against his muscular shoulders. Once she stopped trembling, Beau gently placed her on the ground. He examined the bloody scratches on her arms and legs and tenderly picked away the twigs and leaves that were stuck in her hair.

"*Oh!*" she winced as Beau brushed the side of her head.

"Let me look at this," Beau said urgently. He carefully moved his hand behind her ear and she cringed again. There was blood on Beau's hand as he pulled it away.

"You've got a bad cut there."

"*My head … eet hurtz,*" she said.

Beau started to laugh. "Why are you talking like that?"

"*Why am I talking like how?*" Helen said grumpily. She tried to stand up but fell back against Beau.

"I mean why are you talking like, I don't know … a Russian? What happened to you?"

Helen did not have to answer – Beau knew what had happened – and she did not seem interested in why Beau was there. Helen was back on her feet, urgently searching the woods.

"*Vee must find my friends! DARE!*" she exclaimed, pointing at Patrice near the edge of the woods. Patrice was turning in tight circles and brandishing a guitar over her head, ready to smash the next man who came near her. Not far from Patrice, Anna Tilson was hiding behind a tree. When Helen called out to them, Patrice lowered her guitar and sprinted toward Helen and Beau.

"Oh Helen! Are you all right?" Patrice cried. "I am so, so sorry! I didn't mean to hit you – honestly! I was only trying to scare those Klansmen away and I must have clocked you instead! Are you okay?"

Patrice was about to apologize again when Helen held up her hand. "*Please, no more sorrys. I need quiet now. My head ees pounding.*"

Patrice's mouth fell open when she heard Helen's accent. She looked at Beau for an explanation.

"We know each other," Beau said. "At least I think so."

Gently, Anna asked, "Helen, why are you talking like that?"

"*More questions about dees?*" Helen grumbled. "*I am talking so … I talk! Enough talking about talking!*"

Beau and the women looked up quickly as another Klansman came charging into the forest.

"*Stand back,*" Helen warned as she grabbed Patrice's guitar and smashed it against the log. The Klansman turned and ran the other way. He wanted no part of this crazy woman with the splintered guitar. Patrice let out a mournful groan as she took the ruined guitar and fell to her knees.

"What will I tell Petrov?" she asked, looking up at Helen.

"*Tell him truth – thees geetar ees no good. Come now – let's go.*" Helen started back toward the stage when Beau warned her not to go.

"I think he's right," Anna agreed. "Those lunatics are still out there."

With a grunt, Helen went the other way, stomping off toward Camp Unity as Patrice, Anna, and Beau ran to keep up with her. It did not take them long to reach the edge of the woods where a rock-covered ravine ran alongside the highway. Below them, people were standing on both sides of the road, shaking their fists and cursing at the cars driving away from the concert grounds. The protestors held crudely painted signs – 'Go home Commies!' and 'Folk Music is for Pinkos!' – and some were even throwing rocks at the frightened concertgoers.

Beau held out his arms to warn the women to stay back until a rock cracked against the window of a passing car. Helen could hear the cries of terrified children and with an angry growl she pushed Beau aside and stormed down the hill.

"*I need rock,*" Helen hissed at one of the men by the roadside. Taking a quick glance at Helen, the man said, "Well pick one up! There's plenty at your feet!"

When the man cocked his arm to throw another stone, Helen grabbed his hand and ripped the rock away, wrenching the man's arm behind his back. Howling in pain, he dropped to the asphalt as Helen pressed her foot against his chest.

"*Look!*" Helen snarled, mashing the rock against his face, "*I found rock!*"

"What the hell do you think you're doin'?" another man shouted, rushing over to save his friend. Helen grabbed this man by the wrist and shoulder – just as Petrov had instructed her – and, with a vicious twist, Helen flipped this man on top of the other.

Helen's chest was heaving in anger as she turned in wide-eyed rage at the rest of the crowd. She took one menacing step toward them before rocks and protest signs fell to the pavement and everyone scattered.

"Jesus Christ!" Beau yelled as he came charging down the hill. "Where did you learn to do that?" Anna and Patrice came next, stopping short of the two men laid out on the roadside, groaning in pain.

"Hey listen – we gotta get out of here!" Patrice urged. She tugged at Helen's wrist, but Helen wasn't paying attention. Barreling toward them was another truck.

"Hey – HEY!" Beau shouted, waving his arms as the truck raced by. It pulled off to the side of the road and Clayton Lovelace, another member of the Flying Squadron, leaned out of the cab, calling for Beau to jump on.

"Helen, come on!" Beau shouted as he ran for the truck. "That's Clayton. He can give us a ride home!"

From the back of the truck, Beau waved for Helen to follow him, but she would not move. Soon the truck disappeared at a bend in the road.

Helen knew it was too soon to go back home. She had too much left to do.

She realized how much she had learned at Camp Unity and how good it felt to be this strong, flipping those evil rock-throwers onto the highway. The men were still sprawled on the roadway as a police siren drew closer. Silently, Helen, Anna, and Patrice linked hands and clambered up the ravine to the safety of the woods. From there they would travel west, following the sun to Camp Unity. Their Great Struggle was much closer than any of them had realized and Helen, now vigilant and powerful, was ready for the fight.

"A warning to all enemies of America, at home and abroad, who are planning acts of aggression. This is the story of the gallant men and women who penetrated, and are still penetrating, enemy lines to get secret information necessary for the defense of the United States. This is the story of one of our nation's mightiest weapons – past, present, and future if necessary – the American intelligence services."

TV SHOW ✳ "SECRET FILE U.S.A"

C H A P T E R   E I G H T E E N

FARTHER BACK IN THE WOODS

Henry threw himself against a tree, clutching the neck of his shattered guitar like the muzzle of his old Springfield sniper rifle. The bark felt rough against his back. It felt good.

Up ahead, Anna, Helen, and Patrice were walking to Camp Unity, unaware of the stealthy CIA agent tracking them through the darkening forest, on guard for the danger that could be lurking behind any bush or innocent fern. The last time Henry felt this good – when he felt like a real secret agent – was at Camp X, the CIA training academy.

Long abandoned in the forests of northern Ontario, Camp X was once a children's summer camp before it became another hasty mistake by the CIA. In its race to match the Soviets, the Agency had been desperate to get agents on the ground as quickly as possible so the children's camp was purchased sight unseen and with no time to refurbish it.

Between the biting black flies and a particularly virulent strain of poison oak, Henry and the other CIA recruits were forced to sleep on child-sized bunk beds and crouch over tiny toilets, shaving and shower-ing on their knees and eating breakfast over tables with little bowls and child-size spoons. Camp X made them tough. The British were there to make them smart.

"You fight like a gentleman, you will die like a gentleman!" the offi-cers from MI6, Britain's chief spy agency, would scold the CIA trainees. These instructors were spies of the Old School: cosmopolitan, well read and extremely dangerous in hand-to-hand combat. They had no time for Marquess of Queensberry rules. They knew it was kill or be killed.

Henry was assigned to O Company, led by a renowned drill instructor known simply as "the Major." A legendary expert in Tánsu – the ancient Japanese art of throwing furniture – the Major could turn any piece of office equipment into a lethal weapon. (It was said that the Major once suffocated a man using a single postage stamp.) Henry soon realized that the Agency was grooming him for a desk job – in Cleveland! – safe from injury or anything else that might draw the ire of his famous father, the powerful Congressman C.B. Brownale.

Henry was too proud to complain and he certainly did not want his father to know about his assignment with the "Cleveland Insurance Agen-cy." Here, the chances for heroism were less than none: the CIA's office was located on the second floor of a three-story building, across the street from police headquarters, a fire station and a factory that manufactured gauze bandages and iodine. His desk (rubber-coated) contained neither scissors nor a writing instrument with any kind of point.

Safe and smothering, it was like working inside a giant box of cotton balls.

It would be months before they even let him outside. In fact, his first assignment could not have been safer – an investigation into birthday cards and party favors. The brunt of so many office pranks, Henry figured his first assignment must be just another gag.

"Birthday cards?" he responded skeptically.

"It's true," his supervisor said. "We've located a bunch of blacklisted writers putting Commie propaganda into greeting cards."

Henry gasped. "Are you telling me the Soviets are attempting mind control – "

" – in iambic pentameter," the supervisor said gravely.

He handed Henry a sample card: a little boy was blowing out the candles of his birthday cake and rising above it was a huge, mushroom cloud. Inside was the ominous message, "Make a Wish, Son – Before It's Too Late!"

"Bastards!" Henry muttered. It was so like that Communist scum! Whether it was books, movies, radio shows – and now greeting cards – the Soviets were constantly trying to demoralize America's spirit with *dezinformatsiya.* What was next? Exploding birthday candles? Pin the tail on Trotsky? Musical chairs in the Politburo? Nothing was too low for these ruthless Red bastards.

"We're sending you in undercover," the supervisor instructed. "You'll fit in just fine. You have that look, I suppose. They're all typical writers – failed novelists, unpublished poets, academic alcoholics. They're so desperate for work, they'll write almost anything – restaurant menus, food labels, how-to manuals. Some have even been sports reporters."

Henry shook his head in disgust. He had met some writers before. They were all fragile, worrisome people, willing to do almost anything for a bottle of hooch and a room to sleep it off. They would be easy marks for the Soviet propaganda machine.

"Get inside there, Brownale," the Supervisor said, tossing him a fresh box of number two pencils. "It shouldn't be hard to find a Soviet spy in a pack of deadbeat writers."

Henry nodded. With their greasy, tweed jackets, male pattern baldness, and little concern for personal hygiene, the genuine writers would be easy to spot. To find the Communist ringleader, Henry would have to find more subtle clues, like a dangling participle or the improper use of a subordinating conjunction. Henry smiled ruefully at the idea: Could good grammar defeat the Red Menace?

Henry's ruse was working until his investigation abruptly ended with the Sunday edition of the *Cleveland Plain Dealer:*

I WAS A GREETING CARD WRITER FOR THE FBI!

Hoover's men had planted their own undercover agent among the Red writers and that agent was ready to testify that Henry was a member of this Communist cabal! The CIA had no choice but to pack up Henry's operation and move him out of Cleveland as quickly as possible.

Henry's next assignment would be Radio Free Berlin. That, too, was a bust.

A ten million dollar bust.

After God takes sides in the war between Communism and Capitalism, a scientist makes radio contact with Mars and hears a voice urging Earthlings to return to the Church. Russian peasants tear down Stalin's portrait and the Soviet Union is turned upside down as the Communists are overthrown.

UNITED ARTISTS MOVIE ✳ "RED PLANET MARS"

C H A P T E R   N I N E T E E N

OCTOBER 15, 1949:
the CIA Closes Radio Free Berlin

To: Agency Liaison, Eastern Sector
From: Preston Mathers, Field Debriefing Team
Subject: Debriefing of Agent H. Brownale, Station Chief, Radio Free Berlin

Agent Brownale confirms his unauthorized rendezvous with subjects Anna Tilson and Klaus Vilbricht (21:00 on 8/14/49. Location: Luxemburg Hofbrau, Russian sector, East Berlin)

Subjects Vilbricht and Tilson are known Soviet agents. (See File No. 3978-RFB: Related investigation into the vetting of Subject Tilson as a performer on Radio Free Berlin.)

Chronology: Agent Brownale states that he received a message from Anna Tilson requesting a meeting with Subject Klaus Vilbricht in the Russian sector of Berlin.

(Message from Anna Tilson: "Henry, We need you. No doubt you are still angry with us, but Klaus has vital news that you must hear. Next Wednesday, meet us after dark at the Luxemburg Hofbrau near the Liebknecht Bridge.")

Agent Brownale states Subjects Vilbricht and Tilson arrived at the hofbrau separately. Under questioning, Vilbricht claimed to have made contact with rebel fighters in Belarus. He displayed photographs of Russian artillery that had been destroyed and Russian personnel allegedly killed by said rebels. Vilbricht told Agent Brownale that the rebels needed U.S. support (weapons, food, money) to continue their fight against the Soviets.

Agent Brownale confirmed subsequent and unauthorized contact with his father (Congressman C.B. Brownale) regarding the requested aid. Congressman Brownale then contacted Agency leadership (HQ Langley) urging approval of weapons and supplies along with $10 (ten) million in gold bullion for delivery to Belarus rebels via Subject Vilbricht. (Agency approved shipment, 10/1/49. Voucher #38587389)

The debriefing agent put down his pen and stared at the memo, still incredulous at the report Henry had just dictated.

"So the next thing you heard about the gold was when?"

Henry stared up at the ceiling, still shocked by the memory.

"It was in the papers," Henry said slowly. "First *Pravda* and then the rest. There was a photograph of the gold bricks set out on a table and there were all these Russian generals standing around it."

"Doing what?"

"Smiling."

"What about the rebels?"

"There were no rebels."

"Right. Is there anything else you want to add to this? If not – sign and date it here."

"What's going to happen to me now?" Henry asked.

"I'm not authorized to speak to that, Brownale. But I can tell you something you probably already know: Down at Langley, you are known as a special case."

The two men tried not to look at each other as the debriefing agent packed away his papers.

"So tell me something, Brownale: How does a smart guy like Congressman Brownale end up with a kid as stupid as you?"

Henry had no answer. He had asked himself that question many times. All Henry could do was put his head down on the table and close his eyes, wishing he could simply disappear – just as Klaus and Anna had vanished together. Just like all those bars of gold.

Another agent stepped into the doorway. "What do we do with these?"

"What are they?" his partner asked.

"I don't know. Maracas, I guess."

"Pack them up with the rest of it. That reminds me, Brownale. They said you should keep one of the guitars."

"A guitar?"

"Wait a minute. Let me check that. Right – a guitar or a banjo. And a harmonica, too."

"What are you saying?"

"Look, I shouldn't be telling you this, but they're sending you undercover again. Some kind of folk music thing. I don't suppose it matters, but can you sing?"

Henry was thinking of that debriefing agent and his wise-guy smirk as he followed Anna and the other women through the forest.

Can I sing? Very funny. The better question is can I sing and swallow my pride at the same time?

After the KKK riot at the hootenanny, Henry was certain that his days as Volga the Boatman were over. Another assignment blown! He was still feeling sorry for himself when a rifle butt came down on the back of his skull and Henry collapsed onto the forest floor. FBI Special Agent Walter Thurston picked up Henry's limp wrist and shook his hand up and down.

"Wave nighty-night, Mr. CIA man," Thurston laughed. "Volga the Boatman fast asleep now."

Thurston and the other FBI agents smiled at each other. They knew Mr. Hoover would be pleased that they had bagged another CIA intruder.

"Drive him back to Langley, men. Oh – and leave this around his neck." Thurston handed the other agents a pink ribbon and a postcard signed by Director Hoover. On the card, it read: **Amateurs**!

Russian Spymaster Eisler: You really are a fanatic, aren't you Comrade Cvetic?
Cvetic: I believe and follow the Party line.
Eisler: Oh, don't mistake me. It's good to meet a fanatic now and then.
1951 MOTION PICTURE * "I WAS A COMMUNIST FOR THE FBI"

CHAPTER TWENTY

CAMP UNITY,
September 1950

It was nearly midnight when they came for Patrice.

She heard them coming – she had expected it for days – so there was no surprise when they yanked her off the cot, pulling at her hair and slapping her face. Knowing that they were coming for her, Patrice had gone to bed with all of her clothes on and this made them even angrier. They tore away her clothes and made her stand naked in front of her comrades. She did not resist them.

On the cot next to Patrice, Helen lay still. Unlike the others, Helen did not pretend to be asleep. Instead, Helen stared hard into Patrice's eyes, making her meaning clear: It was me. I turned you in.

Helen was no longer the timid girl stumbling through her first weeks of basic training. After the riot at the hootenanny, Helen sat in the front row of every class at Camp Unity, leaning forward in her chair with her hands balled into angry fists, squeezing and unsqueezing them, determined to drink in every word of Petrov's lessons. There were no more thoughts of

May Day parades or papier mache floats. Helen understood it now. She was part of something larger, something destined to change history.

Through Communism, Helen knew she could help people better their lives (as long as everyone did as they were told). Some people might have to be shoved along – or shoved out of the way – but the Revolution was coming whether the people wanted it or not.

Helen knew she was ready. She also knew the enemy and that she had the power to destroy them. She liked this new feeling and she wanted more of it. It was also having an effect on her libido. Suddenly, Helen was lusting after every man at Camp Unity. They tried to avoid her strength and skill during hand-to-hand combat drills, but they were happy to wrestle with Comrade Helen in the dark.

It wasn't long before Helen saw him at the far end of the lake – a young priest swimming alone.

Father Peter Lamonte was one of a dozen seminarians specially selected for training by the FBI. They would wear a priest's collar by day, but pack a gun by night – undercover agents in the FBI's crusade against the godless Communists – and Father Lamonte was at the top of his class. Helen certainly thought so.

Lamonte was diving off the high board, snapping into a crisp jackknife and cutting into the water with barely a ripple. Helen stood across the lake salivating over him, measuring his dimensions like he was a side of beef. He was beautiful, trim, and athletic with a shock of black hair that curled down his forehead. She also admired his chiseled chin and muscular shoulders.

Her blood pressure was building. She wanted to take him right then. The new Helen would not be denied.

Father Lamonte kept sight of Helen from the corner of his eye. He knew the Communists could not be trusted. He even pitied this poor girl, obviously overwhelmed by the beauty of the Catholic side of the lake. Lamonte stole a quick glance up at the giant statue of Jesus. He was close enough that the Savior's eyes were looking a hundred miles away – far beyond the lake and this young woman staring intently at him. This was a relief to the young priest: he did not want Jesus to know that he was staring back at this beautiful, young Communist.

After his next dive – this one especially high and daring – Father Lamonte came back to the surface, but his young admirer was gone. Disappointed, Lamonte turned back to shore. With athletic ease, he glided across the cool surface, stretching himself taut as his strong hands and legs propelled him through the water – until he stopped with a sudden jerk. Something had pulled hard on the waistband of his swimsuit and then another hand reached out of the water and pulled him underneath. With a wanton smile on her lips, Helen pressed her mouth against his, the young man gasping for air until Helen set him free.

Sputtering out of the water, the young priest frantically spun about, searching for the creature that had molested him. Helen surfaced right behind him, just long enough to snatch a quick breath of air before she dove back under. A last hard pinch on the priest's rump and then Helen was gone, leaving only a trail of bubbles back to Camp Unity.

Helen was still wet when she arrived for Petrov's class on Evasive Tactics and Clandestine Maneuvering. For American Communists, in or out of the water, stealth was their key to survival. Until the Revolution could begin, the Party would have to remain invisible, its members safe underground. No one could use their real name and every order was handed down the line – never up – in order to protect the leaders at the top of the Party. If anyone was captured, no one could say who gave the orders.

For every step forward, there had to be two steps to the side: switching between cars, taxis, or trains; changing hats, coats, and suitcases; umbrellas up, glasses on; fake mustaches in place, wigs and toupees off. Zig-zagging, back-tracking – sometimes fast, sometimes slow – with three right turns if necessary. Party members were both ingenious and patient because every step was being watched by the FBI. That also meant that every step had to be planned in advance! No precaution was too small to ignore. Vigilance!

Vigilance also meant that no plan was complete until it was altered at least three times. It was a constant game of telephone: instructions were carried from one person to the next and meeting places were selected carefully before they were changed at the last minute. Ordering lunch could take until midafternoon. The Reds were so unpredictable that restaurants would often refuse to cater a Communist Party event.

All of this secrecy and paranoia created an even stronger bond between Party members, reminding them that they were special and that their mission was vital to the future of the world. If they weren't special, then why were they being hunted by the FBI?

Many would avoid detection by going "deep underground," leaving their families behind, abandoning homes, disappearing from jobs. One woman refused to visit her sick child in the hospital for fear that she would be exposed to the authorities. Instead of a divorce, another Party member told his wife that he simply had to leave her. It wasn't his idea, he insisted – the Party was making him do it.

He left the house with a big smile on his face.

Naturally, some Party members wondered whether all of this secrecy was necessary – or possibly delusional – but they would never dare ask one another and never would they challenge a superior. After a while, the chase became the game itself. There was a thrill to it. It gave meaning to their lives because, for many Party members, life underground wasn't much of a life.

Helen found it exhilarating. Changing cars, changing lives, hiding under trash, crawling through the mud – just the idea of it was thrilling to Helen. Her zeal was boundless and her Russian accent grew stronger as she honed her skills in guerilla warfare. Vigilance is a skill, Helen learned. It is focus. It is devotion to something larger than yourself. It is the power to win.

But it was not Patrice.

Patrice was too weak for this, Helen decided. She was no use to the Party and, besides that, Helen was tired of Patrice always following her around the camp.

The planning and preparation took nearly a month as Helen practiced Patrice's crooked penmanship during cipher class. The love letter was "discovered" on Helen's pillow and the scandal ricocheted around Camp Unity. By then it was not much of a surprise. The other students had already been talking about Patrice's infatuation with Helen – a rumor Helen started some weeks earlier. Still, everyone expressed their shock at the declarations of love and the unnatural sexual pleasures described in the letter to Helen.

Helen had signed the mash note with a flowery, exaggerated 'P' for sad, lonely Patrice.

"We must make ourselves known as we really are — not as Communist propaganda pictures us. We must pool our efforts with those of the other free peoples in a sustained, intensified program to promote the cause of freedom against the propaganda of slavery. We must make ourselves heard round the world in a great Campaign of Truth."

PRESIDENT TRUMAN *acknowledging Moscow's success in winning the battle for hearts and minds around the world, April 20, 1950*

CHAPTER TWENTY-ONE

DECEMBER 1950:
Martha's Cluttered Kitchen

Martha was starting her day like all the others spent in insufferable Schenectady. Slouched against the kitchen table, she slowly stirred a cold cup of coffee with her finger. She didn't have the energy to pick up a spoon. Her flower-print housecoat was barely buttoned because buttons were more than Martha could manage that morning. It had been an hour since she shuffled into the kitchen and a cold draft still lurked above the linoleum, biting at her toes through holes in her well-worn slippers.

Martha looked about the room. She had never noticed how ugly it was. Who picked this wallpaper? Cows jumping over barns, chickens and pigs dancing down below. So much jumping and dancing, it was making her sleepy again. Another twenty minutes went by before Martha tried to summon the verve to get up and pour herself another cup of coffee. But why bother? The pot was probably cold and the percolator seemed so far away. Her index finger traced the edge of her coffee cup and she sighed as if the cup had disappointed her. Just another dish she would have to clean.

Martha stared blankly at the pile of dishes already looming out of the sink. Cups and plates and saucers trailed out of the kitchen and down to the living room where cigarette butts and the crumbs of half-eaten cake were scattered among discarded napkins, many of them scribbled with half- and quarter-baked ideas from the secret meeting the night before. The morning monotony was syncopated by the clock on the wall; the pendulum wagging its disapproval at Martha – or was it the faucet dripping on top of that Leaning Tower of Dishes?

A wall calendar displayed photographs of the "World's Great Canyons," monumental gorges carved into the earth by the incessant dripping of water. How long would it take, Martha wondered, before the kitchen faucet could drip its way through those dishes, down through the sink, and then out through the floor? Finally, an escape from her miserable life!

Perhaps she should turn up the water and speed things along.

Soon the drip-drip-dripping and the clock tick-tocking receded in her mind. Martha was hearing another sound coming from down the hall. It was the television.

"Mikhail?" Martha called. "Do you want something to eat?"

Michael shouted back, "I ate something."

"What?"

"I ate already."

"I heard you. What did you eat?"

"Cake."

"Cake? What do you mean cake?"

Michael was at the doorway. Cake crumbs covered his mouth and clung to the front of his pajamas.

"Why are you eating cake?"

"I was hungry. There was a piece by the television."

"Oh Mikhail," Martha cringed. It was times like these when Martha wondered how in the world she ever got here? When she married Milo,

Martha had bravely dedicated herself to living a new life: No longer would she be the voice of women in labor, the celebrated "Red Flame of New York." Instead, she would labor exclusively for the comfort of her family. She would be a wife and a mother and she would be happy with that. She would try. After all, Martha Appleton could do anything she set out to do!

But not this! She could not be a housewife! It was just – too – much. The evidence was as plain as the chalk outline around a dead body. She was drowning in housework. The kitchen, the bathroom, and every other room in the house was filled with clutter, the grime so thick it needed hoisting, not dusting. It was all so hopeless.

Martha knew she was never going to be the modern day marvel of motherhood, lovingly stirring a cake with one hand while cleaning the house with the other; never spilling a drop, breaking a dish, or losing her last ounce of humanity. Her once-fabulous life had been replaced by this wheel spinning inside of a cage: cooking, cleaning, shopping, repeat. She found all of it completely intolerable. It hurt her back, her legs, her feet – and her waistline! Most of all, it hurt her pride.

Just when she reached bottom, however, life would somehow find a way to sink her lower. One day, Milo brought home a copy of the union's newspaper and there, on the front page, was a glowing profile of Milo and his life on Tuckahoe Row. Only at the end did the article mention Martha, briefly:

> *"Milo is married to the former Martha Mossbaum, who is remembered for her years of service on the AEWA's Executive Board. Martha was the first woman ever to hold this position. But today she is happy as a housewife here in Schenectady, employing her domestic skills and wifely endeavors to keep our leader well-fed and his suits well-pressed as he battles for the working men and women of Local 1389."*

Domestic skills? Wifely endeavors? Dammit, I'm Martha Appleton! I am not just another Schenectady housewife! I am one of the nation's leading trade unionists! I am a pioneer! I am popular!

Don't they know I am on a secret mission for the Party? Does anyone in their right mind think I would voluntarily move to Schenectady, N.Y. – someone as renowned and beautiful as me? Would anyone seriously think I would marry little Milo Milwaukee unless the Party told me to do it? I was sent here to gather military secrets from General Electric – not to clean house for a bacon-smelling business agent!

Her head snapped up. Oh my gosh, Martha thought. Did I just say that out loud?

Some secrets must never be spoken. Her arranged marriage to Milo, her secret mission in Schenectady – these were things that no one outside the Party could ever know!

That was another problem: Martha had no one to talk to. She wasn't alone, just lonely. She knew about other members of "the underground" – Party members like her who had been sent away on long, secret missions. They went into hiding with instructions to wait until the Revolution began. And there were some, it was rumored, who were dispatched to the underground simply because they were too strange to have around. Some of those crackpots had been in Martha's living room the night before.

Without telling Milo, Martha had reassembled the tiny Communist cell she had formed when she first moved to Schenectady. They had been meeting regularly on the nights when Milo was away – debating, devising, and revising plans for the Revolution. Once more to the barricades: Forward to October!

They were an eccentric bunch to be sure: highly-skilled complainers, jealous of anyone's success, and bitter about their own miserable lives. They wanted more. They all wanted to be in charge and, just like Martha's housework, they were exhaustingly monotonous.

William Foster was right: in capitalist America, women were simply "breeders of slaves and soldiers." Foster had been the leader of the American Communist Party and a progressive voice for the rights of women. Martha had practically memorized his book, *"Toward Soviet America,"* which told the ugly truth about life for women in the West, the oppressive servitude that Foster called "housework slavery."

The only hope existed on the other side of the world – in the Soviet Motherland – where "Socialism liquidates the drudgery of housework," Foster explained. "In the Soviet Union, the attack upon housework slavery is delivered from every possible angle."

Russia, Martha gushed. What a wonderful place it must be!

"Great factory kitchens are being set up to prepare hot, well-balanced meals for home consumption by the millions," wrote Foster. "Communal kitchens in apartment houses are organized and widespread. Every device to simplify and reduce housework is spread among the masses with all possible dispatch."

Devices for the masses – reducing housework with all possible dispatch! This is what she had been telling Milo for years! But would he listen? No!

"It's all right here," Martha insisted as she pushed another Party pamphlet across the table to Milo. Often it was her favorite tract: *Russian Women in the Building of Socialism*," twenty-two pages of treasured insights from the noted Party apparatchik, Anna Razumnova. This wise woman described the great wonders of the Soviet system and the tremendous strides that Soviet women had achieved under Communism.

"You should bring this to work," Martha urged Milo. "People should know about what's happening over there. They should know what's happening HERE – at home!"

Milo would only grunt from behind his newspaper. "Russian women are too hairy," he sniffed as he turned to the sports section. "Their men must be afraid of them."

Martha ignored him. She was too absorbed in the amazing world of Anna Razumnova. She had read Razumnova's brilliant words so often she could recite every line by heart! It was like a travel brochure for a distant paradise.

"The free Russian woman is the trailblazer for the toiling women of the world," wrote Anna Razumnova. "She is beating out a path which her American sister will one day begin to follow. An elaborate system of kindergartens, playgrounds, day care centers, and factory collectives means a great deal in the life of the working woman. They free her from the necessity of spending all her time at home, cleaning, cooking, and mending. While she is at work, she can be sure that her child is being well taken care of, supervised by trained nurses, and teachers who feed them wholesome food at regular hours."

Martha was astonished at the utter genius of the Soviet system: "Wholesome food at regular hours!" Prepared by someone else! Martha could only imagine such a world. In many ways, it was like the world she had left behind in Lake Winnanonga.

Growing up in a household filled with servants, Martha was never expected to cook or to clean. In fact, her parents had never expected her to *learn* such things! When the young women of Lake Winnanonga start their own households, all they must do is supervise the help. No fussing – no dusting! Martha was as far from the privileged shores of Lake Winnanonga as she could possibly be.

Martha did not fully realize how rural Upstate New York could be until the day Milo suggested a visit to the Altamont Fair.

Why? she asked.

So they could watch the pig races, Milo replied. Martha cried in her room for the rest of the day.

Things only got worse once Milo's elderly father moved in with them. Now there were more clothes to clean, another bed to change, more meals to ruin.

"Let's hire a maid," Milo offered.

"A maid!" Martha shrieked. "Are we living on some kind of plantation?"

How could a leader of the Socialist Revolution employ a servant? It was unthinkable! Martha had spent her whole life trying to free the slaves! As a child, Martha had urged the servants to escape her parents' house. She even dragged in shovels from the garden so they could dig their way to freedom.

If she only had a shovel now – or the energy to pick it up – Martha would tunnel her way back to Manhattan!

Cooking was bad enough, but cleaning was worse. Martha's answer was to shove everything into paper bags and then stuff those bags into closets and drawers or under beds and beneath the stairs – anywhere out of sight. But even in that big house, Martha was running out of hiding places. She finally broke down when Milo offered another way to clean the house.

"I need a place to train new employees," Milo fibbed. "Let's bring women into the house for a few weeks of 'training' – cooking, cleaning, etc. – and then a new trainee will take over."

Reluctantly, Martha agreed. But that still left the grocery shopping and this was the job Martha hated most of all.

Shopping for groceries was not only drudgery, it was a public humiliation, pushing a balky grocery cart like a mouse lost in a maze, past dizzying displays of food that she never knew how to cook. Worst of all was the Supermarket – that ugly new "convenience" with the monstrously tall shelves packed with a stupefying number of choices. Martha would sneer at the cashiers, "Are you aware that this much food is a terrible insult to all of the starving people in the world! Why do we have so much and they have so little?"

The slack-jawed clerks would only stare back at Martha, uncomprehending of the social injustice they were obliging. But what else should she expect in this Temple of Consumerism? How Martha resented having to wheel a shopping cart up one aisle and down another, like some beggar at the feet of these greedy corporations, pandering with their slick packaging and phony advertisements!

Martha was a scowling, near-sighted terror as she careened blindly down the aisles, knocking boxes and bottles off shelves. Pulling her glasses up to her nose, Martha confronted a box of PEP Cereal. Such a fraud! On the box, a man was gushing over the vitamins contained in PEP: "The harder a wife works, the cuter she looks!"

Well, oop-poopy-doop, Martha fumed. How disgusting!

With a quick stab of her grocery cart, a row of PEP boxes "accidently" spilled onto the floor.

As she went past the pet foods, Martha naturally thought of her first husband, Harold, that dog. Martha wondered what her life would have been like if she had followed him to Russia. Where could he be now? She could imagine him being much older, still handsome and distinguished, squiring beautiful young women around the nightclubs of Stalingrad. They would be laughing and drinking, dining in elegant restaurants before riding off to the ballet, the art gallery – or Harold's bedroom!

I'll bet none of them are pushing a shopping cart through the dog food aisle!

Her mind wandered back to her hero, Anna Razumnova, the ultimate modern woman – free of children and unencumbered by domestic servitude. There were times when Martha would dream that *she* was Anna Razumnova, the beautiful and mysterious party functionary.

Anna Razumnova, she would daydream. Her name sounded luxurious and seductive, like a fantastically skinny movie star draped in diamonds and furs or a pampered Russian princess, living in a fabulous, mountainside dacha.

An-na-Raz-um-no-va!

Martha decided that she and Anna should be friends – great, great friends. She would write Anna several long letters, inviting her to come to America and then, maybe, Martha's new best friend would invite her to Russia for a long vacation! Far away from the dirty dishes and supermarkets of Schenectady, lounging in a dacha overlooking the Caspian Mountains, Martha and Anna would sip dark Ural coffee and nibble caviar on toast. They would wave to the skiers swooshing down the mountainside and Martha would wonder how anyone could possibly live without caviar on toast!

Martha came out of her daydream just as Michael returned to the kitchen. Cake crumbs of a different color were clinging to his pajamas.

"More cake?" Martha sighed.

"I was hungry!"

Martha put out her cigarette and pushed herself up from the table. Shuffling over in her floppy slippers, she pressed Michael's face deep into her housecoat and rocked him back and forth.

"Mikhail, Mikhail, Mikhail! What am I going to do with you?" She kissed him on the forehead. "You know you shouldn't be eating cake for breakfast!"

"You said you'd make me something."

"Did I? You're right. I forgot."

Oh, where in the world was her energy? She had felt so rejuvenated after her trip to Camp Unity. It had been good to get out of the house and do something for a change – something for the Party: *Forward to October*! It had made her feel alive and useful once more! And when she found out that Milo had been plotting a secret campaign, she felt even more excited. But that was months ago – months and months on top of the years that she had been waiting to rejoin the fight!

This is ridiculous, Martha fussed. When is Milo ever going to confide in me? How in the world can he do this without me? And where is that "Morale Coordinator" – the young woman I met at Camp Unity? Helen, Ellen? So young and inexperienced, perhaps she's been captured by the government!

Martha started pacing the kitchen. Others had been lost to the FBI, even in dumpy little Schenectady. How else could you explain it – all these years of waiting and no one from the Party had contacted her – me! – the Red Flame of New York, for Pete's sake!

Where, she wondered, was Mr. X?

Just before she married Milo, Martha's Soviet controller had told her about an experienced Soviet agent who had been placed in Schenectady years earlier, deep undercover. He was said to be an important official in the city and someday this Russian agent would contact her. But that was more than seven years ago and still not a peep from this unknown "Mr. X."

Seven years of solitary confinement! So where the hell is he?

Martha had invented many fantastic stories to explain why Mr. X had never surfaced. Was he arrested? Killed in a secret mission? Any explanation would be better than what she feared – that she had been abandoned by the Party or deliberately sent away!

Was she one of those misfits, just another oddball conveniently expelled from the Party? If they wanted to send you underground – permanently – you could not go deeper than Schenectady, N.Y.

One day, in a moment of weakness, Martha decided to tell this story to her little cell. She had to do it: she could not stand another night listening to them argue about Party doctrine, the illegitimacy of Harry Truman, or whether slavery was still legal in Utah.

"Please – enough with these conspiracy theories!" Martha shouted over the din. "I have something important to tell you!" For once, there was silence. Every face turned toward Martha.

"We are not alone here!" she said in a conspiratorial whisper.

"I knew it! Those bastards are listening to us, aren't they?" shouted Arthur Klingman, chief writer for the Local's Communist newspaper. "I was reading about this. The FBI can now put a microphone inside a common house fly!"

Klingman smiled at the astonished looks around the room. "They're called bugs!" he whispered.

Some of the cell members gasped and Lonnie Fitzmeyer, the baker's assistant, offered to get a fly swatter from his truck.

"Bugs," snarled the electrician, Morris Steingergard. "*People* are bugs." The room went quiet as they considered this universal truth. People *were* bugs: they were either the hapless victims of the Capitalist system or they were its clueless collaborators – and more than a little stupid. Like the rest of the Communist leadership, the members of Martha's cell prided themselves on seeing things for what they were. Because only the Party's leaders – enlightened people like themselves! – could provide the command and control necessary to set those little bugs free.

Martha and the other cell members knew how important they were to the Cause and they expected, frankly, to be rewarded. How else do you distinguish the leaders from the followers?

That was why all this waiting was so painful!

"Everyone, please – relax," Martha assured them. "When I said we are not alone, I meant the Party has, well ... I'm not supposed to tell anyone."

No one breathed as Martha smiled mischievously. They waited for Martha to tell them what she was not supposed to tell them.

"Well, all right then," Martha said, her eyes wide with excitement. "Somewhere in this city, there is an agent – a super-secret spy who was sent here by the Kremlin nearly twenty years ago!"

"I thought all spies were secret," said Rosie Imperato, the telephone operator.

"Well this one is VERY secret," Martha continued. "My contact told me that he is now a well-established and well-respected member of the community, secretly gathering information to forge the Revolution."

"Then why hasn't he called you?" the electrician asked skeptically.

Martha tried to ignore that question. "The chances of detection must be tremendous. I was told he has access to important information – secrets that are vital to the Revolution. All they told me to do was – "

"Was WHAT?!" shouted Rosie in exasperation.

" – was wait. Dammit, Rosie – just wait! So that's what I've been doing and that is what we must all do! We simply must wait."

"Well, we're used to that," Lonnie complained. "We've been waiting here for years." Sadly, the others nodded in agreement. Life underground was depressing. Martha could see that everyone needed some encouragement.

"We must have faith everyone – faith that one day he will reveal himself to us. I still believe in my heart that Mr. X will come to us soon, just like the Revolution. Until then, we have our faith and we have each other."

Martha held out her hands. Heads bowed, they silently held hands in communal prayer.

Ruining the moment, Lonnie asked, "Do you think it could be the mayor?"

Klingman scoffed at the idea. "Myron Mudlick? Ha! If that idiot is a Russian spy, then we've lost already! America has nothing to fear!"

"So if this fella is Mr. X, then how many names start with 'X'?" Lonnie asked.

"Let's go through the phone book!" Rosie suggested. "It shouldn't take too long."

Martha put her head in her hands, wondering why she ever brought these knuckleheads into her home.

"What about Milo?" Morris asked with a knowing smile.

Everyone quickly turned to Martha. She was so surprised by the idea that she couldn't speak.

"Oh no, no, no, no, no!" she finally laughed. "It couldn't be Milo!" But even as she said it, the thought suddenly struck Martha: Could Milo be Mr. X? She had heard the rumors about her husband and she always wondered how someone like Milo – forever cursing the name of Joseph Stalin – could become the leader of a union run by Communists. What was he hiding? Could Milo be the mysterious Mr. X?

"Listen," Martha said with great urgency. "We can only act on what we know and what we know is that our leaders will never abandon us. If this secret spy – our great Comrade X – is no longer here, then they will send someone else to take his place."

Klingman asked, "What if they already did? Maybe it was that poor man they arrested behind the high school!"

"That bastard Charlie Gaynor. It was all his fault!" Morris snarled. "Him and his Moon Chamber!"

"Star Chamber," Klingman corrected him.

"Same thing: Charlie Gaynor is a rotten bastard." The others shook their heads in disgust.

"Bastard," they muttered together.

"He's nothing like his father was, that's for sure," Rosie said. "Greatest mayor this city ever had."

Martha motioned for everyone to move in closer. She held out her hands and, once more, they bowed their heads in Party prayer. Solemnly, Martha spoke, "Let us keep faith in the wisdom and protection of our leaders. We must make every effort to believe in Mr. X no matter where he is. Because he is the Revolution and someday he will return for our salvation!"

"In the name of the father and the son – " Rosie looked up in panic, realizing what she had just said.

"Sorry," Rosie blushed. "Old habits."

Martha lowered her voice as she gave everyone their instructions.

"With Charlie Gaynor and this new Loyalty Board business, we must be more vigilant. All of us need to watch for any sign of Mr. X. Rosie – make sure you listen to all incoming calls, especially the calls from New York."

"Geez, Martha, I'm doing the best I can," said the telephone operator. "Even the government can't listen to everybody's calls."

Martha turned to Klingman. "Arthur – keep me informed of what's happening down at the plant. This Mr. X might be – "

"He's not there," Klingman interrupted. "I know that for a fact."

Klingman's tone was sharper than Martha expected and he would not look her in the eye as he put on his coat to leave. Martha sensed that Klingman knew more than he was letting on. Nothing happened at the G.E. factory without Klingman knowing about it.

Finally, they were gone, leaving behind the questions about Mr. X, a pile of dirty dishes, and the half-eaten cake.

Martha rubbed the morning fog from her eyes and checked the calendar. It was time for a new "trainee" to arrive and clean the house! Right on cue, there was a knock at the door! Martha practically skated down the front hallway, tossing her glasses onto the shelf before she threw open the door.

"It's about time!" Martha said to the blurry vision on the stoop. Before she could say another word, Martha was snatched off her feet.

"*Martha Mil-vaukee!*" Helen Gamble shouted, squeezing Martha in a powerful bear hug. "*I am home! Now we begin our glorious struggle together!*"

"The only thing red about Lucy is the color of her hair and even that's not legitimate."
DESI ARNEZ BEFORE AN EPISODE OF "I LOVE LUCY," *refuting claims that Lucy was once a Communist*

"EVERYBODY STILL LOVES LUCY"
HEADLINE IN THE *LOS ANGELES TIMES after overnight ratings
and an endorsement from J. Edgar Hoover*

CHAPTER TWENTY-TWO

THINGS HAVE CHANGED

Michael heard the knock at the front door. He didn't move except to turn up the volume on the television. He was not going to answer the door. At this hour of the day, it could only be another "visit" from the FBI.

Agents would park across from the Milwaukees' house and the car would sit there for most of the day. These G-Men were hard to miss – big guys in boxy suits, tall fedoras and heavy, shapeless overcoats. When no one was watching, the FBI squad would check the Milwaukees' mailbox or paw through the trash. They also took note of anyone coming and going to the house on Tuckahoe Row. Other times, they would simply patrol the sidewalk and, being FBI agents, they were always careful not to step on any cracks.

Martha was probably the only Red in America who actually enjoyed the FBI's surveillance. Having "the I" around was like a bridge to her past – back to the good old days when everyone was watching Martha. They made her feel wanted! She still mattered!

She knew, of course, that they were the enemy and Martha was never going to surrender. But fighting back was half the fun and Martha did it with all the grace and ease of a society matron from Lake Winnanonga. Yes, she would match the FBI men in this fight and her weapons would be impeccable manners and charm school refinement.

For the FBI, it was like boxing with Emily Post.

"Oh what a lovely surprise!" Martha would call out to the surprise of the G-Men. Sometimes she would throw open the door before they even had a chance to knock. Gracious and animated – "Why, we have *guests*!" – Martha was the most elegant of hostesses, offering the FBI men cookies, coffee, and sandwiches. From the front stoop, the agents would stare glumly at Martha's boisterous welcome, unsure of what she was up to as she ushered them into her kitchen.

"Why didn't you call first? I had no idea you would be in town!" she shouted gaily, hoping Michael would hear. At first, Martha did this playacting in order to protect Michael. He would have been frightened if he knew that policemen were at the door. After a while though, Michael began to wonder how anyone could have that many "uncles" visiting the house. Still, Martha would insist that Michael shake hands with the agents before he was sent upstairs to his room.

"You should think of the kid," the agents would tell Martha once Michael left the room. "Who's going to take care of him after you're sent to the federal pen?"

The other agents would agree. "Make it easier on yourself, Mrs. Milwaukee. We only want the names of your Party contacts. You do that and we promise never to bother you again."

Only Martha knew the truth: she had no Party contacts. Not real ones anyway.

Eventually, the neighbors took notice of the FBI agents that were continually posted outside the Milwaukees' home. There is definitely something going on there, the neighbors would say to each other. Something was different – possibly dangerous – over there. It wasn't long before

Michael's friends were overhearing their parents talk about "those people" next door.

"Is your dad part of a gang?" Tommy Wasserman asked Michael one day. "My dad says everybody's going to lose their house and all of their money if your dad gets his way."

"My dad says so too," said Benny Collins. "He says 'it's the New Deal all over again.'"

The neighborhood boys all stood quietly, waiting for Michael to answer. Michael was getting hotter and angrier with all of them until finally – WHOP! – Michael hit Tommy with a punch across his head. Tommy yelled so loud that all the boys scattered. Michael stood transfixed as Tommy held the side of his head, crying so hard that his mouth hung open even though there was no sound coming out.

Since that awful day, Michael had spent most of his time indoors, usually in front of the family's new color television set – a 1950 General Electric TeleRama. It was another gift to Milo from the grateful members of Local 1389. The enormous console was nearly six feet long and stood four feet tall with rich, two-tone mahogany and soft, interwoven fabric over the speakers – twin speakers! Television quickly became Michael's escape from his mother, the FBI, and all the problems of life on Tuckahoe Row.

When Helen Gamble arrived that day, Michael was watching "Sepia Tones," a musical variety show for Black singers in Schenectady. But Michael could not concentrate on the show with all that noise in the hallway. He got up to see who was at the door.

"Michael!" Martha shouted. "This is Helen Gamble! Finally – Helen Gamble! She has come here with some very important news, Michael! It's the biggest news to hit Schenectady in years!"

Across the street, FBI cameras clicked away as Martha and Helen hugged in the doorway, jumping for joy. This younger woman, the G-Men noted, was someone new to the Milwaukee household. They decided to investigate things right then. As Martha was closing the door, she spied the FBI agents getting out of their car. Quickly, she pushed Helen and Michael down the hall and into the basement.

"Michael, why don't you take our friend downstairs and show her all of your toys?"

"But I don't have any toys in the base – " CLICK! Martha locked the door at the top of the stairs. Helen and Michael stood in the dark, listening to the muffled voices upstairs.

One of the agents asked, "It's a little early in the day to be conducting Party business, isn't it Mrs. Milwaukee? Where's your friend?"

"She just left. Went out the back," Martha said. Michael was surprised to hear his mother tell a lie.

Martha laughed, "Why are we paying you fellas if you're not going to pay attention?"

"Mind if we look around then? She might have lost her way."

"I certainly do mind!" Martha said sharply. "Unless you have a warrant, I want you to leave right now!" Michael cringed as heavy footsteps moved back down the hallway before they stopped by the basement door.

"You know where to find us Mrs. Milwaukee. We'll be waiting right across the street – every day – and you'd better think about this: Will your son know where to find you once they send you off to prison?"

"ENOUGH!" Martha shouted. "Get out of my house NOW!"

Michael's eyes were filling with tears as the front door slammed shut. Why would they send his mother to prison? When Martha unlocked the basement door, Michael pushed his way past Helen and ran to his mother, squeezing his arms around her legs. Martha's eyes met Helen's.

"This won't be easy," Martha said grimly. "A lot has happened here since you left for Camp Unity."

"Have you had any conversations with him that would lead you to believe he is rather advanced in his thinking on racial matters – discrimination, non-segregation of races, greater rights for Negroes and so forth?"

EXPANDING THE MEANING OF "LOYALTY" *in the investigation of a military scientist,*
Security, Loyalty and Science by Walter Gellhorn, 1950

CHAPTER TWENTY-THREE

FIREWORKS ON A HOT NIGHT IN JULY

The Schenectady City School Board was finishing its monthly meeting when Charlie Gaynor made his big entrance. The board members, the administrators, the parents – everyone knew he was coming. Still, they all jumped when the janitorial cart slammed through the gymnasium doors.

Even in summer, when school was out of session, Chief Custodian Charles W. Gaynor was a constant presence – mopping every hallway and cleaning every bathroom – even checking under desks for wanton wads of chewing gum. Charlie was proud of his dedication. Being conscientious was important, he believed, especially when you cared about the things that most people wanted to ignore. Like wads of chewing gum. And Communists.

When he wasn't cleaning John Brown Junior-Senior High School, Charlie was trying to clean up the rest of the world, one government meeting at a time. He was a regular at every civic session in town: the City Council, the County Legislature, the Board of Estimate, even the Water Board. Wherever there was a microphone or a stenographer, Charlie Gaynor would be there, spouting off on the only subject he ever cared about: "dem-Red-sons-a-bitches!"

Everyone knew Charlie Gaynor, the only son of Stennison Gaynor, the "Red Mayor of Schenectady." For all of his 63 years, Charlie Gaynor had lived under the specter of his father's Socialist legacy. People would ask the boy, "Do you want to be a Communist when you grow up, Charlie?" Not a baseball player or a fireman. No – a Communist! It was like asking a kid, "Would you like to grow up to be an angry, frustrated revolutionary?" Ironically, that's exactly what Charlie Gaynor had become.

"They already took over The G.E.," Charlie sputtered before the School Board on that steamy night in July. "But dem-Red-sons-a-bitches want more than that! You see how they've taken over Europe and China too? What the hell is next: City Hall? This school board? *AMERICA?*"

The Reds were to blame for everything in Charlie's miserable life: growing up without a father, never getting married, and all those lonely nights spent scouring the inside of John Brown Junior-Senior High School. Charlie even looked like old John Brown with the same fiery eyes as that deranged abolitionist, determined to bring damnation to the unrighteous and the un-American.

The gym was sweltering that night and a rolling bead of sweat had reached the end of Charlie's long nose where it hung before the Schenectady School Board, refusing to fall off. (Nothing about Charlie Gaynor ever quit.) The only thing moving was the large electric fan, humming at the front of the gymnasium. Even Charlie stood frozen, just as he was explaining how Communism had created the income tax. His index finger was still pointed in the air when one of the school board members finally broke the silence.

Eunice Fitzmaurice asked reluctantly, "Charlie? Are you all right?"

"QUIET!" Charlie demanded, flinging out his arms to quiet the room. He craned his neck forward, searching the air. That's when they all heard it: it was a small voice – a child's voice – calling for help!

"It's outside!" someone shouted.

In spite of his advanced age and his baggy custodial uniform, Charlie Gaynor leaped over the School Board table and galloped out the back door. By the time everyone else got outside, Charlie was sitting on top of a man, pinning him to the ground. At the edge of the woods, a little girl was crying. It was Eunice Fitzmaurice's daughter, Ellen.

Mother and child ran for each other's arms.

The young man was a stranger in town, a drifter, and his arrest might have been forgotten if Charlie had not pulled a wallet out of the young man's jacket.

"You see! You see here!" Charlie cried. Pressing his knees against the young man's shoulders, Charlie was holding up a membership card of the American Communist Party!

"He's a Commie – a goddamned Commie! He's one a DEM-RED-SONS-A-BITCHES!"

Days later, the police discovered that Charlie's "Communist spy" was actually a vagrant who had stolen the wallet. But by then nobody cared. All anyone would remember was that Charlie Gaynor had actually caught one of dem-Red-sons-a-bitches.

No longer was he just that jabbering, old crank, warning the world of the invisible Red Menace. People now realized that everything Charlie had said was true! He was a new man – an oracle! Suddenly, everyone in town was talking about the brains and bravery of good old Charlie Gaynor.

After that night, Charlie was welcomed wherever he went: the stores downtown, the bars around the G.E., and, most especially, at School Board meetings. They even had Charlie recite the Pledge of Allegiance! "Crazy Charlie" wasn't crazy anymore.

Soon all the politicians wanted to be seen with Charlie Gaynor, the Great Commie Catcher. He was presented with the keys to the city. The Kiwanis named him their Man of the Year and the American Legion honored Charlie with their General Custer Medal of Persistence. But the biggest honor came when Charlie received a phone call from Harold Dietz, the Republican chairman of the county legislature.

Dietz was a desperate man and the most desperate of politicians. For years, he had been stuck on the county board, unable to move up to a more important office. Where he really wanted to be was Albany with a seat in the State Legislature. That would mean more money and much less work, but the Republican Party would not reward Dietz with a promotion.

To the GOP stalwarts, Dietz had been a weak-kneed failure. They demanded to know why so many Communists were still in Schenectady and what was Harold Dietz doing about it? Worst of all, those damned Communists were still running the union down at The G.E.

It was embarrassing to Dietz, but there was little he could do but accept his fate. His political future was at a dead end. He would never escape Schenectady. Then Charlie Gaynor rose up in the sky like fireworks on the Fourth of July. Charlie the Commie Catcher was going to be Harold Dietz's ticket to Albany!

"Charlie Gaynor has done this city – in fact, the entire county – a great service," Dietz told the news reporters assembled in his office. "Mr. Gaynor is an honest-to-goodness American hero. The city and county of Schenectady are fortunate to have an acknowledged expert on radical politics right here in our community and I say it's high time we put that expertise to use!"

"Today I am announcing the formation of the Schenectady County Loyalty Board. All across our great nation – from the federal government to small municipalities – right-minded citizens are creating Loyalty Boards to keep their communities safe during these perilous times! They are helping to bring security to America by ensuring that subversives do not threaten the American way of life. The Schenectady County Loyalty Board will ascertain the necessary facts and circumstances regarding matters of potential social, political, or governmental danger, as well as any other matters deemed to be of vital importance to our local, state and national security!"

The reporters looked at each other. They had never heard such things from a county legislator in Schenectady. One of them asked, "What do you mean by 'matters of possible local, state or national security'?" Dietz pretended not to hear the question.

"In addition to Mr. Gaynor, the Loyalty Board will be comprised of Mr. Montgomery Hughie, the distinguished publisher of *The Ledger* newspaper; his Right Holy Bishop James Carney and, of course, Schenectady Mayor Myron Mudlick. Together these four men will be our champions in the fight for civic integrity and American justice here in Schenectady! Now, let's hear a few words from the members of our Loyalty Board. I'd like to first ask Bishop Carn – "

Before the Bishop could step forward, Charlie Gaynor rushed in front of Dietz and grabbed the microphone with both hands.

"Thank you very much, Legislator Dietz, for this great honor," Charlie sputtered. "As Chairman of the Loyalty Board, I intend to use every fiber of my being to protect my fellow Schenectaders from the dangers posed by the Communist menace. You can count on me, Schenectady!"

The other members of the Loyalty Board looked at each other in surprise. No one had said anything about Charlie Gaynor being the chairman! When no one objected, Charlie continued his pledge.

"I shall use every muscle in my body – every bone and every corpuscle – to the never-ending pursuit of dem-goddam – "

Dietz made a loud cough, reminding Charlie not to mention any "sons-a-bitches," Red, blue or otherwise. Dietz had also been firm on one other point: the Loyalty Board was not to investigate Local 1389. The union was a powerful force in local politics and Harold Dietz was looking for every vote he could get – Communists included.

Charlie went back to his speech. "Like Mr. Dietz was sayin', this city is filled with submersives and it'll be our job to flush 'em out or flush 'em down as the case may be." Charlie showed his gap-toothed smile, waiting for someone to laugh at his joke. When no one did, the janitor cleared his throat and tried again.

"We have a saying in the world of custodial engineering, 'Whether it sticks or smells or floats like a boat, you can't clean shit without muscle and soap.' And that's what I intend to do with this here Loyalty Board."

Dietz gave out a low groan, Bishop Carney crossed himself and Mayor

Mudlick checked his watch. Everyone else stood in disbelief until Montgomery Hughie began to laugh.

"Ha! That's a good one, Charlie!" the publisher laughed as he turned to his reporter. "Make sure you write that one down!"

Dietz stepped forward to end the press conference, but Charlie wasn't finished.

"And them Commies in Local 1389 had better watch out 'cuz there's a new sheriff in town! And now, if you are ready gentleman, FOLLOW ME!"

Drawing his arm forward like a saber, Charlie marched out of the press conference with the reporters quizzically falling in behind. The room quickly emptied, leaving the other members of the Loyalty Board staring at Dietz and wondering what he had gotten them into.

"Are you sure this is what you want?" Mayor Mudlick quizzed Dietz. "Charlie Gaynor – the chairman of your Loyalty Board?"

Dietz pretended to be shocked by the question. "I thought this is what *you* all wanted!"

"The Loyalty Board, certainly," said Bishop Carney. "But I question the appointment of this … janitor!"

Dietz grinned, reaching for their hands. "Gentlemen – please. What's the worst that could happen?"

Hughie laughed again as he looked out the window: Charlie Gaynor was striding up State Street hill with a gaggle of reporters and cameramen racing to catch up. They were pestering Charlie for answers – who would be the Loyalty Board's first target? Would it be Local 1389 and Milo Milwaukee? Was anyone going to jail? But Charlie would not speak until they were standing in front of John Brown Junior-Senior High School. Teachers and students pressed their faces to the windows, wondering what all the commotion was down below.

Charlie pointed a bony finger up to the school. "Somewhere in here, gentlemen – somewhere in this school – Communists are teaching our young people the lessons that the Kremlin wants 'em to learn! And so I ask you: Is this America? Will this be our future or can we save our young people from the clutches of dem-Red-sons-a-bitches?"

No one asked Charlie to explain what he was talking about. Likewise, none of the reporters asked for any proof. They were too busy writing down every word that was pouring out of the Chairman's mouth.

"Members of the Fourth Estate, pay heed – my name is Charles W. Gaynor – that's G-A-Y-N-O-R – and I want you to spread the word to dem-Red-sons-a-bitches. From now on, they had better watch out. I caught 'em once and I'll catch 'em again! Tell 'em the Schenectady County Loyalty Board is on the job! That is all for now, gentlemen. Good day!"

With that, Charlie turned on his heel and marched into the school, heading straight for the Principal's office. A few minutes later, he emerged with the keys to Room 116: Charlie was moving out of the broom closet and into his very own office, complete with a secretary and his own telephone! Soon, Charlie's name and his new title were being stenciled on the office door:

CHARLES W. GAYNOR
Associate Superintendent
Public Safety and Facilities Management

From that day forward, both the principal and the superintendent were consulting Charlie on every decision in the district. The football coach needed Charlie's permission to turn on the stadium lights. The cafeteria menu could not be changed without a preliminary sniff and a sample taste for Charlie. The swim team had to share their pool with Charlie and his late-afternoon "swim-bath." Everyone knew where the real power rested in the Schenectady school system – with the Great Commie Catcher, Charlie Gaynor.

They soon learned of the files Charlie was compiling on every teacher in the city, carefully indexing their political views, their private affiliations, the books they read, the clubs they belonged to, and their overall moral character. Teachers quickly realized that what was important to Charlie

Gaynor had better be important to them, too – like civil defense drills and pledging allegiance to the flag. Certain books were kept off the shelves and specific names and historical events were no longer mentioned in their classrooms.

The lesson plan was clear: America was the world's greatest country and Communism was its greatest threat. No questions necessary.

This was true everywhere except in the classroom of history teacher Francis T. Figgins. Since arriving at John Brown in 1939, *Doctor* Figgins had always been the odd duck, cautiously regarded as "a character" by his fellow teachers. Dr. Figgins directed the school's Dramatic Arts Club and he was adviser to the Student Poetry Society, as well as founder of the Young Philosophers Club. But Figgins was best known for his dramatic classroom lectures in which he would dress as a famous figure from history.

But Niccoló Machiavelli? Immanuel Kant? These were not the sort of people Charlie Gaynor would consider famous – or even American!

People like Francis Figgins made Charlie suspicious. Figgins was always using fifty-cent words that Charlie could not understand, words that were meant to make you feel small and Charlie Gaynor did not like feeling small.

"Long-haired snooty bird," Charlie would grumble whenever he saw Figgins.

Back in Charlie's office, Harold Dietz had sent over a list of names for a "loyalty review." All of these names were political enemies of Dietz. Charlie shoved that list aside. The Loyalty Board – Charlie's Board – had smellier fish to fry.

It was time to write up his own list – a new, secret "watch" list, a list so secret that the only person who knew about it was Charlie Gaynor. At the top of the page, Charlie wrote "Red Sons of Bitches" and the first name on that list was Dr. Francis T. Figgins.

"Reactionary politicians have managed to instill suspicion of all intellectual efforts into the public by dangling before their eyes a danger from without … Every intellectual who is called before one of the committees ought to refuse to testify, i.e. he must be prepared for jail and economic ruin, in short, for the sacrifice of his personal welfare in the interest of the cultural welfare of his country … If enough people are ready to take this grave step they will be successful. If not, then the intellectuals of this country deserve nothing better than the slavery which is intended for them."

ALBERT EINSTEIN *in a 1953 letter to school teacher William Frauenglass*

CHAPTER TWENTY-FOUR

MARTHA AND HELEN
GET TO WORK

Milo was at work and Michael was at school when Martha and Helen began their campaign to "reawaken the Communist zeal" in Schenectady.

"I think I've found just what we need," Martha said, pouring Helen another cup of cold coffee. "All the teachers are talking about that lunatic Charlie Gaynor and how he's running the entire high school! Imagine a janitor telling teachers what they can and cannot teach! They're all afraid of what he might do to them. Don't you think that's great news?"

Helen looked confused. Martha smiled knowingly.

"One of my sources tells me Charlie Gaynor has drafted a 'secret' hit list and his first target is a history teacher named Francis Figgins. This is just what we need! We'll make this fellow Figgins a martyr for academic freedom! For personal freedom! It's the sort of fight that will rally the people and show them the power of collective action. Win or lose, we win!"

Grabbing paper and pencil, Martha quickly listed all of the things that she and Helen would have to organize: handbills, posters, speeches. "And a slogan! Every campaign needs a memorable slogan. It has to be something catchy. How about: There's No Stinkin' Reason to Fire Francis Figgins?"

At school a week later, Francis Figgins was surprised by the handbill taped to the door of the Teachers' Lounge. In bright red letters, it read: REMEMBER FIGGINS!

That's odd, thought Figgins. Since when do you remember someone who is still among the living? Then Figgins grew indignant. Was this some kind of joke? He tore down the handbill and inspected the small lettering at the bottom of the page: "Sponsored by the Social Awareness Committee, AEWA Local 1389."

The AEWA – the union at General Electric? This is a complete puzzle, Figgins fretted.

Over the heads of the other teachers, Figgins called out, "What makes those lay-abouts at General Electric think I am deceased?"

"Well they can dream too, can't they?" cracked Lou Reynolds, another of the school's history teachers.

"A young woman brought it over from the union," said the librarian, Alice Walters. "She wanted you to know that 'You are not alone.'"

"Yes you are!" shouted Lou Reynolds.

"I saw those handbills on all the street lights coming to work this morning," the librarian added. "They must be all over town."

"Extraordinary!" Figgins marveled. "Did she leave her name?"

"No, just this phone number." She handed the note to Figgins just as the principal's secretary came to the door. "Dr. Figgins? Principal Farnsworth would like to see you in his office."

The room went quiet as the teachers turned to Figgins. A feeling of dread – but very little empathy – hung over the Teachers' Lounge, for Francis Figgins was not at all popular among the faculty. He had strongly objected to their formation of a labor union and now he refused to pay its monthly dues.

"We're professionals, for God's sake," Figgins sniffed. "Why are we behaving like Teamsters? What difference will there be between me and some loutish longshoreman!"

"About 150 pounds," Lou Reynolds observed.

Reynolds and the other teachers thought Figgins was actually saying that he was smarter than they were. He had a doctorate in World History. You are simply you. You may need a union, but I never will.

Figgins was not feeling so determined as he walked down to the principal's office. "We'll remember you Figgins!" Lou Reynolds chirped. "For a while anyway."

"Francis," began Principal Farnsworth, "you've been here at John Brown for a very long time and I respect that very much. I respect *you*! This is difficult, but I feel I should inform you that next Thursday afternoon, I will be appearing before the Schenectady County Loyalty Board."

"That is outrageous! What right do they have to investigate you?"

"Me? Oh no, no, no, no," the Principal laughed. "I'm being called as a witness. The hearing is about you!"

"About ME!? I was never told about any such thing! Now you're going to be a witness against me? At a secret hearing!" With every question, Figgins' voice was rising higher and higher.

"Now listen to me, Francis. I am not against you and I am not going there as your enemy. I'm sure all this is very routine – or as routine as things are nowadays. But there's no harm in answering their questions, don't you think?"

"Well, I certainly have questions!" Figgins exclaimed. "How does everyone know about this except me? This is Charlie Gaynor again, is it not?"

Principal Farnsworth frowned and then looked past Figgins toward the open office door. Farnsworth got up from his desk and checked to see if anyone was listening. The coast was clear. Farnsworth quickly nodded 'yes.'

"Well, don't believe everything you read!" Figgins declared, throwing down the 'Remember Figgins' handbill. He stormed into the hallway, ready to charge into Charlie Gaynor's office when one of the junior janitors called out his name.

From out of his coveralls, the janitor removed a greasy sheet of paper and handed it to Figgins. Puckering his face, Figgins pinched the paper between two outstretched fingers and gingerly held it up to the light.

"It's a soo-pee-nee," the janitor said. "From the Associate Superintendent, Mr. Gaynor."

"Are you certain? I thought he could only write in crayon."

Under the letterhead of the Schenectady County Loyalty Board, the subpoena read, "The presence and ipso facto personage of Mr. Francis T. Figgins, PhD, is to be presented, dead or alive, at a duly constituted hearing of the Schenectady County Loyalty Board, at 9 a.m. and not a minute later, on Tuesday, May 15, 1951. God Bless America. That is all."

The subpoena was signed, 'Charles W. Gaynor, Chairman.'

"Hmmmph," Figgins sniffed. "I should have thought he would scratch his name with an X."

Figgins looked down at the janitor, expecting him to laugh at this cutting remark, but the janitor only wiped his nose and shuffled away. Suddenly, Dr. Figgins was feeling very un-witty.

And very alone.

What on earth is happening? Figgins felt himself beginning to panic. Remembering the note from the union girl, he hurried back to the Teachers' Lounge and dialed the number. After four rings, a woman answered the line.

"*Dah?*"

"Yes, hello. This is Dr. Francis Figgins, I am the senior instructor in American and World History at John Brown Junior-Senior High School. Someone left me a note to call this number."

"*Oh, yes, Doktor Feegins,*" said Helen. "*Our union wants to help you.*"

"Well, thank you, Miss – ?"

"*Gam-bell.*"

"Miss Gam-bell. Yes, well … I don't know what to say about this. I certainly did not expect to be put in such a position! It's all very disturbing."

"You must be berry angry."

"Yes, well, these are the slings and arrows of outrageous fortune!"

"Outrageous arrows … yes," Helen replied.

Now Helen was getting worried. Perhaps this would be a tougher fight than Martha had imagined. They needed a sympathetic victim – a heroic martyr – not a prickly professor spouting Shakespeare.

"This is but a test," Figgins continued, "as the Bard has instructed: 'Cowards die many times before their deaths; the valiant never taste of death but once.'"

Now that was more like it: a valiant death! Helen perked up. Martyrs die valiant deaths! Perhaps there was a fight here after all.

"Dok-tor Feegens, we would like you to be our special guest at this year's May Day parade. All of your friends will be dare to support you."

Friends, thought Figgins. I have friends? All of this was very strange, but he was too confused to object. Sadly, he was grateful for the support – even from friends he did not know.

"Vee vill fight together. A valiant death, dah?"

A valiant death? "Of course," Figgins choked as he hung up the phone. He laid his head down on the table. Nearby was Lou Reynolds, standing at the mimeograph machine, smiling over his shoulder at Figgins.

"Cheer up Francis," Reynolds said. "It's times like these when it's good to have friends."

Figgins looked up in confusion. "Friends? I don't even know those people!"

"Yes, you do, Francis. You work with them every day."

"What on earth are you saying?"

"The union, Francis – the union that you think so little of. It's the union that stands behind people when they're in trouble. But you never had any use for that kind of thing, did you? You always had to do things your own way."

Figgins had never been spoken to this way, least of all by Lou Reynolds.

"What do you want me to say?" Figgins asked. "The union told me that I would have to teach my history classes the same way that you and the others teach. So I said, 'No, I am my own man and I will not be told how to do my job – least of all by a labor union!' What does it matter to the union how I choose to teach my classes? I don't criticize the way you teach and I don't question how effective you are at doing your job, so why should you and your union care what I do?"

Reynolds sat across from Figgins. "Because we all have to stick together, don't you see that? Sticking together means we stand together or we fall together. That's what a union does. The rules have to be the same for everyone."

"Conformity," Figgins sighed. "Yes, uniformity is so much easier to measure. Set the bar at the same height and then everyone will make it over safely, isn't that right? It seems like everyone wants me to conform. And what if I don't want to do that, Mr. Reynolds – what then? What's going to happen if I don't – how would you union fellows put it – knuckle under?"

Reynolds smiled as he turned back to the mimeograph, which was spitting out more copies of the tombstone handbills: REMEMBER FIGGINS!

"Well, whatever happens, Francis, you know I'll never forget you!"

In the Garden of Eden, there were "no union dues, no labor leaders, no snakes, no disease ...
Only as millions of Americans turn to Jesus Christ at this hour and accept him as Savior, can
this nation possibly be spared the onslaught of a demon-possessed Communism."

"SATAN'S RELIGION," a sermon by the Rev. Billy Graham

CHAPTER TWENTY-FIVE

MAY DAY 1951

May Day was like Christmas for the Communists: a worldwide celebration of union strength and community solidarity. Members of Local
1389 celebrated each May Day with a huge parade – always the longest
and largest in Schenectady – and, afterward, tens of thousands of people
would gather for a picnic, games, and union speeches at the riverside. Fireworks always finished the night.

In the spring of 1951, the fireworks came early.

Along the entire three-mile route, the sidewalks were jammed with
spectators long before the parade stepped off. You could hear the parade approaching from blocks away, the drums of the high school marching bands,
and cheers for the war veterans lining up for one more march. Next came
the fraternal orders – the Elks, the Kiwanis, and the Moose – just ahead of
an enormous float celebrating Local 1389, draped in a banner proclaiming
"AEWA Local 1389 – Bringing the American Dream to Schenectady!"

In celebration of its many victories, the union float featured the symbols of 1950s prosperity: a neat modern house surrounded by a white

picket fence stood in the center of the parade float with a miniature car parked nearby and, inside the house, children were gathered around a large television set from G.E. This tableau of middle class success was punctuated by Santa Claus himself – Milo Milwaukee – popping out of the chimney to throw kisses and candy to the crowd.

With hot dogs and beer waiting for everyone at the picnic, the entire procession moved at a lively pace. But the parade always moved a little faster when it passed the Cathedral of the Holy Shepherd, a fearsome fortress of stone and stained glass, topped with horrible gargoyles and strange messengers of God gazing down from a monumental steeple. The most frightening figure of all stood at the top of the cathedral's granite staircase, his feet firmly rooted to the enormous portico that stood fifteen feet above the parade. It was the Bishop – the Right Rev. James B. Carney – who caused May Day marchers to avert their eyes and march a little faster. Bishop Carney towered over them like a stone-faced sentinel, guarding the doors of his Cathedral and silently praying that Union Avenue would open up and swallow every one of these godless heathens.

Standing next to the Bishop was a new priest in the Schenectady Diocese.

"Isn't this sickening?" the young novitiate muttered as the war veterans passed by.

"Look at those poor boys," Bishop Carney agreed, pulling tighter on his rosary. "Just a few short years ago they were saving the world from Hitler. Now they can't even save themselves from this – "

"Indignity."

"Yes – indignity. And saddest of all, they don't even know what they've lost."

"Silently surrendering to the godless Communists!"

"Without a shot being fired."

"Not a single shot."

"And what of those boys still fighting in Korea?" the Bishop asked. "How would they feel about this?"

"Betrayal!"

"Of course!"

"Shame, shame, shame."

The shrill blast of a police whistle signaled that the Communists were coming. The two priests bowed their heads as the Reds came into view, carrying a banner that stretched from sidewalk to sidewalk, proclaiming "It's Not a Party Without the Party!"

As usual, the Schenectady Reds were dressed as Russian peasants, adorned in their finest drab. On red-draped floats with crimson bunting, they waved posters and banners proclaiming Communism to be "Twentieth Century Democracy – for America and the World!" Other banners followed along:

"From Moscow With Love – Your Uncle Joe"

"See What Communism Can Get For You!"

"Read Marx: Be Well Red."

When they passed the Cathedral, the old-time Communists would never quake in the Bishop's shadow. In fact, they only got louder. You could measure the noise by the length of the Bishop's frown. Except in the parade of 1951. That year an unexpected hush fell over the Communist contingent as it drew closer to the Bishop. No one was singing "The Internationale." There were no shouts of revolution and workers' rights. Instead, there was a softer sound – the sound of small voices chanting, "Let – us – learn! *We want to learn*! Let – us – learn! *We want to learn!*"

The priests stepped forward to get a better look: row upon row of children – their wrists and necks bound by cardboard chains – staggered down the street like a galley of beaten slaves. Close behind was a wagon covered in red, white, and blue tissue paper. Set in the middle was a gray box that was surrounded by more children. These kids were on their knees and they seemed to be in mourning.

"What's in that box?" the new priest asked.

"It's not a box," the Bishop said morosely. "It's a prison."

The "grieving" children were rocking back and forth, their little hands covering their faces as they pretended to sob for the prisoner locked inside the cardboard cell. Two older boys, brandishing toy machine guns, stood guard and pressing his face through the bars was the hapless prisoner, Dr. Francis Figgins.

"*Free Francis Figgins!*" Helen was calling through a megaphone, urging the crowd to join in. "*Free Francis Higgins! Sign the Petition – to Free Francis Figgins!*" Soon the crowd was chanting in unison as the children wailed and moaned in agony from the pain inflicted on poor Dr. Figgins.

"*Ladies and gentlemen,*" Helen shouted, "*your children deserve a chance to learn in our schools! If you care about academic freedom, then sign the petition to free Francis Figgins! Free him from the witch hunt of the Schenectady County Loyalty Board. Your child's education is at stake! Sign today or they will be burning books tomorrow!*"

When Helen said, 'They,' she jabbed her finger up at Bishop Carney. This got under the Bishop's collar. As a young man, Carney had been an amateur boxer and he never let a challenge go unanswered. When Helen jabbed her finger again, it was like a bell had rung for the opening round: Bishop Carney moved toward the Cathedral stairs until the younger priest grabbed his robe and pulled the Bishop back.

At the end of the block, the jail guards threw open the prison door and pretended to beat Dr. Figgins with their toy guns. The other children – and now their parents – looked on in horror. They eagerly signed the petition offered by Helen and soon everyone was chanting, "Remember Figgins! Remember Figgins!"

"When did the Loyalty Board start investigating a teacher?" asked the new priest.

"We didn't," Bishop Carney answered icily. He turned on his heel and stormed back into the Cathedral as the parade continued into downtown, past the soup kitchen and the second-hand clothing store, the credit union and the medical clinic – all of them created by the Morale Coordinator Helen Gamble (with secret guidance from Martha Milwaukee).

In addition to the Thursday night bowling league, the International Book Club and the Friendship Film Series, production was about to begin on Red Star beer and the Red Star Television Network. Soon news of interest to local Communists would be broadcast on WRED-TV along with original programming like "Bowling for Rubles" and the game show, "What's My Lie?" There were even programs for the kids, like the puppet show "Socko and Vanzetti."

Meanwhile, an even bigger project was underway in Schenectady and throughout much of the world – a campaign so insidious that the Catholic Church had assigned this new priest to the Schenectady Diocese.

Fresh from his FBI training at Lake Unity, Father Peter Lamonte's mission was as simple as it was strange and ironic: stop the spread of peace.

"I've got a brother in Stalingrad, I thought you knowed
I've got a brother in Stalingrad, way down the road
On the many things we can agree, and he wants peace just like me
I'm gonna put my name down."
"PUT MY NAME DOWN" ✳ *Song by Woody Guthrie and Irwin Silber*

Monogram Studios has dropped plans to film the life of Hiawatha "for fear that a picture about Hiawatha's peace efforts might be regarded as Red propaganda."
NEWS COVERAGE IN SEPTEMBER 1950

Workers Break Back of Peace Plea Signer A Milwaukee auto worker is thrown into the street for supporting a "Communist" peace petition.
NEW YORK TIMES ✳ JULY 26, 1950

CHAPTER TWENTY-SIX

DECEMBER 1951

Beau Duffy was feeling woozy, suffocating in the overheated church and his undersized collar. St. James Church was not much bigger than a chapel, far too small for its large congregation and the factory-sized radiators boiling on either side of the pews. It felt like a Catholic rotisserie, reminding everyone of the eternal flames that awaited sinners on the other side.

Every Sunday, the new parish priest, Father Peter Lamonte, made sure you got the point: Communism was the fastest route to hell.

"What is happening to AMERICA?" shouted the muscular priest, slamming a heavy fist into the Bible. The jolt startled the altar boys and the head of every parishioner snapped to attention. Built like a linebacker, Father Lamonte was no gentle shepherd.

"America is truly the land of opportunity because we are a nation of *free* people – free to choose what we believe and who we choose to follow. But not in Russia, my friends!"

"Here we go again," Beau muttered.

"No, not in Russia," Lamonte bellowed as he tromped down the center aisle, his sausage-sized finger wagging at the congregation. Every Sunday that finger seemed to be pointing at big Beau Duffy with his melon-sized head looming above the prayerful. Beau was an easy target because everyone knew he worked for Local 1389 – an auxiliary of the international Communist cabal, according to Father Lamonte.

"Right here in Schenectady, there are forces among us who threaten the very freedoms we hold dear. It is the Red Menace – the Communists of the Amalgamated Electrical Workers of America – make no mistake about it. For Local 1389 is the slime that oozes down Erie Boulevard. Its evil is manifest in Milwaukee Hall!"

Raising his hands in surrender, Lamonte plaintively asked, "So – is there nothing we can do?"

"That question is now being asked in Eastern Europe because those poor people are suffering behind the Iron Curtain. They have no way to fight back. They lost that chance years ago when they failed to heed the warning signs! And that is what I am bringing to you today, my friends, an urgent and dire warning.

"If you love America, if you want to protect the freedoms that we enjoy today, then pray for the memories of the Church leaders who have been imprisoned, tortured, and killed by the godless Communists. For Cardinal Mindszenty in Hungary – pray for us. In Poland, Father Tomasz

Rostworowski – pray for us. In Yugoslavia, Cardinal Stepinac – pray for us. They died as so many others have perished before them: crushed by the acolytes of the Kremlin – killed for their faith in God and their desire for freedom here on Earth. Oh, dear God, when is this going to end?"

Seemingly exhausted from his rage, Father Lamonte rested his hands against the pew where Beau Duffy sat with his mother and young sister. The priest glanced at Beau, but there was no reproachment in his eyes. It looked more like an invitation – a plea for Beau to join Father Lamonte and his fight against the Reds. But Beau was too angry to return the priest's supplication. Father Lamonte strode back to the pulpit, bowing his head low as he pressed his large forearms against the lectern.

"Let me remind you that tomorrow morning there will be a memorial service for Kenneth Stevenson, a young man from our parish who recently lost his life to North Korea – killed by a Communist bullet, killed in the defense of our liberty. Killed by the same forces that proclaim they want peace!"

Father Lamonte held up a piece of paper. "Have you seen this, friends? Can you believe it – these Petitions for Peace? Have these hypocritical Communists asked you to sign their so-called Pledge for Peace? I beg you not to do it! Peace has no meaning when it is offered by the enemies of God! Frankly, it is un-American to be talking about peace at a time like this. When those ungodly Communists ask for your name, I want you to say NO to peace!"

Beau's little sister looked up at her mother, not understanding why a priest would be opposed to peace. Her mother was also confused. Bowing her head, she put a finger to her lips to silence the child.

"A peace petition is cold comfort for the family of Kenneth Stevenson!" Father Lamonte cried. "'You won't have to bury your sons,' the Communists are whispering. 'You can save your boys if only you sign this piece of paper.' If we beg them for peace, then they will stop killing our young men. After they take over the world, of course!"

The altar boys scattered as the priest charged toward the congregation. "Put down your weapons, America, and the next thing you know Korea is gone and then the rest of Asia has fallen. Before you know it, America will be overrun by the Communist horde – this union-swarming parasite – this marionette of Moscow!"

"Yes, that's when the people of Schenectady will learn what the rest of the world already knows: that life under Communism is nothing but a living hell. Then we'll all be wondering how it ever happened here. We will shake our heads and ask ourselves, 'How could we have been so foolish?' Why did we listen to our friends and neighbors who thought they could bargain with the Devil and the misguided souls in Local 1389, disciples of the International Communist conspiracy?"

Beau's mother bowed her head and Beau could feel the eyes of the entire congregation on him – their eyes boring straight into his soul – and Beau just wanted to tear it all down! He wanted to throw Helen and her entire Commie gang right into the street! Tear down Milwaukee Hall, rip down the church, burn down the whole damned city!

Beau pulled at his collar, straining to catch his breath in the stifling heat. He had to get away from peace petitions, from Father Lamonte, from the church, the city, and everything in it.

He had to get out now!

Beau stumbled out of the pew, lurching down the aisle until he fell against the massive oak doors at the back of the church. Pushing them aside, Beau felt the frigid air press against his face. The church service stopped and everyone turned to stare at Beau Duffy. They saw a sorrowful man trying to escape his guilty mind. Beau's mother put her hands to her face and began to cry.

Outside the church, Beau was walking in angry, mindless circles, his giant steps churning through the snow as the sound of organ music filled the air. The congregation began to sing the closing hymn and a few parishioners were walking out of the church when they saw Beau Duffy glaring back at them. The frightened congregants rushed back inside.

Beau fumed, "I'll handle it, he says! That son of a bitch, Milo. I'll handle it! Well, he hasn't handled a goddamned thing!" Beau looked back at the church where the sign read: "Be a Calm Me. Not a Commie."

Like hell, Beau vowed. He wasn't going to be calm anymore. He was going to do something about all this Communist crap and he was going to do it today!

"Excuse me, sir?" Beau turned to see a young woman holding a clipboard toward him. "Have you signed the Petition for Peace?"

"Have I what?" Beau gasped. A moment later, the clipboard was shattered against the sidewalk. Father Lamonte and the congregation shook their heads at the sight of Beau Duffy chasing a young woman down the sidewalk, peace petitions blowing across the churchyard, as Beau tried to apologize. But all the parishioners could hear was the young woman crying, "Leave me alone! Leave me alone!" as she ran away from Beau.

Petitions for Peace were a masterstroke of Cold War propaganda. The Soviet strongman, Joseph Stalin, had launched a worldwide con – a bait-and-switch on a global scale – pedaling world peace and international friendship to the West, while his armies were erecting barbed wire around Eastern Europe. Eight million prisoners trapped in a Communist gulag, their food, homes and property plundered – all to feed Stalin's armies and his Five Year Plans for Russian prosperity. Stalin's propaganda was another means of control.

The Russian people had an ancient fear of the outside world and the memories of the Nazi invasion were still fresh in their minds. Stalin kept this fear churning by taking away their food, taking away fathers and mothers, jailing husbands and sons. With his peace campaign, Stalin was creating more fear and paranoia: America will invade! America will bomb us! America must be stopped and only I can stop them, the Soviet leader assured his people. Anyone who didn't believe him was taken away and shot. The peace petitions, of course, made no mention of this oppression or Russia's backing of the North Korean Communists.

Millions of peace-loving people responded around the world. Almost overnight, the peace petition campaign gave Stalin a virtual trademark on the words 'peace' and 'brotherhood.' From Schenectady to Senegal, "Partisans for Peace" went door to door to promote the myth that Russia stood for peace and not the gulag. It wasn't long before the Schenectady Committee for World Peace and Understanding was boasting more than 600 members, each of them scrounging signatures from friends, neighbors, relatives, or strangers on the street.

Backed by the Social Awareness Committee of Local 1389, the peace committee offered toasters, percolators, televisions, and other "Peace Prizes" for the comrades who collected the most signatures. The competition became frantic – and even dangerous. Names were taken off mailboxes, gravestones, and phone books. Out-of-towners were accosted as they stepped off the bus. Someone tried to block a major roadway, demanding drivers sign a peace petition before they could pass. After a while, the best way to start a fight in Schenectady was to ask someone if they supported peace.

Just when it seemed impossible to find any more names, word spread of a nationwide grand prize – a free trip to Russia! – for the most signatures collected by May Day. This is what Martha had been waiting for: a chance to finally meet her hero, Anna Razumnova!

Imagine – an afternoon at the dacha, relaxing in the sun with wine and caviar, spending hour after hour discussing Martha's groundbreaking work in America, her importance to the American labor movement and, of course, her quiet leadership of this new Revolution in Schenectady. Today, comrades; tomorrow, the best of friends!

Martha had to find more names!

It was then that a young man stepped forward with a brilliant proposition. Wide-eyed and achingly earnest, John Anderson was an English teacher in the Junior High School and his idea surprised even Martha.

"What if all the school children wrote letters to Chairman Stalin and to President Truman, asking them to be friends and to support peace together? We all want peace and our children should want this too. Isn't this what America stands for?"

Soon the local school children were bolstering the Campaign for Peace, adding their names in crayon and pencil. By Christmas, the kids were making greeting cards, wishing peace and goodwill for both countries. Anderson proudly mailed these cards to his own family and friends – cards that were soon in the hands of the Schenectady County Loyalty Board.

Peace, equality, social justice? These were things the Soviets wanted! Was John Anderson trying to spread Communism in our schools? the Loyalty Board demanded. Several witnesses – teachers and parents – were called to testify and they, too, suspected that John Anderson might be some kind of subversive.

In closed-door hearings, the Loyalty Board kept up the pressure.

"Would you say Mr. Anderson's feelings regarding race relations are stronger than those of the average person?"

"Have you ever heard John Anderson criticize the United States government?"

"What kind of music does John Anderson listen to?"

When the evidence was gathered, along with the gossip, the rumors and innuendo, the Loyalty Board brought Anderson in for questioning.

"Is it true that you signed a petition opposing the dismissal of Dr. Francis Figgins?"

"Yes I did," Anderson said meekly. He tried to pick up his head and confront his inquisitors in the eye, but he could not do it. John Anderson was no longer wide-eyed and earnest. He was just aching.

"And what about this?" Charlie Gaynor was holding one of the Christmas cards that Anderson had mailed to his friends. "'Peace on Earth; Good Will to Men.' Isn't that what the Soviet Union is advocating in its phony peace campaign?"

Anderson did not know what to say. "Isn't that what everyone wants, peace and goodwill?"

The Loyalty Board stared back at him in disbelief. How could anyone be so naive?

The case was soon closed and a report delivered to the Schenectady City School Board. Later that year, John Anderson would be denied tenure as a teacher and soon he was out of a job.

Of the thousands of petitions for peace that were signed by the citizens of Schenectady, none of them were signed by John Anderson. He had taken someone's advice: "Don't sign those peace petitions," they warned. "It might get you into trouble."

"The word Communist, at least in Texas usage, has come to mean practically anybody the rest of us don't like — a regrettable perversion of the old-fashioned son-of-a-bitch."
TEXAS NEWSPAPER PUBLISHER *HOUSTON HARTE*

CHAPTER TWENTY-SEVEN

THE LEDGER NEWSROOM:
January 1952

Dear Uncle Sam,

Why is there so much more Communist activity here in Schenectady? At Bingo last night, a Communist won the $1,000 grand prize and declared that everyone should have a share. I'm not sure I like the idea of sharing prizes, especially the grand prize. Does that make me a bad person?

— *Suspicious in Scotia*

Dear Suspicious,

Communists are very crafty people. They talk about peace even as they prepare for war. They say they want to share their riches, but how long will there be Bingo nights once the Reds tear down our churches? No, you are not a bad person. Your question reflects the savvy wisdom of a patriotic American. Of course

you should keep all of your prize money because
that is the reward for true competition. It is the
American way. The Communists want to take our way
of life and Bingo is

"Bingo is … Bingo is what?"

Montgomery Hughie sat back from his typewriter. The newspaper publisher took an angry puff from his pipe. He tried again, typing "Bingo is a game of numbers and letters providing more mathematics and literature than the average American consumes in a lifetime." Hughie flung the paper out of his typewriter and threw it into the trash.

Bingo, scoffed Hughie. Ridiculous! You had to hand it to the Catholics: they knew how to squeeze every last dime from the faithful. "They should call it the Wednesday Night Collection Plate," Hughie muttered as he went back to his typewriter.

"Bingo is five little letters … five letters that spell 'liberty.' Oh for Christ's sake, Montgomery! What the hell is that?" Hughie ripped another page out. "Bingo doesn't spell anything except *Bingo!*"

Hughie stormed over to his office door and shouted into the newsroom, "What the hell is Bingo?!" The startled reporters and frightened editors drew back from their desks, expecting another phone book to be hurled across the newsroom. Snarling at their incompetence, Hughie bit down on his pipe and slammed the door.

Hughie was searching for inspiration. He looked out his window overlooking State Street and rising above the downtown were the familiar smoke rings puffing from the mechanical mouth above the Otis Cigar Shop.

"That's odd." Hughie checked his watch. It was 8:17 a.m. "Smoke's not supposed to appear for another 13 minutes. What the hell is going on over there? Van Lueven!"

The newspaper's city editor, Tom Van Lueven, crept into Hughie's office. After 27 years in *The Ledger* newsroom, Van Lueven was a broken, nervous man. The editor took his place next to the publisher's desk, slipping into what was known among the newspaper staff as "Old Sparky."

The stiff, hardwood chair had a tall back and leather straps on both arm-rests – an exact replica of the electric chair in Sing Sing prison.

Nearly every day, there was another execution in *The Ledger* newsroom and Montgomery Hughie would deliver the volts himself.

"Get somebody over to the cigar shop right away!" Hughie thundered. "There's something wrong with their billboard. That last puff was almost fourteen minutes early!"

Van Lueven had survived decades at *The Ledger* by not telling Montgomery Hughie anything the publisher did not want to hear. It was strange for a newspaperman, but Montgomery Hughie hated bad news.

"Well, Mr. Hughie," the editor began cautiously, "the answer may be in today's paper."

"You got the story already?"

"Actually, sir, it's an advertisement – on page five."

The publisher opened the paper and immediately fell back into his chair. "Great Jumpin' Jehoshaphat! What in God's name is *THAT*?"

The large advertisement read, 'NEW TO DOWNTOWN SCHE-NECTADY – The International Friendship Cinema! Located in the for-mer Otis Cigar Shop, tonight's double feature is 'Citizen Stalin' and 'Jezebel – The Lady in Red.' Half-priced tickets available for Red Fist card holders!'

"I'm sure it was inadvertent," Van Lueven offered meekly. Across the desk, Hughie's face crossed from red to purple as the newspaper crumpled between his constricted fingers.

"A Communist advertisement!" Hughie bellowed. "IN MY NEWSPAPER!"

Under his breath, Van Lueven said, "Bingo!"

Hughie had not been this angry since he caught a Communist news-boy selling copies of the *Daily Proletariat* in front of *The Ledger*. He was so furious, Hughie ordered his driver to run the boy over. He was a Hughie, after all, and for four decades the Hughie family had been using their newspaper in a vain attempt to destroy the local Communists.

Editorials, news articles, and even the obituaries were written to skew-er the Reds. Whenever a Party member died, Hughie would place their death notice under the headline: 'More Good News.' More recently, the paper had been running photographs of suspicious-looking people in a new feature called, "Who Is That Stranger?"

"Is there someone you don't recognize – someone who may be a threat to public safety? It is the responsibility of every American citizen to report danger whenever they see it! Call *The Ledger* newsroom and we'll find out: *Who Is That Stranger?*"

But Hughie's newspaper seemed powerless to stop the Reds. While the rest of the country was cowering under the lash of Joseph McCarthy, Schenectady had become a Mecca of open Revolution: Communism celebrated in broad daylight! For the rest of that morning, Hughie sat glumly in his office, searching his mind for some way to win back his city.

From out of the wadded-up newspaper, Hughie noticed a familiar face: the bulldog grimace of FBI Director J. Edgar Hoover. Hughie spread the newspaper onto his desk. "Hoover Declares FBI Ready to Assist Local Efforts in Combatting Communism."

Of course – the FBI!

Within seconds, Montgomery Hughie was on the phone to the Schenectady field office of the FBI. Special Agent Walter Thurston answered the line.

"That's what I said: Lock 'em all up!" Hughie demanded. "Save the taxpayers some money, skip the trial, and just deport them! Better yet, let's just shoot 'em and get it over with! They're a menace and they're getting bigger every day! What I'd like to know is, what is the FBI going to do about it?"

"Confidentially, Mr. Hughie, we are just waiting for the word," Agent Thurston said. This surprised even Hughie.

"You can't print this, Mr. Hughie, but I want you to know that Director Hoover is ready to undertake just those kinds of extreme measures. Our men have tracked the whereabouts of tens of thousands of suspected Communists, fellow travelers, and others with disloyal, un-American proclivities and when we get the 'go' sign – and that could come at any moment – we are ready to bring them all in."

"And then what?"

"They will be permanently detained."

"You mean like the Japs during the war?"

"Precisely sir, those same internment camps have been carefully maintained and they are ready for reoccupancy as we speak."

"Interesting," the publisher mused. This was exactly the kind of bold action that was needed in Schenectady and it got him thinking: what if an emergency could be declared right away? Not a major one, of course, just something large enough to justify the mass arrest of every pinko in Schenectady. Perhaps every member of Local 1389?

"Agent Thurston, I need you to come to a meeting of the Schenectady County Loyalty Board. We can't seem to make any headway against this Communist blight, and frankly, we need your help."

The Loyalty Board was set to meet two nights later at a "secret location" – Charlie Gaynor's basement apartment.

That night, Charlie waited eagerly for the signal – three knocks (one loud, two soft), then two seconds of silence before three more quick knocks. Instead, a single sharp thud struck the door, shaking the pictures on the wall. Charlie peeked through a crack in the door, just wide enough to see a tan overcoat stretched across the massive chest of Chief Inspector Wotan Volk.

"Anyone follow you?" Charlie whispered. With one short punch, Volk knocked open the door, stopping hard against Charlie's face.

"Sorry, Charlie. I forgot the password."

"Jesus, Detective! That hurt!" Charlie grumbled as he rubbed his cheek. "We gotta be careful nowadays. Dem-Red-sons-a-bitches will do anything to stop our work!"

Volk could only grunt at such nonsense. He looked around Charlie's dark, subterranean lair. The hulking detective hunched his shoulders as he lumbered into the kitchenette, throwing open cabinets and drawers.

"You got anything to drink?"

"I don't think drinking is a good idea tonight, Detective. The Bishop will be here any minute."

"The Bishop can take care of himself. I'm the one who's thirsty. And don't call me Detective. I'm the Chief Inspector."

"Right – Chief Inspector. Is the mayor coming?"

"The mayor can't make it tonight and the Chief's busy too."

"Well, it's a privilege to have you here."

"Yeah, right. A privilege."

Volk stalked around the apartment, putting his nose in the air as his hat brushed against the low ceiling. "I hope they like cheese, Charlie. It smells like you got a lot of it in here."

"It's hard to keep things dry in a basement apartment."

"Well how about opening a window? You're gonna kill us all," Volk said, waving his hat against the fumes. "I thought these meetings were supposed to be in the County Office Building."

"Not secure enough. Like I said, dem-Red-sons-a-bitches will do anything –"

"Right, right, right. Well, I think we'll be safe. Tonight is their bowling night."

"I think I hear something!" Charlie sprang for the door. Volk went back to his search for a drink.

"Excellency!" Charlie exclaimed as he opened the door to Bishop Carney. "Thank you so much for coming, sir!"

The Bishop began wiping his hands as soon as he pulled them away from Charlie's sweaty palm. Barreling in behind the Bishop was Montgomery Hughie.

"My God, Charlie! Fix those stairs, will you! Damn near broke my neck. Oh, forgive me, Excellency. I didn't see you there." Hughie quickly made the sign of the cross as the Bishop nodded forgivingly.

Next in the door was Special Agent Walter Thurston, carrying a large satchel. Volk eyeballed the FBI agent suspiciously. The lawmen took seats at opposite ends of the table as Montgomery Hughie brought the meeting to order.

"We all know that our mandate as a Loyalty Board has been limited. We have not been allowed to investigate matters concerning General Electric and Local 1389 and, while I strongly disagree with this restriction, that has been the policy. So tonight I have asked Special Agent Thurston to show us how we can be more effective given our present circumstances."

Thurston opened a briefcase stuffed with files. "In here, gentleman, you will find all the ammunition you need to nail those Red bastards. Oh, forgive me, Father. I didn't see you there. The light's kind of dim."

"Yes, a blessing," sniffed the Bishop.

"After my conversation with Mr. Hughie, headquarters has instructed me to offer you gentlemen certain pieces of information that have been developed by our dedicated field agents. They have been collecting files on the activities of certain individuals here in Schenectady, both members and non-members of Local 1389. Under normal circumstances, the Bureau does not share this sort of intelligence. However, Director Hoover has instructed me to make this material available – discreetly – to your Loyalty Board."

Charlie's eyes lit up. "Sweet Mother of pearl, look at all this. We're gonna get some action now!"

Everyone echoed Charlie's enthusiasm – everyone except Volk. He sat silently in the shadows as Thurston passed the FBI files around the room.

"As you can see, gentleman, the FBI is well-equipped to keep you thoroughly informed about the activities of these un-Americans. We have the resources, the experience and the know-how to uncover even their future schemes – the very things this Loyalty Board was meant to expose. To be frank, gentlemen, what the FBI is lacking is an effective means of disclosing this information to the public and that's where you come in. With our files and your standing in the community, we can bring the public's attention to these undesirable persons before they cause further damage."

"What can we do with these?" asked the Bishop, holding up membership lists, petitions and other records from Thurston's briefcase.

"What you need are names, Padre – names on paper," Thurston said. "For instance, here are petitions collected by the Communists and their various front organizations. Like this one from the Schenectady Women's Garden Club."

"The Garden Club?" exclaimed the Bishop.

Thurston checked the file. "That's right, your Excellency. According to our files, these ladies were secretly taken over by the Reds in the summer of 1949."

"How do you know this?"

"Well let's just say that wherever there's a Communist, there's usually an FBI informant in the same room. Sometimes more than one."

Hughie reached into the file labeled "Schenectady Petitions for Peace." He read the preamble out loud, "We the Undersigned do hereby call upon the United States Government to stop its war mongering and join co-operatively with the Russian people to bring peace and harmony to all nations of the world."

"Ha! Peace and harmony," Charlie scoffed.

Then Montgomery Hughie's eyes grew wide as he read the first name on the list. "Marjorie Whitetower – that's my secretary!"

"And no doubt an agent planted in your organization by the Communists," Thurston said grimly. "With these lists, gentlemen, your Loyalty Board can expose the rot that is infecting your city, your schools, and your businesses. Finally, you can bring law and order to Schenectady."

The room shook as Detective Volk slammed a bottle of White Rose down on the table.

"May I remind you gentlemen that we already have law and order in Schenectady."

"No offense, Chief Inspector," Hughie said, "but you must admit, the Communists in G.E. – this Social Awareness Committee – they really have gone too far. They have to be stopped!"

"I don't think we've met," Agent Thurston said, extending a hand toward Volk. Volk did not stand up and his face remained in the shadows. His hand stayed in his pocket. Volk wasn't in the mood to shake hands.

Thurston smiled. "I've heard a lot about you, Chief Inspector."

"What's that supposed to mean?" Volk snapped. Everyone turned toward the big detective, surprised by his menacing tone. Thurston kept smiling.

"I've been meaning to come down to the station to meet with you and discuss our latest investigations."

"Can't wait," Volk said sarcastically. "Just so you know, Agent Thurston, there is a lot more at stake here than the antics of some nutty rabble-rousers. You may not be aware of this, but there is a very good reason why we have laid off the union. When it comes to the Reds, General Electric wants to keep things quiet and they've got a billion reasons – maybe ten billion. That's how much the company stands to lose if the Pentagon gets spooked by your investigation into garden clubs, soup kitchens and whatever else the FBI thinks is subversive. There's nothing to investigate here, Thurston – at least nothing that's worth G.E. losing this defense contract. Take it from me: You're wasting your time and you might be costing us all a lotta money."

Volk planted his ham-sized fists on the table and leaned over the Loyalty Board members. "Think twice, gentlemen, before you do the FBI's dirty work. If this were so easy, then why does the FBI need your help?"

When no one had an answer, Volk shook his head. He downed a slug of White Rose and then another. The bottle fell off the table as Volk slammed the door on his way out.

Agent Thurston turned back to the Loyalty Board. "We've seen this kind of thing before: local law enforcement is unable to meet the challenges created by the rapid spread of Communist cells. It's embarrassing, of course, but you can't ignore the problem and I don't need to tell you that once these things get out of control, you will need stronger measures to defeat this threat. If you want my opinion, what Schenectady needs most of all is a loyalty oath."

The Loyalty Board members leaned forward, eagerly nodding in agreement.

Three months later, in the spring of 1952, the Schenectady City Council and then the County Legislature unanimously approved the new Loyalty laws. Anyone seeking a government license or a special permit had to declare their allegiance, under oath, to the United States of America. Taxi drivers, fishermen – even strippers and bartenders – were soon lined up at the County Clerk's office, their left hand on the Bible and their right hand raised to God, declaring "I am not currently a member of the Communist Party, a Communist front organization or a member of any group sympathetic to the aims of the Communist Party." The penalty for perjury was a $500 fine and a year in the county jail.

"Loyalty Permits" for individuals and organizations brought names, addresses and other tasty morsels for the Loyalty Board to chew. When the Garden Club was denied a permit for their annual flower show, Club President Ethel Fleetwood was ordered to appear before the Loyalty Board.

"Mrs. Fleetwood," Charlie Gaynor asked, "are you aware that the Smith Act makes it a crime to belong to an organization that advocates the overthrow of the United States."

"Oh my, no. I did not know that. But I would never belong to such an organization. My boys fought in the wars, you know – both of them! And only one of them came back."

"Then tell me, Mrs. Fleetwood, why would you sign a petition circulated by an organization certified as subversive by the United States Attorney General? An organization, in fact, that is dedicated to the violent overthrow of the very government you say you love?"

"The Garden Club?"

"Did they not circulate a so-called Petition for Peace?"

"Yes – because I don't want another mother to lose a son like I did!"

"Why didn't you ask who was behind this petition? If you had asked, Mrs. Fleetwood, you would know that the sponsors of this petition are known to be a dangerous threat to the United States!"

"And now you think the Garden Club is dangerous?"

"Let me ask the questions here, Mrs. Fleetwood."

"It was my neighbor's idea, Betty LaFever. I didn't know Betty was involved with anything dangerous to the country!"

"Betty LaFever, you say?" Charlie Gaynor smiled. "Please ... tell us more about her."

"A man is going about his business. A heavy hand falls on his shoulder. He is under arrest. Why? Perhaps he has criticized the political system that has taken over his country by force. And some stool pigeon has reported him. For this is happening in a police state where no one is free to debate what is good for the country. One must accept without protest the ideas of the men in power. Communist countries are police states. And we must never let the Reds turn our free America into that kind of fearful place. FIGHT THE RED MENACE."

"POLICE STATE," *one of 48 bubble gum cards sold by the Bowman Gum Co. of Philadelphia*

CHAPTER TWENTY-EIGHT

THE SATURDAY EVENING POST

After finishing the sixth grade, Michael Milwaukee would spend the summer of 1952 learning about cruelty, the lies that parents tell their children, and, finally, about Communism.

It started with Little League baseball. Michael was the youngest and smallest player on the team, but he could hit the ball like older boys twice his size. Other teams soon heard about this pint-sized phenom and on Opening Day, Milo and Martha were in the stands cheering loudly for their boy's first at bat.

Michael would not remember much of what happened next.

He was aware of the ball flying past him – first his belt, then his nose, and then his chest – and with each pitch the umpire yelled "Strike!" until the third strike and then "You're out!"

Michael never swung the bat. He was so frightened, he could not move. All he could see was the enormous face of the umpire, Mike Muldoon, leering over him and smiling in a way Michael had never seen from an adult – angry and gleeful all at once. And never had he heard such terrible things – words a child would never expect to hear from a grownup.

Until he met Umpire Mike Muldoon.

Michael was waiting for the first pitch when suddenly he was aware of a shadow passing over him. Michael looked up and there was Muldoon, leaning in so close that Michael could smell his horrible breath. "Here comes the little Red bastard," Muldoon growled. "Since when do Commies play baseball, you little shit?"

Michael tried to see if Muldoon was smiling, straining to see past the sunlight behind the umpire's mask, when – FFWOP! – the ball smacked into the catcher's mitt.

"Steeerike one!" Muldoon shouted. The umpire adjusted his face mask and whispered to Michael, "Like I said, kid – Commies can't play ball."

Did he say Commies? Michael could hardly think straight as the noise from the dugouts grew louder, the other players jabbering at Michael to "swing batter-batter." He tried digging in for the next pitch, but the ball shot past him again. And then again.

"Steerike three – yer out!"

Michael stood still for a moment, unsure of what to do next, when he heard Muldoon chuckle, "Go back to Russia, kid. They're gonna send your parents there soon enough!"

The next thing Michael heard were the howls of laughter coming from the boys in both dugouts and then he felt the warm pee running down his leg. Michael looked down in horror as a wet stain spread across his pants. He dropped the bat and bolted toward third base, not knowing where to run. When he saw a hole in the fence, Michael made his escape, running three and a half miles back home, stopping only once to tear off his pants and throw his jersey into the bushes.

Sunshine reflected against the tears in his eyes, making it difficult to find his way home. Stumbling past his grandfather near the back door –

unable to breathe – Michael raced upstairs to his bedroom and threw himself onto his pillow. He felt the ball cap still perched on his head and with a new rush of fury he charged into the bathroom and threw his cap into the toilet. He pulled at the lever – once, twice, three times – as the hat swirled around the bowl and jammed into the drain, water spreading across the floor. Desperately, Michael pushed open the window and threw the water-logged baseball cap, all of his baseball cards, his Yankee pennants, and his new baseball shoes into the backyard.

Finally, he locked the bathroom door and climbed into the tub, filling it up to the brim. Martha was soon at the door.

"Michael?" his mother knocked urgently. "Misha, darling, are you okay? Misha?"

Michael slowly sank into the tub until the water covered his ears and his mother's voice disappeared underwater. All he could hear was his breathing – far from 'Misha,' safe from Mike Muldoon and everything else in this stupid world.

Near the middle of August, Michael went to the barbershop with Tommy Wasserman. It was good to be outside again. Since his run-in with the umpire, Michael had quit the baseball team, preferring to stay in the house for most of that hot summer. Out in the sun again, Michael and Tommy flew their bikes down the streets, jumping over the curbs, slipping in and out of the parked cars. They had money in their pockets for a haircut and then an ice cream cone.

Waiting in the barbershop, Michael thumbed through a copy of *Boy's Life* while Tommy looked at pictures in a worn copy of the *Saturday Evening Post*. Michael was engrossed in the latest chapter of "Space Conquerors!" when Tommy gave him an elbow.

"Is that your dad?" asked Tommy, holding up the magazine.

Michael took a quick glance before tossing it back.

"Very funny – he doesn't wear a dress," Michael laughed.

"Not that! Here," Tommy said, pointing to the photograph on the opposite page.

The photo covered half of the page: serious men were lined up against the walls of what looked like a courtroom and all of them were staring at the small man, sitting alone at a table. It was Milo Milwaukee.

Michael pulled the magazine closer. Above the photo, the headline read, "Do Commie Unions Open Doors to America's Defense Plants?"

Michael's eyes shot back to the photo. His father looked so young, a face Michael only knew from the wedding pictures hanging in the dining room.

"Labor boss Milo Milwaukee testifies before the House Subcommittee on Communist Influence in Organized Labor," the caption read. "Subcommittee Chairman Conrad B. Brownale is investigating alleged control and intimidation of American labor unions by Communists and whether this subterfuge poses a danger to America's defense industry."

"What's he doing there?" Tommy asked.

Michael was feeling dazed. First his mother – now his father? Milo was a Communist too?

Grabbing the magazine, Michael ran out the door, leaving his bicycle and Tommy Wasserman at the barbershop. He ran blindly, not knowing where he was going, until he found himself back on Tuckahoe Row. Michael stuffed the magazine under his shirt and crept into the Milwaukees' backyard. Behind the tool shed, he found a shovel and started digging.

The long handle of the shovel beat against the shed as Michael worked frantically to get rid of this magazine. He had to bury that picture! The noise brought Michael's grandfather out of the house. The boy was pounding the loose soil back into place just as his grandfather peeked around the corner.

"Burying some treasure, Mikey?" his grandfather smiled. "Are you a pirate or a gangster?"

Michael could not look at his grandfather. He was too ashamed and too frightened. He threw down the shovel and ran into the house. Michael was still in his room when Milo came home from work that night.

The house was quiet and no one answered when Milo announced that he was home. He went out to the backyard and found his father asleep on the chaise lounge. Nearby, the shed door was open and a shovel was laying in the grass.

"Pops," Milo said, shaking his father awake. "Where's Martha? Where's Michael?"

"Michael went inside. He was playing pirates." The old man pointed to the shed and then put a finger to his lips. With a mischievous smile, he whispered, "We buried treasure back there!"

Milo walked around to the back of the shed where a small mound of earth was covering the torn pages of a magazine. Shaking away the dirt, Milo was surprised to see his younger self staring back at him.

"Shit," he said.

Milo looked around the large yard and the old trees that surrounded it. There was the swing set and the tree house he had built for Michael and the oversized fence that Martha wanted for privacy. On all sides of the property, there were thick rows of trees and bushes. Milo turned toward the garage and then looked up at the big house, nearly tall enough to be seen above those trees. This place had always felt protected, safe from the rest of the world. Until now.

Tears filled Milo's eyes. He realized the house, the fence, the trees, nothing was big enough to protect his family. The outside world had followed them home. Accusations and suspicions had trailed Milo and Martha for years and now they were pressing in on Michael too.

Milo felt ashamed and, for the first time in his life, he knew he had failed his son. A father is supposed to protect his children. What good was this big house – what good was *he* – if he could not guard his family?

Milo had seen this day coming and he had taken careful steps to break away from the Communists – setting up Helen Gamble as the Morale Coordinator, letting the Social Awareness Committee get so big – and so annoying – that the members of Local 1389 would finally throw the Commies out. But his great plan had only succeeded in making the Communists stronger. Helen had done everything Milo had hoped for, but he had not counted on one thing: the people – most of them anyway – liked what the Communists were doing.

Helen had been absolutely relentless – organizing meetings, gathering petitions and creating programs for every conceivable need in the city. Somehow she made it all seem so natural and reasonable. No one was calling it Communism. This was peace, brotherhood, and good citizenship – a slice of the American pie. There was no rebellion and there never would be.

"Christ," Milo muttered. "What have I done?"

And what do I do next? he wondered. Is it too late to stop this?

Milo looked at the magazine again. He had to smile at the cocky young man sitting at the witness table. The photograph did not show how scared he was – seated in front of Conrad Brownale, the Great Red Hunter, and a room packed with reporters and federal investigators.

Had anything really changed after so many years? Milo still felt trapped, just as he was in that hearing room, unable to tell Congressman Brownale what he really thought about the Reds – how he was only pretending to be one of the Communists, using them to get what he wanted: a big shot life with a big house and a big yard.

A bigger liar.

On that day in front of Congressman Brownale, Milo had somehow managed to dodge his way through a barrage of angry questions – accusations, really – and never once did Milo have to plead the Fifth. By the end of the hearing, even Congressman Brownale was impressed. He called Milo into his office for a private chat.

"You strike me as a sensible young man," the congressman said. "I would think someone as smart as you would give more thought to the sort of people you have running your union. You should also be thinking about your future. You'd be doing your union a great favor if you changed sides and you'll be saving yourself and your family a lot of heartache. Things won't end well if you stay with this Mickey Mouse union, but you already know that, don't you?"

Milo tried to be polite but all he could think about was the hallway outside Brownale's office. Could he escape this meeting without being seen by anyone from the union? If the Communists knew about this conversation, they would mark Milo as a snitch – someone they could never trust again.

Another traitor, another Frankie Pepper.

"Think about what I told you," Congressman Brownale told young Milo. "If you ever need my help, you give me a call."

Milo threw the *Saturday Evening Post* into the trash. He went back inside the house and for several minutes he stood at the bottom of the stairs listening to Michael cry in his room.

How could he explain what he had done and why he had done it? He wanted Michael to know the truth. Could he explain to him what a Communist was? Mostly, he wanted Michael to know that his father was trying to make things right. He would find a way to break away from the Communists without losing everything they had.

Not losing Michael would be the first and most important thing of all.

After so many lies, could even a child believe in him again?

It was time for a new plan, Milo decided. Helen and her Social Awareness Committee were irritating but not irritating enough. Something more had to be done to throw out the Reds. But first Milo had to take care of something else – something he should have done weeks before. He picked up the phone and called Beau Duffy.

A week later, Mike Muldoon was taking off his chest protector and loading his umpire equipment into the car when a Louisville Slugger came crashing down on the back of his neck. His chin hit the back bumper before his head cracked against the dusty parking lot. Beau Duffy was just getting started.

He dragged Muldoon behind the car. With one foot on the umpire's head, Beau scanned the ballfield and then the parking lot. No one was there to see Beau reach back and kick Muldoon hard, crushing his left eye. Beau kept kicking and punching until he was too tired to beat the umpire anymore. By then, Mike Muldoon wasn't moving. Beau reached back for one last kick – not as hard as the others, but strong enough to leave three bloody teeth in the dirt.

When Mike Muldoon got out of the hospital, his dog – painted red from snout to tail – was waiting for him by the front door, next to an envelope with three bloody teeth inside.

Muldoon would not be calling balls and strikes for the rest of that summer and he did not call the police either. And Mike Muldoon would never call anyone a Communist ever again.

"We parents and the teachers and the principals do not like the horrors created by the comics. Are the Commies behind these books which appear in print by the thousands?"

LETTER FROM A CONCERNED NEW YORKER *to the national magazine of the American Legion*

CHAPTER TWENTY-NINE

MIKE MANGLE TO THE RESCUE

After that miserable summer, Michael was sure things could only get worse. The first week of a new school year always meant another essay on "What I Did On My Summer Vacation." What could Michael write except, "This summer I discovered that my parents are Communists, probably Communist spies."

Was this his fate – to be voted "Most Likely to Visit His Parents in the Federal Pen?"

First confused, then frightened, Michael was getting angrier at the mess his parents had made. He hadn't spoken to Tommy Wasserman since that day at the barbershop and, as Michael walked to school that first day, he was certain that Tommy had told all their friends about the magazine article and the picture of Michael's father.

And what about Sandra Pepper? Michael would gladly welcome some attention from the beautiful Sandra – even if it was only her scorn.

Three blocks from school, Michael spotted a dirty paperback lying by the curb. The pages were stiff and stained and the cover was torn in half. But there was enough left for Michael to find something he desperately needed: a hero!

The paperback was a *Mike Mangle Murder Mystery*. It was like no book he had ever seen before: Mike Mangle, the private eye with a gun, two fists, and the guts to use all three. The book was as messy as the story it told. When Mike Mangle wasn't cracking someone's head open, he was peppering the room with a fusillade of vengeful gunshot. Either way, his target was always the same: those filthy, no-good Communists!

Michael was entranced, glued to the magical words that flew out of this stained and profane paperback. It was "Take this!" and "How do you like that?!" as Mike Mangle dispatched one Commie creep after another. Michael felt a warm tingle run up his legs and into his hair.

Between the senseless violence and the staccato dialogue, the ungrateful dames and the Commie traitors, Michael had found a world where might meant right and if somebody didn't like it, then Mike Mangle was ready to stamp their ticket to Hell. He was tough and ruthless – a killer on a mission. Here was a man who knew what to do with a Communist!

"Pardon me, you weak-kneed liberals. Don't talk to me about Constitutional rights. I'm here for what's right and wrong!"

Michael knew it immediately: Mike Mangle was the most. For the next twenty minutes, Michael's face was buried in the pages of this discarded, disgusting paperback. His feet had not moved, but Michael felt like he was flying.

"The Commies had better get wise. The only place left for them is that hot house called Hell. Make 'em climb the six foot ladder – down, down, down, baby. Send them back to the mud and the maggots where these worms belong. But first give 'em your best knuckle sandwich 'cuz it's gonna be a long trip and they ain't comin' back. Die, Die, Die, Die, Die!"

This is what we should be learning in school, Michael realized. Soon, he was buying more Mike Mangle paperbacks. The *Black Knight* and *Captain Gruesome* were great comic books, but Mike Mangle was the most potent superhero of all! And Mangle was just an ordinary mug. Sure, he was quick with the ladies and fast with a gun, but Mike Mangle was just a regular Joe – just like Michael Milwaukee! They didn't go looking for trouble, but when they found it, Mike Mangle and Mike Milwaukee knew what to do.

BAM! – SLAM! – POW!

Michael jumped at the sound of a car horn behind him. A police officer had pulled over to the curb as Michael had his nose in another Mike Mangle Mystery.

"You'd better get along to school, son," the officer said. Michael shrugged, his lip curling into his best tough-guy smirk.

Don't rush me, Flatfoot. I'll get to school when I get there.

Michael tucked the paperback into his pocket, pushed back his shoulders, and slowly headed for school.

Sandra Pepper, I'm comin' for you, doll.

Michael would carry his favorite Mangle paperback wherever he went. His mother would always find his comic books – *Zombie Mad Men, Reform School Girls,* or *Combat Goons* – hidden under his bed or tucked inside his school books. But she never found those Mike Mangle paperbacks. They were safe – the two Mikes – as long as they stuck together.

Until Mrs. Perry.

Michael had not counted on her.

It was during math class and Sandra Pepper was at the blackboard working on a math problem. Michael, meanwhile, was working on a problem of his own: how was he going to get Sandra Pepper to notice him? As Sandra concentrated on her math problem, Michael concentrated on Sandra Pepper.

He pushed the Mangle paperback under his math book so he could give all his attention to this junior high school beauty. Under the fluorescent lights of Mrs. Perry's classroom, Sandra's long, golden hair shimmered as it fell off her shoulders and down that velveteen dress. That dress was Michael's favorite, the blue one that fit her tighter than a lunch lady's hairnet. He liked how Sandra twisted her feet around, pushing herself up onto her toes as she rubbed the chalk against the blackboard.

Why don't you put down that chalk and come over here, little lady? I'll help you figure out your problems.

SLAP!

Like a gunshot echoing across the classroom, the Mike Mangle paperback had fallen to the floor. Mrs. Perry scooped it up before Michael could rescue his hero. He covered his face with his hands as the teacher examined his treasure. Turning to a random page – this one had Mangle shooting a woman in the eye after she had double-crossed him – Mrs. Perry's mouth fell open. She stared down at Michael in horror, unable to comprehend the violence in this filthy novel.

"Michael Milwaukee, where on earth did you get such a thing?!"

None of the kids could see what Mrs. Perry was holding, but from the look on her face, they knew it had to be something very bad and really, really good. The teacher thrust her finger toward the door, banishing Michael to the principal's office. Casually, Michael stood up on one foot and pushed back his chair with the other. He gave his belt a tug and slowly loped toward the door.

An afternoon in the slammer? No problem, Mrs. Perry. I've done hard time before.

Sandra Pepper turned from the blackboard just as Michael sauntered past her – and then he stopped, just long enough to give Sandra a wink and that Mike Mangle smirk. Sandra Pepper felt a warm tingle run up her legs and into her hair.

Then it happened, the dream of every boy in the seventh grade: Sandra Pepper smiled. The only thing standing between them was three feet of linoleum and a stubby piece of chalk. Their eyes locked together while the eyes of everyone in the classroom were locked on Sandra and Michael. Even Mrs. Perry could feel the electric surge running between them.

The chalk rolled out of Sandra's hand and fell to the floor like an empty shell from Mike Mangle's .38.

Bang, bang, kid: you got me.

The chalk rolled toward the door where Michael snatched it up. He drew a big heart on the blackboard before tossing it back to Sandra. The chalk felt warm in her moist hands.

Michael snapped open the classroom door – like Mangle flicking off the lid of his Zippo lighter – and then he was gone, an unsolved problem on the blackboard and the flame of a new love burning inside Sandra Pepper. Sandra turned to her teacher, "May I please sit down now, Mrs. Perry?"

Outside the principal's office, Michael felt a terrible knot building inside his stomach. He suddenly realized that Mrs. Perry had confiscated his Mike Mangle paperback! For the first time in weeks, Michael was without The Mangler by his side!

He slumped against the wall, powerless. Samson without his hair.

Then something familiar caught Michael's eye. He squinted into the distance, leaning closer toward the open door across the hall. There was something on the wall that filled Michael's heart with wide-eyed wonder. Silently, he walked across the hallway, transported on air, as he was drawn to this miraculous vision. Between a framed photograph of Senator McCarthy and a Gilbert Stuart print of George Washington, there was the face of Ace Thompson, the face on the back of the Mike Mangle paperbacks!

Thompson was the actor who played Mike Mangle in the movies and now here he was – inside Michael's school!

From underneath a snappy fedora, Ace Thompson smiled the cocky, cynical smile that epitomized the icy coolness of America's toughest private eye – a smile that said, "Sorry I have to plug you, sweetheart. I hate to waste a good bullet on a bad dame."

Michael was so intent on Ace Thompson that he did not notice that he was standing inside Charlie Gaynor's office, just a few feet from where Charlie was taking his mid-morning nap. Michael whispered, "Make 'em climb the six foot ladder – down, down, down, baby."

The words of Mike Mangle roused the old man from his sleep. Half-awake, Charlie stared at Michael as Michael kept staring at the magnificent picture on the wall.

"Do you know who that is?" Charlie asked.

"That's Private Eye Mike Mangle," the boy said with great reverence. "He's the best."

"Damn straight he is. He knows how to handle dem-Red-sons-a-bitches."

Michael responded with the lines he had memorized from the book: "Send them back to the mud and the maggots where these worms belong."

Charlie grinned. "But first give 'em your best knuckle sandwich."

Michael followed, "Cuz it's gonna be a long trip and they ain't comin' back."

Then the Commie-hating kid and the Commie-cursing man chanted together: *"DIE, DIE, DIE, DIE, DIE!"*

"A few days ago, I read that President Eisenhower expressed the hope that by election time in 1954 the subject of Communism would be a dead and forgotten issue. The raw, harsh, unpleasant fact is that Communism is an issue and will be an issue in 1954."
SENATOR MCCARTHY

CHAPTER THIRTY

A WARRIOR RETURNS TO WASHINGTON
January 20, 1953 – What a Glorious Day!

"This is just too *exciting!*" J. Edgar Hoover squealed as he jumped out of bed. He could not write anything more in his diary. The big day – the *biggest* day – had finally arrived!

Inauguration Day had the capital celebrating the ascension of a new president – General Dwight David Eisenhower! Finally, after six long years, President Harry Truman would just be an unpleasant memory. Six more hours and America would once again have a true leader – a mighty champion! – a president with dignity and gravitas. From the mold of George Washington came Dwight Eisenhower and once again America would have a warrior-king!

After leading his country in battle, Eisenhower would now lead the nation in America's war against the "Commonists." Hoover was so gleeful he wanted to prance down Pennsylvania Avenue and sing from the top of the Washington Monument! Election Day had restored order to the kingdom along with Hoover's faith in the American voter.

Giddy since Election Day, the FBI Director could be heard singing around the office and no one could remember the last time Hoover had anyone deported!

The noble Eisenhower, like Constantine the Great, was triumphantly returning from battle to lead his people and Hoover would be there, as always, to serve the new emperor. There was much to prepare – FBI dossiers and briefing memos! – but his first assignment for the president was a genuine surprise.

"McCarthy," said Eisenhower's press secretary, Warren Pillsworth. "We have got to do something about McCarthy." Others in the president's circle were quick to agree.

"This is a new administration. It's time to rein him in."

"Every week it's another attack on the State Department! It's like he's working for the Soviets!"

"Did you see him the other day, leering over the French ambassador's wife? He had her bent so far back, it looked like she was dancing the limbo!"

"Was he drunk?"

"When isn't he?"

Hoover sat silently, awkwardly, shocked to hear his fellow Republicans talking so harshly about a genuine star of their party. The FBI director also considered McCarthy a friend and a protégé. It was Hoover who first urged the new senator to take up the sword against Communism and no one in the long line of Congressional Red Hunters had ever accomplished so much and so fast. Now, after three years in the spotlight, McCarthy's act was wearing thin.

There was room for only one star in the Republican Party and that star had to be the new president. Obvious as that was, McCarthy was not getting the message. He had even questioned Eisenhower's commitment to fighting Communism! The Eisenhowers were at breakfast when McCarthy's accusation first hit the newspapers: "McCarthy Scolds Ike for Not Caring About Commie Threat."

As soon as the president read the news, Mamie Eisenhower was showered with her husband's orange juice.

And McCarthy kept it up, jabbing once more at his favorite punching bag – the U.S. State Department. Those weak-kneed know-it-alls had given China away to the Communists, McCarthy scolded, and the State Department was still harboring more Red saboteurs. McCarthy asked the press: Was President Eisenhower going to repeat the thoughtless mistakes of Roosevelt and Truman? When was someone going to take action?

McCarthy's accusations became so frequent that Mamie Eisenhower moved to her husband's side of the breakfast table.

As much as Eisenhower tried to ignore him, McCarthy would not keep quiet. Something had to give. The new White House was determined to put an end to McCarthy and his traveling circus.

All eyes turned to Hoover. Hoover created this Frankenstein – what was he going to do to stop it?

"Let me handle McCarthy," Hoover assured the president and his men. "He always listens to me."

Eisenhower smiled. The King was pleased and for J. Edgar Hoover there could be no greater reward.

Back in his office, Hoover called Special Agent Walter Thurston.

"I need to get McCarthy out of Washington. *Give them that picture!*"

"The problems of the United States can be summed up in two words: Russia abroad, labor at home."

GENERAL ELECTRIC EXECUTIVE IN 1946

CHAPTER THIRTY-ONE

IN G.E.'S CORPORATE TOWER
Overlooking Schenectady

"What the hell is he waiting for?"

Philip Reedy, the CEO of General Electric, stood before a gargantuan window, thirty stories above Erie Boulevard. A low, mournful groan slowly filled the Executive Suite as Reedy slid his hands up the window until his body was pressed against the glass and his arms raised in surrender.

Reedy pleaded again, "What is Milo waiting for?"

Standing a safe distance away, George Schidell could only shrug his shoulders as he glanced anxiously toward the office door and then quickly back to his boss. Halfway around, Schidell's head snapped back for a second look: all the other G.E. executives had slipped out of the Executive Suite, leaving Schidell alone with the boss, frothing at the window.

Reedy was staring down at Milwaukee Hall, the headquarters of Local 1389, and the picture painted on its roof – a cartoon of angry union men grabbing hold of General Electric's mascot, "Ready Kilowatt," and screwing his light bulb head into the ground. In bright red letters, a banner screamed up at Reedy: SCREW YOU, G.E.! RAISE OUR PAY!

The rooftop cartoon was a remnant of the Great Strike of 1946, one of the longest walkouts in the company's history. Seven years later, the cartoon was still taunting Philip Reedy.

"It's the middle of winter and it's still there! How much longer do I have to look at that goddamned cartoon?" It was another question George Schidell could not answer.

As the chief of General Electric's Security Division, Schidell's mind was always on safety – usually his own. When Mr. Reedy was agitated like this, Schidell knew that silence was usually the safest reply.

As his boss continued to stew, Schidell tried to calculate the number of steps it would take to reach the door. Anything more than three extended steps and escape would be impossible. Schidell counted four, maybe five, long steps. He was trapped.

"Milwaukee knows how much this could cost us, doesn't he?" Reedy barked. "The contract – Milo knows about the contract, right?"

Schidell muttered, "Yes sir. He knows about the contract and he knows the Communists are – "

"Are what?" the CEO snapped.

"Not very helpful." Schidell lowered his head, wishing he could melt into the carpet and leave Reedy alone with his fury.

"Helpful? Ha! They're a goddamned disaster! Does he understand how big this contract could be? Hundreds of millions – hell, BILLIONS – of dollars! A technology this advanced – flying high-altitude, spy planes over the Russians, the Chinese, over whoever and wherever we want – this could be the greatest goddamned weapon since – "

"Since?"

"Cannonballs!" Reedy shouted.

"Yes sir – cannonballs."

Reedy paced in front of his window and with every step he was getting more agitated. Schidell was prepared for moments like this. He had gone to the library to research the defensive mechanisms employed by small animals when they are confronted by an angry predator. The pigeon-toed sloth, for example, can control its respiration so completely that its blood will temporarily stop flowing and its skin turns to a morbid, unappetizing gray. Schidell gulped a chest-full of air and waited to see if his boss would ignore an inedible sloth lying on the floor.

"So what the hell is he waiting for?" Reedy turned to see Schidell's face matching the color of the crimson carpet. "Schidell – what the hell are you doing? Why can't you answer me?"

Gasping for breath, Schidell panted, "Are you talking about the Communists – or the union roof, sir?"

Reedy threw up his hands. He was ready to give up. He bowed his head against the glass and sighed. At this window, the G.E. boss had once enjoyed moments of quiet solitude, precious minutes away from the rat race of corporate earnings and factory production schedules, where he could take in the natural splendor of Upstate New York. To the west, trailed the Mohawk River and the Erie Canal as it journeyed toward Utica, Syracuse, and then farther to Buffalo. To the north, Reedy could see the tips of the southern Adirondacks and the wilderness that stretches into Canada. Now, Reedy could not lift his eyes beyond poor Ready Kilowatt, his face contorted in pain and his big cartoon eyes pleading to be rescued.

The strike of 1946 had been a nine-month siege that began soon after World War II. There were strikes all over the country that year as workers demanded a greater share of corporate profits, including the overtime wages they had been paid during the war. On the other side, manufacturers like G.E. were lobbying the government to continue the war-time freeze on wages but halt the price controls that had trimmed their profits since the start of the war.

When G.E. refused to negotiate with the AEWA, the union called a strike. It lasted longer and was more rancorous than anyone expected, tearing the company – and the city – apart. The strike abruptly ended on a Tuesday night after Philip Reedy invited Milo for dinner at the Mohawk Club. The company relented with a slight pay increase to the workers, along with a secret "peace bonus" to Milo. The Little Giant was named the exclusive insurance broker for every policy written on each and every member of the Local – all 40,000 of them. No one, not even the Communists, knew about the hefty commissions that Milo was paid for each of those insurance policies.

Recalling the Strike of '46 would always bring a smile to Milo's face. He might have been a Commie, but as far as Philip Reedy was concerned, Milo Milwaukee was a Red who was willing to negotiate. Once the strike was settled, the company enjoyed a year of record profits. The only thing bigger was this impending contract with the Defense Department.

"Milo said he would do something about the Communists and that was what – six years ago?" Reedy squawked at George Schidell. "Does he think the Army will do business with a company that's tied up with a Commie union? They don't need another goddamn Rosenberg scandal – or a hearing before Joe McCarthy! Hell, the Army doesn't want McCarthy up their ass any more than we do! Speaking of that loudmouth," Reedy leaned over his desk to check his calendar, "has he been taken care of this month?"

Schidell nodded. The monthly bundle of cash and G.E. stock certificates had been delivered to a Post Office box in Madison, Wisconsin – protection money that Reedy paid to keep Joe McCarthy away from G.E.

Staring out the window again, Reedy wondered if he could simply drop a bucket of paint onto the union roof and cover up that awful cartoon. And what if he missed? Reedy scanned the street and the sidewalks below. Thirty stories away, cars and people moved silently along the street like single-celled organisms wriggling under a microscope. Even if he did miss – and the paint can landed on one of those wriggling organisms – would anyone really notice?

Rules, rules, rules, Reedy sighed.

"Goddammit, Schidell, I asked you a question! What the hell is Milo waiting for? Schidell? Schidell! Where the hell – ?"

George Schidell was gone. The pigeon-toed sloth had reached the door with four long steps and a silent turn of the knob.

At the other end of Erie Boulevard, Frankie Pepper was also looking out his office window. He stared longingly down the hill, past Milwaukee Hall, and then farther down the street to the front gates of General Electric. His window was smaller than Philip Reedy's, but Frankie Pepper had much bigger dreams.

"What the hell is he waiting for?" Frankie Pepper asked.

Pepper's accountant, Maury Zegranski, looked up from his ledger. "Waiting – who?"

"You know, Milo – the Local," Pepper responded dreamily, imagining thousands of G.E. workers pouring out of Milwaukee Hall with their union cards in hand and striding up the hill to join Frankie Pepper's struggling union.

"His members are ready to dump Milo and those goddamned Commies. I just know it. Maury, I can feel it."

"Better be soon," Zegranski muttered as he closed the financial ledger and the small, unbalanced numbers that barely filled one page. Frankie Pepper's tiny union, the International Union of Electrical Workers, was nearly broke. If the members of Local 1389 did not defect soon, then Pepper's upstart union would be a bust.

Everyone knew things were desperate for the IUEW, but only Frankie knew about the $50,000 "advance" that Frankie had taken from the local loan shark, Mickey Scarpino. He had no way of repaying Scarpino without the monthly dues from thousands of new members. Still, there were times when Frankie would have welcomed just one face at his door: if his old union brother, Milo Milwaukee, his ex-best friend, would come to say hello then Frankie would be glad for nothing else.

Frankie could never forget that night when he gave Milo the news: he was leaving the AEWA. Pepper was in trouble with the Feds and leaving the Red-controlled AEWA was his only way out. Would Milo want to come along and make a fresh start, maybe help his old pal create a new union, free of Communists and Communism?

Milo had no love for the Communists, but he could only see Pepper's decision as a betrayal of their friendship and an attack on their union. Without a word, Milo turned his back on Frankie Pepper. Three years later and the two rivals had not spoken a word to each other. Each new day only stoked Pepper's obsession to take back Local 1389.

"Things are changing, they're changing fast. Christ, faster every day!" Frankie shouted at Maury, sitting just one desk away. "Who the hell does Milo think he is anyway – Superman? He can't just lift up the Earth and hold back time, am I right?"

"He flies backwards."

"Backwards?" Pepper asked incredulously, yanking his feet off the desk and flinging cigar ash onto his satin vest. "What the hell are you talking about: backwards?"

"Superman," Maury said. "He doesn't lift up the Earth. He holds back time by flying backwards around the Earth."

"And that's my point!" Frankie insisted. "Milo is out of step – he's flying backwards! The rest of the country is heading the other way – MY way. You see what I mean, Maury? It's progress, I'm talking about – progress! We're flying this way, not that way!" Frankie threw up his arms for a Superman takeoff, sprinkling more ash across his expensive three-piece suit.

The best suits and the finest cigars: whatever the big shots at G.E. were wearing, smoking, or doing, that's what Frankie Pepper wanted as well. He dressed the part because he knew that someday he would be back at the G.E. conference table, once more negotiating with the great Philip Reedy. Someday he would be in charge again, no longer dreaming through a tiny window at the wrong end of the street.

"All that dues money – Ha! What's Milo going to do then?" Frankie said, rubbing his chubby palms together. "Dammit Irene – turn down that music, will you? I can hardly hear myself think."

"Must be a terrible echo in there."

"Very funny, Irene. Always the comedian."

The secretary lowered the volume on a recording of "The Stars and Stripes Forever." From Sousa marches to Kate Smith's "God Bless America," patriotic music was always playing on the sidewalk speaker outside the headquarters of the IUEW. The music matched the union's patriotic slogan: "Made in America Where Americans Are Made." Frankie Pepper wanted the whole world to know that his union stood for loyalty to the good old U. S. of A. – not like those bums down the street, those goddamned Reds in Local 1389!

The AEWA may have been Red, but Frankie knew Milo wasn't. Milo was no more a Communist than Frankie was.

So where is the gratitude? Pepper wanted to know. How dare Milo turn his back on me, that little phony! I'm the one who showed him how to trick the Communists. If it wasn't for me, Milo Milwaukee would still be working the goddamn factory floor!

They had started work at G. E. on the very same day and together Milo and Frankie climbed off the assembly line and into full-time jobs with the union. They were the best of friends, together so often that people called them "Filo." They shared beers, laughs, and even girlfriends. They also shared a strong dislike for the Communists who controlled Local 1389, secretly mocking the old Wobblies for their thick accents and their creepy devotion to the Workers' Revolution.

They were young and cynical, and it was easy to make fun of those crusty anarchists. Still, they did have to respect the Reds. The Commies made the union strong and nothing got done without them. They wouldn't let you try anyway: the Reds controlled every important job in the AEWA leadership, including the Schenectady local. Milo and Frankie both longed for those union jobs with the white shirts and silk ties, better pay and shorter hours. To escape the grease and grime of the factory floor, Frankie and Milo would have to play the game: they would sell themselves as true-blue Reds.

Frankie was the first to act. He discovered that some well-timed applause at a Party speech would always draw the notice of the old-line

Communists. Whenever someone was spouting the usual revolutionary nonsense, Frankie would not only pretend to be interested, he was the first to exhort his comrades to storm the barricades! Forward to October! Nobody was more enthusiastic than Frankie Pepper.

He learned all of the Reds' slogans and mimicked their blind, undivided loyalty to the Kremlin, attending dozens of boring Party meetings, passing out their literature, and collecting money for magazines and other "activities" by unspoken friends of the Revolution. The Communists all agreed: that Frankie Pepper, he's okay.

From shop steward to the executive council then on to the district leadership, Frankie moved quickly up the union hierarchy. Soon he was out of Schenectady altogether, first as a district director and then as a board member of the AEWA International. With each step up the line, Frankie found it easier to embellish his Party bona fides. He would smile silently whenever a comrade would mistakenly vouch for Frankie's Communist credentials. From comrade to comrade, Frankie was pushed higher and higher up the leadership ladder, gaining greater power with each promotion. He was surprised at how quickly he gained their trust and he did it without ever becoming one of them.

Frankie would do damn near anything for the Reds, but he drew the line at signing his name. It was the one thing Milo and Frankie had promised they would never do: they would never sign a Communist membership card, a petition, or anything else that officially connected them to the Communist Party. A signed document was all the FBI needed to throw you in jail or even throw you out of the country. Signing a Party document was like signing your own death warrant.

Their charade continued as Milo was elected leader of Local 1389. By then, Frankie had made it all the way to the top – he was elected president of the national organization, the International AEWA. No one knew or even suspected the truth, that two non-Communists were now leading one of the most-fervently Red unions in the country. One of them might have gotten away with it, but not both of them. The truth had to come out. Ironically, it was Frankie who blew the whistle on himself.

Headlines tore across the country on the day Frankie announced that he was leaving his job as union president: "AEWA Prexy Bolts, Vows to Fight Reds with New Union." Frankie met with reporters the next day.

"My heart is first with my country which is why I can no longer represent an organization whose first allegiance is to Russia – a dictatorship sworn to overthrowing the nation I love. I hope my union brothers and sisters can see the truth and will follow me out of the AEWA."

It was for God and country, Frankie declared. It was also for the FBI and a federal grand jury.

The Justice Department was holding a perjury indictment over Pepper – charges that he had filed a false declaration with the National Labor Relations Board. Under federal law, union leaders had to swear that they were not members of the Communist Party. He may not have had a Party membership card, but there were plenty of ex-Communists who would testify that Frankie Pepper was fiercely loyal to the Party. Frankie was a Red, whether he liked it or not.

Through with this double life, Pepper moved back to Schenectady, vowing to take back the union at G.E. So far, there weren't many takers. Schenectady was still Milo's town.

Frankie lit another cigar as he thought about Milo, that little faker, strutting around with his ridiculous pompadour and his fat, Commie wife. He wondered if Milo knew the truth about his marriage to the "Red Flame of New York" – how it was Frankie who arranged their first meeting and how he pushed Milo into proposing to Martha. It was just another favor to the Communists. Another step up the union ladder for Frankie.

It had also helped Milo, of course. If he had not married Martha, the Communists would never have made Milo the boss of Local 1389. And still he puts up with that Commie nonsense!

"Oh, what is he waiting for?" Martha got no answer from the mirror. It had been more than two years since Martha discovered Milo's secret plans – his plot to reawaken Communism in Schenectady. Two years! For all that time, Martha had carefully stayed behind the scenes, steering Helen's ambitions and the activities of the Social Awareness Committee, all the time waiting for Milo to confide in her – to bring the Red Flame of New York into the fight! Back into the limelight! Still, after all this time, Milo never said a word. This was all so confusing to Martha.

Surely, Milo must know what I have been doing – how I've guided young Helen and helped her reignite the Communist fervor in Schenectady? How can he be so selfish, getting me to do all of his work and never once thanking me? Where was the gratitude? Where was the credit?

Where was the adoration?

Enough of this, Martha decided. I'm tired of waiting for Milo! Tired of waiting for my trip to Russia! Tired of asking, when will it be MY turn again?

Martha rolled herself across the bed. The clock said 7:45. Milo was out of town on business, Michael was locked away in his room, and Helen was meeting with the Young Communists Club at Union College. They were organizing another night of bowling or ping pong or whatever the hell they were planning.

Was anyone planning something for Martha?!

Ping pong nights – how ridiculous, Martha fumed. As a matter of fact, how were bowling leagues and bake sales going to overthrow Capitalism? How do we defeat the industrial pigs, the war instigators, and their base agents with puppet shows on television? Martha grew angrier the more she thought about it. Angrier at Milo! Angrier at Helen – especially with Helen!

What would the Party think if they knew what was going on here? Using the Party's treasury on beer and pretzels. No Revolution was ever born from such fluff and nonsense! This was all Helen's fault! There must be an accounting for all of her ridiculous actions!

Following the Party orthodoxy – never wavering left or right – that is the most important responsibility of any Party member. It takes courage – the courage to do what must be done, regardless of the consequences!

Things had to be put right, Martha vowed, and she was the only one who could do it!

Vigilance!

Martha got on the phone to Camp Unity.

"Comrade Petrov? This is Martha Milwaukee – in Schenectady. You will not be happy to hear what I have to tell you."

"I would prefer, if you would allow me, not to mention other people's names. Don't present me with the choice of either being in contempt of Congress and going to jail or forcing me to really crawl through the mud to be an informer."
HOLLYWOOD WRITER LARRY PARKS *testifying before*
the House Committee on Un-American Activities

C H A P T E R   T H I R T Y - T W O

A WHOLE LOT OF TROUBLE

Milo needed a new plan. Michael had been treating him like a stranger ever since he found that magazine at the barbershop and it was the magazine that got Milo thinking: Would Congressman Brownale fulfill his promise from all those years ago? Would he help Milo break from the Communists? Milo traveled to Washington to see whether C.B. Brownale would be true to his word.

In the shadow of the Capitol, there stood a decrepit gardening shack, listing to one side. A hand-painted sign above the cracked, dirt-covered door read, "Congressional Maintenance Facility." As he had been instructed, Milo pulled on the door – it was heavier than he expected – and peered inside the shed. Rakes and shovels were propped against bags of grass seed and fertilizers. Still, something seemed out of place. As Milo's eyes adjusted to the dim light, he noticed that this maintenance shack was remarkably clean and tidy. That's when he spotted the large Marine standing at attention six feet away.

"Take this across the street," said the guard, handing Milo a red and white tag with the number 139 stamped on it. The guard pointed Milo back toward the Capitol building.

The sunshine was gleaming off the Capitol dome as Milo pushed his way through a hedgerow along the northeast side of the building. There he found a long, metal staircase leading to an elevator loading dock. Milo pushed the button and the floor began to shake. As the doors opened, Milo was pulled inside by a rush of air. Without pressing another button – because there were no buttons to press – the elevator car descended six floors below the House of Representatives. When the doors opened again, Milo found himself inside a shimmering white hospital ward.

Milo stopped one of the nurses, "Pardon me, but I'm here to see Congressman Brownale." The nurse handed Milo a hospital gown, along with a cap, mask, gloves, and, finally, slippers to cover his shoes. Now wrapped in sterile cotton, Milo was led down a wide hallway, passing doors numbered in red and others in blue. The nurse stopped at number 139.

"A Republican, right?" the nurse asked. Milo nodded. She motioned for Milo to pull up his mask, but when the nurse opened the door, Milo found himself covering his eyes from the piercing white light. He stepped cautiously into a room crisscrossed with intravenous tubes, catheters, inhalation bags, gauges, and monitors buzzing and beeping as doctors, nurses and hospital technicians moved busily around the room. Between the sporadic chirps and pings of the instruments, there was a heavy, almost mechanical sound of someone breathing. Milo moved toward the noise before he was cut off by a tall, young man wearing an oxygen mask as large as a diving helmet. Through the glass, Milo could see the concern on the young man's face.

"You can't be here very long," said the hollow voice echoing inside the helmet. "The Congressman is not well."

"Are you his doctor?" Milo asked.

"No, I'm the Congressman's Chief of Staff. Stay here, please." The Chief of Staff turned on his heel and walked toward the congressman's bed. Milo stayed behind as medical personnel raced about the room. Milo had never seen so much health care in one place before.

"Perhaps I should come back at another time?" Milo asked, but the Chief of Staff waved him forward.

The aide whispered, "Remember – he doesn't have much time."

When Milo's eyes grew wide in surprise, the Chief of Staff apologized. "I meant he only has a minute before he's scheduled to vote. Please be brief."

Milo was incredulous. "Vote? Can he even walk?"

"For now, we use one of these." The Chief of Staff pointed to a wheelchair that was wrapped inside a large wooden desk. The desk was an exact replica of the desks used by congressmen in the House chamber six floors up.

"We call it Portability. It's going to be the next big thing in health care. All the members have them."

"There are more congressmen down here?" Milo asked.

"Many of them are quite elderly and the government recognizes the value of a robust health care system. With today's technology, House members can survive – I mean, serve – their constituents for as long as medical science will allow. The only term limits down here are the ones up there." The Chief of Staff pointed his thumb toward the ceiling. "He's ready for you now."

The nurses and technicians stepped away and then, finally, a makeup artist made room for Milo to approach. There was Congressman Brownale, his face and body pierced by the tentacles of a dozen medical devices. It might have been the makeup, but Milo had to admit, Congressman Brownale looked pretty good for a man in his condition.

He's probably better off than I am right now, Milo told himself.

"Hello Congressman," Milo smiled. When the Congressman didn't respond, Milo spoke a little louder. "Do you remember me, sir?"

"Of course I do," Brownale growled. "And stop shouting at me. I'm old, not deaf!"

"I'm sorry you're not feeling well."

"What's that?"

"I said, *I'M SORRY –*" Milo got the joke as he saw the Congressman smiling back at him.

"You haven't lost your sense of humor."

"Young man, I never had a sense of humor," Brownale said soberly. "I just have a good sense of what's foolish in the world. You should too – a smart guy like you, running around with those juvenile Communists, conspiring in their ridiculous, secret meetings. Talking about peace and love one minute and the next minute, they're planning to blow up the banks and overthrow the government! Infantile nonsense! It would be pathetic if it weren't so dangerous. I understand that things have gotten worse for you lately."

"That may have been my fault."

"Damn right, it's your fault."

"I thought if the members could see how crazy the Reds are then maybe they would throw them out of the Local."

"Mr. Milwaukee, please. Save the theatrics for us politicians."

"I guess I'm also worried about McCarthy."

"You should be. He's a wild man. Completely unpredictable – except for the headlines he gets every day. He's so big now, he's practically running the government!"

"But he hasn't done anything!"

"When has that ever mattered? This is Washington, for God's sake!"

Congressman Brownale signaled for a nurse. She brought an oxygen mask up to his face and, after three deep breaths, the congressman sat up in his bed.

"Well, you should be worried, especially about McCarthy. People think he'll be president one day. Not me. I know what makes him run and it's not the White House. Joe McCarthy needs only three things: a generous bottle of gin, a well-done steak, and a woman with nothing to lose but her dress. Believe me, he won't last – men like him never do. But he's still got a few more years left in him, the lucky son-of-a-bitch, and that could be trouble for you, Mr. Milwaukee. So you'd better think of something fast, otherwise, Joe McCarthy will be riding up to Schenectady with all those television cameras and his big bag of shit and it's all going to fall on you and the boys at G.E. What's Philip Reedy going to do then?"

Brownale rested his head back against his pillow and closed his eyes.

Is that it? Milo panicked. It looked like the congressman was falling asleep – or worse! Milo leaned over the bed. "Do you remember what you told me all those years ago – after the hearing? You said I should never trust anyone in a room full of Commies and that if I ever needed a way out, I could call on you for help. That's why I'm here today. I need your help."

Brownale frowned. He did not like to be reminded of promises he never expected to keep. "Let me ask you something and I want the truth: Are you prepared to do whatever is necessary to get rid of those Reds? I mean, for good?"

"Yes, I really am. I've been trying for years and I know it's going to happen sooner or later. I don't want to lose control of the Local when it does."

Brownale smiled. "And what about your wife?"

"Martha's out of that business."

"Are you sure about that? Because what I'm going to suggest is going to get some people – possibly friends of hers – into a whole lot of trouble. Very serious legal trouble. Disloyalty is a crime, and some people will have to be sacrificed if you and your union are going to survive."

Milo did not hesitate. Yes, he nodded.

"Then I have something in mind." Brownale gestured to his Chief of Staff. "Percy, get a message to my son. Tell him to meet Mr. Milwaukee as soon as possible. Milo, my son Henry can help you. I would do more if I could, but right now – " With that, the congressman lay back against his pillow and closed his eyes. The Chief of Staff tugged at Milo's elbow. It was time to go.

As Milo left the room, he turned back to see Congressman Brownale being lifted off the bed and wrapped in a hospital gown – a gown, that from a distance, resembled a crisp suit and necktie. Then his aides slipped Brownale into the wheelchair made to look like a Congressional desk.

Milo stepped into the hall where a red light was flashing on the ceiling: it was time for the congressmen to vote. The hallway quickly filled with hospital orderlies pushing other congressmen in their wheelchair-desks. C. B. Brownale gave a "thumbs up" as he wheeled past Milo.

When the hallway was clear, Milo rode up to the hearing room where he had testified all those years ago. Everyone in the union had praised his performance that day: Milo stood up to Brownale's questioning. He refused to save his own skin. Milo would not give in.

That Milo, he's okay!

Milo looked at the empty witness table, remembering how lonely it felt to be up there alone surrounded by the cameras and the accusations. Then it suddenly hit him: it was going to be different this time. He was going to have to sacrifice some members of the Local if he was going to get rid of the Communists. Milo would have to choose someone to turn in. How many Communists would he have to expose? Would Martha be one of them?

He tried to push the idea aside, but Milo knew it was inevitable. After all these years – after all the pretending and the hiding and the lying – Milo Milwaukee was going to be naming names.

Dr. Parker: Jim, it's only the beginning.

Jungle Jim: You mean we've got to do this all over again?

Dr. Parker: Not right away, but at other times, in other places — wherever free men seek the weapons of peace.

BATTLING COMMUNIST SPIES, "Jungle Jim" (Johnny Weismuller) convinces island natives to leave their homes so America can test an atomic bomb. ✱ *1953 motion picture, Savage Mutiny*

CHAPTER THIRTY-THREE

SECOND BANANA NO MORE

"It's a fraud, really. Everyone knows it. Honestly, how can any legitimate government declare itself unfriendly to bananas – in Guatemala, for heaven's sake!"

Henry nodded again, at least he tried to. In the stifling heat of the jungle, Henry's head flopped back and then forward again as if it were coming unhinged. It was even harder to keep his eyes open as Durston, this PR man for American Banana, kept on yammering.

"You know these Communists, Henry. They're all the same, really. The Russians, the Chinese – even these local boys. All the same. The problem isn't revolution – it's evolution! They are mere savages, let me tell you. It wasn't so long ago when they would just as soon eat you as shake your hand. And now they want to run a government?"

"Hmmm?" Henry grunted as his head bounced up again.

"And for what?" Durston continued. "All they're really looking for is a chance to muck things up – especially a successful commercial venture like ours! Pour on the petrol, light the match and call it progress! 'Look here, good people: We bring you fire! You'll be warm tonight, but you'll have no job come the morning!' No plantation means no plantation jobs, am I right, Henry? No picky, no money! Henry – ?"

Henry could not stay awake. His head was throbbing from the sweltering humidity and Durston's ceaseless droning, pushing Henry further into this tropical stupor.

Durston had been the first person Henry met upon his arrival in Guatemala and, in all that time, this company shill had stopped talking only long enough to catch a hurried breath and flash that smarmy, company smile. Durston was like a human metronome: speak, smile, repeat. Even the flies were snoozing on Henry's shoulders.

Suddenly, Durston launched himself down on the bench next to Henry. "Keep sharp there, old boy!" Shoving an elbow into Henry's ribs, Durston said, "It's nearly three o'clock, you know! I appreciate you seeing me off and all, but I can't have you falling asleep on me. Here – have a banana."

Henry waved the fruit away. Bananas had once been the only thing Henry could eat but now he couldn't stand the smell of them. Durston tried to cheer Henry up with another performance of his "trick" – thrusting an entire banana into his mouth and then withdrawing just the peel. Swatting at the flies, Henry was not amused.

Disappointed, Durston tossed the wet peel over his shoulder and onto the stacks of hard, green fruit that were ready for shipment to America. While the bananas were headed for groceries up and down the East Coast, Durston was off to Dayton, Ohio and the headquarters of American Banana. He would have little progress to report: The Communists – or so they were labeled by the company – had seized control of the Guatemalan government and its new president was now threatening to nationalize the plantations and packing operations of American Banana. In response, the American government launched "Operation Slippery Peel," a CIA operation to overthrow the Guatemalan regime and install puppets with friendlier strings.

Henry Brownale was one of the hundreds of CIA agents sent to South America. After failing in Cleveland, then in Berlin and finally as Volga the Boatman, Henry's punishment was this posting in Guatemala.

Durston was peeling another banana when he flew to his feet. "Oh my goodness, Henry!"

Henry was off the bench in less than a second. Tarantulas were known to hide among the bananas and Henry was sure that something must have crawled onto Durston.

"Sorry to startle you, old man, but I was told to give you this message. Straight from Washington they told me. Completely slipped my mind."

As Durston pulled his hand from out of his vest pocket, Henry's eyes locked onto a small, cream-colored envelope. He immediately recognized the Congressional seal embossed on the envelope and his father's name on the back. Snatching the note from Durston's hand, Henry gave only a passing notice to the long, hairy leg – thick and muscular – that was reaching over Durston's shoulder. That leg was followed by other prickly tendrils, each connected to a round body that was large enough to be served at Wimbledon. Silent and graceful, the tarantula continued over Durston's shoulder and down his arm. By then, Henry was already on his feet, walking briskly toward the airfield as he ripped open his father's message.

"Come home at once," the congressman had written. "You are needed in Schenectady. Urgent – Reds must be stopped! Further instructions upon arrival. Your father – C.B."

Dropping the note onto the airport tarmac, Henry jumped onto the gangway – leaping for joy! – and the next flight home.

Goodbye Guatemala! Henry Brownale was off to Schenectady, N.Y. for redemption, for more of his father's approval and, finally, for a chance to defeat some Communists. Henry was not looking back – even when Durston's screams echoed across the jungle.

> "It was a little thick to hear administration spokesmen denounce Senator McCarthy for imputing guilt by association when the loyalty boards, operating under a presidential order, had for two and a half years, been condemning men on grounds of 'sympathetic association' with organizations arbitrarily called 'subversive' by the attorney general."
>
> *THE LOYALTY OF FREE MEN,* 1951 ✳ BY ALAN BARTH

CHAPTER THIRTY-FOUR

ONE WEEK LATER AT THE SCHENECTADY
County Loyalty Board

On Hoover's orders, Special Agent Walter Thurston was back before the Loyalty Board. This time, he was carrying a single envelope.

"Gentleman, I have a message from the highest authority. In this envelope is a photograph that will have great importance to loyal Americans here in Schenectady."

As Thurston tipped over the envelope, two female legs appeared and then the rest of Martha Milwaukee slid onto the table. It was a picture from Madison Square Garden when a younger Martha – wearing her tightest and reddest dress – was holding out her arms to embrace her fans at a raucous union rally. Off to one side of the stage, a man stood transfixed, his mouth agape and his eyes busting out of his head, like he was gawking at a movie star. Martha was all of that and so much more.

"Holy moly – who is that?" gushed Charlie Gaynor.

"That, Mr. Chairman, is none other than Mrs. Milo Milwaukee!"

"Really!" said Montgomery Hughie. "I never would have guessed it. I mean – look at her! She's … she's – "

"A knockout!" said the Bishop. He quickly marked the sign of the cross and the others followed.

Agent Thurston smiled. "In those days, she was known as the Red Flame of New York. Since moving to Schenectady, she has been out of the public limelight, but, in all honesty gentlemen, we still consider her to be as dangerous as a four-alarm fire. In fact, there is considerable evidence linking her to the recent spate of Communist activity here in Schenectady."

"What do you want us to do?" Hughie asked.

Thurston looked gravely at the Loyalty Board. "Gentlemen, it is now High Noon at the OK Corral. For a job like this, you have got to bring in a big gun."

"A big gun?" Charlie asked.

"The biggest," Thurston replied.

A reverent hush fell upon the Loyalty Board as a single name echoed around the room: *McCarthy*!

"Some people have the idea that a YCLer is political minded, that nothing outside of politics means anything. Gosh no. They have a few simple problems. There is the problem of getting good men on the baseball team this spring, of opposition from ping-pong teams, of dating girls, etc. We go to shows, parties, dances, and all that. In short, the YCL and its members are no different from other people except that we believe in dialectical materialism as a solution to all problems."

RECRUITMENT PAMPHLET FOR THE YOUNG COMMUNIST LEAGUE

CHAPTER THIRTY-FIVE

THAT SAME DAY IN A DOWNTOWN ALLEY

Helen was gluing posters on the buildings downtown when she heard a familiar voice calling from the alley.

"*Excuse me, Miss. Where can poor man get bowl of soup?*"

"*PETROV!*" exclaimed Helen, throwing her arms around his rumpled beard. "*What are you doing here? I am so happy to see you! I want you to see all the things we are doing!*"

"*Shush, little one!*" said Petrov, pulling Helen off the street and down into the alley. "*I have heard what you are doing. So I have come to see for myself.*"

He took a poster out of Helen's hands.

"*What is this? 'Come One, Come All to the Hootenanny for Peace!' Well, well, well.*"

Petrov threw the poster into the snow and grabbed Helen's sleeve – hard – jerking her farther into the alley.

"*Petrov, what is the mat-* ?" Before Helen could finish her question, everything went white. The blow from Petrov's hand came from over Helen's shoulder, slamming against the side of her head. Staggering from the shock and pain, Helen tried to hold herself against the brick wall as Petrov lunged toward her. Again he slapped her, this time across the face, sending her backward into the snow. Helen raised her hands to deflect the next blow as Petrov pulled Helen off the ground and pinned her against the wall. The tiny eyes that had once delighted Helen now burned with insane fury.

"*Petrov don't!*" Helen pleaded, straining to pull away from him. She kept her voice low, not wanting to draw anyone's attention. "*Tell me what I have done? Please Petrov. Listen to me – everything ees okay!*"

Mocking her pleas, Petrov smiled viciously, "*No, everything ees not okay! You think we trained you for this – hootenannies and puppet shows? Dancing clowns on the television? Bowling parties for ignorant workers? This ees what Party money has been buying – singing songs and making beer?*"

Helen slid to her knees, holding her head against the pain, as Petrov stepped back, seeming to calm himself. He put his hands into his pockets and glanced down the alley toward the empty street. Seeing no one, Petrov charged at Helen again, his hands coiled to strike. Helen covered her face with both hands until Petrov pulled them apart, pressing his savage face against her skull.

"*This ees not what we want, Comrade Gamble! You have failed us!*" Petrov reached back and smacked Helen across her nose. Her eyes went white as blood splattered across the wall.

"I'm so sorry! Please! Please!" begged Helen, trying not to cry. "What do you want me to do? Tell me!" Helen's face was numb, her head throbbing in pain. Her Russian accent was gone.

She was certain that Petrov was not finished. Helen tried to escape but all she could do was crawl toward the street, pushing her knees through the icy slush. Petrov's boots stepped in front of her, and Helen collapsed into the snow, sobbing.

"For now – enough!" Petrov smiled as he lifted Helen onto her feet. His voice was gentle again. *"You made many terrible mistakes, Comrade Gamble, and now you have been taught harsh lesson. You will not forget this day. You must remind yourself of all the things we have taught you. Always you will be vigilant and remember: The Party must come first. Not soup kitchens and bowling parties. Do not disobey me, Comrade, or there will be much worse for you to come."*

Petrov released his hands from Helen's shoulders and she fell to her knees. Pressing herself against the brick wall, Helen curled into a ball, praying that Petrov would walk away.

"ARE YOU LISTENING?" Petrov growled, grabbing Helen's hair and dragging her through the snow. Near the street, Petrov pushed Helen's face against the frozen wall and, with a wave of his finger, he instructed her to stand still. Helen struggled to keep from crying, knowing that any noise might spark another beating.

"Who ees out there?" Petrov commanded as he straightened his hat and smoothed the creases of his coat. Helen shook her head – no one was nearby. Petrov took one step onto the sidewalk before he wheeled around and jabbed his finger into Helen's face.

"Be ready for my next visit, Comrade Gamble! I expect great changes when I return. Do not fail me again."

Petrov disappeared around the corner and Helen fainted into the snow. The sky was turning dark when she was jolted awake by the sound of a dog sniffing at her shoes.

"No, no, no!" Helen shouted, pushing herself away from the shadowy figure. Her head was stinging and her nose caked with blood. The frightened dog whimpered away as Helen pushed herself up and onto her feet. She slid roughly along the alley wall, stumbling over the paste bucket and posters scattered in the snow.

Find your way home, she told herself, lurching forward in the dark. Just make it home.

And then what? Should she tell Milo what happened? Was he in danger too – and what about Martha? She must talk to Martha, Helen decided, never suspecting that it was Martha who had betrayed her.

Martha will know what to do, Helen told herself. Martha will know. Until then, I must be more vigilant.

"Joe couldn't find a Communist in Red Square — he didn't know Karl Marx from Groucho — but he was a United States senator. Talking to Joe was like putting your hands in a bowl full of mush."

"I'd call up Joe and say, 'This was in the Milwaukee Journal, is this what you said? 'Sure,' Joe would say, 'I'll say that for you, or do you want me to say something else? Tell me what you want and I'll say it.'"

Former newspaper reporters who covered McCarthy
JOE MCCARTHY AND THE PRESS BY EDWIN R. BAYLEY

CHAPTER THIRTY-SIX

MAY 2, 1953

Fifty-seven passengers, four motormen, one conductor, and three Pullman porters were riding the Empire Limited as it pulled out of Union Station and rolled north to New York. The passengers had different reasons for leaving Washington, traveling to divergent destinations and, like the train crew, most were leading unexceptional lives. They were the same as people all around the world. Whether they were riding in first class or coach, every one of them was a liar.

There were storytellers and embellishers, tax cheats and wife deceivers, job-seeking equivocators, false witnesses, con artists, misleaders, broad-brushers, swindlers, plagiarists, piecemealers, phonies, mixers, perjurers, assumers, bigots, bamboozlers, tricksters, and plain old fibbers. There also was an economist and a meteorologist. They got paid for lying.

They had lied to themselves, to their husbands or wives, mothers and fathers, sisters and brothers, grandparents, cousins, bosses, subordinates, police officers, judges, neighbors, sons and daughters, to the rich and to the poor, to friends and, most of all, to strangers. They were human and they were good at it.

A lie can be the dawn of a new day, a lover's promise, a story at bedtime, and it will nearly always work because somebody, somewhere, is forever willing to take it – and they will probably take it again tomorrow.

For some, lying is just good business, starting with "Honestly" and ending with a firm handshake. "Take it to the bank. You can count on me!" Eye to eye, lie to lie.

Among the repeat offenders, lying is simply easier than telling the truth. After enough lies, the truth can feel unnatural and there is always a good excuse for avoiding it. What's true can be too complicated or too simple or simply inconvenient. Or boring. Life is never boring for someone who lies.

While commerce depends on it and politics thrives on it, there was one man on the Empire Limited who had built his entire career upon it. When it came to lying, Senator Joseph R. McCarthy was the Undisputed Heavyweight Champion of the World and, in the spring of 1953, he was still standing, bruised but eternally undefeated. The chicken farmer from Grand Chute, Wisconsin was proof that anything is possible and, if you say it often enough, people will believe almost everything you tell them. They will trust you. They will vote for you. They will make you a star.

But every star must fade and a black hole awaits even the brightest stars. Joe McCarthy was heading for his. But the inevitable never interested Joe McCarthy. He could barely see beyond his dinner that night. This train ride to Schenectady was no different. McCarthy did not reflect on his stardom or the possibility of his mortality. He was thinking of only one thing – Martha Milwaukee. Until he got to Schenectady – until he had her in his bed – Joe McCarthy would do what he enjoyed doing most and that was being Joe McCarthy.

America's most-flamboyant politician was holding court in the train's Club Car, one leg stretched across a table, a drink in one hand, and the Daily Racing Form in the other. There was no need for a crown or scepter because there was no question about who was the King here. All eyes were on Joe.

He leaned back and blew smoke rings over the heads of the reporters. (He was very good at blowing smoke at reporters and over most everyone else.) Traveling with the press – "his boys," McCarthy would chirp – made Joe feel like a winner. It was just like the old times and it had not felt that way for most of the past year. Joe McCarthy, the people's champion, was starting to lose his punch.

Among the reporters, even those regulars who had stuck with Joe from the beginning, only a few had agreed to take this long trip north. Most would be getting off in New York City. No one wanted to ride all the way to Upstate New York – what was the point? Three years ago – even a year ago – any self-respecting newshound would have jumped at the chance to be close to Joe, watching him carve up some hapless Red and leave them crying and twitching in the witness chair. Not anymore. It wasn't fun anymore. It wasn't news anymore.

Same smoke, smaller fire.

An old joke among reporters is "You don't let the facts get in the way of a good story" and for a long time Joe McCarthy had been a very, very good story. He was such a big story that he had become his own "beat." Newspapers and magazines were assigning a reporter – sometimes two – just to birddog McCarthy wherever he went. Their only job was to report on every crazy thing Joe said or did as McCarthy scoured the Earth for Communist spies, hidden pinkos, and their fellow travelers.

By 1953, it had become routine, like ringing a dinner bell. Feeding time, boys! All McCarthy had to do was open his yap and the press guys, acting more like stenographers than reporters, would write down every word he said. Sometimes they would even fill in the blanks when Joe wasn't able to make his point with the usual McCarthy flourish or when his "facts" did not square with reality. Everybody wanted a good story, so some of the press guys would help Joe be Joe.

After all, McCarthy was a United States Senator and he was chasing the repugnant Communist scourge – what more do you need to know? His office and this crusade gave Joe instant credibility, at least enough to get him into the papers. Day after day.

Once he took off on his Red Scare campaign, the McCarthy beat was a breeze, a guaranteed ticket to the front page. You might even get the "Wood" – a headline so large that they used huge blocks of wood for each letter on the print press.

So everybody was a winner: the reporters, the papers and, of course, Joe himself – slayer of the fearsome Communist dragon. If only he could find the darn thing! Joe was very good at searching for Commies, but he was not so good at finding them.

Sure, there were days when it was only Joe being Joe, hollering about Communists here and Commies there. And it was hard not to smile when McCarthy was carrying on about this great national peril when he was only questioning an obscure government librarian or another fourth-tier bureaucrat. Still, this was considered front page news because Joe McCarthy, when he was at the top of his game, was Barnum and Bailey and Harry Houdini all rolled into one – a three-ring circus under the Big Top capped by another miraculous escape from the truth.

Even when he was caught in a lie, Joe would simply top it with a taller tale, calling reporters late in the evening, just before their deadlines, with some fantastic, unprovable news – too late to verify the facts, but too juicy to pass up. It was always great theater and who doesn't want a good story?

A lie can stretch around the world, but it cannot last forever. For all of his bluster and noisy investigations, Joe McCarthy had yet to uncover the Great Communist Plot. Not even a small one. Joe was still ringing the dinner bell, but by 1953, fewer reporters were willing to answer it. Pavlov's dogs would have been better at sniffing out Communists.

Increasingly, the reporters and their editors were having their doubts about old Joe and his flamboyant claims. They kept those suspicions to themselves, seldom questioning McCarthy about his flimsy accusations. So the McCarthy headlines continued to roll off the presses.

In the time it takes most senators to pass their first bill, the press had made Joe McCarthy a media sensation and a national political heavyweight. More than a few senators now owed their seats to Joe's intervention just before Election Day. In some parts of the world people wondered, with more than a little shock, whether this reckless loudmouth might be the most-powerful politician in America.

Joe had become so big so fast it was hard to remember that it all started in such a small way, at a sleepy luncheon of meatloaf and a medley of garden vegetables served to the Republican Women's Club of Wheeling, West Virginia. They were a ripe assortment of blue hair, grapefruits, gravy, and biscuits. Only a couple of reporters were in the room that day because the chance of anything getting into the paper depended more on the meatloaf catching fire than what this junior senator might say at the annual Lincoln Day address.

They figured wrong.

Forkfuls of peach cobbler were suspended in midair and excited glances moved around the room as this burly, young legislator stood bug-eyed at the podium, hollering about "enemies from within" and how "the god of war" was spreading across the world "all the way from the Indochina hills." The ladies who lunched were not expecting so much passion and urgency from their monthly speaker. It was so much more exciting than their previous meeting when the local Fire Chief had discussed fire safety and cotton knitting materials. This speaker actually brought the fire!

"I hold in my hand the names of 205 Communists," McCarthy shouted, waving something – a list? – but only for a moment before it disappeared into his pocket. That's when the roller coaster began. As soon as McCarthy left the podium, news of his speech was picked up by a few radio stations and then the small-town papers before it reached the national wires. The news was sensational: Joe McCarthy had a list of Communists secretly working inside the U.S. State Department! This was treason and everyone wanted to know more.

The young senator did not make that easy. Any time a reporter got too close or asked too many questions, McCarthy's "list" was quickly tucked away. The mystery grew as fast as the news. Soon, Joe McCarthy was on the front page of every newspaper in the country – radio and television stations, too.

As Joe told and retold his story, those "205 Communists" steadily shrank until the number dropped to 57. Years later, the reporters who knew him best figured that Joe had settled on 57 because that was the number on his favorite bottle of ketchup. It was just another thing to love about Joe McCarthy, like all of the stories they would joke about, especially the ones they never printed: about the crazy nights of booze and broads, staying out past dawn, the Bloody Marys at breakfast. All of it made the press guys want to be around Joe and he wanted to be around them.

So the boys piled onto the train for one more ride with Joe:

To where – Schenectady? What the hell is in Schenectady? I'll jump off in New York, check in with the desk and then catch the next train back to D.C. We can leave Schenectady to the wires. Not much chance of news happening up there anyway. Where is it – a mile from the Canadian border? Joe will have a better chance trapping a beaver than catching any Communists.

Until they got to New York, Joe would take care of everything else. As the night stretched into the morning, Joe kept the alcohol flowing and the conversation lively.

Deal the cards. Come on, let's have another round.

They liked the guy, some even felt sorry for him. He had been good to them for so long, it was sad to see it end like this. They knew the real Joe – not the guy everyone attacked as a demagogue and a thug. Joe McCarthy was actually a helluva nice guy – even when he was accusing the press of working for the Kremlin. That was just part of his shtick, the press guys would say with a nod and a wink.

Did you see him after that one hearing where the woman was bawling her eyes out and screaming for Joe to leave her husband alone? Well, what does Joe do after the hearing? He invites the two of them out to dinner – the lady and her husband! McCarthy had just called her every name in the book and she had thrown it right back at him and now Joe was offering to take them out for a steak! She couldn't believe the guy! But that was Joe: A typical politician. He just wanted to be liked by everybody, even a Communist.

After building him up for all these years, now the press was taking him down – slowly. It should have happened long before this, but no reporter had ever written the whole story of Joe McCarthy, about his half-truths and outright lies, the phony histrionics and, worst of all, his dirty, distorted accusations. Newspapers crave something new, something different, and what was missing now was the news. It wasn't there anymore. The Great Red Hunter was shrinking right in front of their eyes, inch by column inch. The headlines got smaller and the stories grew shorter until they dropped off the front page and now they were moving farther back into the paper, closer to the funny papers and then the obituaries.

Still, McCarthy could not stop his "crusade" any more than he could stop being himself. He would always be the loudmouth, tough-talking Marine. He had been doing it his way since he was first elected a county judge, long before he connived his way into the United States Senate. Now he was "Tailgunner Joe," the big-hearted Irishman who cared more about his country than he did about the details. Take no prisoners, leave the facts behind.

With or without the press, Joe McCarthy could not be measured in headlines or news bulletins. He was that unquantifiable commodity of American culture – he was a celebrity. He was electric. People could only wish they were Joe McCarthy, even for one day, and Joe McCarthy was determined to take every day he was given.

On the train to Schenectady, McCarthy pretended not to care about the feckless press or what those big shots in Washington truly thought about him. He just wanted to enjoy this train ride, secretly anticipating his liaison with the Red Flame of New York. Besides, he liked having the boys around, even if they were only stopping in New York. He was still King of the Club Car.

The party might have been smaller, but it continued throughout the night until the Empire Limited bumped and rocked its way into Upstate New York, past the farm fields and small towns; the small people flying by the window. Joe McCarthy put his hat over his face and fell into a deep sleep, dreaming of Martha Milwaukee as he fondled her picture in the warmth of his pants pocket.

Her dewy image cradled Joe during his nervous, fitful slumbers, shielding him from the constant nightmares he had been suffering of radiating hydrogen bombs, his face melting through his fingers, running blindly from the terrible secret that only he knew – the biggest lie in the unimaginable life and legend of Joe McCarthy.

"I don't care how high pitched becomes the screaming and squealing of the left wing elements of press and radio … as long as I am in the Senate, this task is not going to become a dainty task. If lumberjack tactics are the only kind of tactics that crowd understands, then take my word for it, those are the kinds of tactics we're going to use on them."
SENATOR JOSEPH MCCARTHY *on Feb. 23, 1952, defending his rough methods*

"Nobody loves Joe but the pee-pul."
SONG OF SUPPORT *among McCarthy boosters*

CHAPTER THIRTY-SEVEN

HEAL MY CAT!

Everyone – even the Communists – wanted a look at Joe McCarthy. Nothing this intriguing had come through Schenectady since a two-headed bear was hauled down the tracks for a permanent exhibition at the State Museum. At every stop, that train and its smelly caboose attracted hundreds of hunters, taxidermists, and other curious onlookers. But the two-headed bear never drew a crowd like the one that came out for Joe McCarthy, the two-faced politician.

Every Republican in the region, along with some vote-hungry Democrats, packed themselves onto the train platform in downtown Schenectady, back-slapping and elbowing each other for a photo with Tailgunner Joe: your patriotism certified in an 8-by-10 glossy. At least everyone assumed that Joe McCarthy would be standing on the platform. Only the men on the Empire Limited knew differently.

As the train arced away from the Hudson River, chugging west from Albany to Schenectady, McCarthy's men were already at work. They had less than an hour to perform another Resurrection. Like a dead bear, McCarthy was out cold, having passed out somewhere north of Poughkeepsie. To wake him, McCarthy's team usually started with a cold, wet towel before moving onto several hard slaps to the face. When there was too little time – or when McCarthy had consumed too much booze – the staff would dress and shave him while he slept. Even on a moving train, shaving that steel-wool beard was easier than getting McCarthy dressed. It was like pulling clothes onto a big bag of rocks.

When the package was finally complete and the train was entering the station, it was time to get the Senator into position. Grabbing legs and arms, his hat and his head, McCarthy's men carried him out of the first class coach, shuffling quickly past the sleeper berths and over the heads of the Club Car diners before adjusting him vertically behind the exit door. A pie-stained tie was thrown around his neck as two men crouched behind McCarthy, holding him in place, as the train door was opened and the crowd went wild.

"Mr. McCarthy! Mr. McCarthy!" A woman holding a cat pushed her way to the front of the crowd. "Please Senator – the poor dear is not well! Please Senator, heal my cat!"

Blinking in surprise, McCarthy leaned heavily against the train car door. "I am sorry, madam, but I am afraid I cannot assist you in this endeavor. For I firmly believe, strongly, that no feline is worth saving. Cats are the Communists of the animal kingdom! They are lazy, disloyal, and forever waiting for a handout. One more shall not be missed." Before his staff could pull him back, McCarthy took hold of the cat.

"You know what I think?" he shouted to the crowd. "I think everyone should have a dog because dogs are trustworthy and loyal. Dogs are true-blue Americans!" Raising the cat over his head, McCarthy shouted, "There's only one thing we should do with cats and that's feed 'em to the dogs!"

The cheering suddenly stopped and the "Welcome Joe" banners sagged a little as McCarthy's men sprang into action. Grabbing the cat and cueing the band to play a Sousa march, they shoved the senator into a waiting car and hit the gas.

"What did I say?" McCarthy pleaded. "It was only a cat!"

McCarthy's men sped around the block before stopping at the rear entrance of the Hotel Van Arsdale. As soon as the bottles of booze and trays of food arrived from room service, the door to the Presidential suite was locked for the night. It was 8:30 the next morning when Donald "Duck" Robertson, McCarthy's chief investigator, answered a heavy knock on the door. It was Chief Inspector Wotan Volk reporting for duty.

It would be Volk's job to "guard" McCarthy during his three days in Schenectady. There might be trouble from the Communists – at least that was the rumor spread by McCarthy's men. The real reason was Martha Milwaukee.

Joe McCarthy had traveled 400 miles to spend a night with the Red Flame of New York and it was Volk's job to get her there.

"Is he up?" Volk grumbled, unable to see anything inside the darkened room.

Robertson poked a thumb over his shoulder, past the black patch that covered his missing eye. Volk followed the one-eyed investigator inside, kicking his way through a carpet trail of drained liquor bottles, high-ball glasses, and empty clothes. At the back of the room, Volk could see the shape of a large body, half-covered in a sheet, with two big feet dangling off the end of a sofa. The Chief Inspector pulled open the curtains and sunlight poured into the room. McCarthy pulled the bed sheet over his head, groaning like a 250-pound child.

Volk snapped, "The hearing is at nine, right? That doesn't leave us much time."

Duck Robertson still would not speak. He shrugged his shoulders and held up his hands as if to say, "What can I do?"

Now Volk was getting annoyed. "Then what time should I get her there? The Milwaukee woman – what time does she testify?"

Robertson signaled for Volk to follow him outside.

"Martha Mossbaum is not going to testify," Robertson explained. "The boss wants her back here tonight – sometime after eight."

Glancing over at McCarthy, Volk gave a sour look of disgust. "He wants her back *here* – in the hotel? What am I supposed to do with her until then?"

With another shrug, Robertson went back into the room and picked up a newspaper, holding it close to his good eye. The paper was full of news about McCarthy and his plans to grill the Communists of Local 1389:

McCarthy Ready for Showdown with G.E. Reds
Joe Vows to Expose Commie Unionists
Leaders, Members of Local 1389 Now Forced to Testify

But there was no tension or excitement in the Presidential suite. The only sound was Robertson going through the paper and the intermittent snorts from Joe McCarthy's snoring. Both were interrupted by a train whistle blowing from the nearby station: passengers were boarding the Lakeshore Limited to New York City. Volk glanced out the window and then his body stiffened. Martha Milwaukee, dressed in a tight, blue suit and tremulous high heels, was getting on the train!

"Sonofabitch," Volk muttered as he bolted for the door. By the time Volk reached the sidewalk, the train had left the station.

It didn't matter. Volk knew where she was going – even if Martha Milwaukee did not have a clue.

"The famine was the final climactic chapter in my Russian education. I went to Russia believing that the Soviet system might represent the most hopeful answer to the problems raised by the World War and the subsequent economic crisis. I left convinced that the absolutist Soviet state ... is a power of darkness and of evil with few parallels in history ... For murder is a habit."

AMERICAN REPORTER WILLIAM HENRY CHAMBERLAIN
Confessions of an Individualist, 1940

"Mr. Duranty thinks it quite possible that as many as 10 million people may have died directly or indirectly from lack of food in the Soviet Union ... The Ukraine had been bled white."

NOTES FROM A PRIVATE MEETING WITH WALTER DURANTY,
Moscow correspondent for the New York Times, September 1933.
Duranty never reported the famine – in fact, he often denied its existence. While Duranty would excuse or cover up other crimes by the Stalin regime, his coverage from 1931 was honored with a Pulitzer Prize.

CHAPTER THIRTY-EIGHT

THE TENTH DIRECTORATE

On the Lakeshore Limited, Martha rested her head against the seat and smiled contentedly. She was finally on her way – back to New York, back to the people that she knew best and who loved her the most!

Martha had been summoned to a meeting of the Tenth Directorate of the CPUSA. After all these desperate, lonely years, Martha was going home! Despite the years of waiting – never knowing if the Party would ever call her back – Martha felt no bitterness. She knew this day would come and now, finally, it was here.

You should have seen the looks on their faces, Martha gloated. The members of her little cell were simply in awe when Martha told them the news. The Tenth Directorate wants to see me! To meet with the Tenth Directorate was like having an audience with the Kremlin itself because this was the office in charge of all Party activities in the entire Northeast. It was the North Star of the Communist Party-USA and Martha Milwaukee, its once and future star, was returning to the Party's constellation of heavenly bodies!

She looked out the window as the train rolled east toward Albany and past the courthouse where Joe McCarthy would soon be holding his inquisition of Local 1389.

"Good luck to you Joe!" Martha said to herself. "You had your chance. Sorry you missed me, pal!" Like the other Communists in town, Martha was going to lay low and avoid a subpoena to testify. Even Milo was in hiding. After a few days away, Martha knew she would be back with a new and very important assignment from the Party. Joe McCarthy would just be a distant memory.

No more waiting around for Milo and his "secret" plans. Let Helen take care of the bake sales and bowling nights! Martha Mossbaum Milwaukee was far too important for such nonsense.

She looked out her window at the fields of carefree cows, munching grass and blinking at the passing train – passing into history! Martha closed her eyes, imagining the exotic locales where they would be sending her next. Moscow? Paris? Who knows where? Just the idea of it made Martha tingle with excitement! As she opened her eyes, she caught the man across the aisle looking at her. Admiring her, Martha knew. He tried to avert his eyes, but Martha caught him peeking. She closed her eyes again as a tiny smile crossed those movie-star lips.

That's right, Martha girl. You've still got it.

The Tenth Directorate was located in the Manhattan headquarters of the Amalgamated Cobblers and Shoelacers Building, five blocks from

Grand Central Station. Martha reminded herself to be careful: she must not be followed! She had to get rid of Cow Eyes from across the aisle. He might be an admirer – *or he could be the FBI!*

In her younger days, Martha might have slipped out of a window – even on a moving train – if that was her only chance to escape. But that was many years and many pounds ago. She remembered how her former husband, Harold the Louse, had shown her how to suffocate a man with a bag of peanuts. But was it the bag or the peanuts?

As Martha considered her options, the train conductor came down the aisle, collecting tickets. He punched Martha's ticket and then, strangely, the conductor pressed what felt like another ticket into her hand. For just a moment, the conductor looked her straight in the eye.

A signal!

Martha glanced quickly over to Cow Eyes. He was reading a book (or pretending to). As the conductor continued down the aisle, Martha carefully disguised the secret paper in her palm. There was probably a message written on the back, but Martha – naturally, vainly – had left her glasses at home. She decided to take the message into the ladies' washroom where the light was better.

"Hey there – stop!"

Oh my God! Martha froze. Cow Eyes was calling to her! She turned around slowly.

"You'd better leave a stub on the rack," he said with a smile. "Otherwise, you might lose your seat!"

This was no FBI agent. She could spot a lovesick pigeon from a mile away. Flashing that Hollywood smile, Martha sashayed back to her seat, rocking those big hips left and right, toward Mr. Cow Eyes.

"Aren't you just the sweetest thing?" Martha purred as she smushed his lips into a pucker. "Now you guard my seat, won't you? I'm going to freshen up!" With a graceful pirouette, Martha sauntered away with what she hoped would be her sexiest catwalk. But those quaking heels and the lurching train left her clinging to every seat as she stumbled to the washroom. As soon as

Martha closed the door, Loverboy gathered his belongings and fled to another car. He did not want another pucker from this strange woman.

Inside the washroom, Martha opened the folded ticket.

'When the train stops, change into clothes under the sink in Club Car bathroom. Wait for five knocks on door.'

Martha went back to her seat, her face flush with the excitement. She had not felt this way in years – even in the years before Schenectady. Late-night rendezvous, secret mail drops, coded messages: Harold had talked to her about these things, but he never gave her a chance to practice any real spycraft. Now, riding on this train, passing secret messages, and plotting escape routes, Martha felt like a modern-day Mata Hari – a mysterious, cosmopolitan lady of international intrigue. The household drudgery of Schenectady was more than a hundred miles away as the train entered the tunnel at Grand Central Station.

In the dark, Martha made her way to the Club Car washroom. She found a note attached to the bag of clothes: "Drop your clothes in trash bin."

Martha could not believe it. She had just bought this suit! It was something special for her meeting with the Tenth Directorate and now she had to throw it away? Martha decided to put her new clothes in the bag and bring them with her. She was certain no one would mind. Anyway, who would dare criticize the Red Flame of New York?

The contents of the bag were the next surprise – only a pair of gray flannel pajamas. Perhaps the idea was to make her look inconspicuous. When Martha felt the train jerk to a stop, she knew there was no time to lose. She took off her new suit and struggled to pull on the pajamas.

Martha put her ear to the door. The only sound was her breathing – heavy and halting – until suddenly five sharp raps struck the door. With her brightest smile and her eyes wide with excitement, Martha threw open the door.

Everything went dark!

A cloth hood was shoved over her head and a handkerchief was wrapped across her mouth as she was yanked through the door. Martha's feet were lifted off the floor and she was carried down through empty train cars until she felt herself going down a flight of stairs. They were outside the train now. It was colder and yet somehow she could still feel the darkness. The sounds of the train were replaced by cavernous, mechanical noises, along with heavy footsteps scuffing along the greasy, tunnel floor.

Martha tried to talk through the handkerchief. "Fellas, can't I just close my eyes? I promise not to peek." No one answered her.

She heard someone count to three and then she felt a sickening weightlessness as her body was thrown onto a pile of bags. She was now in the back of an open-air truck. When she tried to sit up, a large hand pushed her back down. Now her nerves were on edge and she jumped at the sound of the truck engine firing up. The vibration nearly lifted her off the truck bed and then, with a jerk and a shift of gears, the truck started to move forward, speeding out of the tunnel.

Dammit Martha, she scolded herself. How could she have been so easily tricked? The damn FBI! She was surprised that they would man-handle her this way, but nothing was past those awful G-Men. She was their sworn enemy and this was war, after all.

Suddenly, Martha could feel sunshine against the cloth hood. The noise of city traffic and crowds on the sidewalk filled her ears as light and shadow passed over her face. She thought about her new clothes – the ones she had placed in the bag.

"Did you fellows remember to bring my clothes?" Martha asked sweetly.

"Shut up," a voice said gruffly. "And don't move."

Someone pulled a tarp over Martha, blocking all the light and most of the sound around her. The truck raced forward before taking a sharp turn to the right and then to the left. Martha tried to remember each turn as the truck pinballed across several short blocks.

Wouldn't it show them if I can figure out where they are taking me? But Martha soon lost track as the truck took several more turns before lurching to a stop. Martha could hear more voices, but she could not understand what they were saying. The air quickly filled up around her as the tarp was torn away.

Two men hoisted her over the side of the truck and dropped her back on her feet. Without warning, her knees buckled as someone grabbed her by the throat and tugged the hood away from her face. Here was the train conductor glowering at her from just a foot away. They were standing inside a dimly-lit garage and Martha could see the shadows of two other men, one of them as big as the conductor, standing by a door.

"Walk," the conductor commanded. "They are waiting for you."

Martha took a few short steps before she was able to straighten herself and move toward the door. The conductor was holding Martha's hands behind her back, pushing her down a narrow hallway. There was a light coming from a doorway at the end of the hall and Martha could hear voices – then many voices – coming from the room up ahead.

As she moved closer to the light, the voices grew softer and then, one by one, the people stopped talking and the lights went out. Martha had figured it out by then: this must be a gag! They're getting quiet so they can shout "Surprise!" when I come into the room! Now, with each step, Martha was feeling a rush of excitement. Meeting with the Tenth Directorate!

They know I've arrived, Martha smiled. Maybe they'll sing The Internationale? That would certainly bring out the tears!

As she turned the corner, a blinding spotlight hit her in the eyes. She was accustomed to this from her speeches in large auditoriums so Martha kept her head up, smiling as always, as she carefully followed her feet to the edge of the stage. She guessed that a podium or microphone would not be far away.

Then Martha became aware of the cold silence. There was no applause, no cheering. She could feel the tension and, from the low-hanging lights in the back of the room, Martha saw silhouettes but no faces. No one was moving. She could not see or hear anything more than the harsh spotlight burning through the silence, but she could feel their eyes on her.

Through a loudspeaker, a voice commanded, "Comrade Mossbaum – sit down!" It was a man's voice, clipped and angry.

"Mossbaum?" Martha said to herself. They must know that I'm no longer married to Harold! She turned clumsily from one side of the stage to the other, trying to see past the spotlight, when two big hands reached out of the darkness and pushed Martha onto a small metal chair.

Martha was trying to make sense of this. Why are they calling me Mossbaum? And what way is this to treat a star? None of this was making sense. She started to perspire. Maybe this is still a gag.

Maybe.

"Harold?" Martha called out, wondering somehow if her ex might be nearby. People in the audience started to laugh. Then it was silent again.

"Harol – " Martha choked as the hood was shoved over her face again.

"Shut up, Comrade, will you please?" It was the conductor growling in her ear. "Do not say another word, do you understand me?" When Martha nodded, the hood was pulled away.

Martha looked down at herself. Perspiration had soaked through the gray pajamas. She let a frightened whimper escape her throat and it echoed across the room. Someone coughed in the back.

"Who's there?" Martha demanded. She leaned forward, straining to raise a hand to shield her face from the spotlight. "Where am I? Comrades?"

"Sit still!" ordered the voice through the speaker. "Comrade Mossbaum – do you know why you are here?"

"I received a message that you wanted to see me – for a meeting. An important meeting with the Tenth Directorate."

"This is not a meeting. You have been ordered to appear before a tribunal of the Military Board of the Tenth Directorate of the Communist Party USA. You will now listen to the charges and the evidence against you!"

Martha squeezed the sides of the chair, feeling like she might fall over. She could not understand what was happening. Charges? Evidence against her? She started to get up when the conductor grabbed her shoulders and shoved her down again. This time, he pulled her hands behind the chair and handcuffs closed around her wrists.

Martha tried to stay calm, but she could feel herself starting to cry.

"Why are you doing this to me? What have I done?" Tears ran down her face and her pajamas were now dark from the sweat pouring off her body. Martha tried to hold back a sob but it burst out of her mouth as a choking, wet cough.

"Silence!" the voice demanded. "We will now read the charges brought against you. Martha Mossbaum: You are charged with conspiracy as a member of a counter-revolutionary organization."

"Wait – wait!" Martha pleaded. "Why do you keep calling me Mossbaum? My name is Milwaukee, Martha Milwaukee. If this is about Harold, I haven't seen him in years. He left me long ago – long before I married Milo. And let me remind you, I married Milo on your orders. Orders from the Party!"

"Silence!" the voice shouted as Martha continued to protest.

"And I did not question those orders even though it meant I could no longer live in New York and you should know this – all of you – because I have been waiting up there for such a very long time, waiting for your instructions – just a signal or something. Please tell me what you want me to do!"

"The second charge against you: That Martha Mossbaum organized an anarcho-syndicalist organization with other enemies of the people – a gang of known wreckers, subversives, and spies – and that you supported their criminal behavior with Party treasury."

Martha was dumbfounded. "What – my cell in Schenectady? My little Party cell? I swear, they are all loyal Party members! They were sent underground – by the Party – like me!"

Martha could hear laughter from somewhere behind the spotlight. She lowered her head as her body slumped forward, pulling the handcuffs against the back of the chair.

"Charge Three: That you have associated with and shared Trotskyist ideas with now-exposed enemies of the party."

"What enemies?" Martha demanded.

"Anna Razumnova, Harold Mossbaum, Rosalene Imperato – "

"Rosie – the telephone operator?"

"And other persons expelled, imprisoned, or liquidated by order of the Supreme Soviet."

Martha felt the blood rush down to her feet. She had no feeling in her arms.

Harold – liquidated? Anna Razumnova imprisoned? For what – when?

"Harold's dead?" Martha cried, her eyes searching in the light. "Why would they kill Harold? And Anna? What have you done to Anna?"

The voice did not answer.

Martha's heart was racing. What are they going to do to me? Are they going to kill me too?

"Michael!" Martha cried out. "Misha? Mommy's here!"

She was sobbing now, tears smearing the makeup she had taken so long to apply. Martha hung her head, whispering over and over, "I didn't say goodbye to my baby. I never said goodbye to Michael!" The spotlight burned into Martha's eyes.

Then she passed out.

It was hours later when Martha woke up on a small cot. She was in a different room, not much bigger than a closet. She heard voices outside the door. One voice was louder than the rest. It was a man's voice, deep and commanding. He sounded angry.

"It doesn't matter! Out of the way – now!"

A woman called out urgently, "Comrade, *wait!* On whose authority? There are procedures we must foll – " Something heavy fell against the wall. In a fright, Martha shot up in the bed, her back pressed against the wall as the struggle continued outside the door.

The woman spoke again, but this time her voice was strained like she was choking. "Stop! You can't!" Then the door jerked open and an enormous man came in. His face was in shadow and behind him, Martha could see a woman pushing herself up off the floor.

"Get up," the man ordered Martha.

"What are you – what's happening here?" Martha cried. Suddenly, she felt her new clothes – the ones she had bought for her trip to New York – fall against her face. They felt wonderful!

"Get dressed, Mrs. Milwaukee," Wotan Volk said as he went back into the hallway. "I'm taking you home."

Once dressed, Martha stepped cautiously out of the small room. At the far end of the hallway, a group of people were cowering against the wall. Backing away from Martha was the angry woman who had been thrown to the floor. She scowled at Martha, but most of her scorn was directed at Volk, Martha's protector, as Volk and Martha slowly backed down the hall.

Who is this woman? Martha wondered. What have I done to make her hate me this much?

Martha stumbled down the hallway, clutching Volk's overcoat, as the big man kept his eyes on the angry crowd behind them. Martha had to hurry to keep ahead of Volk. Glancing back, Martha could only see Volk's massive shoulders brushing against the walls of the narrow passageway. Then she heard the cursing, the Party members muttering insults, but none of them were loud enough or bold enough to challenge the authority of Wotan Volk. Soon, they were in Volk's car driving back to Schenectady.

Martha was going home. She was safe and although she did not know it yet, she was saved.

"Comrades! The kulak uprising in your five districts must be crushed without pity. The interests of the whole revolution demand such actions, for the final struggle with the kulaks has now begun. You must make an example of these people.

(1) Hang (I mean hang publicly, so the people see it) at least 100 kulaks, rich bastards, and known bloodsuckers.

(2) Publish their names.

(3) Seize all their grain.

(4) Single out the hostages per my instructions in yesterday's telegram.

Do all this so that for miles around people see it all, understand it, tremble, and tell themselves that we are killing the bloodthirsty kulaks and that we will continue to do so. Reply saying you have received and carried out these instructions.

Yours, Lenin.

P.S. Find tougher people."

TELEGRAM FROM VLADIMIR LENIN, *August 10, 1918*

CHAPTER THIRTY-NINE

MARTHA LEARNS THE TRUTH

Nothing was spoken until they reached Kingston and then the silence and the questions became too much for Martha. Softly, she said, "I want to thank you for what you did back there."

Volk did not respond. This annoyed Martha greatly. She sat up against the front seat and repeated herself. Volk ignored her again, switching hands on the wheel and driving a little faster.

Martha was, of course, a fervent Communist, but she also had been raised in a household where people learned their manners. Even large people, whose upbringing she frequently questioned, should not be excused from the necessary conventions of polite society.

"I don't know if you can hear me up there," Martha said sharply, "but you really scared those people, you realize."

Still, the big cop said nothing.

"Frankly, I think you may have blown this whole thing out of proportion. For all we know, they were probably just testing me."

Dismissing that nonsense, Volk grunted something that Martha could not hear – or was he laughing at her?

"Honestly!" Martha exclaimed. She fell back against the seat, disgusted with Volk's refusal to speak. And then she started to think. It was several more miles before she spoke again.

"I have been waiting a long time to meet you."

This got Volk's attention. He looked at her quizzically in the mirror. Martha knew she had found her Mr. X.

"Why didn't you find me before now?"

"I didn't know you were lost," Volk quipped. Martha was looking intently at Volk. Lowering his head, Volk pulled his hat down and kept his eyes on the road.

"They told me about you. They said, 'We have an important agent in Schenectady,' and that I should wait for you. But they never told me your name or where I could find you."

"I doubt they were talking about me," Volk looked at her in the mirror again. Firmly, he said, "Listen Mrs. Milwaukee, I want you to forget about what happened here today. And forget about me, too. After tonight, you don't know me, and you won't ever see me again."

Martha pulled herself up against the front seat. "What were they going to do to me?"

"Who knows? They probably didn't know either. That's when people can get hurt."

After another mile, Volk laughed. "That bunch in the Tenth Direc-torate – they've always been a little nuts. Not as crazy as Stalin, of course, but crazy all the same." Volk smiled at Martha, but she did not smile back. Instead, she snapped, "How can you speak that way about our Supreme Leader – and about our comrades? How dare you be so flippant!"

Volk grimaced as he squeezed the steering wheel tighter. He wanted to jam on the brakes and drag Martha out of the car. After what had just happened to her, Volk wondered how anyone could be that stupid. He pushed the mirror aside and kept on driving. Slowly, his anger drained away as the sun disappeared behind the Catskill Mountains. He glanced back at Martha, her arms still crossed against her chest, scowling like an angry child.

"You really don't know, do you?" Volk said, shaking his head with disbelief. Martha turned away from the mirror. "Tell me, Mrs. Milwaukee, how many people used to come and hear you speak? Ten thousand? Twenty thousand?"

Martha smiled at the memory. "I don't know if it was that many," she laughed. "I probably filled the Garden once or twice. The Cow Palace too, of course."

"Okay. So, I want you to picture each one of those people and then imagine every one of them dead at your feet. Tortured, shot, poisoned, garroted, hanged, starved – every possibly way that a person can be killed by another human being – then think about that happening over and over again, a thousand times more for years, decades."

"What are you talking about?"

"Shut up for a minute. I want you to think of all those faces that once looked up at you on that stage and imagine those same eyes staring at you from behind prison bars, pleading for some humanity. But there is no mercy – only beatings and torture, day after day, until these prisoners reach their last breath and then they are spared for one more day of tor-ture. Finally, they give up and they die – dumped in a pit as if they never existed. That's where they are now, Mrs. Milwaukee – thousands of un-marked graves holding millions and millions of your 'comrades' – all killed by your Supreme Leader. You nearly got it yourself today. Lucky for you, I got there in time."

Martha stared back at Volk, sniveling, her face streaked with tears. Volk did not like to see a woman cry, but he got angry when he realized Martha's tears were only for herself.

"Let me ask you a question, Miss Red Flame: How could so many people die – so many millions of your beloved Russians, Poles, Czechs, and Slavs, starved and tortured by the Kremlin's killing machine and somehow you don't know a thing about it? The great masses you're always talking about and millions are trampled day and night by Stalin and the Supreme Soviet. How do you not know this? All of you loyal Party members – it's incredible! I don't know what's worse – to live through that horror or pretend that it never happened!"

"You're mad! Who told you these things?" Martha demanded.

"Tell the truth, Mrs. Milwaukee: Just how ignorant are you?"

"I've heard these lies before! What kind of Party member are you to be repeating this slander?!"

That was too much for Volk. He jammed on the brakes and the car swerved to a stop in the middle of the road. Martha screamed as Volk reached back to grab her.

"This is what it's like, Mrs. Milwaukee!" Volk shouted. "Nothing but darkness all around you, the fear surrounding every part of you because you know something's out there and it's coming for you – but there's nothing you can do to stop it! Nothing!" Martha screamed again as Volk slammed his fist against the horn and the car burned its tires against the asphalt.

"Stop your hollering, Mrs. Milwaukee! You're not going to die – not tonight! Too many others have gone before you and millions more will die because of lunatics like you. The great unwashed of the Soviet Socialist Republic, millions and millions of innocent people, moving along an assembly line of death! But you're safe, Mrs. Milwaukee. No one's coming after you, comrade. Not tonight anyway. Thanks to me, you can go back home to your family, back to your idiotic dreams and your fairy-tale Revolution!"

For the next two hours, Volk recited the atrocities of Stalin's Red Terror: the decades of purges, starvation, and destruction as Stalin bent the world to suit his needs. Tortured themselves, Stalin and his men remembered the lessons of persuasion taught in the Tsarist prisons. Once in power, the Bolsheviks created their own devices to break people – first for money, then for information and, finally, they tortured simply because that was that way things had always been done.

There was the "parilka," a sweat room filled with so many men and women that they were forced to stand against one another, without ventilation, one naked body crammed against another in the choking heat and the vicious lice. After standing for hours – and then for days – crippled by swollen feet and gnawing thirst, prisoners would collapse to the floor or they were dragged off to the next torment: the "conveyor." Here they were forced to run (as if that were possible) through dozens of rooms along long corridors. Interrogators sat at desks in these rooms, demanding money or information, and when the cursing and insults did not produce these results, the prisoners were forced to run to the next desk – and then the next. Prisoners would remain on the conveyor for hours.

When they fell, they were beaten and when they had nothing to offer, their children were arrested and tortured in front of them. There was no rising of the masses; no triumph of the working class. There was only Stalin and his cronies, killing their enemies, killing innocent people, and then killing each other – one loyal Party member murdering the next and then waiting for their turn to die, all in the name of Communism.

Martha offered no protests, no Marxian principles or Party line rationalizations. Now she knew the truth.

It was close to midnight when they arrived on Tuckahoe Row. Volk stopped his car at the far end of the street. They got out and stood together in the shadows.

"Remember what I told you, Mrs. Milwaukee. You don't come looking for me and you don't talk to anybody about me or what happened to you today – especially to that squirrelly bunch of Reds you bring into your house. I already heard about that Mr. X business. Just forget we ever met, have you got that?"

"I … I don't, I don't know what to do," she stammered.

Volk straightened up and smoothed the hair under his hat. "I know you've been through a lot today, but you might as well hear the rest of it. That cell of yours? None of them were sent underground. They were so useless, the Party just sent them away to get rid of them."

Martha was silent for a moment. "And what about me?"

"You were a different story, but after today, what does it matter? Yes, they wanted you here. That labor guy – Frankie Pepper – he arranged the whole thing."

"Frankie Pepper!" Martha exclaimed.

That bastard arranged my marriage to Milo! Frankie Pepper wasn't smart enough to arrange a sock drawer much less a marriage – MY marriage! My life!

Volk reached into the trunk of the car and took out a stack of letters, bound together with twine. "Here – take them. They're yours."

"What are they?"

"Letters from Anna Razumnova."

There in her hands – letters from her hero? Martha felt like crying again. She looked up at Volk, her eyes expressing gratitude that she could not put into words. The letters felt heavy in her hands. Letters from Anna Razumnova!

Volk looked up at the massive houses along Tuckahoe Row. Some had lights on, standing tall against the night.

"It's strange. In Russia, these would be the houses of the Party elite, people like Anna Razumnova. It was worse for them, you know – the Party functionaries. They only worked to serve Stalin until the day that someone would inform on them and then they would be taken away, gone without warning. Sometimes there would be a trial; otherwise, they were gone without any trace of what had happened to them. No chance for them to say goodbye. They were only given time to confess to a crime they never committed and then another bureaucrat would sign the papers and the machine was set in motion. Human beings ground up like raw meat."

Volk leaned against the car. The story was too enormous, too exhausting.

"I've seen the ones they leave behind – the wives and daughters, mothers and sons. They gather every morning at the NKVD prisons, praying for some bit of news, some small hope. If they knew what was happening inside those prisons, they would pray that it ended quickly. It never did. Torture can take a very long time and Stalin is an expert. He knows how to make it last."

Martha shook her head. "That's not how it's supposed to be. That's not what Communism is supposed to be! The Party is there to lift people up, to help every man and woman achieve a happy life. It's what we've been trying to do here."

"Here? Give me a break. Just look at what you've done to this city, Mrs. Milwaukee. You have brought Joseph McCarthy here! Not the Local, not your husband – YOU! And get this Mrs. Milwaukee: He wants you! That's right, Martha. Joe McCarthy told me to bring you to him tonight, just like the women they bring to Stalin's bed to be raped and then thrown away with the garbage. I saved you in more ways than you can imagine."

"I don't understand," Martha gasped. "McCarthy came here – for me?"

"Don't flatter yourself, sister. There are a lot of things you've been missing – starting with that revolution you're always jabbering about. But you're right about one thing: This is not what Communism is supposed to be. Marx never saw this coming. It was Lenin and the rest of those kooks. But don't kid yourself. Don't pretend it would have been any different if someone like you was in charge. I've known people like you before, always insisting that they would do it right – that they could make Communism work and make it beautiful – if only they had the power. And that's the problem, Martha. The power. That's the disease.

"You need that power, otherwise, people are not going to do what you tell them to do. They won't go along with your Five Year Plans and your collective farming and everything else to run their lives. You might have to get rid of those complainers – those counter-revolutionaries. But you would have the best of intentions, am I right? Maybe Stalin isn't such a bad guy either. Don't you see, Martha? It doesn't matter who is in charge – it could be almost anyone – and you still can't control it. Communism is just another name for a gun or a knife or a prison because no one can stop it. It kills freedom. It kills people. I figured that out a long time ago and ever since then, things have been working out just fine for me – that is, until you knuckleheads started making all this noise, taking over the downtown, the stores, and the clubs.

"You'd better think about this: If you want to help Schenectady – and that means helping your husband, the union, and everybody else in your life – then you'd better give up these fairy tales about saving the proletariat. This is a one-company town and that company is looking to win the biggest military contract anyone has ever seen. The last thing G.E. needs is you stirring up a noisy revolution and giving Joe McCarthy more reasons to hang around here. Believe me, you of all people should want to get Joe McCarthy as far away from Schenectady as possible."

"What am I supposed to do?" Martha cried. "I can't control Helen Gamble! I can't stop Milo!"

"Milo? You don't have to worry about Milo!"

"Oh no, you're wrong. He's been up to something. Helen told me."

"Whatever you say, Mrs. Milwaukee. Just think of something and do it fast."

Volk pulled down his hat and got back in his car, leaving Martha alone in the dark.

"What can I do?" Martha repeated, her voice cracking, realizing that she had been living a horrible lie.

She looked down the prosperous street, down to her house near the middle of the block. She could see the nightlight in Michael's room. She also noticed her neighbors watching her from their windows, wondering what Martha Milwaukee was doing out there in the night. Martha sighed.

Someone was always watching. Later that morning, the FBI would be back again. But tomorrow was not going to be like every other day, Martha decided.

Things were going to change. She would make sure of it.

"The evidence also discloses that secret members of the Communist Party played an important part in placing other secret communists in various positions in the public service which could be strategic, not only for espionage but also for propaganda."

ENGLAND'S ROYAL COMMISSION *Investigating Communications Between Public Officials to Agents of a Foreign Power, June 27, 1946*

CHAPTER FORTY

COCONUTS

Volk drove downtown to give McCarthy the bad news: Martha Milwaukee would not be sharing his bed that night. The Chief Inspector was glad to disappoint him. Volk wasn't pimping for anyone, much less a goddamn politician.

The whole business was seamy, especially the locale. Volk could smell the sweet, musty decay of the Hotel Van Arsdale as soon as he walked in the lobby, past the sleeping bellboy and the grease-stained wallpaper peeling itself from the walls, trying to make a break for it. Once the finest hotel in town, the Van Arsdale was only a little better than the $5 hookers who prowled the back alley. Even the famed Coconut Room was a wreck. It once featured the biggest of the big bands – from Duke Ellington to Jimmy Dorsey. Now, the Coconut ballroom looked like a rest home parked inside a saloon. The marble entranceway was still framed with tiny, embalmed monkeys hanging from pink-marble palm trees – a reminder of those strange and swanky nights when celebrities mingled with gangsters after a day in Saratoga. But now there was a smell about the place, a heaviness in the air, the rooms disinfected with vinegar and bleach and the customers drenched in liniments and camphorated oil.

In the center of the parquet dance floor was an enormous Oriental carpet that once belonged to Mae West. It was said that every stain on that rug could tell a story, but now the ancient carpet was as faded as the nightly regulars who were propped against the bar. From out of the Tiffany mirror, their bleak reflections were bathed in soft green neon, dressed up like the half-filled bottles of Rémy Martin and Johnny Walker. The drinks, like the lights, were not very strong and still these barflies kept falling to the floor like the ersatz coconuts.

But for all its dreariness, the Coconut Room had miraculously come to life once more, at least for one night. Joe McCarthy was in town, surrounded as always by news reporters, his personal staff, and some newfound pals from Schenectady – local politicians, a rich potential contributor, and of course some local dames. Everyone was thrilled to be out with a celebrity. They were all looking for some laughs, a hustle, or a story that no one would believe.

The senator and his guests were in high spirits, or at least they tried to be, shouting above the noisy demonstrators who were marching outside the hotel. The protestors chanted, "Hey – ho, what a show, Joe McCarthy has got to go," along with other Communist couplets. Most were members of Local 1389, directed by Helen Gamble and the Social Awareness Committee, mocking McCarthy for his investigation into "Communist Influence in the Defense Industry." The same crowd had been at the federal courthouse earlier that day, trying to disrupt a closed-door session, the first day of a two-day hearing by Tailgunner Joe.

McCarthy had no trouble ignoring them. He had his mind set on a glorious evening with Martha Mossbaum Milwaukee, the Red Flame of New York! Every few minutes, he would check the picture of sexy Martha, smoldering in his pants pocket, rubbing tightly against his sweaty thigh. McCarthy had spent weeks studying every curve and bump in that picture and now his patience was disappearing – mostly from the castigating stares of Montgomery Hughie. The newspaper publisher sat across the main table of the Coconut Room with his hands in his lap and his coat still buttoned, seemingly invulnerable to McCarthy's sense of fun.

Hughie had been wearing that scowl since earlier in the day when McCarthy's long-awaited investigation of Local 1389 went swirling down the toilet. He had placed great hopes on these hearings, firmly expecting that Joseph McCarthy, the nation's most ferocious Red Hunter, would finally reveal the Great Communist Conspiracy inside General Electric. McCarthy did not even come close. Now the publisher watched in horror as the junior senator from Wisconsin tried to balance a wine bottle on his chin and a cork on his nose.

Junior indeed, Hughie huffed.

"Let me tell you something, Monty," McCarthy bellowed across the table, "you fellas in Schenectady sure know how to have a good time. God knows, you're well rested!"

Hughie smiled stiffly. He was in no mood for McCarthy's pie-in-the-face humor.

So this is what all the fuss is about? Hughie wondered. This is the man who has captured worldwide attention as the foremost enemy of Communism? Boozy and unshaven, McCarthy looked more like a wet circus seal. This should have been the day Local 1389 received a public undressing, a full-scale interrogation of those subversive Reds and their takeover of General Electric, finally bringing an end to Local 1389 and the entire AEWA!

But that didn't happen. If anything, the Communists had won the day. Hughie was aghast as every witness, all of them members of Local 1389, pleaded the Fifth Amendment, refusing to answer even the simplest question. What was their name? Where did they live? What day is it today? Those arrogant cretins smiled their insipid smiles while McCarthy tapped his little gavel and demanded order from the raucous crowd. Worst of all, McCarthy never called Milo Milwaukee or any union leader to testify!

What about his wife, the Red Flare or whatever she was called? All of them, the entire Commie quagmire, had gotten a pass! With this boozy, late-night horseplay, it was obvious McCarthy did not care about the Reds in Schenectady or anywhere else. He had another audience to entertain and McCarthy was determined that the show must go on!

Leaning far back in his chair, McCarthy was examining the crystal chandelier above the Coconut Room when the chair toppled backward and a bottle of Red Velvet was launched off the table. With just one hand, the senator nimbly snatched the bottle out of the air without spilling a drop! McCarthy turned to the crowd, expecting a round of applause for his circus trick, but no one seemed to notice.

"Well what the hell?" McCarthy whined. "Come on you guys – that was some catch! What, are you takin' the Fifth? Hell, I just CAUGHT a Fifth! You get it?"

McCarthy tried to laugh but the noise sounded more like a sickly cough that ended with a loud snort through his nose. A fine mist of McCarthy's phlegm flew across the table and sprinkled Montgomery Hughie's face.

"Hughie – where you going?" McCarthy shouted as the publisher got up to leave.

"I'm sure you'll need to get to bed soon, Senator. An awfully big day tomorrow."

"Well hell, Hughie, right now I'm trying to have an awfully big NIGHT! But hey now, Hughie, don't go! Don't go. We're just getting started – honest."

The publisher cleared his throat. "Well thank you, Senator, but I have to be getting back to the paper. I wish you good luck at tomorrow's hearing. Thank you for having us over."

"Just the way I like 'em, Hughie: Over easy!" McCarthy laughed. "Well, good night then, Mr. Publisher! And make sure you have my paper ready for me bright and early, my good man. I want a great big headline on the front page! Something like – I don't know – 'Schenectady Loves Joe'!"

Hughie stalked out the back door as Wotan Volk entered through the front. Like the petrified monkeys hanging from the doorway, everyone stopped and stared at the giant cop, his enormous girth filling the marble archway of the Coconut Room. McCarthy jumped to his feet, expecting to find Martha Milwaukee hiding behind Volk's tent-sized coat. Seeing no bumps or curves, McCarthy flopped back on his chair.

"So this is the great Inspector Volk," McCarthy growled. "Jesus – you are a monster! Where the hell have you been?"

"New York," snarled Volk, grabbing one of the bottles in front of McCarthy and pouring himself a tall drink. Looming over McCarthy and his startled guests, Volk curled his lip as he took in the scene. Every table was covered with languid bodies and empty bottles. Volk was about to swallow his drink when he felt a hand on his sleeve, pulling him down toward the table.

"So, you gotta surprise for me – upstairs maybe?" McCarthy whispered, his gaseous breath blowing over Volk's face.

"I'm afraid the party is down here tonight, Senator. I see Mr. Hughie just left you."

"You are correct, sir! Mister Hughie has gone ka-blooey! I don't think that guy likes me very much. But, hey – he's a swell guy, a great American! Someday I hope he can get that stick out of his ass."

Everyone at McCarthy's table howled with laughter and McCarthy accepted their adoration until he tumbled backward over his chair, slapping his head against the parquet floor. Volk pulled him up and tried to fold him into the arms of Duck Robertson, but McCarthy wasn't ready for bed yet. He wriggled free from Robertson and climbed on top of a table.

"Friends, Romans, countrymen: I offer you a toast to Schenectady, the Not-So-Electric City! *Ha*!" This time, the senator tumbled off the table and Robertson was ready to catch him. Draped over Robertson's shoulder, McCarthy was taken up to his room and his empty bed in the Presidential suite. It had been a long and unproductive day: McCarthy did not catch a single Communist, not even Martha Mossbaum Milwaukee, the only Red he truly wanted to capture.

Outside the hotel, the protestors were falling out of line until there was only Helen, Arthur Klingman, and a new man – a stranger – standing together in a circle, still cursing the name of that bloodsucker, Joe Mc-Carthy. Then Henry Brownale lifted his hand and the chanting stopped. He brought a finger to his lips and the silence drew Helen and Klingman toward him.

"Comrades, it is I – Vladimir!" Henry announced. He then spoke the code words they had been expecting: "My bowling ball is ready."

Together, Helen and Klingman responded, "You are the King of the Hill!"

Milo Milwaukee's plan – his *new* plan for extinguishing the Reds – was about to begin.

"She got an affection from him ... When you are in love with a person, you don't care whether they are red or green. Love knows no bounds."

DEFENSE LAWYER FOR JUDITH COPLON, *a clerk for the U.S. Justice Dept. seduced into spying for the Soviets*

CHAPTER FORTY-ONE

WALL TO WALL

Arthur Klingman, editor of the local Communist newspaper, invited "Vladimir" to stay with him during his time in Schenectady. The three of them – Klingman, Henry Brownale, and Helen Gamble – walked to Klingman's apartment above Schicksal's Butcher Shop.

"Watch where you step," Klingman warned as he opened the door for his guests. Helen and Henry paused at the doorway because the room looked strangely out of balance, like a library turned on its ear. Towers of books and magazines, leaflets, instructional manuals, political tracts, newspapers, and Party propaganda were stacked from the floor to the ceiling. Henry and Helen stepped into the room cautiously, feeling the floor sag with each step as they followed Klingman along a narrow passageway between the paper columns.

It had taken Klingman nearly eight years to create this paper jungle: hoarding, clipping, and sorting every article he could find on history, philosophy, self-improvement, the sciences, and politics. The walls were covered with key passages, annotated with circled questions and exclamation marks. Still more clipping and sorting remained among the stalagmite stacks and twine-bound bundles, bulging bags and boxes bursting with paper, piled together from wall to wall.

Dr. Livingstone had been lost in just such a jungle.

"You can sleep over there if you like," Klingman said before he disappeared around a bend. Henry turned to see where Klingman had pointed, but it was Helen who caught Henry's attention. Now that they were in the light, Henry could not look away from her as she disappeared and then reappeared between the columns of books, magazines, and newspapers. She was the most beautiful woman Henry had ever seen and when she smiled at him, Helen chased away every other thought from his mind.

Suddenly, Henry had no idea what he was doing in Schenectady. Maybe it was simply to be with Helen.

"When do we get started?" she asked, and the question startled Henry. He could only smile back at her blankly, lovingly. Then he realized her meaning: she and Klingman were ready to help "Vladimir" steal secrets from the research labs inside General Electric – secrets, they assumed, that would be shipped off to Moscow. For Helen, this would be a chance to demonstrate her vigilance, to accomplish something meaningful for the Party – something, she hoped, that would make Petrov happy the next time he came to Schenectady.

Helen was hoping this Soviet agent, Vladimir, and his plans for sabotaging G.E. would keep her safe from another beating. Henry, as usual, mistook Helen's eager expression.

Is this young woman interested in me – romantically? That would be a distraction – a pleasant one – but Henry knew he had to stay focused on his mission. Milo Milwaukee was counting on him and so was Henry's ailing father. Stamping out the Communists was even a greater cause. This was a mission to save America!

Henry had not met or even spoken to Milo. It was Congressman Brownale who described the plan: Get close to the local Commies and then catch them in the commission of a crime, preferably something treasonous. Who and how, it did not matter.

Henry had no doubt that he could entrap some Communists – until he saw that magnificent face. Suddenly his mission became much more complicated. How in the world could he put Helen Gamble and that lovely face behind bars?

"Our tormentors used to say that one 'must become stiller than water and lower than grass.' They had the means to make a person like clay in their hands — clay which they could form as they wished."

I WAS A COMMUNIST PRISONER BY PASTOR HARALAN POPOFF, *one of many*
Bulgarian clergymen imprisoned in 1948 on bogus spying charges

---

"He heard screams. That's all. Simply one night he heard screams."
The daughter of a Moscow diplomat explaining why her father left the Communist Party.
WITNESS BY WHITAKER CHAMBERS.

CHAPTER FORTY-TWO

THAT SAME NIGHT,
Back on Tuckahoe Row

Martha rushed in through the back door, clutching the letters to her chest. She looked in on Michael, then his grandfather, and finally Milo. Everyone was asleep. Everyone was safe. Most precious of all, the letters from Anna Razumnova were still bundled in her arms. In the darkness, it seemed as if Anna was calling out to her.

Martha raced downstairs. If she did not hurry, Anna would be gone.

As Martha drew closer to the basement door, the moonlight briefly illuminated the letters in her hands. There was Martha's name and the address on Tuckahoe Row, scrawled in jagged handwriting across the front of each envelope before they disappeared into the darkness as Martha hurriedly closed the door. Turning on the light in the laundry room, the official stamp LUBYANKA PRISON appeared across the front of each envelope. Martha's hands were shaking as she opened the first envelope. Inside was a single page of coarse paper with tiny letters cramped together in urgent strokes:

Comrade,

Thank you for your kind letters. I am sorry to be writing to you now after so much has happened. As you may know, I am no longer secretary to the 1917 Party Committee. I have been convicted of unspeakable crimes. Unable to defend myself, I was sent to a corrective labor camp and now I am in Lubyanka Prison. There is both torment and shame to be convicted of a crime without evidence and no opportunity to confront my accusers. I write to you in hopes that you can convince Party leaders to examine the record and stand behind my cause. I am the victim of lies and baseless accusations, in part, I am sorry to tell you, because I knew your husband. It was this friendship that I now regret. Comrade Armov testified that I was recruited by Harold to be a spy for England. I have never talked to Harold about anything except our work for the Collective and there was no proof presented to support Armov's outrageous lies! It did not matter. My conviction is the result of my own vigilance. Following the trial of Zinoviev, Kamenev and David, I called on Party members to be suspicious of anyone who fails to report associations with known enemies of the People. Soon after my speech, the Party proclaimed your husband to be such an enemy and, because I knew him, this relationship has been used to destroy me. Please Martha, if you are still there, I beg you to help me now. My spirit is strong but my body has suffered. Please save me.

Your comrade, Anna

Down on her knees, Martha's body shook in terror as she squeezed Anna's letter in her hands. She quickly grabbed another envelope and ripped it open and then another and another, but all of these letters were censored with thick black lines covering Anna's shriveled handwriting. Others were torn into ragged pieces. Only one envelope remained.

Martha carefully unsealed it, desperate to find her friend again. This time the letter was intact. It was Anna's last letter to Martha.

Dearest Friend

I know you have tried to help me, but there is no more hope. I cannot remember my life before this. All I hear now are the screams of the other prisoners and I touch the scars from tortures I have suffered. I remember how I had prepared myself for such things, knowing that one day I might be captured by the fascists. But I never thought such things could happen from inside the Party! By my comrades! As they brutalized me, I could not imagine meeting insult with insult or defending myself while I was beaten and made to stand for hours without food or water. I knew this because we were comrades! I see the truth now. I was foolish to believe in such things. My silence must have given them strength because they kept on hurting me, thinking I was guilty. Maybe I am. It gives me no pleasure when I see them now, the guards who abused me. They sit in the cells beside my own. We are all prisoners together, comrades once more. This is a barbaric joke because you are my only true friend. From your first letter I have always dreamed of meeting you, my American comrade. I know this will never happen now but it makes me smile when I dream about you in my heart. Do not forget me. You tried to help when no one else could save me.

My Love Always, Anna
A day in Spring, 1950

Clutching her chest, Martha screamed into the floor until her body shook and there was no more sound left in her throat.

Three years ago! Three years of Anna suffering while Martha wrote ignorant letters to her, gushing about Russian coffee and vacations in the mountains! All of her stupid dreams and Anna Razumnova was already dead.

What a fool I have been, Martha cried. Now she understood what had happened at the Tenth Directorate, what the Party had become. This is what Communism has always been. Evil.

No more, Martha declared.

I will stop it now. And I will stop them: Helen, Klingman – all of them. First, I must stop Milo.

CHAPTER FORTY-THREE

TEN-POUND HANGOVER

Joe McCarthy reached across the bed and felt the rumpled sheets, the place where Martha Mossbaum should have been the night before. This trip had been a disaster and he still had to get through another hearing – a public session this time – with more bullshit from those union thugs. What was the point?

He angrily threw a pillow against the window, but it fell limply to the floor.

The next thing in his hands was *The Ledger* newspaper. Through blood-shot eyes, McCarthy read the front page headline:

SENATOR PALOOKA:
McCarthy Can't Land Single Punch vs. Reds.

McCarthy's rage pushed aside his hangover. This time, he opened the hotel window and threw the paper into the street – and then the pillow. Both of them landed without a sound. Infuriated, McCarthy threw down the sash and felt some satisfaction as the window cracked against the sill. He stumbled into the bathroom to slap cold water onto his face.

Staring into the mirror, a bitter, unshakeable truth crystallized in his brain: he had traveled 400 miles to Schenectady, N.Y. and all he had to show for it was a ten-pound hangover and insults from a two-bit newspaper. McCarthy gargled the last of the Red Velvet before hurling the bottle out the bathroom door. This time, there came a sharp, satisfying crash as the bottle shattered against the wall.

It was not the only thing Joe McCarthy would smash that day.

McCarthy aide: Why, for instance, would you say the Communist party will someday
be the salvation of this country?
Union witness: Why should I say that?
McCarthy aide: Why would you say that?
Union witness: I shouldn't say that.
McCarthy aide: Is that one of the things that you say which you shouldn't say?
Union witness: I have never said that, because I don't know that much.

Confusion at McCarthy hearing into "SUBVERSION AND ESPIONAGE IN
DEFENSE ESTABLISHMENTS AND INDUSTRIES," *Nov. 13, 1953*

C H A P T E R   F O R T Y - F O U R

OPEN SESSION IN
THE FEDERAL COURTHOUSE

The courtroom was nearly full when the G.E. executives straggled in,
their heads bowed low, one following the other like a line of regretful
school boys, reluctant witnesses to Joe McCarthy's final hearing. It was
hard to tell who were the defendants in this make-believe trial – the
G.E. brass or the members of Local 1389. Without a word or a glance
toward anyone else, the General Electric managers quickly filled the last
two rows of the gallery.

News photographers sprang to their feet, flashbulbs popping, as the
company president and CEO Philip Reedy entered the courtroom. An
excited murmur spread through the gallery as Reedy reluctantly pulled off

his hat and looked straight into the cameras. Next to Reedy, a G.E. public relations man looked on in horror as Reedy turned his head from one side and then to the other as the cameras kept on clicking. The PR man whispered urgently, "Mugshot! Mugshot!" Realizing his error, Reedy quickly dove under the bench, pretending to tie his shoes.

The cameras turned to the rest of the General Electric brass. They quickly pressed their faces into stony, Mount Rushmore expressions. To further accentuate their ardor for America, each of the company men was dressed in all-American colors: a red tie, white shirt, and a true-blue business suit. They would have carried apple pies baked with amber grains if that would convince America's greatest patriot, Senator Joseph McCarthy.

Patriot, my ass, groused Philip Reedy, furiously fingering the brim of his hat. Reedy was seething at the betrayal by this miserable ingrate: McCarthy had broken his long-standing bargain with G.E. For the past three years, the company had been paying "consulting fees" of more than a million dollars and, in return, McCarthy was supposed to stay the hell away from G.E.

But here he is, Reedy fumed, bringing his three-ring circus to Schenectady, elephant crap and all – and just a week before the company would be hosting a procurement committee from the Pentagon! Now this cheeseball is conducting a public hearing less than a mile from the company's headquarters! If he had not been bribing a United States senator, Reedy would have pressed criminal charges.

Cannonballs!

The CEO looked at the union men seated in front of him, noisily, joyously banding together to oppose Joe McCarthy. Reedy had to admire them. Unlike his cowering lieutenants, the men from Local 1389 were bravely defiant. They had toyed with McCarthy at the previous day's hearing and now they were back for more.

Philip Reedy would have loved to join them.

"All rise!" shouted Duck Robertson. Right on cue, "Hizzoner" Joseph McCarthy, puffing out his chest, waltzed into the courtroom, wearing a judge's robe and carrying a gavel as big as his cornball smile. McCarthy strode to the bench and fell heavily into the judge's chair, swiveling into position eight feet above the gallery. Slowly, he turned to his right and scowled at the press – because there weren't many reporters in the courtroom – and then he swiveled back to the left to face the crowd. Looking down on his targets, McCarthy felt like he was back in the air again, flying across the Pacific in a Douglas SBD Bomber – Tailgunner Joe ready to mow down the enemy!

His head was aching after that long and pointless night in the Coconut Room, not to mention his neglected libido. Now McCarthy wanted his revenge. It didn't matter if it was the Commie unionists or these corporate pinheads – somebody was going to pay.

McCarthy drew his eyes across the line of GE executives at the back of the courtroom like a hungry lion choosing the first Christian to be consumed. "Call the first witness," the Senator barked.

"Eugene Pielewinski," responded Duck Robertson.

Pielewinski, one of the union stewards, casually took his seat at the witness table. As he took the oath, Pielewinski smiled up at the bench as McCarthy squeezed his gavel, wishing his hands were wrapped around Pielewinski's neck.

"Mr. Pielewinski," McCarthy growled. "I have given you 24 hours to consider your situation. Yesterday, you could not seem to recall your own name or even the city you were born in. Now you are back here today with that idiotic grin on your face. Does this mean you are ready to answer my question – are you now or have you ever been a member of the Communist Party?"

"It's like I told you yesterday, Senator: You ain't got no right askin' me about my politics. In fact, I was thinkin' about this last night – who says you can sit up there wearin' a judge's robe and holdin' that gavel? You ain't no judge, Senator."

McCarthy rapped the gavel as Pielewinski turned and gleefully gave the 'ok' sign to the rest of the Local. Then Pielewinski turned back to McCarthy and leaned into the microphone. "And I got a question for you Senator: What are you wearin' underneath that robe?"

McCarthy's jaw hit the bench as the courtroom exploded in laughter.

"Silence! Silence!" McCarthy shouted, hammering the gavel so hard that it snapped in two. The gallery laughed even louder as McCarthy frantically searched for something else to pound – or throw – to silence the union rabble. Finally, he took off his shoe and desperately smashed it against the bench to the delight of the union men.

A tiny smile pressed against the corners of Philip Reedy's mouth. This might be worth a million dollars after all.

"ENOUGH!" McCarthy bellowed, finally taming the crowd. "Apparently, Mr. Pielewinski, you are unaware that I was a judge before I was elected to the United States Senate and from where you are sitting, you should be more respectful of that fact! For the purpose of today's hearing, let me remind you that I will be the judge, jury, and quite possibly the executioner!"

Someone in the gallery blew a raspberry. McCarthy glared at the crowd. He was about to hammer his gavel until he realized that he was only holding the broken handle. Pointing the stick at Pielewinski, McCarthy demanded, "I'll ask you again, sir! Are you now or have you ever been a member of the Communist Party?"

"I will not answer, Senator McCarthy, because all you're trying to do is break my union and I ain't gonna help you. I am going to stand by my rights as an American citizen." The union steward then reached into his jacket and read from a piece of paper. "Senator McCarthy, I am hereby invoking my rights under the Fifth Amendment of the Constitution of the United States of America." The members of Local 1389 jumped to their feet, cheering and applauding until McCarthy stared them back into their seats.

"Which Constitution would that be, sir? The Russian one? Let me ask you another question: Do you believe that a union dominated by the Communist Party should be allowed to represent workers in defense plants and research laboratories where top-secret military work is underway for the United States government?"

"Like I said before, Senator: I will take my Fifth Amendment rights as an Amer – "

McCarthy shot to his feet, shouting, "Fine then! This witness is excused!" Pointing at Reedy and the G.E. executives, McCarthy said, "Are you listening back there? Because this, frankly, is a rather fantastic picture! I find it incredible that in this day and age we still have people of questionable loyalty working inside a defense plant with ready access to secrets vital to our nation's defense! We have only just gotten rid of the Rosenbergs and now we have another Communist cabal pledged to destroy the United States! In this case – amazingly – we have subversives working right under the noses of America's most-trusted business executives! Are you also the most clueless? Let me remind everyone here: The Communists stole our atomic bomb! What are they looking to steal from General Electric?!"

McCarthy squinted at Reedy, pointing the gavel handle at him like the barrel of a gun. No one in the back row moved as eyeballs to the left and to the right strained to see how the boss was reacting to McCarthy's impertinence. Ever so slightly, Reedy nodded at McCarthy while his fingers continued to rub hot circles around the brim of his hat.

Message delivered, the two men silently agreed.

McCarthy smiled broadly as he leaned back in the judge's expansive chair. "But I did not come all the way to Schenectady to make a speech. I came here looking for answers. So I ask you, the gentleman of General Electric, please stand up and be heard! I won't require you to take the oath. I only want clarification about the security procedures inside your company, how someone in your employment can come here today and plead the Fifth Amendment and then, without a worry in the world, they can expect to be back on the job tomorrow! All I am asking is a simple question about their loyalty to America – a question that touches on the very security of your company and the very sanctity of our nation! Do any of you gentleman have an answer?"

The union men, the reporters and everyone else in the gallery turned to see what the G.E. men would say. The executives nervously examined the courtroom walls, the chandeliers, and the lint that had to be plucked from their true-blue suits. Only Philip Reedy kept his eyes locked on McCarthy.

In his mind, Reedy was counting all of the bags of cash and the hefty stock certificates that had filled that fat bastard's wallet, month after month, for the past three years. And now to be humiliated in public! How did this country bumpkin swindle one of the largest corporations in the world?

As the silence continued to hang over the courtroom, McCarthy stood up and leaned far over the bench, taunting Reedy to speak. "I'm waiting – "

Slowly, the chief of G.E. Security, George Schidell, rose from his seat. There was no strength in his legs and yet Schidell felt his body rising upward, propelled by a force that was beyond his control. Even Reedy was surprised to see the timid executive standing in the shadow of Joseph McCarthy.

Schidell tried to move his mouth, but nothing was coming out. Finally, he was able to clear his throat and squeak, "Your honor, senator, judge sir – if I may – "The Senator broadly shook his head from side to side and Schidell slowly sank back in his seat.

"I can wait," McCarthy said as he signaled for the next witness: Anthony Chicatelli.

"Perhaps you will answer my questions, Mr. Chicatelli. Tell me, sir – were you born in this country?"

"Uh-no sir," Chicatelli answered in a thick Sicilian accent.

"Do you have any special grievance against our government, Mr. Chicatelli? Do you, for instance, condone the Communist Party? Do you agree with its stated objective to destroy the very Constitution behind which your union has been hiding?"

Chicatelli looked over his shoulder and gave the men a wink.

"I'm-uh sorry, Senator McCarthy, but could you-uh please repeat-uh the question?"

The gallery was in hysterics as McCarthy threw the gavel handle to the floor. He held his hands out to Chicatelli, pleading for an answer.

"What kind of American are you, Mr. Chicatelli? Do you not covet the shelter and protection of Lady Liberty? Do you not take pleasure in her bounty – the richness and warmth of her embrace? She lies before you, sir, beseeching you to love her – to be one with her!"

Chicatelli leaned in close to the microphone. "I-uh don't think I can-uh do that, Senator. I'm a married man!" The laughter echoed through the courthouse. Reporters, court officers, and even some of McCarthy's team had to laugh at that one.

McCarthy shouted, "Enough! Enough I say!" Bowing his head, Mc-Carthy spread his arms out across the desk, trying to catch his breath. "Let me ask you this way, Mr. Chicatelli, and please remember sir, you are under oath. Other than the usual complaints that we all have, do you feel that you are getting a fair shake here in this country?"

"I certainly-uh do and it's all because of my union. They have been-uh good to me and I think that all-uh you want to do is rip-uh apart my union! I tell you now: I had enough-uh this business and so I say-uh to you, good day sir, and a good-uh riddance to you, Mister Senator!"

Chicatelli did not reach the end of the aisle before a nod from McCarthy had U.S. marshals surrounding Chicatelli.

"I am citing you for contempt of Congress, Mr. Chicatelli!" McCarthy shouted over boos and catcalls. "Good-uh day and good-uh riddance to you too, Mr. Communist!"

"Anyone else?" McCarthy glowered at the spectators. "What about you veterans in the audience. As you know, I am a veteran myself. As veterans, all of us should be proud to answer any question about the security of our nation. If you have nothing to say, then so be it. But remember: By remaining silent, you are really saying much more than you realize. To state it plainly, when a witness takes the Fifth Amendment, there is no stronger proof of his membership in a subversive organization like the Communist Party! If you are not a member of the Party, you can simply say so and there may be nothing more to incriminate you. But you cannot get stronger testimony than when you plead the Fifth. Veterans – please! Am I right?"

No one answered as the crowd stared back at McCarthy.

"Well, I'm not surprised. Why should anyone care when there are no consequences? Here in Schenectady – here at General Electric – there are no penalties for such loathsome behavior. Please then – take the Fifth, be a Communist, pass vital secrets to the enemy – no one cares! Nothing will happen to you! Am I the only person who hopes to see a new policy at General Electric and at every other defense works in this country? What we need are companies who will stop coddling Communists! We need companies that will adopt Fifth Amendment policies that protect us from untrustworthy workers. When will we see such a day here in Schenectady?"

McCarthy glanced at Montgomery Hughie and the publisher was smiling and nodding at McCarthy's fiery speech. This was the Joe McCarthy that Hughie had been waiting for: the real Tailgunner, blasting these union bastards to hell!

"Frankly all of this makes me sick. How about you gentlemen in the back there? How does it make you feel, Mr. Reedy, or will you be taking the Fifth as well?"

The audience gasped. Even the union men realized that McCarthy had gone too far. Reedy shot to his feet and, with a flick of his thumb, the G.E. entourage followed their boss out the door.

"Come back when you have an answer please!" McCarthy shouted. "And take the Fifth Amendment with you!"

The hearing continued until early that afternoon. Seven more witnesses repeated their allegiance to Local 1389, the AEWA and the Fifth Amendment. By then, even Montgomery Hughie had had enough. McCarthy was also ready to go home, confident that he would at least get good headlines, if not a Communist. That was some consolation even if it wasn't worth the long trip to Schenectady or the lump on the back of his head, still throbbing after his swan dive in the Coconut Room.

McCarthy adjourned the hearing and returned to the judge's chambers, where he flopped onto the couch and drained a bottle of scotch from the judge's liquor cabinet. Soon he was fast asleep on the train back to

Washington, dreaming about Martha Milwaukee and her sumptuous body draped across the witness table.

"I want you," Joe calls to her. He reaches for his gavel only to find a broken stub in his hand. Meanwhile, the Red Flame is floating into the sky, wrapped in the clouds above General Electric, its enormous neon sign flashing NO, NO, NO. Martha calls back to him as she floats away, "You can't have me, Joe! I'm taking the Fifth! I'm taking the Fifth – "

"The Fifth, the Fifth," McCarthy mumbled in his sleep. "Dammit Reedy, do something about the goddamned Fifth!"

"The long struggle against communism in this country is liberally strewn with the wrecks of well-meaning but badly informed and blundering anti-communists. *When in doubt — confer first with known experts and authorities* ... You cannot expect to outwit and thwart (the Reds) by reading a couple of pamphlets or even a book. You simply have to know your stuff."

"THE WAY YOU CAN FIGHT COMMUNISM" *THE AMERICAN LEGION MAGAZINE* ✶ *August, 1948*

CHAPTER FORTY-FIVE

GODDAMN GOLDMINE

The next day's paper summed it up: McCARTHY HEARINGS TAKE THE FIFTH -- On Commie Question: Union Refuses, Company Snoozes, Public Loses.

For publisher Montgomery Hughie, the hearings began as a great flop before ending on a brighter note. Not as bright as flames pouring out of Milwaukee Hall, but bright enough for now. Where there was smoke, now there was fire. The headline on Hughie's editorial was **Hope for Our Future**:

"If you ever wanted to run away with the circus, you had your chance yesterday when a three-ring parade of pinkos, Reds, and union hooligans marched into the federal courthouse, all of them eager to taunt and berate United States Senator Joseph R. McCarthy. The Wisconsin legislator parked himself behind the bench of U.S. District Court Judge Marvin Benjamin with the stated intention of exposing the dangers of Commie-led Local 1389 and how it threatens our national security inside the

General Electric Corp. It was the second day of McCarthy trying to elicit answers from the Reds, who once more skillfully hid behind the Fifth Amendment and refused to cooperate.

Nothing says 'guilty' like a Commie taking the Fifth, charges Senator McCarthy, and we think so too. What about the leaders of General Electric? Where do they stand or will they continue to sit on their hands? The company should take steps – appropriately demanded by Senator McCarthy – to fire anyone who is more concerned with self-incrimination than with our national security. What good is the Fifth Amendment and the rest of our Constitution if America is reduced to rock and rubble, destroyed by the very weapons we created?

Let us have no more hand-wringing about Constitutional rights, of innocence before guilt! We can't imagine that Joseph Stalin worries about Constitutional rights in Russia! Sometimes it's best to shoot first and consult the law books later.

Please, Senator McCarthy, come back soon and finish the job before it's too late!

"Sure – hurry back, you drunken bastard," Hughie muttered, flinging the newspaper across his desk. He was thoroughly disgusted by McCarthy's drunken carousing, pawing every woman and molesting every bottle within his reach.

Tailgunner Joe? *Tailgroper* is more like it, the publisher scowled. We finally bring Joe McCarthy to Schenectady and all he wants to do is drink and fornicate!

Hughie yelled into the newsroom, "Doesn't he get enough of that in Washington?" The reporters and editors bent a little lower over their typing and scribbling as the publisher stalked around his office looking for something to throw.

That's when Hughie noticed a headline on the *Saturday Evening Post*: **Wisconsin Town 'Invaded' by Communists**. Hughie quickly thumbed to the page picturing grim "Russian soldiers" leveling their rifles at a man in his pajamas. The caption read, "*Mooseburg Mayor Barney Thompson is rousted from his bed shortly before dawn. He quickly surrenders to the 'invading' Russian army during Mooseburg's 'Red Scare Days,' a two-day dramatization of what life would be like if Communists captured this small Wisconsin farm town.*" Hughie fell back into his chair.

"Brilliant!" he whispered.

We'll show these Bingo-playing mouth breathers what Communism is really about – not those lovey-dovey peace petitions, folk songs, and bake sales. We'll show them what Communism looks like from the barrel of a gun. We're going to scare the crap out of 'em!

"Van Lueven!" Hughie shouted. "Get in here – *NOW!*"

Like a tired boxer lurching into the ring for one more beating, City Editor Tom Van Lueven shambled into Hughie's office. He started his apology even before he took his seat on "Old Sparky."

"I'm sorry about today's funnies, sir. One of the guys thought it would be funny if Sluggo dropped his pants in front of Nancy. Honestly, it won't happen again."

"No, no – not that. This!" Hughie pointed to the *Saturday Evening Post.* "Here's what we're going to do in the Bulldog: I want a banner headline across page one, something like: 'Red Menace At Our Doorstep – City Will Host' ... No, wait a minute – make it: 'Senator McCarthy Invited to Witness Commie 'Takeover' of Schenectady.' Give it the wood and send in Johnson for the rewrite. I'll give him the story myself! Boy, what a story! We're going to make history!"

In the next two editions of *The Ledger,* the citizens of Schenectady learned of Montgomery Hughie's plan to stage a "Communist takeover" of the entire city: the police department, City Hall, the television station – everything would be "captured" by the Soviets in a city-wide pageant of Red menace and mayhem. Mooseburg would be the model: the faux siege had been so realistic, the mayor of Mooseburg died from a heart attack.

"Even better!" thought Hughie, imagining Mayor Mudlick clutching his chest as Red Army soldiers skewered him with their bayonets. What a fitting end to a political gasbag like Mudlick.

Under Hughie's byline, the news was soon spread across the front page:

RUSSIAN REVOLUTION TO HIT SCHENECTADY:
'Commietown' Will Demonstrate Horrors of Soviet Regime, Joe McCarthy Invited to Lead City as 'Supreme Commissar'
By Montgomery Hughie, Ledger Publisher

Under the auspices of the Schenectady County Loyalty Board, the City of Schenectady will soon be transformed into "Commietown," an all-day demonstration of what America would be like under the Commie tyrants of the Soviet Union. Ledger Publisher and Loyalty Board Vice Chairman Montgomery Hughie said the event will take place to coincide with U.S. Senator Joseph McCarthy's imminent return to the Electric City.

Shortly after the newspaper hit the streets, Hughie got a frantic phone call from Schenectady Mayor Myron Mudlick.

"Goddammit Hughie!" the mayor shouted. "Who the hell are you to turn my city into a passion play for those Commie-bashing friends of yours? If you want to play dress-up, do it on your own time and not the city's!"

Hughie hollered back, "Listen to me, you conniving little weasel. Commietown is going to be the biggest thing to hit Schenectady since Edison invented the electric bread slicer! This is going to bring in every newspaper and television station from across the country and every politician too. You're going to see the governor, senators, congressmen, you name it and that's going to mean more business than this town has seen since your mother welcomed home the Fourth Infantry."

"Really?" Mudlick gasped. "Tell me more – !"

"We're gonna have tourists from all around the state and all of them will be renting rooms, buying meals, drinking, eating, and spending. Spending, spending, spending! Listen to me, Mudlick, there's money to be made in Communism! I'm telling you right now, we're sitting on a goddamn goldmine!"

"All right, you old rag monger, I'm with you! Now how do we get McCarthy back here?"

"Didn't I just tell you? We're going to draw every newspaper, magazine, and television network in the country! He'll be begging us to come back! Mooseburg today – Schenectady tomorrow!"

C H A P T E R   F O R T Y - S I X

HENRY NEEDS A COVER STORY

Now that he had a place to stay, the next thing "Vladimir" needed was a job. This was arranged by Milo, still unseen and unknown to Henry Brownale. Henry also needed an alias for his new life in Schenectady – something masculine and daring, like Dirk or Gunner. Almost anything would be better than plain, prissy Henry.

Henry recalled an actor from an old R.K.O. picture, Nick Lansing. In the movie, Lansing played a suave British agent caught in a web of deceit and double-dealing. Henry liked the story and he liked the actor's name even more. From then on, the mysterious Vladimir would be known as dashing Nick Lansing.

"Nick" was assigned to Building 25 on the General Electric campus. Amid the clattering of conveyor belts and noisy steam compressors, Building 25 pushed out a continuous stream of large appliances, hundreds every day. Henry's job would be at the end of the line, cleaning out the refrigerators, ovens, and washers before they were packed for shipping.

"The job is pretty simple," a foreman shouted over the rattling metal.

"You take a rag, hose down the box and then you wipe it clean. Got it?"

It wasn't long before Nick received another set of instructions, this time from the union steward in Building 25.

"Here's the deal – while you're scrubbing and cleaning and all that, you gotta be watching to see what's going on around you," said the union steward. "If the line is going too fast, it's my job to slow it down – and I might have to cause a little accident for the foreman to get wise. We call it a 'Skippy.' So keep your eyes open and be ready."

Henry nodded, not really knowing what to expect. He grabbed a rag and got to work.

The assembly lines at G.E. were managed like an enormous Swiss watch. A worker's every movement, in every type of job and for every action required for that job, had been measured to the tenth of a second using scientific, time-motion studies. One and seven-tenths of a second was needed to grab a rag, three seconds to soak the box, six and three-quarter seconds to clean the box, three more seconds to rinse, and then another half-second to step back and prepare for the next appliance. The company knew how fast people could work and the assembly lines were timed to move just a little faster.

On Henry's first day, the line went so fast that a woman fell onto the conveyor belt and nearly died. Even as she was pulled off the line, the work continued. Time did not stop so the line did not stop. An hour later, the union retaliated with a Skippy. If falling workers could not get the company's attention, then a Skippy would.

"Be ready," the union steward called to "Nick." Henry nodded, still unsure about what was going to happen. The line moved so much faster than Henry could have imagined. As simple as his job was, Henry could barely get in and out of a box before the next refrigerator or stove was on top of him – one machine following another along this giant, inhuman conveyor. The pace seemed to be getting even faster when suddenly the woman alongside him shouted, "Next one!"

"What's that?" Henry asked as the other workers stepped back from the line. One unfinished appliance and then another piled against the next machine until they all fell off the line and onto the floor. Henry dove out of the way as refrigerators, stoves, and ovens stacked up against each other, their smooth metal shells crushed and gouged in a massive heap.

The foreman got the message: slow down the line, otherwise, no appliances were going out that day. Soon, everyone was back at work, the noise of the machinery mixing with the chatter of workers along the line. By the end of his first week, Henry had never felt such satisfaction. He was part of a team, a regular guy doing a regular job. He came back to Arthur Klingman's apartment exhausted, but supremely happy.

"I have something for you," Klingman announced before he disappeared behind his stacks of newspapers and magazines. Henry expected another book on Marxian philosophy so he was surprised when Klingman returned with a shoe box in his hands.

"Here they are, Vladimir. The high-security badges you asked for."

"Well, well, Comrade. Very ... impressive," Henry said, carefully pulling his hands behind his back. Those security passes could open doors to the most sensitive and highly classified buildings at G.E. – places where secret military hardware was developed. Stealing those badges was a major federal crime so Henry was not going to touch them even as Klingman tried to push the box into his hands.

"Our friends will be pleased with your work," said "Vladimir," backing up against a tower of magazines. "I see you have no trouble accessing the most sensitive areas of the factory."

Klingman smiled. It was true. Everybody at G.E. knew Klingman. This familiarity allowed him to roam freely from building to building – even in the research labs and work rooms – as Klingman delivered copies of the *Daily Proletariat*, the Communist newspaper of Local 1389 ("*Read by Reds Since 1932*").

Klingman was the paper's chief writer, editor, photographer, printer, and newsboy. After the evening press run, Klingman was up early the next morning, roaming the factory floors, the work rooms, and loading docks, peddling his Communist newspaper for a penny. People were glad to buy the paper because that meant Klingman would be off to his next customer. Otherwise, Klingman would stay and talk – lecture, actually – and always on the subjects he was most passionate: the ugly, unjust Capitalist system against the pristine virtues of Communism and the Soviet Union.

Klingman had opinions on any topic you could name but he could always tie them back to Communism's Great Struggle. He was an anarchist's anarchist. When he wasn't proselytizing at the plant, Klingman was educating the masses from a soapbox in front of the Otis Cigar Shop. His audience might be just the pigeons pecking at the sidewalk, but shouting from that soapbox made Arthur feel like he was speaking to the entire world. The truth had to be told: the world outside of the Soviet Union was a place of great injustice. Klingman believed his entire life had been one great injustice.

Shorter than the tallest jockey, Klingman looked even smaller because of a severe curvature in his spine. It left him permanently stooped and unable to walk without alternately twisting his shoulders and switching his hips. But it was Klingman's head that drew most of the gawking. It was nearly oval in shape – more like an egg turned on its side – and balanced between two pointy shoulders. He was almost completely bald except for a tuft of red hair at the top of his head – a Kremlin-spouting Kewpie doll with large, mismatched eyes and a small ball of flesh where his right ear should have been.

His missing ear, his head, his politics, his entire life: nothing was ever right with Arthur Klingman. It began with the day he was left at the doorstep of Our Sisters of Sacrifice. Arthur soon learned that he was a great disappointment to the Sisters and all the other orphans. They did little to hide their disgust for the humpbacked boy, which seemed particularly unfair to Klingman. He was the one who had to live that way.

From grade school to high school, the insults and the mockery never stopped. Even the young parish priest, the future Bishop Carney, would shake his head whenever he saw the boy.

"He's no Lucky Lindy," Rev. Carney would remark sadly. If Rev. Carney said it once, he must have said it a thousand times – loud enough to make Klingman turn his good ear away whenever Rev. Carney was near. Klingman wasn't sure what it meant, but he grew tired of hearing about this Lucky Lindy.

Someday, the orphan promised himself, Arthur Klingman would be bigger and luckier than this "Lindy." With Vladimir's arrival in Schenectady, Klingman wondered if that time was now.

"When will we be going in?" asked Klingman, still displaying the stolen security badges.

"Into the plant?" Henry blanched. "Well, I – "

BUM-BUM-BUMP! Three sharp raps struck the floor from the butcher shop below. The butcher was sending them a warning: the FBI was coming! Footsteps echoed in the hallway as three stocky men, dressed in identical snap-brim hats and long overcoats, came running up the stairs to Klingman's apartment.

"Vladimir, quick – hide!" whispered Klingman, shoving the security badges between some newspapers while Henry jumped behind a column of *Look* magazines. Klingman threw open the door before the G-Men could announce their arrival.

"Arthur!" called one of the agents. "We hear you've got a new roommate! Mind if we step inside and say hello?"

"He's not here right now and, no, you can't come in. I'm cleaning right now."

The agents gazed at the towering stacks of books and papers that covered the apartment.

"You're gonna need a bigger broom, Arthur."

Another agent cracked, "Arthur – listen! I think I hear a voice crying for help! Sounds like your friend might be under that pile in the corner."

"I'm right here," Henry announced, stepping out from behind the magazines. Henry's eyes went over each of the FBI agents until he stopped at the man in the back. Henry nearly gasped as he spied his old nemesis, FBI Special Agent Walter Thurston.

Thurston chuckled, "Well, well. Look who's here!" Klingman turned to Vladimir in surprise.

Henry blustered, "I told you in Pittsburgh to stop following me! You FBI guys never learn, do you?"

"Oh yeah, Pittsburgh," Thurston smiled, relishing Henry's embarrassment. "Why don't you come down to my office sometime and we can discuss those old times in Pittsburgh. What do you say?"

"He's got nothing to say to you!" Klingman protested. He tried to close the door, but an agent put his foot in the way.

"Whatever you say, Arthur," Thurston replied. "All you Commies end up singing in the end, don't they boys? When you're ready to talk, comrades, we'll be right outside waiting for you."

"Thanks for the advice," Henry snapped, shoving the door closed.

Henry stumbled to the couch and flopped down on a pile of Party brochures. His face was white and covered in sweat.

"You should have told me the FBI was around here! Those badges were right in front of them!"

"Be strong, Vladimir," Arthur boasted. "This is what we must do for the Revolution, am I right? Forward to October!"

Klingman looked at his comrade in astonishment. Clearly, Vladimir was someone the FBI had been pursuing. Perhaps he was more important than Arthur realized.

And if Vladimir was important, then I must be important too!

"Important, but a little nervous," Klingman was telling this story several hours later, standing in the shadows of the G.E. loading dock.

"Nervous how?" asked Wotan Volk.

"I don't know. Just nervous," Klingman said. "After the FBI barged in, he didn't want to talk about the badges."

"FBI? Arthur, do you want to tell me what's going on?"

"I'm trying to! So when Vladimir calmed down, he said I should put away the badges and instead I should look into getting the floor plans for Building 29 and also 62. Of course, that won't be a problem – not for me, anyway."

"For God's sake, Arthur, what are you thinking? There's nothing more secure than those two units! They'll arrest you for just looking at Building

62! If you steal the floor plans, they'll send you to Leavenworth and throw away the key!"

"Of course they're secure. That's why they want me to get inside, isn't it?"

"Who, Arthur? Who is *they*?"

"Us, of course! What do you think Helen and I have been doing all this time? We're working for the Party and from what I've seen, this fellow Vladimir has come to us straight from the Kremlin!"

"Stop it, Arthur! Just stop it," Volk said impatiently. "You don't know who this guy is so you can't be sure if he's working for Moscow. If I wasn't told about him, then chances are he's working for the Americans – the FBI, the CIA, somebody. So what happened with the FBI?"

"It looks like they've been tracking Vladimir since Pittsburgh."

"Okay, we have people there. I'll check him out. In the meantime, don't be doing any more favors for this Vladimir, understand? And what about Martha Milwaukee – has she said anything more about me?"

"You mean that Mr. X business? I told you before, she has no idea you exist. But I haven't seen her for the past few weeks. She cancelled our last cell meeting – twice, as a matter of fact."

"Go talk to her, Arthur. Find out what's going on."

"You know something, don't you? What's happened?"

"Stop with the questions and go see Martha. I think she's got something important to tell you. It might help you figure out this Vladimir business."

"You always talk in puzzles, Chief Inspector."

"That's what cops do, Arthur," Volk said as he got into his squad car. "And then we put the pieces back together."

Wotan Volk was not the only one who knew secrets. Klingman had already put together the secret life of this big cop – or so he thought. Still, Klingman did not know the whole truth about Wotan Volk and how dangerous those secrets could be.

CHAPTER FORTY-SEVEN

ALL THE WAY

Martha had told no one about her terrible trip to New York and her abduction by the Tenth Directorate. Only she knew about her rescue and how she had learned the truth about the Party. Now it was time to fight back, for Anna Razumnova and all the others.

She had to stop Milo and Helen, but she would have to do it quietly. Michael, however, immediately saw the change. Suddenly, Martha was smiling and happy – at times, nearly hysterical with joy – racing around the house, washing and scrubbing places she had never cleaned before. Even Michael's clothes smelled cleaner and somehow the frozen foods at dinner were tasting fresher.

As she scrubbed and cooked and polished, Michael could hear his mother muttering to herself – "And they thought they could fool old Martha, did they? Well, they were *wrong* and they're not going to get away with it! No siree. I know too much now, let me tell you, and *no one* is going to stop me!"

It got stranger a few days later.

Michael was finishing a bowl of Sugar Jets cereal one Sunday morning when Martha threw the telephone book onto the table.

"Michael," she announced, "we have a choice to make."

"About what?"

Thumbing through the Yellow Pages, Martha said, "We have to hurry. We don't have much time to get there."

"Get where?" Michael asked again.

"Church!" Martha responded, her voice both excited and apprehensive. "So let's go through the phone book and see what's in town."

"You two going to a show?" Milo asked as he padded into the kitchen, still in his pajamas and his pointy hair parted down the middle. Yawning and pawing at his two-day-old beard, Milo smiled at Martha and Michael waiting for an answer about "the show."

"Are you trying to be funny?" Martha spit back. Milo stopped scratching his stomach and looked at her in surprise.

"Jesus, what's with you?"

"That's exactly right, Milo: Jesus! Yes, Jesus Christ. And please do us a favor and do not use His name in vain unless you truly mean it – and we both know that you don't!"

Michael tried to slip out of his chair, but Martha pulled him back to the table.

"Michael and I are going to church today because today is Sunday and Sunday is the day when all the churches have their ceremonies."

"Not all of them," Milo said, his head inside the refrigerator. "Are we out of milk?"

"Churchgoing families – families that believe in something good and decent – they know that you're not supposed to drink milk on Sundays."

"Michael," Milo said firmly, "why don't you let your Mom and me talk for a minute. I want to hear more about drinking milk on Sundays."

"You stay here, Michael," Martha said, pulling the phone book between them. "We have to choose a church! Here they are. Should we try the First Free Baptists? Or the Ess-pick-a-palions? How about the Church of Ladder Day Saints – now they sound exciting!"

"Gosh, Mom, do we have to? I was going to play ball with the guys."

"Play time can wait," she scolded. "Heaven knows – now isn't that a nice expression? – heaven knows, Michael, I have been neglecting your moral upbringing for far too long and that is going to change right this instant! It's time we started living like normal people – normal Americans! – and go to church. The only question is, which one? How about the Refreshing Spring of Our Christ the Lord and Savior? Or the Lutherans? My, they sound serious."

Michael slumped in the chair, dejected and trapped. When Milo reached down to tousle the boy's hair, Michael squirmed away from his touch. That surprised Milo, but he pretended not to notice as he shuffled down the hall.

"I hope you find what you're looking for, Martha. And Michael, I hope you get to play ball someday. For myself, I will be enjoying a glass of this most-foul liquid – the Devil's elixir: Chocolate milk!"

"Ignore him, Michael. Your father has been doing some very foolish things lately. Hopefully, he'll think twice before he makes things worse."

Hearing this, Milo stormed back to the table, looking for Martha to explain herself. Instead, she got up from her chair – slowly – and towered over her diminutive husband.

"Michael, go up to your room and get dressed for church. Your father would like to talk with me."

"Yes, Michael – go," Milo said. "See if that Pioneer uniform still fits you."

"Ha-ha. Very funny, Milo. But I'm not buying that act anymore."

"And what act is that, Martha?"

"You pretending to hate Communism. Yes – THAT act. Why don't you finally confess your sins, Milo? Let the whole world know what you've been doing! Tell everyone about the darkness in your heart and your devious plans to promote Communism inside the union. Go ahead – tell us how you're trying to spark a Revolution right here in our own community. Let's hear it! What have you got Helen Gamble doing for you this week?"

Martha's accusations nearly sent Milo tumbling backward. It was as though his own voice was coming out of Martha's mouth. Here she was, the most fanatical Communist Milo had ever known, and now she was talking like Billy Graham!

She thinks I'm seriously plotting a Revolution? Because of Helen Gamble? How does she know about Helen?

Within seconds, Milo realized that he had no alternative. If he wanted to preserve his secret battle against the Reds, he had to play along with her. He had fooled the local Communists for years and now he would have to fool Martha as well.

Milo shoved Martha into a chair. "Listen to me," he said menacingly. "There are things happening right now that are bigger than the two of us and people are going to get hurt if we're not careful. Like asking too many questions, have you got me? Our family – you, me, and most of all Michael – will suffer the consequences if you don't watch what you say. Am I making myself clear, Martha?"

Martha and Milo looked up as they heard Michael running up the stairs. He had heard every word of Milo's threat.

"There! Are you satisfied?" Milo seethed. "Once again you've brought our son into this."

"No, Milo – you brought this into our house a long time ago and I hate it! I just hate it! All you care about is the Party, don't you? All those years of secret plans and plotting with Helen and all the while telling me how evil Communism is. Well I'm nobody's patsy – not anymore – and especially not for you! If you really cared about Michael and me, you would tell Helen the truth about the Party!"

Milo had to stop himself from saying what he really wanted to tell her. He had to respond like a Communist – to throw out some sort of Soviet slogan or Party epithet, but his mind went blank. How was he going to act like a Red if he couldn't talk like one?

Milo pointed a finger up at Martha. "Don't you dare say a word to Helen, do you hear me? The Party has big plans for her and if you interfere, Martha, I don't know what will happen – to her or to us."

"Oh believe me, Milo, I know what can happen. I've seen it for myself. So spare me the lecture because I can't waste any more time on your sickness! I have to go to church now and let me tell you something, Milo: I'm going to go all the way with this and I mean *all the way!*"

Up the stairs Martha shouted, "Michael, get in the car! I've made a decision: We're going Catholic!"

"The power of Marxist-Leninist theory lies in the fact that it enables the Party to find the right orientation in any situation, to understand the inner connection of current events, to foresee their course, and to perceive not only how and in what direction they are developing in the present, but how and in what direction they are bound to develop in the future."

HISTORY OF THE COMMUNIST PARTY ✳ *Moscow, 1945*

CHAPTER FORTY-EIGHT

HENRY ALONE

"Vladimir! Vladimir!" sobbed Klingman, stumbling up the stairs to their apartment. He held the newspaper up to Henry: '**STALIN DEAD!**'

But Henry's eyes were drawn to another face on the page. It was his father.

REP. CONRAD BROWNALE, RED-HUNTING REPUBLICAN, DEAD AT 81

"Congressman Brownale is predeceased by his wife, the former Arlene Droefelle, and survived by a son, Henry Conrad, of New York City."

Klingman could see the shock on Vladimir's face. Their Supreme Leader was dead! Henry took the newspaper from Klingman's hands and quickly folded it in half. It would be difficult to explain the resemblance between himself and the Commie-bashing congressman pictured on the front page. The photo was taken in 1934, the year C.B. Brownale first ran for office. His father was about Henry's age at that time. As the photograph showed, father and son shared the same flat, thin lips, a strong chin, a receding hairline, and eyes that seemed to be looking far into the distance. His father had always been searching for his next conquest while Henry had spent most of his life questioning the choices he made and fretting about the opportunities he might have missed.

What had he missed with his father?

"Vladimir" put his arm around Klingman, who was crying enough tears for the both of them. Their Great Leader, Joseph Stalin, was no more, the victim of his own reign of terror. Stalin's guards did not save him because they were too afraid to enter his bedroom. Other guards had been killed when they disobeyed Stalin's orders: no one could enter without Stalin's permission. The guards cowered outside the door as the Man of Steel died alone in his room.

Henry tucked the newspaper under his arm and grabbed his lunch bucket. It was time for work. Klingman followed him out the door, hoping Vladimir would offer some insight into what would happen now that Stalin was gone.

Vladimir had nothing to say. Henry only stared into the sky, holding back the tears that suddenly appeared for the death of his father. Covering his face with the newspaper, Henry waved goodbye to Klingman and headed off to G.E.

Klingman walked the other way, toward Tuckahoe Row. He had to talk to Martha Milwaukee. She would know what to do now that Stalin was dead.

Henry opened the newspaper again and stared blankly at his father's picture. As a cloud slipped away, the sun fell across the page and his father's face disappeared in the brilliance. In that moment, Henry realized that he was now the last of the Brownales. Or was he dead too? If not for Milo Milwaukee and FBI agent Walter Thurston, no one knew Henry was in Schenectady. To the rest of the world, there was the mysterious Vladimir and there was Nick Lansing, a new employee at General Electric. But Henry Brownale was gone, just like Volga the Boatman and all of his other roles for the CIA.

There was something strangely pleasant about this situation. Henry felt free. No longer Henry the Ever-Obedient Son. Could he now remain in Schenectady and be with Helen forever?

With his lunch bucket whistling against his coveralls, Henry put his face up toward the sky and with each step, he was feeling more like dashing Nick Lansing, the newly-promoted apprentice on the sheet-metal press. Near the factory gate, Henry came upon a group of G.E. executives, each of them sporting a natty suit and a corporate tower grimace.

"Hmmphh," Henry grunted dismissively as he swaggered past them. "Guys with ties."

The noise in Building 25 quickly filled Henry's head, pushing out thoughts about his father, the Communists, and even about Helen. It was time for work, real work. Henry was now assigned to the other end of the refrigerator box line. Here the job was too noisy for chatter between the workers. This was a job for men and they saved their conversations for lunchtime in the taverns along Orchard Street. Heavy glasses of beer would be lined up along the bars, waiting for the noon whistle and the men to arrive. Along this assembly line of beer, no one talked about politics or union grievances. Here, they discussed baseball, car engines, and fishing or they simply enjoyed the fraternal comfort of a midday beer. Or two.

Lunchtime left everyone in a good mood and the rest of the afternoon would sail along under the pleasant thrum of the factory floor. The only thing left on their minds was the five o'clock whistle and the end of their shift. As Henry headed home that night, he thought about his father and all of the things they should have said to one another, all of the questions Henry wanted to ask but never had the courage to try.

It was too bad Helen never had a chance to meet his father, Henry decided. Such a beauty, Helen would probably be the only Communist who could make the old man smile.

Henry found himself back on Orchard Street that night and he stayed there for seven more beers, toasting the man he had never known and dreaming about the woman he could never leave.

"Sobbing, she told us the story of Alice Abramovitch ... Her husband had been arrested early in the purge. She and her child stayed on, waiting every night, as did so many, to be arrested between midnight and 2:00 a.m., which was the hunting time for the NKVD. When the feared knock finally came at Alice's door, she took her child and ran like a frightened and cornered animal from one door to another in the hotel, begging the comrades to keep the child ... They looked at her in distress and closed their doors in fear. To shelter the child of a woman about to be arrested was treason."

THE DECEPTION BY FORMER SOVIET SPY HEDE MASSING *describing the horrors of the Great Purge, 1935-38*

CHAPTER FORTY-NINE

SEVEN MILES OUTSIDE THE CITY

The Chief Inspector was at ease, pouring his morning cup of imported coffee, heavy and very dark. Very un-American. It was steaming out of an Imperial Samovar, the same urn that had been used by the Czar and the rest of Russian royalty before the Revolution.

Wotan Volk sniffed the thick aroma rising from the porcelain cup, pinched between a meaty thumb and the forefinger of his shooting hand. Volk could kill with either hand, both were strong and steady. But this was no time for guns. Relaxing in his study, Volk once more raised the delicate cup to his lips for a long, satisfying sip. He closed his eyes, leaning back against the velvet embroidery of his gold-encrusted swan couch, another artifact from Russia's czarist past.

What would Tsar Nicholas be thinking as he relaxed in his palace? Did he realize the danger lurking outside his door, the Bolshevik mob plotting his assassination? It was around this very couch that the Tsar and his family had gathered in their final moments on Earth, surrounded by their jewels and opulent furnishings, before the blood and the screams and the terror, when everything and everyone was burned in the palace court-yard. Their deaths were the birth of the Communist Revolution. Mass murder was just beginning.

It was long before sunrise and Volk was enjoying his coffee as he did every morning before work. Work – that was something the Romanovs never did. If they had learned to work, even a little, perhaps there would never have been a revolution. The Samovar hissed in reply as Volk took another drink.

Imperial Samovars were made by hand. Melded from copper, bronze, iron and brass, each one was elegantly embellished with gold, rubies, emeralds, and sapphires. Because Samovar designs were unique to each craftsman, no two urns were exactly the same. That kind of individuality could never be tolerated by the Communists. They destroyed the Samovar factories and imprisoned the craftsmen, ensuring that these beautiful urns – symbols of the Romanov Empire – would never be seen again.

Never. Always. Must. Forever. The Communists always dealt in abso-lutes. They had no sense of proportion. Everything was taken to extremes. Look what they did to poor Marx. His manifesto was nothing more than a children's fable, a world that could never exist. "From each according to his ability, to each according to his need." Man helping his fellow man? Such nonsense, the Samovar hushed. As if coffee this luxurious could be enjoyed by just any man.

And who decides what is enough? What Five Year Plan can sensibly ration the world's riches? The world – the real world – could never abide so much selflessness and cooperation – and so much planning! It is so much easier to take something for yourself and kill if you must. For each according to his wants, to each according to his grasp.

The Communists were proof of that. They showed how life is full of fallible, imperfect people, each one malleable, corruptible, and even monstrous. That is the nature of humans. Give them enough power and they become dictators. Give them enough fear and they will terrorize.

Communism was not just a failed experiment in social justice, the Soviets had turned it into a brutal excuse to kill, torture, and steal – all in the name of Progress, the Party, and the Revolution. Mostly, in the name of Stalin.

This is what happens when people give up their freedom to the State. Personal freedom becomes nothing more than a commodity to be consumed. And it doesn't stop there: Communism needs more to survive. More sacrifices, human and otherwise. People with lives and loves, families and art, truth and humanity – all of it must be destroyed in order for Communism to live.

Communism only feeds the State. Everything else must die.

It was time to put down the dainty porcelain cup. It may have been the coffee or simply thinking about his homeland, but Volk's temper was starting to build. He closed his eyes again and tried to relax.

What can be done about it now? he sighed.

Volk had built a new life for himself and thinking about his success always improved his disposition, especially in the morning, surrounded by the many treasures that adorned this house – a mansion, actually – bordered by farms and uncultivated pastures far outside the city. He could feel the eyes of the Russian icons hanging on the walls above him. His favorite – the portrait of Prince Baratyansky – dominated the mantel above the fireplace, his ivory skin matching the palisander panels on the walls and the Chinese silks draped about the windows.

Volk was a collector, but not of the refrigerators, radios, and dishwashers that he filched from the loading docks of General Electric. Those appliances were simply another form of currency to expand his collection of priceless relics from Russia's past, the Russia that had been trampled by the Bolsheviks. It had been many years since Volk had left home and he was determined to never go back.

He had been sent to America as part of an exchange program between the "sister cities" of Schenectady and Volgograd in southern Russia. Long before the Cold War, the two cities had sponsored police officers, clerks, and other municipal officials for a year-long stay in their sister city, a gesture toward world peace and international understanding. The Russian delegation was carefully selected, including the young Wotan Volk, newly recruited to Russia's secret police, the NKVD. His mission was to find some way to remain in Schenectady following his year in the exchange program. Once established, Volk would then infiltrate the weapons factory at General Electric and send Moscow the plans and specifications for the latest American armaments.

That was 17 years ago – the year Schenectady suffered the bloodiest summer since the Dutch first cleared the land of Indians, trees, and anything else that was inconvenient to the business of making money. Three brutal murders, each one seemingly random and disconnected from the others, all took place during a single, horrific week.

None of the victims, nor the murders, seemed to fit a pattern other than the gunshots and knife wounds that nearly severed the head of each victim. People in Schenectady were afraid to leave their homes. The terror was felt by everyone. Just before the city called in the FBI, the young detective from Russia single-handedly solved each of these unspeakable crimes.

No one stood trial, however, because Wotan Volk delivered the verdict himself: a .38 caliber slug to the back of the head. He had to shoot, Volk explained, because the killer was reaching for his gun – the same gun Volk had used to commit all three of these murders. Everyone was too relieved and too grateful to ask many questions. With the supposed murderer now dead, there was no need for further investigation. A grateful city hailed Wotan Volk as a hero and Chief McGuire asked him to stay on after the other Russians had returned home.

After Volk officially joined the Schenectady Police force, he was soon working on his next targets: first, General Electric and after that, the Russian secret police.

Volk took another sip of his rich Russian coffee. He would wait, as he always did, for the sun to rise before he would get dressed and head downtown for work. It was always a good day when the light would slowly fill his study, creeping over the Fabergé eggs, then twinkling like the Eastern Star against the armorial glass flute. Yes, life was good, Volk reminded himself with a sigh of satisfaction.

He had worked hard to lose his Russian accent as he moved up the ranks of the Schenectady police force. He had also been diligent in his reports back to Moscow. His controllers in New York were pleased with Volk's frequent, if trivial, dispatches about military contracts and aviation research inside General Electric. Nothing of great consequence, but just enough to make the NKVD believe that Volk was doing his job for Mother Russia.

These informative tidbits came easier once Volk informed General Electric that there was a spy inside the Schenectady plant, the same spy who was now the Chief of Detectives in the Schenectady Police Department. The company's CEO, Philip Reedy, personally agreed to Volk's offer: discreet cash payments would be deposited in the First National Bank of Schenectady and, in return, Wotan Volk could assure Philip Reedy that there would be no espionage from the NKVD, the KGB, or any other foreign agency. General Electric would pay a spy to catch a spy.

Collecting salaries from G.E., the NKVD, and the city of Schenectady – with pensions guaranteed from all three – Volk would never have to worry about money. For a little extra, there were the "aftermarket" sales of G.E. appliances. Clearly, Wotan Volk was doing very well and he was about to do even better.

Special Agent Walter Thurston had recently approached Volk about a new business venture. Thurston recognized the potential profits that could be made from the thousands of dossiers collected by the FBI. With the Red Scare in high gear, no corporation wanted dangerous subversives on their payroll. Would G.E. be interested in learning more about its employees – perhaps $1,000 for every file that Thurston and Volk would deliver? It would be like printing money, the two lawmen agreed.

Above the fireplace, Prince Baratyansky seemed to be winking at this enterprising detective. Communism can provide a good life, Volk mused, as long as you're not living among Communists.

A moment later, Volk's worry-free life would end with a knock at the door.

It sounded more like someone – or something – scratching against the wood. Perhaps a farm animal had wandered onto his property and was using the doorknob to satisfy an itch. Volk peered through the bullet-proof glass: no one was there. Then he looked down to see Arthur Klingman, up on his toes, straining to reach the iron door knocker.

Klingman?

There was no car outside and no city bus traveled this far. Klingman must have walked more than seven miles to get there.

How did he find me and what the hell does he want?

The oak and steel door opened slowly, just enough for Volk to be heard.

"What is it?" he demanded.

Klingman took a step back, raising his head to where he expected to find Volk's face.

"Martha Milwaukee – she told me everything!" Klingman sobbed. He startled Volk by grabbing hold of the heavy door and pushing it aside. "She said it's all been a lie! None of it is true!"

"What are you talking about?"

"Russia, Communism – it's all lies! There is no justice there. No peace. No prosperity. No equality! It's just the opposite! She says it's all a nightmare and Martha says she can prove it!"

Tears were running down his face as Klingman tugged at the ball of flesh on the side of his head.

"And that's why you're here?"

"Just tell me what's going on! Did Stalin truly starve his people? Does he torture and murder them? Martha said millions of people have been eliminated – exiled to labor camps, tortured, slaughtered! How could this happen?"

"Do you believe her?"

"I don't know what to believe. I have to, I suppose. She said the Tenth Directorate even tried to kill her! How is that possible?"

"You run a newspaper, Arthur. Find out for yourself."

"All I'm asking for is the truth!"

"What are you saying? After all these years – after all your worthless propaganda – now you want the truth?"

"What do you mean 'propaganda?' I only wrote what I was told to write – what everyone in the Party was thinking!"

"Thinking, huh?" Volk smiled. "But now you've gone so much farther, haven't you comrade? Thinking up big plans with your new pal, Vladimir – this great Soviet spy. Why don't you ask him for the truth? Ask him why we should be loyal to these butchers?"

"I have only done what was asked of me!"

"Then why are you worried? Your conscience is clear, am I right? When you wrote about the Five Year Plans, you actually believed that Stalin had somehow magically created Russia's heavy industry – out of what? How did he do this? Certainly not by taking food away from his own people, am I right? Not by starving children and their grandparents! Not by sending innocent Russians to die in Siberian gold mines! He would never! It was all from Stalin's genius, isn't that true? 'A worldwide powerhouse created overnight!' That's what you wrote, isn't it? Well get wise, Arthur. The Russia you love so dearly was built on top of the dead – millions of men, women and children destroyed for the glory of Joseph Stalin and the great Soviet Socialist Republic!"

Klingman slumped against the wall. His complicity and shame were overwhelming. All of his life was built on a lie. Countless hours spent on the street corner, trumpeting the virtues of the glorious Soviet system, shouting until his voice went hoarse; typing and editing his newspaper every day, writing columns and tributes to thieves and murderers!

"Why – why didn't you tell me? I thought we were friends! How can Martha Milwaukee care more about this than you!"

Volk pulled Klingman off the floor. "What did she say about me? Did she send you here?"

"What? No – she doesn't even know you exist! I'm the only one who knows the truth or what I thought was the truth. I don't know anymore. Are you part of this too?"

Volk threw open the door and with one hand he tossed Klingman outside. Klingman did not protest. He looked up at Volk with his pathetic, mismatched eyes. Too sick to speak and too confused to think, Klingman walked the seven miles back home, past the corner where he had proclaimed the greatness of Soviet society. Above him were the banners advertising the upcoming Red Scare Days: "*Commietown is Coming: Will You Be Ready?*"

Back at his typewriter, Klingman wrote his final editorial for the *Daily Proletariat*:

The Beast is Dead, but the Monster Still Lives

Russia is no longer ruled by the so-called Man of Steel. Joseph Stalin is dead — a death which might suggest that he was human after all. Sadly, the only thing human about Joseph Stalin was his mortality. For those of you still blinded by the Party doctrine, you may not know that Stalin was something far less than a man.

He was not a "super man" as the Party has insisted. He was only the latest tyrant to massacre millions of innocent people. Perhaps he was the greatest of his kind. We won't know that for many more years. They may still be counting the bodies and, by then, there will be a new leader of the Supreme Soviet.

Will that leader be just another monster? Did Stalin have an apprentice, someone trained in the mechanics of torture, starvation and fear? In case you don't recognize this, these are called questions. As members of the Communist Party, you have not been allowed to use them, along with your brain, your free will and any other part of your humanity.

You had better get used to hearing more questions. They will open your eyes and unplug your ears. They

```
will lead to horrible accusations because the world
will demand an accounting of Stalin's crimes. For
myself and the people who read this newspaper, we
also are guilty and we will continue to be until the
Party is destroyed.
```

```
    My eyes are open now and I am ready to face the
consequences.
```

The word shot up from New York soon after the *Daily Proletariat* hit the streets: get rid of Arthur Klingman – immediately. Milo and the local Communist deputy, Ira Glabberson, were sent to retrieve the keys to Klingman's office. They found Klingman standing by the window, looking like a man desperate enough to jump. Klingman turned and smiled as Glabberson stepped closer. Klingman opened his mouth and swallowed the office key.

"Be patient, comrades," Klingman laughed. "Everything comes out in the end."

Klingman walked home feeling heroic, but his defiance did not last very long. What was left now? Without the newspaper, what was he going to do with his life? He felt empty and defeated. Who was going to listen to him now?

As he neared his apartment, Klingman was shocked to see newspapers, magazines, and books flying out of the windows above Schicksal's Butcher Shop. The street was covered in paper – Klingman's papers!

"Bastards!" Klingman cursed. Party thugs are trashing my belongings! All of his writings – his precious thoughts and words – were being thrown into the gutter! As Klingman ran toward the butcher shop, it was Boris Schicksal who came flying out the door.

"Klingman! What the hell were you thinking?" the butcher cried. "All of those books, the magazines, and newspapers – they must have weighed three tons! You nearly brought the roof down on me! On my wife! On my meat!"

The two men jumped aside as an Underwood typewriter came flying out of the window and smashed against the pavement. Klingman walked slowly over the debris, his entire life spread beneath his feet. He looked up to the window just as a single newspaper clipping came floating out of the sky, zig-zagging on the breeze, until it came to rest on Klingman's nose. It was an article from *The Ledger* newspaper dated March 2, 1932, the day that newspapers all around the world announced the awful news: **LINDBERGH BABY KIDNAPPED!**

The baby boy of Charles Lindbergh – "Lucky Lindy" – had been stolen from his crib. Klingman looked at the headline and then once more at the date: March 2, 1932 – the same year Klingman was born. In fact, it was the same month the nuns had found him on their doorstep, March of 1932!

Klingman had to sit down on the curb as more paper came fluttering down around him – just like the ticker-tape parade that celebrated America's first transatlantic aviator. Suddenly Arthur Klingman realized who he was and where he had come from! The thought was absolutely shattering!

The sky above Klingman's head was the deepest blue he had ever seen – the kind of blue sky his father must have witnessed as he bravely piloted the Spirit of St. Louis across the Atlantic. Lucky indeed. It was the reason why Rev. Carney had taunted him all those years ago – that poor little Arthur Klingman, abandoned by his parents, was no Lucky Lindy. But now here was the truth: Klingman knew where he belonged and that his life truly mattered. Once forgotten, now he was found!

Arthur Klingman was the Lindbergh baby!

CHAPTER FIFTY

NOBLESSE OBLIGE

When Henry came home from work, he did not expect the crowd milling around Schicksal's Butcher Shop. People were stepping over heaps of books and magazines and in the center of this mess, surrounded by news reporters, stood Arthur Klingman.

For once in his life, everyone was listening to Arthur!

"I realize now the errors of my ways – the lies and the propaganda that blinded me to the truth. With the revelation of my true birth family, I am now ready to make amends. No longer will I be a puppet for the Communist Party. I stand before you now a full-fledged and fervently-loyal citizen of these United States, grateful to finally learn the truth about my heritage. I am truly reborn."

"What's he saying?" Henry whispered to people in the crowd.

"Something about him getting rich," a man responded.

"He's the Lindbergh baby!" a woman said excitedly. "Not a very handsome baby, I must say."

Henry gasped, "He's the Lindbergh – ? Oh, for Christ sakes!"

Grandly, slowly – because this is the way patricians gesture when they speak – Klingman turned his knobby head from one side of the crowd to the other, holding out his tiny hands to welcome the world's adulation. "As a member of one of America's leading families, I fully embrace our obligation to help all Americans to achieve the same kind of success that my family has attained. It is our noblesse oblige, if you will. Do you want me to spell that for you, fellas?"

The reporters stared blankly at Klingman. They were skeptical, of course. It was difficult to believe that the Lindberghs had gotten rid of their baby by staging a kidnapping. But this had been a slow news day and the reporters knew that this was a big story – big enough to make the national wires. So no one challenged Klingman for evidence and Klingman offered no explanations. Besides, the newsmen knew better than to spoil a good story. No need to ask a lot of picayune questions because here was a crowd and the people were getting excited because the reporters were there and the reporters were getting excited because the people were there so this had to be news!

The Lindbergh baby right here in our town!

Klingman was also amazed at the hubbub around him. He could hardly believe his good fortune. Every word he was speaking was going straight into the reporters' notebooks. It was an intoxicating feeling watching all those pencils scribbling furiously, filling page after page with Klingman's glorious words!

"Before I leave for New Jersey to reunite with my family, I pledge to remain here in Schenectady and to right the wrongs I have committed on behalf of the Communist Party! I will stand as a Lindbergher should and testify before Congress, before God, and before my fellow Schenectadians to proclaim that Communism is an abomination against God and man and it should be wiped off the face of the Earth or my name isn't Arthur Charles Lindbergh!"

There was a smattering of applause as the crowd, like the reporters, puzzled over what they had just heard. That's when Boris Schicksal stepped in. The butcher had long been a devoted Communist, but everyone has to make a living.

"No more questions. No more questions!" Schicksal shouted as he led Klingman back to the butcher shop. The crowd followed them inside where Mrs. Schicksal was ready at the counter. On sale that day was bologna.

This was too much for Henry. He raced to the back door and pulled Klingman into the slaughterhouse.

"The Lindbergh baby, huh? You honestly believe you are the son of Charles and Ann Lindbergh? Arthur, you realize the Lindberghs already found their baby? There can't be two Lindbergh babies!"

"Then they were wrong – or ashamed or something because the newspaper said a plane, looking very much like the plane flown by my father, was seen over Schenectady just a day before I was found by the Sisters of Sacrifice. Besides, the Bishop told me himself."

"The Bishop told you what?"

"That I was no Lucky Lindy."

"Because you're not!"

"We'll see about that! The Lindberghs may have abandoned me once, but wait until they see me testify in front of Joe McCarthy and all those TV cameras! I can't wait to blow the lid off your little conspiracy, Vladimir! Then we'll see who's a Lindbergh or not!"

Henry yanked Klingman up against a bloody steer hanging from a meat hook. But Klingman was not going to be pushed around anymore.

"Take your hands off of me, you dirty Commie! How can you live with yourself – you and the rest of that scum! Killing innocent children – starving them to death! – all the while claiming to be this paradise of peace and freedom. You're the murderers – all of you! Tell me, Vladimir: when are you going to tell Helen the truth?"

Henry could not believe what he was hearing. Klingman was talking like J. Edgar Hoover at an American Legion convention! But what could Henry say? He was still pretending to BE one of those murderous Reds.

"Arthur, you'd better think twice about this. If you testify before Mc-Carthy, people are going to come after you."

"Is that some kind of threat, Vladimir? Well save it, Ruskie. If I were you, I'd hightail it back to Leningrad – and don't say I didn't warn you!"

With that Klingman picked up his suitcase and started for the door.

"Where are you going?"

"I can't stay here anymore. Honestly, how could anyone from MY family live over a butcher shop? You must be out of your mind!"

Henry watched Klingman switch and twitch his way down Genesee Street, heading for more trouble than either of them could imagine.

How did things ever get so mixed up?

Klingman was going to name names and Henry was going to be one of them: accused of being a Communist spy by the Lindbergh baby!

"The communists have never relied on numerical strength to dominate a labor organization. Through infiltrating tactics they have, in too many instances, captured positions of authority. Communists have boasted that with five percent of the membership, the communists – with their military, superior organizational ability, and discipline – could control the union."

TESTIMONY *by FBI Director J. Edgar Hoover*

CHAPTER FIFTY-ONE

BETWEEN COMRADES

"How's things?"

"Okay, I guess. You?"

Ira Glabberson looked less than 'okay.' Milo looked worse.

"So … what do you think of this 'Commietown' business?"

"Not happy about it," said Glabberson, the Communist Party chief within Local 1389. "The Tenth Directorate doesn't know what we should do about it."

"The Tenth – ?"

"Directorate. Remember – the Party's regional office in New York? They don't know whether to fight this thing or use it for propaganda. Maybe a training exercise. Of course, with McCarthy coming back here, that raises other possibilities, other risks."

Milo nodded, pretending to understand.

"Milo, you look tired."

"I'm all right, I guess. I was just thinking that you and I should talk more often. The union and the Party go hand in hand, of course."

"Of course."

"So what's been happening lately?"

"Oh – so much. So, so much!" Glabberson fell back against his chair, his hands measuring the enormity of it all. "There is great turmoil, of course, about the fate of Comrade Zhdanov. Zhdanov, as you know, was the first deputy to Vice Premier Shtemenko until he was denounced by Zhukov. This led to charges against Zhdanov, Zinoviev, and Shtemenko until Zhukov realized his mistake: he had meant to denounce Comrade Zhadanova, not Comrade Zhdanov. An honest mistake, under the circumstances."

"Clearly."

"Now there are rumors that Khrushchev may be leaving the Party."

"What for?"

"I hear he's opening a shoe store."

"And what's happening over here?"

"The American Communist Party must decide on a new delegation for the Communist International, particularly the chairmanship. Many are favoring Voznesensky, and if not Voznesensky, then it should be Poskrebysheva or Dzherzhinsky."

"And who do you like?"

"O'Brien."

"Good choice."

"Moscow, of course, will make the final decision. In fact, I was expecting a message in today's pouch, but instead I get this in the mail." Glabberson held up an official-looking document. "Another notice from my bank!"

"The bank? Ira – is everything okay?"

"No, not at all," Glabberson choked.

"Sorry, it's not my business," Milo apologized.

"No, it's all right. I could use some help, actually. Advice, I mean, because Milo you know a lot about – "

"Money? Well, I suppose so."

Glabberson threw his face into his hands. "Oh, I'm so ashamed! I can't pay the bills! Now Morris needs braces and Rhonda wants a new car."

"Can't you get a raise?"

"From the Party? Fat chance. Party leaders all have second homes, but I've had to take a second job and I still don't make enough! I'm close to losing the house! But the worst of it is this: I made an appointment to see Mickey Scarpino."

"The loan shark! Ira, you can't take money from that crook! It's too dangerous."

"I know, I know and just as I was walking to his clubhouse, I see Frankie Pepper coming out of there. I turned around as fast as I could and walked the other way."

"Did he see you?"

"I don't think so."

"Listen, I think we can arrange a loan for you – from the union Pension Fund. Or the Insurance Fund. Don't worry about a thing, Ira. Strictly between friends – comrades, right?"

"Milo, I can't thank you enough. If there's anything I can do for you, just say the word!"

"Actually, I do need a small favor from you: Just a little refresher on how to talk to the members, the way a Party member should speak to a comrade. Some of the current lingo, you understand? I can't even talk to Martha lately so I was hoping you could help me with that."

Across town, other favors were being traded across a table at the Montefiore Social Club.

" – so I was hoping you could help me … again," Frankie Pepper said. Mickey Scarpino stirred his espresso until his fist struck the table and the hot drink landed on Pepper's pants.

"Why you need more?" the gangster scowled. "I help you too much already – and what do I get for this? Your puny union is no bigger than it was two years ago."

"Now, Mickey, that's not true. We're getting closer, I can tell you that. Milo can't hold us off much longer."

"Closer to what? And why you are calling me Mickey?"

"Sorry, Mr. Scarpino. The members – the workers at G.E. – they're getting tired of being called a bunch of Communists. They're ready to dump Milo and come over to my union – I mean, OUR union. Honestly, I can feel it."

"I got something else you can feel, Frankie Pepper." Scarpino grabbed Frankie's tie and pulled him down onto the table. "I give you $50,000, you chiseler, and you tell me I make three times more. So where is my money, Frankie Pepper?"

"Here's the thing," Frankie said, his head still pinned against the table. "This 'Commietown' business, it's going to bring Joe McCarthy back to Schenectady and that could be the break we've been looking for."

Scarpino held tight to Frankie's tie as he whistled over his shoulder. From out of the back came one of Scarpino's thugs. It was The Mouse, the smallest and toughest member of Scarpino's gang.

"This here is The Mouse," Scarpino said. "He is one of my best. Now you listen carefully, Frankie Pepper: The Mouse is going to help you get rid of Milo Milwaukee so then you will take over the Local and I will get the money you have promised me. You get me these things or The Mouse is going to take you and Mr. Milo for a swim in the river."

A few weeks later, loan sharks and cement shoes had been forgotten once Arthur Klingman made the news. Klingman, the Star Witness, had the ammunition to put Milo Milwaukee behind bars.

There was only one thing for Frankie Pepper to do now: keep Arthur Klingman alive.

"Our ideas may be new and strange to you. Probably you have never seen or met a Communist before. We don't ask you to agree with us but to listen with an open mind and not to accept as gospel truth the sensational tales of stool-pigeons and planted agents who will be the Government's chief, if not sole, witnesses. Centuries ago, Judas became the symbol of such infamy, a forerunner of those who join a group of sincere and honest people, advocate its teachings, carry out its practices only to betray it."

OPENING STATEMENT BY ELIZABETH GURLEY FLYNN, *an avowed Communist,*
on trial in 1952 for "advocating the violent overthrow of the government"

CHAPTER FIFTY-TWO

THE WITNESSES

Life would change quickly for Arthur Klingman. He would soon be joining a growing fraternity – a profession really – one that was both reviled and acclaimed in America's fight against the Communists. Arthur Charles Lindbergh was about to become a witness.

An informant.

A rat.

With hundreds of congressional committees, grand juries, deportation hearings, and loyalty board investigations, professional witnesses were vital to the unmasking of Red subversives. Like Klingman, these witnesses were usually former Communists, disgruntled with the Party or threatened with arrest or deportation by the American government. For others, it was simply a matter of survival: they needed the work and government agencies and private corporations were willing to spend outlandish sums to expose the Communists and their fellow travelers. Providing testimony against the Communists was a sure way to make a decent living and business was getting better every day.

Most in demand were the witnesses who could name the most names, who told the most hair-raising stories, or displayed a razor-sharp memory for colorful – unverifiable – details. Legislators, their investigators, and especially the press were captivated by their dramatic testimony. These witnesses seemed preternaturally clairvoyant, even omniscient. They could somehow remember specific conversations between people they had never met and from places they had never been.

They were lying of course. Telling the truth was not a job requirement for a professional informant.

For the more celebrated and successful Witnesses, there were still more ways to get paid: book deals, television and radio appearances, even product endorsements (cleaning soaps and solvents, security systems, bug spray).

Careers were launched. Stars were born.

It wasn't long before husbands and wives were testifying together. The Mattesons of Syracuse were the Fred and Ginger of these formerly Communist couples, dancing across the country from hearing to hearing, vouching for the Red bona fides of hundreds of supposed Communists. The Mattesons always swore on a Bible and they were paid just as religiously. "Fred and Ginger" even tried to organize a professional society – a union of sorts – to raise the fees and other benefits for Witnesses such as themselves.

There were so many Witnesses, professional and newborn, that informants were often testifying against each other. Even the most-meticulous and best-rehearsed informant would eventually crack. They could only remember so many stories, tell too many lies. They drank, they divorced, they gave away friendships, and old loyalties. Some wanted to quit until the FBI waved more money at them or they were threatened with their own indictments.

So they continued to talk: "I solemnly swear to tell the truth, the whole truth, and nothing but the truth, so help me" and then help me some more. The government helped them plenty.

No one in authority ever questioned the authenticity or truthfulness of these informants. Just the opposite. Whenever doubts were raised or lies exposed, the government would rally around their Witnesses and attack anyone who threatened their legitimacy. Too many convictions depended on the infallibility of these informants. The reputations of too many government officials were also at risk.

Inevitably, contradictions would arise in a Witness' repeated testimony – after all, how many times can you tell the same story without changing a few details? Serious discrepancies could result in perjury charges, embarrassing headlines, and appellate reversals. It could also mean the end of the gravy train for a fallible Witness. To prevent "mistakes" from happening, the government hired memory experts and stenographers to remind the Witnesses of the many stories they had told, along with the names they had produced during the course of so many hearings. This chicanery was justified because there was a higher purpose at work here. The war against Communism was too important to quibble about a fib here or mistake there.

Convicting Communists – and making it stick – that was the first and most important consideration. The damage to innocent people was considered collateral damage, simply the cost of doing this important business.

Frankie Pepper was explaining all of this to Arthur Klingman, describing "the wonderful opportunities" that lay ahead of him as a Star Witness – the chance "to set the record straight and put those Communists where they belong." And, of course, there was some money to be made.

But it was hard for the union boss to sound enthusiastic since Pepper could only whisper his encouragement as they stood together in the dark, tiptoeing up the back staircase of Pepper's house so his wife and daughter would not see the strange little man who was now living in their attic. For Klingman, it was more hiding than living, but at least he was safe. While many were calling Klingman a hero, no one was saying that in the taverns on Orchard Street or on the factory floors of G.E. There, they had other names for him: Klingman the Rat, Klingman the Traitor, and Klingman the Dead Man.

It was generally assumed that Klingman would crack under the questioning by McCarthy's men. Once he started talking, how far would he go? Would Klingman mention friends, co-workers – even the people he feared?

The men in the Local were already on edge since the company had issued a new policy regarding the Fifth Amendment: any employee refusing to testify would be fired on the spot. It had everyone asking the same questions. Whose name would Klingman be giving to the Senate investigators? Who would be next on Joe McCarthy's hot seat and the first to be fired?

And some were asking a more sinister question: Who was going to wait to find out? Getting rid of Arthur Klingman would answer a lot of questions.

At Wotan Volk's country estate, where pieces of a Fabergé egg lay shattered on the floor, that question had already been answered. Wotan Volk would not wait any longer.

CHAPTER FIFTY-THREE

EVERYBODY!

To the Daughters of the American Revolution, Arthur Klingman was their "Plymouth Rock of 1954." The Elks Club inducted Klingman into their prestigious honor society, the Antler and Hoof. The Gold Star Mothers did what mothers do best: they cooked and baked for him. Arthur was a hero before he had done anything heroic.

The press was also fawning over him. Lengthy articles appeared almost daily, even more frequently than the radio and television news reports on Klingman's upcoming testimony. Frankie Pepper acted as his go-between, arranging Klingman's calendar to accommodate the flood of media requests and public appearances, the testimonial dinners and autograph seekers. While Pepper sifted through all of these requests, Klingman remained in Pepper's attic.

From the window, Klingman would watch Frankie retrieve the mail each day – the invitations and the death threats. Pepper tried to clean up the red paint that had been thrown onto the mailbox. But nothing could disguise the blood-red trail that ran down the sidewalk.

"You get used to it," Pepper said, straining to smile for Klingman. He did not mention the dead rat that had been nailed to the front door the night before. "Still and all, you probably will want to stay inside tonight, right? McCarthy and everyone will be here tomorrow for 'Commietown,' so you'd better rest up."

Klingman nodded as he took the paint-splattered letters out of Frankie Pepper's hands. In the middle of the stack was a postcard stamped 'Mr. X.' It was a signal to meet Wotan Volk.

That night, Klingman set out for the G.E. loading docks, slowly winding his way through the back streets, carefully avoiding pedestrians and potential eyewitnesses. With his distinctive gait, it would be easy to recognize the Star Witness so Klingman kept his head down, stirring the pressure and anxiety in his head. He did not notice the snow that was falling or the footprints that trailed from Frankie Pepper's house.

With a muffler wrapped around his head, Klingman also missed the sound of footsteps behind him.

A green sedan was parked in the shadows when Klingman arrived at the loading docks. This was not Volk's usual car. With the engine running, Klingman nervously crept up to the window. It was too dark to see anything other than Volk's silhouette, that massive hulk jammed against the steering wheel. Klingman jumped back in fright as Volk tapped on the glass.

"What the hell?" barked the muffled voice. "Get in the car."

Klingman was still climbing onto the front seat when Volk pressed hard on the gas, whipping the car west toward the Mohawk River.

Volk laughed stiffly, "You don't look so good – even for you, Arthur. Too many chicken dinners with the bluebloods of Schenectady?"

"Not tonight. I'm seeing McCarthy's men tomorrow."

"So, tomorrow's the big day, huh? Well, I hope you're ready. It's gonna get rough, you know."

"Rough? Why should it get rough? I'm their star witness!"

"You're a star all right, Arthur. What are you gonna say when they ask you about all your friends down at the plant? Everybody knows old Arthur."

"I'll just tell them the truth. They already know who's in the Party. They just need to hear it from an expert like me."

"An expert – right." Volk lit a cigar the size of a firecracker. "Then what about Martha – or Milo?"

"There's nothing to say about Martha. She's changed – you know that. She knows the truth now. I won't be talking about her."

"What if they don't care that Martha Milwaukee is going to church on Sundays or that she's the all-American housewife? What if it's Milo they're after? You can't avoid talking about Milo, can you Arthur?"

Volk's big cigar was filling the car with smoke and choking the air out of Klingman. He reached for the handle to roll down a window, but the lever was gone. So was the door handle.

"And what about Helen?" Volk pestered. "They'll want information on her too – especially her. And that means talking about her boyfriend, right? What's his name, Vladimir?"

"Boyfriend?"

"Sure, your old roommate. They're a pretty hot item, those two. What – you didn't know that? That's right. You don't travel in those circles anymore, do you?"

Klingman was getting angry. Vladimir doesn't deserve Helen! Here was another reason to hate that Commie snake. And Volk too.

The Chief Inspector drew in a long breath before filling the car with more smoke. "Still, it's not every day that a Russian spy comes to town, right?"

"Except for you, of course," Klingman snapped.

Volk jammed on the brakes, grinding to a stop in the middle of the road. The big cop was squeezing the steering wheel, glaring into the dark, as Klingman squirmed in his seat, anxiously searching the road for another car barreling around the corner. He glanced to his right: the Mohawk River was running fast below the road. Helplessly, Klingman pressed against the door, hoping to find an escape, when Volk fired up the engine and, with a jerk of the wheel, the car shot forward.

They were heading farther west, speeding away from the lights of the city. Clinging to the hillside, the car skidded around hairpin curves as Klingman struggled to stay in his seat, trying not to reach out and grab hold of Volk. He dare not touch the detective when he was this angry.

"Don't be a wise guy, Comrade. You still didn't answer my question: what are you going to say tomorrow? Are you going to tell them about me?"

Klingman pleaded, "What's the matter here? Why would I say anything about you? No one knows about you, so there can't be any questions, right? Listen – please, can we stop the car now?"

Klingman was desperately struggling for air as Volk shot off the road, stopping heavily above an empty field. They were at the far end of the G.E. complex. Volk came around to the other side of the car and yanked open the door. Klingman tumbled onto his knees, gasping for breath as the frigid air burned against his throat. Volk stood over Klingman and nudged him with the toe of his boot.

"These are not nice people, Arthur. McCarthy is not going to take 'no' or 'I don't know' for an answer. So don't be a dope: You can't plead the Fifth."

"I've got nothing to hide."

"Oh yeah? Then what about those badges you lifted?"

Volk remembered the stolen security badges! Did he know about the floor plans too?

"Well, all right, sure – then I'll tell them about Vladimir. And Helen too. Why shouldn't I?"

"Maybe we should tell them first. Follow me, Arthur. We can do it right now."

"What are you talking about?"

"Helen and Vladimir – they're right down there." Volk pointed to a small brick building in the middle of the field, nearly a hundred yards away. "Vladimir's been hiding out here since you moved in with Frankie Pepper. I wonder if Helen is out here again tonight?"

Klingman squinted into the dark. He recognized this small stockade, half a mile away from the nearest G.E. security office. A single light was on inside. It was no surprise that Volk would know what – or who – was in there. The detective knew more about the G.E. plant than even Klingman. Still, Klingman's heart sank at the idea that Helen had fallen for Vladimir.

"They don't want to see me – not now. Is that why you brought me out here?"

"No – there's more. Come on, I'll show you." Volk started down the hill, wading through the muddy, snow-covered marsh along the hillside. Klingman stayed by the road until Volk turned and waited for him to follow. Still, Klingman refused. He couldn't face Vladimir and especially not Helen.

But Klingman could never resist Volk. He slowly tramped through the mud and the cattails, muttering to himself about the messy snow and the cold.

"What's the matter, Arthur? Don't like being told what to do?" Volk laughed as he gave Klingman a shove. Klingman looked up at the bigger man, his confusion melting into anger. "What are you gonna do when they push you around tomorrow, Arthur?" Volk gave Klingman another shove, harder this time.

"You can't fight back, you know. You never could. So what are you gonna do – mutter to yourself like some strange little fruitcake?" Volk shoved him again. "Or will you spill your guts?"

"Stop it!" Klingman shouted, rubbing his shoulder.

"They're gonna want names, Arthur! So who's on your list? Who's it gonna be?" Volk pushed Klingman so hard it sent him backward into the snow. Volk was looming over him now, his face covered by the full moon shadow, as he pressed a boot on top of Klingman's ankle. "Take me through the list Arthur. It will be Helen and Vladimir and Glabberson and then who? Who's next, Arthur?"

Volk reached down and with one hand he plucked Klingman off the ground. The little man's eyes were wide with fright as Volk shook him back and forth, his tiny feet swinging in the air.

"Tell me Arthur – who's it going to be? Tell me!"

Klingman was too frightened to speak so Volk threw him back on the ground, the snow burning against Klingman's face and hands. He tried to shout something – to make enough noise that someone in the blockhouse might hear him – but the stockade suddenly disappeared from view as Volk pressed his boot against Klingman's neck, filling his nose and ears with mud and snow. Volk kept pushing with his foot, shouting "Who, Arthur? Who?"

Volk was tired of waiting. A massive hand grabbed Klingman by the coat and lifted him up to Volk's face. "Answer me, goddammit! Who are you going to name? WHO?"

"EVERYBODY!" Klingman shrieked. "Everybody! You, them – everybody! EVERY –"

Klingman fell hard against the snow as his screams echoed across the river. Climbing to his knees, the air suddenly rose up around Klingman as Volk's huge overcoat swirled overhead, the big man turning on one foot as he pulled a Mauser revolver from its holster. Volk set his feet in the snow and stretched the gun toward Klingman's face.

"Get up," he commanded.

Klingman scuttled to his feet, his head leaning toward the gun, when the white-hot light exploded in his eyes and the night disappeared into nothingness.

Volk walked down to the river and then back again, leaving deep, clean footprints from the oversized boots he was wearing. These peasant-style boots, the type worn in Russia, had been trimmed with fur but now they were decorated with the bloody shards of Klingman's skull.

Volk stood over the body, staring into the bullet hole gouged between two lifeless eyes. He would leave Klingman there. The other body – the one he had left in the trunk – would have to be dropped someplace else.

Beau Duffy had been determined to get Klingman in front of Joe McCarthy's hearing. Finally, someone was going to testify against those goddamned Reds and Beau was going to make sure it happened. Beau stayed in shadows as he followed Klingman to the G.E. loading docks that night. Trying not to scare the little man, Beau had walked for several blocks on tiptoe – which was difficult for a man of his size – and in his concentration, Beau did not hear the sound of someone lunging at him from behind, not until his body doubled over from the searing pain of Volk's knife slicing into his back.

An hour later, Beau was still breathing when the car trunk was opened again. Beau struggled to raise his hand against the knife that plunged deep into his heart. His eyes shut slowly as Volk closed the trunk and the light disappeared.

"These people are working day and night — laying the groundwork to overthrow YOUR GOVERNMENT! The average American is prone to say, "It can't happen here." Millions of people in other countries used to say the same thing. Today, they are dead — or living in Communist slavery. IT MUST NOT HAPPEN HERE!"

IS THIS TOMORROW? AMERICA UNDER COMMUNISM! ✳ A COMIC BOOK
PUBLISHED IN 1947 BY THE CATECHETICAL GUILD

CHAPTER FIFTY-FOUR

THE NEXT MORNING:
The Start of Commietown

"Listen for the cannon fire, Senator. When you hear the boom, that will be your cue."

"Jesus Christ," McCarthy winced. "It's been booming all morning."

It had been another long night and the cannons were already firing inside McCarthy's skull. The senator held a hand up against the light. "Why is it so damn bright in here? I thought this was radio! And can somebody get me a Bromo?"

McCarthy looked through the studio window. No one was paying attention to him. He grabbed the microphone off the table and yelled, "I said, can somebody get me — " and then the ice picks went back to work inside his brain. Gently, he put down the microphone. Shouting was a bad idea.

The Supreme Commissar of Commietown lowered his head against the table and closed his eyes, hoping the walls would stop spinning around the studio.

"It's radio *and* television, Senator."

McCarthy moaned, "I don't care if it's coast-to-coast and straight to the moon. Can't somebody please turn down the lights?"

"Then the audience won't be able to see you."

"I don't want to be seen."

"Sir?"

"Can't we do this in the dark? That'll scare the hell out of 'em." McCarthy tried to laugh, but his face hurt too much to smile.

"Like I said, Senator, your cue will be the cannon fire."

"Himmp!" whimpered McCarthy.

Across town, in the courtyard outside City Hall, a line of American Legionnaires was standing at attention. Dressed in Russian military regalia, each man had a rifle locked to his side as the platoon stood ready for instructions from the Legion Commander, Alden Reynolds. The commander, however, was not paying attention to his men. Instead, Reynolds was nervously eyeing the hulk of rusting, blackened metal that stood a few feet away. It was the Revolutionary War cannon known as "Old Saratoga" and, for 150 years, it had sat next to City Hall, ignored and neglected. No one had tried to fire the weapon since King George had been the target.

Until now.

Reynolds had been dreading "Commietown" for months. It all began in the spring when Reynolds was suddenly gripped by patriotic fervor – he had to be part of Schenectady's Red Scare Days! – and without thinking clearly (or thinking at all), the American Legion commander volunteered to light the fuse on Old Saratoga. He even requisitioned his own custom-made cannonball.

Since that day, Reynolds had been haunted by a recurring nightmare: surrounded by George Washington, Ben Franklin, and the other Founding Fathers, each of them shaking their heads at his stupidity, Reynolds slowly approaches Old Saratoga, the cannon now snorting and pawing the dirt like an angry Braham bull. The dream always ended the same way, exploding in a fiery flash of white light with Reynolds screaming, "Matchstick!" and waking his wife and the neighborhood dogs. Now the awful day had arrived.

This was no dream.

A hundred onlookers stood nearby for the start of Commietown and across from them a gaggle of newspaper and radio reporters, wire service men, newsreel photographers, and television cameras were huddled together. Also in the courtyard were local dignitaries, including the Common Council and members of the Board of Education. Several of them brought along their children and the kids, like everyone else, were getting impatient. So far, Commietown had been a very quiet siege. The press had been expecting tanks and artillery for the Red Army's invasion of Schenectady. They wanted action and they were about to get it.

Alden Reynolds nodded gravely toward the Legion's vice commander, Perry Ohlright, who was standing guard by a wire cage filled with pure white homing pigeons. Ohlright's hand was poised to fling open the door, letting the birds fly free once the cannon was fired.

Reynolds' mind was flashing back and forth between the cannon, the birds, the press, and the dignitaries as he tried to weigh his options, still kicking himself for volunteering for this nonsense. The "Red Army" soldiers could also see the fear in their commander's eyes. No one knew whether the cannon would fire a shot or simply explode. Imperceptibly, the soldiers shifted their toes through the snow, sliding farther away from Al Reynolds and Old Saratoga.

"Let's go!" shouted one of the newsreel cameramen. "Hell, if it blows up, we'll get a better picture."

Reynolds slowly advanced on the ancient cannon, his hands shaking so badly that he dropped his matches into the snow. Reynolds feigned exasperation, holding the wet matches up to the crowd as he silently thanked God for saving his life. That's when Perry Ohlright came waddling over with a dry box of matches. Reynolds glowered at Ohlright until the vice commander slowly retreated to his post by the pigeon cage.

As the fateful match was struck, Reynolds ceremoniously lifted the flame high over his head, hoping the wind might snuff it out. But the fire endured. With a heavy sigh, Reynolds shut his eyes and slowly dropped the match toward the fuse. The explosion was so tremendous that Reynolds nearly wet his pants and the blast echoed to New Baltimore. The resulting shockwave frightened the pigeons so badly they refused to fly. Perry Ohlright flipped over the cage and tried shaking the birds out.

Sensing a public relations disaster, Reynolds decided to improvise. He marched briskly toward the rifle brigade as the stunned pigeons fluttered helplessly in the snow. Whispering instructions to his men, Reynolds snapped to attention and thrust his sword high into the air, just as the dazed pigeons caught flight and winged into the sky above City Hall.

"Fire!" Reynolds commanded and within seconds, the crowd gasped in horror as bloody pigeon parts came raining down upon them. Children were crying and women screamed at the carnage of wings, beaks, and feathers falling over the courtyard.

Charlie Gaynor decided to step forward. Commietown's "Minister of Truth" scowled at the pigeon-speckled bystanders.

"You foolish Americans!" he bellowed. "Do you see it now? This is what life will be like now that we – the great and powerful Communists – have taken over your city! If you do not obey, Communism will mean death to you all and the first to go will be the pigeons!"

Through loudspeakers set up around the city, a craggy voice suddenly filled the air. The Supreme Commissar, Joseph McCarthy, began his address to the prisoners of Commietown.

"Citizens of Schenectady – your attention! Your homes and businesses are now in the hands of the International Communist Party! You must now follow us, your Russian overlords! I am your Supreme Commissar – Joseph McCarthy, your fearless Commander in Chief!"

McCarthy was starting to feel better now. Shouting was clearing his head.

"So listen here, you American swine! You can forget your so-called Bill of Rights. That does not apply here! Surrender your guns! Surrender your freedom! Do what we say and only a few of you will get hurt! Go now to City Hall for your food ration coupons, your city driving permit, and your identification papers! And prepare your children for a wonderful day at school! Tell them to wear a heavy coat because we do not provide heat in our schools! If they want heat, we will burn their books! You are about to witness Communism in all of its oppressive glory! Comrades, welcome to Commietown!"

The broadcast went silent for a few seconds until a hacking cough came over the air. "Okay … okay. Are we off – we're off the air? Good. That oughta scare those milk drinkers, huh? Har-Har-Har … ooohhh – Jesus, my head!"

Back at City Hall, the Minister of Truth was still barking orders. Charlie shouted, "You there! Clean up those pigeon pieces! Gather them up and bring them to the stockade. The Enemies of the People will have to be fed!"

"Now wait just a minute!" protested Ed Lyons, the Common Council President. Lyons' wife was gingerly picking bloody pigeon feathers off her coat when Charlie went nose to nose with her husband. "Listen here Charlie Gaynor, you can't tell me what – "

"Silence!" Charlie screamed. "Take him away!"

The Red Army soldiers dutifully grabbed the Council president and dragged him through the snow.

"Dammit Charlie! I've got to get to work!"

"Daddy!" cried his daughter, Emily.

Hands on his hips, Charlie smiled viciously at the chaos all around him. "Say goodbye to your daddy, little girl! Say goodbye to democracy everyone! Ah-HA, HA, HA, HA, HA! I love it!"

A photographer from *The Ledger* ran up and was snapping photos of little Emily Lyons until Montgomery Hughie shooed him away. The newspaper publisher pulled Alden Reynolds aside and signaled for Charlie to join them. The Minister of Truth goose-stepped over.

"Charlie, what the hell are you doing?" Hughie hissed. "You're a Russian – not a Nazi! Knock it off with the goose-stepping!"

Charlie snapped into a salute. *"Jawohl, mon capitaine!"*

"Listen you two – that was damn near a complete disaster. We've got reporters from all over the country here so let's shape up, do you hear me? And I mean right now! Let's be the best goddamn Communists anyone has ever seen!" Hughie shook his head grimly as he stalked back to his office. But as he turned the corner onto State Street, a smile returned to the publisher's face.

The opening ceremonies would be quickly forgotten because Communism was already changing life in Schenectady! Long lines were forming outside the stores and restaurants. Ration coupons were as scarce as the food choices and, on the street corners, newsboys were hawking copies of *The Red Word*, the official newspaper of Commietown. (Even the funny papers followed the Party line: Dagwood stabbed the Boss in the back and took over his office.) The deaths of Liberty and Justice were listed on the obituary pages and the advertisements were just as gloomy: "You could buy this car – but where would you go?"

With the newspaper now under Soviet control, the faux Communists moved next to capture the radio station, the telephone office and City Hall. Their first stop was the home of Mayor Mudlick. It was a little after nine a.m. when the mayor, wearing a terry-cloth bathrobe and teddy bear pajamas, walked out of his house with his hands in the air. Mudlick was instantly surrounded by rifle-toting soldiers of the Red Army as news cameras recorded the mayor's surrender.

"Stop – stop!" a photog from *Life* magazine cried. "Mayor, can you go back inside and when you come out this time, try to look like you're afraid. Don't be smiling and waving to the crowd – you're being captured by the Red Army!"

The other reporters and photographers soon joined in, directing the action in order to stage the best pictures. After five trips in and out of his house, Mayor Mudlick finally got it right and the crowd cheered as the Red Army took him away.

Martha Milwaukee was not among the spectators. She was still at home, fretting about Joe McCarthy's hearing the next day and the subpoenas that would soon be delivered to members of Local 1389. Would Milo be pulled in to testify this time?

Martha knew she had to do something before things went too far. Milo could be in real danger this time. Someone – maybe Arthur Klingman – might implicate Milo in whatever the Communists were up to and that could mean prison for her husband!

Martha could kick herself. She should never have told Arthur the truth about Communism! What would happen to her and Michael if Milo was put away?

She stared at herself in the vanity. Yes, someone has to stop McCarthy. Our family has too much to lose! Martha got herself ready.

Far from Schenectady, J. Edgar Hoover was immersed in the same feeling of dread.

We've got too much to lose, the FBI Director told himself. The President is counting on me! I have got to do something about McCarthy!

I can make him listen, Martha assured herself. First though, she had to stop shaking, otherwise, she would never be able to put on her makeup.

Yes, something had to be done. Hoover looked at himself in the mirror. If not you, J. Edgar, then who else is going to do it? He turned his head and frowned. The mirror did not lie: he had lost more hair.

Martha brushed her hair, teasing it taller. Everyone's counting on you, she told herself. Whatever the Local has done – whatever the Communists are plotting – ruining more lives is not the answer. She reached for the foundation to cover up the age spots.

A new complexion – a new outlook on things – a new understanding of what must be done. Hoover looked around the table, not sure of what to do next. The eyebrow pencil added thickness and shape until the mirror reflected sharp, fashionable arches.

What will I say to him? He's a United States Senator! Well I'm no pushover, Martha vowed. With long, soft strokes, she applied her eye shadow – always subtle and alluring.

Alluring and subtle: two words never used about Joe McCarthy!

Hoover smirked at himself in the mirror. McCarthy was about as subtle as a crutch. After all of Hoover's warnings – and for all of his promises to lay low – McCarthy had really capped it this time, announcing a full-blown investigation into the United States Army. He was now questioning the loyalty of America's top military commanders!

Hoover reached for more powder. The President was so angry he stopped inviting Hoover to the weekly war games that Eisenhower and the Joint Chiefs would play in the White House basement. That had been such great fun – pushing the plastic soldiers, tanks and rockets across the floor – but now he was excluded! All because of McCarthy, that oaf!

Martha put down the eyeliner. Yes, somebody has to stop that man.

And that somebody is me, Hoover grimaced.

"You ready, kid?" Martha asked herself. She guessed that she was, as much as she would ever be.

Hoover picked up the phone.

"You ready?" he barked.

"Just give us the word, Chief," Agent Thurston replied.

"Then do it," Hoover growled. "Do it today!"

"When a Communist heads the government of the United States — and the day will come as surely as the sun rises — the government will not be a capitalist government but a Soviet government and behind this government will stand the Red Army to enforce the dictatorship of the proletariat."

WILLIAM FOSTER, *former chairman of the American Communist Party*

CHAPTER FIFTY-FIVE

LATE AFTERNOON IN COMMIETOWN

Like perps in a police department lineup, the children stared blankly into the cameras. They were surrounded by colorful circus clowns, teddy bears, and polka-dotted elephants dancing on the walls and, like the children seated on the floor, these cartoon characters radiated with nuclear brilliance — their tiny eyes frozen in place — as the lights of 14 television cameras illuminated the Children's Reading Room of the Schenectady Public Library.

This was Story Time with the Supreme Commissar, Joseph McCarthy.

The leader of Commietown held a hand up to his eyes, struggling to see past the fog of the lights and the miasma of the previous night's drinking. McCarthy was vaguely aware of the small objects gathered around his feet. Through this haze, the Commissar thought he recognized an assortment of tiny airline liquor bottles, all of them within easy reach — just the thing to take the edge off in the late afternoon.

The senator reached for what he thought would be a refreshing nip of scotch, but he quickly withdrew his hand when he felt a small head of hair in the palm of his hand. To his left, a photographer for *Time* magazine was coaxing one of those hairy little "bottles."

"Come on, little girl," the photographer urged. "I want to take your picture with Senator McCarthy. Now, try to look sad, will ya? You're being held prisoner by this bad man!"

The girl pouted and McCarthy scowled as they held up a copy of the Communist Manifesto, the cameras clicking and flashbulbs popping.

"All right, fellas – enough!" McCarthy growled. "I'm sure you boys and girls have heard what happened this morning – how your city was taken over by us, the Communists! While we're deciding the fate of your parents, I thought I would come down here to the People's Library and read you kids an early bedtime story. It's an important story – important for every young Communist because it will teach you the value of hard work and the benefits of government-sponsored, er … motivation. The name of this story is 'The Little Red Train That Could.'"

McCarthy held the picture book up to the cameras and began to read:

"The Little Red Train was at the station, loaded from boxcar to boxcar with miners headed for Siberia. The miners were actually political prisoners carrying shovels, picks, and axes. It was all so heavy that the Little Red Train could not move! Someone needed to push, but the miners were too sickly and starving to help the Little Red Train. It was stuck on the tracks!

"Then the Little Red Train remembered the sworn duty of every industrious worker of the Soviet Socialist Republic: Everyone has a job to do whether they are a prisoner or not! Whether they are starving a little or starving a lot! Everyone must work or they will be shot!"

The children's eyes grew a little wider as McCarthy smiled viciously over the top of the book.

"And so the Little Train started to pull. 'I know I must! I know I must,' puffed the Little Red Train. And it pulled and it pulled and soon it was climbing up and over the Ural Mountains – all the way to the prison camps of eastern Siberia! And for all those miners, that was the end of the story. Well now, boys and girls, what did the Little Red Train teach us about our duty to Mother Russia?"

A little boy held up his hand. "Can I go to the bathroom?"

"Hell, I gotta take a leak too!" said McCarthy, tossing the book aside. "Which way to the Little Comrades' room?" At the doorway, McCarthy looked over his shoulder. No one was following him. He continued on tiptoe into the basement and the World History section of the library. And there she was: Martha Milwaukee. She had one leg up on the stacks of Ancient History and the rest of her was leaning across the Dark Ages.

"Martha?" McCarthy gasped. This was not the woman whose picture he had been ogling. Many years – and many more pounds – had been added to the Red Flame of New York.

"Of course it's me, silly!" Martha said in her most coquettish voice. "Were you expecting somebody else?"

"Sort of," McCarthy grumbled. With a heavy sigh, McCarthy closed his eyes and reminded himself: I know I must. I know I must.

And then she was on him.

"MmmmmMmmmmMmmmmm," Martha hummed as she mashed her lips against his, squeezing McCarthy so tight that the air came squeaking out of him. He was just getting his breath back when Martha yanked him out the back door, pulling him toward the blue Continental parked behind the library. McCarthy took the keys.

"Comrade," he leered, "finally we are together!"

Comrade? Martha wondered. She looked more carefully at McCarthy's Commietown costume – a gray wool coat decorated with Soviet ribbons and garish medals. He was just staying in character, Martha guessed.

"Yes, together, Comrade!" she exclaimed. "Take a right at the end of the driveway. I've got just the place for us, my darling!"

McCarthy raced out of the parking lot, the engine revving up the hill as Martha leaned across the front seat and nibbled on his ear. She was glancing out the window just as the car reached the sidewalk and that's when Martha's eyes met the incredulous stare of Helen Gamble. Helen was pulling a .45 revolver out of her sleeve – ready to plug Commissar McCarthy in the head – when the sight of Martha Milwaukee canoodling on Joe McCarthy's ear was too much for her. The gun slipped out of Helen's hand and the bullets rolled aimlessly across the sidewalk. The two women continued to stare at each other through the back window of the Continental as the car sped down the street.

"Everything all right?" the Senator asked Martha.

"I guess so," she said as the car moved quickly along Union Avenue, past the library and the black sedan idling by the curb. Behind the wheel of that car was Frankie Pepper and in the back seat was Mickey Scarpino's tiny hit man, The Mouse.

Pepper exclaimed, "Holy cow! That was Martha Milwaukee – with Joe McCarthy!" He turned back toward the library. "And what the hell is Helen Gamble doing back there?"

Near the front of the library, Helen was reaching for the gun, but Henry got to it first.

"Vladimir – what are you doing here?" Helen cried. She tried to snatch the gun back but Henry was too strong. He grabbed Helen by the arm and pushed her across the street to where Rosie Imperato, Helen's getaway driver, was waiting.

"Shut up and get in the car," Henry ordered.

"What is wrong with you?" Helen protested. "That was our chance!"

"No chance at all," Henry snapped. He nodded across the street as the cops and news reporters came pouring out of the library, all of them searching for Joe McCarthy.

"Get in the back," Henry ordered Rosie. "I'm driving."

"Who's this mug?" Rosie asked.

"Do like he says, Rosie. But hurry, Vladimir – drive! I can still see them up ahead."

Rosie leaned over the front seat. "Will someone please tell me what's going on?"

"That's Joe McCarthy in the blue Continental," Helen shouted, "and he's got Martha Milwaukee with him!"

"He's *what*?" Rosie exclaimed. "McCarthy's kidnapped Martha?"

"It didn't look that way to me. I was just taking out the gun when I saw her kissing him! I was so startled, I dropped the gun!"

"Duck!" Frankie Pepper shouted to The Mouse as Henry, Helen and Rosie sped past. The Mouse, slouching in the back seat, did not move.

"So this was your plan?" The Mouse asked flatly.

"Nothing to worry about," Pepper said as he hit the gas and joined the chase. "We both know what to do. Things just got a little more complicated, that's all."

"You told the boss it was 'beyond simple.' Mr. Pepper, let me tell you something: We are way past simple."

It was true – this was not what Frankie had planned, but what else could he do? Klingman had disappeared the night before so Frankie went to Plan B. He had to kill Joe McCarthy and he would make it look like Milo pulled the trigger. Frankie memorized his story for the cops: Milo, the Red-crazed killer, was determined to stop McCarthy's investigation into Local 1389. He would do anything – even kill a United States Senator – if that's what Milo needed to stay in power.

The true killer would be Scarpino's button man, The Mouse. Dressed in a baggy suit and pointy pompadour, the little gangster gave a passing resemblance to Milo Milwaukee. All they needed now was a witness before The Mouse could bump off McCarthy.

"We can't miss," Pepper promised Mickey Scarpino.

"I never miss," the crime boss agreed. "That's why you're going to drive."

Several blocks away, McCarthy's right ear was still enjoying Martha's nibbling. "I like that," McCarthy cooed. "Nice to have some company for a change. With what I have to do nowadays, it can get awful lonely."

"Tell me about it," Martha said. "Especially in a town like this. But you, Joseph McCarthy – you should be so proud of what you've accomplished!"

"Not bad for a chicken farmer from Wisconsin, huh? Sure, I've done okay. It's just that it keeps getting harder every day. Keeping up appearances, I mean. Now they've got me going after the Army – the goddamned United States Army! That's not easy, let me tell ya. I don't know what they'll expect me to do after that. Go after the Navy, I suppose."

"You have to be strong. We know who the enemy is and we just have to keep on fighting!"

"I'm trying. I really am. I just wonder if they appreciate what I'm doing."

"The American people? Of course, they do."

"No," McCarthy laughed. "I mean Moscow."

"What – ?"

"Hmm?"

Reporter: Do you think that Senator McCarthy can show any disloyalty exists in the State Department?

President Truman: I think the greatest asset that the Kremlin has is Senator McCarthy.

CHAPTER FIFTY-SIX

DO YOU HAVE A DUCK?

Flabbergasted, Frankie Pepper turned to The Mouse, "Did you see that crazy Commie back there – Helen Gamble? I think she had a gun. It looked like a goddamned gun!" The Mouse said nothing.

"A gun! A gun! A goddamned gun!" Pepper repeated as he sped after Helen, Henry, and Rosie. "Helen Gamble was actually going to kill a United States senator! I really don't believe these Reds! They're all nuts!"

"Stop," said The Mouse.

"Were you watching her?" Pepper continued. "She had a clean shot, but she didn't shoot. Why didn't she shoot?"

"Stop!" The Mouse said louder.

"I could not believe it. She had a clear shot – a CLEAR shot!"

"STOP!"

Frankie Pepper flew through a red light. The cop at the corner turned on his siren and soon had Pepper pulled over. Up ahead, the other cars were turning off Union Avenue and disappearing from view. Pepper put his head against the steering wheel, shaking his head in disbelief. First, he had lost Klingman and now McCarthy was gone. Frankie wondered if he should drive The Mouse down to the river and just get it over with.

"License and registration, please," said the motorcycle cop.

Pepper smiled up at the officer. "Hey there, Tommy. I guess I missed that light back there."

"Jesus, Frankie – where's the fire? You coulda killed somebody!"

"I'm sorry Tom, really I am. It's just that we're kind of in a hurry."

The cop looked into the back seat. "Who's that with you? Is that Milo?"

The Mouse waved his hand as he turned away from the officer.

"Nice to see you guys back together," the officer said. "I don't know if I can let you go on this one, Frankie. Let me see your license and registration."

"Sure thing, but hurry it up will ya? Milo is really upset – his wife is missing, maybe. We're not sure what's happened to her." As Pepper talked with the cop, The Mouse slipped out of the car and ran down the avenue, hiding behind parked cars as he searched for McCarthy and the blue Continental. When he reached the river, The Mouse spotted the car on the other side, parked at the Mohawk Motor Lodge, a collection of paper-thin bungalows known for its hourly specials and "no questions" check-in policy. In the dusk of early evening, a neon signed blinked above the motel office: "Featuring the New Whirl-a-Bed!"

"I've never tried a Whirl-a-Bed. Sounds like fun, huh?" McCarthy said as he came back with the room key. "Christ, let's get inside. Colder than a witch's tit out here."

On this frigid night, Martha Milwaukee paused for a moment as she tried to return McCarthy's smile. She was still not sure what McCarthy meant when he said Moscow was proud of him. Why would Moscow like anything about Joe McCarthy, the Great Commie Hunter? Standing outside a cheap motel in Scotia, New York, all of it reminded Martha that she was a long, long way from Lake Winnanonga.

She felt the evening air bite against her face, still sore from the wiry hairs of McCarthy's five-o'clock shadow. Then she thought about Michael and Milo and what she had to do. She took in a deep breath: you've come this far Martha. You've got to finish this.

Martha had still not decided what she was going to do with McCarthy. A bagful of liquor was in the back seat of the Continental and in her pocket she carried a bottle of sleeping pills. In case of real trouble, Martha also had Michael's baseball bat. But did she have the courage to kill this big Wisconsin farm boy?

"You bring the booze?" McCarthy called from the cabin door. "Here, let me help you carry that."

"I've got it, Joe. I've got it."

"Ok, ok. Just trying to help!" McCarthy laughed, holding his hands up in mock surrender.

Rosie gasped, "Jesus, will you look at that: Martha has taken him prisoner!" Rosie, Helen, and Henry were parked next to the motel office. Down the hill, they could see Martha follow McCarthy into the Whirl-a-Bed bungalow.

"What's she got in the bag?" Helen wondered.

"I can't tell," Henry said. "It's getting too dark to see that far. I'd better take a closer look. You two stay here."

As Henry crept around the motel office, The Mouse was crossing the bridge into Scotia. He was halfway across when Pepper pulled up in his car.

"That was terrific!" Pepper exclaimed. "That cop thinks that was you! I mean, Milo. He thinks Milo is after McCarthy!"

Gasping for breath, The Mouse pointed over to the motor lodge.

"The bungalows?" Pepper asked. Then he saw it too: the blue Continental was parked near a cluster of four cabins. Pepper pulled into the motor lodge parking lot, stopping on the other side of the office from where Helen and Rosie were parked.

Rosie grabbed Helen's arm. "Look over there! That's Frankie Pepper and – oh my gosh – that looks like Milo sitting next to him!"

Helen was speechless. Frankie Pepper was dedicated to destroying the Local. How could Milo be with that man? Then again, how could Martha be with Joe McCarthy? Helen was about to run out the door when she saw The Mouse scurrying down the hill toward the blue Continental.

"We gotta get Milo out of here," Rosie urged. "Whatever Martha is up to, we can't let her take Milo down with her!"

That's when Helen put it all together. "It's that bastard Frankie Pepper! He brought Milo out here to set him up!" Helen threw open the door and charged over to Frankie Pepper's car. She rapped hard on the glass and Pepper screamed in surprise. Pointing at Pepper, Helen drew her finger across her throat. "You're a dead man, Frankie Pepper!"

Frankie had heard about Helen Gamble's temper. He had to think fast.

"Miss Gamble, I'm so glad you're here! Down there – it's Milo! He's got a gun and he's mad as hell. He's looking for his wife – and Joseph McCarthy!"

Rosie cried, "Oh my God, oh my God, of my God! He's gonna kill 'em both!"

"Come on," Helen said, grabbing Rosie by the hand. They raced down the hill as Frankie Pepper followed, stumbling through the snow. To Frankie, it felt more like dancing! This was starting to feel like a plan!

Inside the Whirl-a-Bed cabin, McCarthy found the light switch and then he saw his breath filling the unheated cabin.

"Christ, there's no heat in here! Come on, baby, let's go someplace else."

"Now wait a minute there, Mr. Senator," Martha snarled playfully as she jumped in front of the door. She grabbed McCarthy by the shoulders and threw him back against the wall. "I don't think I can wait that long. I want you right now!"

"Ouch! Take it easy, will ya!"

"Take me, you big lug," Martha growled. "Here – let Momma warm you up." Martha gyrated against McCarthy as she pinned him to the wall, buttons and zippers and Russian medallions clicking together. Martha was smiling wickedly as she leaned back and spun McCarthy onto the Whirl-a-Bed. Taking another step back, Martha leaped on top of McCarthy.

"Joey, Joey, Joey," Martha said urgently. "What do you want me to do to you?"

"Let me catch my breath first!"

"Of course, darling. Would you like to have a drink?"

"I don't think that's it. Try it again."

Martha sat up on the bed. "What are you saying?"

"The password," McCarthy said. "They told me to say, 'Do you want a duck?' Not a drink."

Martha stared blankly at McCarthy.

"No, no – wait a minute. That's not it," he puzzled. "Would you like to have my duck?"

"I think it's time we both had a drink," Martha said. She unscrewed the bottle of Mont Blanc Muscatel while McCarthy pushed a handful of quarters into the Whirl-a-Bed. The bed began to whir and buzz before it slowly lifted off the floor, spinning to a tinny recording of "Mood Indigo."

McCarthy rested his head on a pillow. "This Commietown business is something else, isn't it? So what do you think of my uniform? I'm the Supreme Commissar, you know."

"Very elegant! And they gave you a sword!" Martha gushed.

"Funny isn't it? They used to fight battles with sabers like this one. Boy, how things have changed! It wasn't so long ago that I was shooting Japs from the bottom of a B-52 and now even that's considered old-fashioned. Nowadays, everybody's thinkin' about the Big One."

"You mean The Bomb?"

"Do you worry about it?"

"What – about the Russians bombing us? Once in a while I suppose."

"I think about it all the time," McCarthy said somberly. "It scares the hell out of me. I can't sleep some nights just thinkin' about it. That's how I first got interested in the Party."

"You know they'll bomb us the first chance they get. They're maniacs!" Martha said.

"You better believe it and the Russians won't back down for nothin'! So … have you got an escape plan?"

"I suppose I'd run to my son's school. They seem to know what to do. I'm sure they already have things set up for important people like you."

McCarthy nodded. "They pretty much guaranteed me a way out of the country before anything happens. It's only fair given the chances I've taken for them."

"Of course! I suppose a lot of people in Washington will be given a chance to get out."

"Don't you know it. And there's a helluva lot more of them than you might think. I haven't met any of them yet – not as far as I know, anyway. Of course, I can't be askin' too many people if they have a duck, you know what I mean? Might raise suspicions."

Martha was only half listening as she struggled to open her bottle of sleeping pills. If she could keep him sedated and locked up for the night, maybe they would call off the hearing the next morning. No McCarthy, no hearing, no trouble for Milo.

If that didn't work, there was always the baseball bat in the car.

Meanwhile, out in the cold, Helen and Rosie were darting between the cabins, tracing snowy footprints left by The Mouse.

"Milo! Milo!" Helen whispered into the darkness. Helen stopped when she heard the sound of somebody thrashing about in the snow. Behind the Whirl-a-Bed cabin, they found The Mouse facedown in the snow with Henry sitting on top of him.

"Vladimir, get off of him – that's my boss! That's Milo Milwaukee!"

Henry jumped up in surprise. After all these months, Henry Brownale was finally meeting Milo Milwaukee!

"Oh gosh, I'm so sorry – I didn't know! I mean, he had a gun!"

Slowly spinning on the Whirl-a-Bed, Martha and Joe McCarthy heard the commotion outside.

"Listen!" McCarthy whispered urgently. "They've followed us out here!"
"Who?"

"I don't know who, but somebody! Oh Christ, what are we going to do?"

"Relax, will you, please?! I'll see who's out there." Martha opened the door a crack. "Helloooo? Is anybody out there?"

"Martha – it's me, Helen Gamble!" Helen ran to the front of the cabin, but Martha quickly shut the door.

"Don't come in Helen! I can't let you in right now!"

"It's okay, Martha, I don't need to come in. But you'd better come out – and I mean right now! Do like I say, Martha. Get out here now!"

"Who else is out there?"

"Milo is and he's pretty sore about this! Come quick, Martha, and I'll get you out before he sees you!"

Grabbing her coat and just one shoe, Martha ran out the door as Rosie Imperato came sprinting for the car.

"RUN MARTHA! He's got a GUN!" Rosie screamed.

"A gun!" McCarthy cried, slamming the cabin door shut as angry voices rose up from behind the bungalow. This time it was The Mouse.

The filth and venom pouring out of the little man made Henry and Frankie take a step back. The Mouse did not appreciate Henry tackling him in the snow. Henry could understand why "Milo" was so upset. What husband wants to find his wife cheating on him? Still, Henry knew that his first responsibility was to the United States government and, even though he had quit the CIA, Henry had sworn to do everything in his power to protect the life of a United States Senator. Henry made sure the gun was out of Milo Milwaukee's hands and safe inside his pocket.

When The Mouse had quieted down, Pepper suggested, "I think Milo should have a chance to say something, don't you? A devoted husband like Mr. Milwaukee deserves the opportunity to see what has been going on between his wife and another man. Don't you agree, Mister … say, what is your name?"

Henry had to think about that one. "Nick. Nick Lansing."

"Oh yes, I've heard about you," Pepper smiled. "Well, let me introduce myself. I am Francis Aurelius Pepper, Business Agent for the one and only, truly-patriotic union in the city of Schenectady. Isn't that right, Milo?"

"Whatever you say," The Mouse muttered.

As they walked to the front of the cabin, Henry whispered to The Mouse, "I'm so sorry for tackling you, Mr. Milwaukee. But don't you worry: Everything is going according to plan." The Mouse stared back at Henry in disbelief. Another plan!

Pepper gently knocked on the cabin door. "Senator? Senator McCarthy? Could we have a word with you, Senator?"

"I'm not here," said McCarthy, hiding beneath the Whirl-a-Bed.

"Senator, please. Milo Milwaukee – Mrs. Milwaukee's husband – is out here and he wants to talk to you about what happened here tonight – or what might have happened here tonight. Please, Senator, just open the door."

"Somebody said there's a gun."

"No, no – Mr. Milwaukee does not have a gun. Not now, anyways. It is perfectly safe."

The lock clicked and the door slowly opened.

"Thank you Senator," Pepper said soothingly. "Milo, why don't you sit on the bed there, while I speak to Senator McCarthy."

The Mouse took a seat on the rotating Whirl-a-Bed and cradled the bottle of Muscatel. With every rotation of the Whirl-a-Bed, The Mouse took another hard swig from the bottle – now mixed with sleeping pills – and glowered at Henry with every turn.

"Jesus," whispered McCarthy as the three men moved to the far end of the room. "This guy Milwaukee is really sore, huh? You've got to make him understand: Nothing happened here tonight – not really. I mean, look – I've still got my coat on!"

Frankie and Henry tried not to stare at McCarthy's naked legs.

"He'll calm down," Pepper said, nodding toward "Milo."

"Say – you're that union guy I met the last time I was in town."

"That's right, Senator: Frankie Pepper, leader of the International Union of Electrical Workers and let me say on behalf of all the hard-working members of the IUEW, we are grateful to have you back in Schenectady. This time, we know you'll finish off those Commies in Local 1389."

McCarthy turned to Henry. "And what's your story?"

"I'm the guy who saved your life, Senator."

"Like hell!" Pepper exclaimed. "Senator, I followed these two characters out here because I was certain they were planning to do you harm. Both of them are dangerous, radical lunatics. Milo there runs the Commie Local and this character, I'm told, is a genuine Russian spy!"

McCarthy's eyes lit up.

Henry pleaded, "Wait a minute here! There's a lot more to this story. You've got to believe me, Senator."

"A Russian spy, huh? Well, you can tell me all about it when you testify tomorrow morning."

"Testify?" Henry blanched.

"You hear that Milo?" Frankie Pepper announced. "You and Nick here are going to be on the hot seat tomorrow with the rest of your Commie pals." Pepper was beaming as he took a seat on the Whirl-a-Bed. As Pepper and the gangster Mouse wrestled for the remaining Muscatel, Henry pulled McCarthy closer and whispered, "Senator, you don't understand what's happening here! My real name is Henry Brownale and I was sent here by my –"

McCarthy smiled and pulled him closer. "Comrade, comrade – there's nothing to worry about. I am with you – you are with us, do you know what I'm saying? So just play along, okay? Tomorrow, you plead the Fifth and then everything will be fine. You've got a duck, right?"

Henry could not believe what he was hearing.

"No, no, Senator, please – this is not some part of Commietown! I'm being serious: I am an agent – at least I once was an agent – for the Central Intelligence Agency and I came here because –"

"Well then, you be ready to testify tomorrow morning, Mr. Russian Spy," McCarthy proclaimed loudly as he walked back to the Whirl-a-Bed. Frankie Pepper was smiling broadly, imagining all of the union dues that would soon be coming his way. The Mouse, meanwhile, was flat on his back, passed out from the Muscatel and sleeping pills. Joe McCarthy leaned over the bed and tried to roust him awake.

"Mr. Milwaukee? Mr. Milwaukee! I'd like to apologize to you personally for all of the unsubstantiated confusion you might have, uh …

witnessed here this evening, along with the personal trauma you may have suffered as a result of the unnecessary gunplay here tonight. I want you to know that I am convinced you are completely innocent of any and all charges."

"Innocent? Unsolicited?!" Pepper shouted. "Senator, HE was the one who brought the gun out here – a gun to shoot YOU!"

"Be that as it may, I think it's only fair that I postpone any testimony from Mr. and Mrs. Milwaukee until such time as these unforeseen circumstances are more … foreseen. Don't you agree, Mr. Milwaukee?"

"No, no, no – I do not agree!" Pepper protested. "You have to make Milo testify! You have to make them ALL testify! I mean, think of how the press will react! The city is packed with reporters and now you're giving a free pass to the biggest Commie in all of Schenectady? Don't you see – Milo and his wife are behind this whole racket!"

"No sir, I firmly believe that the Milwaukee family has been thrust into a situation far beyond their control and, despite what you may have heard about me, I am a man who is willing to forgive and forget. Mr. Milwaukee –" McCarthy extended his hand toward the Whirl-a-Bed, waiting for The Mouse to spin back around. " – Mr. Milwaukee, I hope you are that kind of man too." McCarthy shook The Mouse's hand before he spun away again.

"With that gentlemen, I bid you all a good night!"

"Stop right there, Senator. I can't let you do this."

McCarthy and Pepper turned to Henry – and the gun he was pointing straight at them.

"What the hell are you doing?" McCarthy demanded.

"All of this has got to stop and it's going to stop right now," Henry said firmly. "Mr. Pepper was telling you the truth, Senator. If you don't get the Communists out of G.E., the reporters are going to crucify you. But there's one thing he didn't tell you and that's that Milo Milwaukee is not a Communist. I don't know why his wife came here tonight – maybe she was trying to convince you that Milo is not really a Red after all or maybe she just wanted to take the blame. That doesn't matter now because tomorrow morning, Senator, you're going to stand next to Milo when he brings Local 1389 out of the AEWA and into Frankie Pepper's union."

"He is?" Pepper exclaimed, nearly swooning off the Whirl-a-Bed.

"Have we got a deal, Senator?" Henry said, still holding the gun on McCarthy.

"I guess so," McCarthy said. "Deal."

"Deal!" said Frankie. "What do you say, Milo?"

The Mouse hoisted the bottle of Muscatel into the air. "Thass a deal!"

CHAPTER FIFTY-SEVEN

ONE HOUR LATER ON TUCKAHOE ROW

Someone was knocking on the back door.

"Christ Almighty," Milo grumbled as he threw open the door. "Have you got any idea what time – who the hell are you?"

"Who are you?" Henry replied. Henry looked hard at the small man in his pajamas and pointy hair. Then Henry looked down at The Mouse, asleep in Henry's arms.

"I'm Milo Milwaukee. Wait a minute – you're Agent Brownale, aren't you? Didn't I tell you not to – "

"Not to come around here, that's right. You also told me to take care of your Communist problem and now I've done that."

"What are you saying?"

"Be at the federal courthouse tomorrow morning at nine o'clock, Mr. Milwaukee. Joseph McCarthy and Frankie Pepper will be waiting to stand next to you when you move Local 1389 into the IUEW."

"Frankie Pepper's union? Why the hell should I do that?"

"Because Mr. Milwaukee, you just shook on it."

Kathie Bleeker: "What are you rebelling against, Johnny?"
Johnny Strabler: "What have you got?"
THE WILD ONE, 1953

CHAPTER FIFTY-EIGHT

MEN!

The phone rang at Helen's. It was Rosie, in a panic.

"Helen – is Vladimir with you? The cops are lookin' for him. It's cuz of Arthur – they found him dead by the river."

"Slow down – slow down! Arthur's dead?"

"So you steer clear of Vladimir, the cops, and anybody else 'til I find out what's goin' on, okay? I gotta go!"

"Wait – what about McCarthy?" Helen asked, but Rosie had disconnected the line. Stunned by the news, Helen sat on her bed unable to move, the dial tone still buzzing in her hand.

Poor little guy, she thought. Sure, Klingman was a lousy traitor, but you had to feel sorry for him just the same. Now the cops think Vladimir did it? He didn't seem capable of doing anything, much less kill somebody.

Helen jumped at a sharp knock on the door. Looking out the window, all she could see was an enormous trench coat and a tent-sized hat slouched toward the door. It was that city detective, Wotan Volk.

"Miss Gamble," Volk said politely as Helen opened the door. He admired her nerve. Of all the Reds in Schenectady, this young woman was probably the toughest and possibly the most dangerous Communist of all. That was the way Klingman had told it.

"I'm Chief Inspector Wotan Volk. Do you know the whereabouts of someone answering to the name of Vladimir?"

"I don't know any Vladimir."

"Let's try this again – where is Nick Lansing?"

"Why?"

"Because I'm asking."

"How should I know?"

"Listen sister, I ask the questions, you follow? If you see him, stay away from him. He's a killer. If there's any sign of him, you call me at Police Headquarters, understand?"

"Is that it?"

"No – take this." Volk slapped a subpoena into her hand. "Be at the federal courthouse at nine a.m. Senator McCarthy wants to see you. If Nick Lansing is smart, he'll be there too."

"So you can arrest him?"

"Eventually."

"Take your time, Detective. I hate to see a civil servant break a sweat."

"Why, you got some mouth – " Volk took a menacing step forward before Helen slammed the door in his face. He could have punched his way in, but instead Volk left a pair of fur-trimmed boots on Helen's front porch – a "clue" that would help close the case on Arthur Klingman, another murder that would soon be solved by Chief Inspector Wotan Volk.

Helen walked aimlessly through the house and when she reached her bedroom, her thoughts went from Klingman's murder to Petrov's threats to harm her again. Could she be next: would they kill her for baking cookies and handing out turkeys instead of preparing the masses for Revolution? The calendar on the wall was covered with large, black X's, marking each day that Petrov had not returned to Schenectady. She still had nightmares of the beating she took in the alley. How many more days before Petrov would be back?

She had to do something – something significant – to demonstrate her commitment to the Party and its Revolution. Vladimir! Helen cursed. He was supposed to help her do this! Wasn't that why he was sent here – to steal vital secrets from G.E.? But Vladimir was only good for talk: constantly asking her what her day was like, what she was having for dinner, and what she was going to do after dinner and then on the weekend and, during all this, he's looking at her with those adoring, worshipful eyes! *THIS* is who the Party sends for such an important mission?

The best you could say for him was that he was handsome. Sort of handsome. Helen thought she might have been interested in him at first, but not anymore. She was sick of him now, this lovesick schoolboy always talking but never doing!

She was finding that all men were trouble. You can't rely on any of them, especially the handsome ones. She had a chance to kill Joseph McCarthy, but no! Vladimir screwed that up.

Martha too. What was going on with her last night – jabbering on about the evils of Communism and all the mistakes she had made and how everyone was wrong about the Party? What about the evils of McCarthy and the rest of these Capitalist bastards?

What about me saving her life last night?

I will have to do this myself, Helen decided.

Perhaps Klingman's murder is the answer! Could she convince Petrov that SHE had killed the little weasel? Bumping off a rat like Klingman would certainly please Petrov. It might even impress the Party leaders in the Tenth Directorate. Maybe that would keep her safe from another beating.

This idea gave her some comfort – something she had not felt for a very long time – and it helped Helen fall asleep. It was only a short while later when Helen woke to a tapping sound on her bedroom window. As she had expected, it was Vladimir.

She helped him take off his coat and when he embraced her tightly, Helen was angry at herself for not pushing him away.

"All right then," Helen said impatiently. "Tell me what happened! Is McCarthy dead?"

"Dead? No, not dead. But he might as well be. Helen, I think the man is off his nut. First thing tomorrow, I'm going to tell Moscow that the all-powerful Joseph McCarthy is headed for a rubber room!"

Helen looked doubtful. "He may be nuts, but he's not crazy. You're the one driving me crazy! Why are we wasting so much time here? We should have finished him off at the library! I would have done it if you hadn't stopped me."

Henry took the revolver out of his belt. "Relax, will you? I have more experience with this sort of thing." He looked around the room as if he were searching for a place to stash his gun. Slowly, he made his way into Helen's bedroom, hoping she would follow.

Henry put the gun on the table next to Helen's bed as Helen waited outside the room, making no secret of her annoyance with him.

"Experience?" she snapped. "How many months have we been waiting for you to use that 'experience' and we're still waiting! Now look what's happened!"

"It hasn't been my fault. I had to wait for instructions from – "

"Klingman is dead, Vladimir! You pushed him right into McCarthy's arms and now he's dead!"

"Dead? How can he be – "

"Dead. Did you hear me this time? He tried to help you and all you did was push him aside. 'Not now Arthur. We have to wait Arthur.' We've all paid a price for your hesitation and now Arthur is dead!"

Henry stared blankly at Helen.

"You can't be surprised," she said flatly. "To tell you the truth, I'm not all that sad about it. He was going to put us both on the hot seat!"

"Poor little guy," Henry muttered.

"Please – enough already! He was willing to put you and me in prison, so let's be honest, he had it coming! And the cops think you did it. Well – did you?"

Henry turned away from Helen. He wanted to tell her the truth – he wanted to tell her everything, especially about his secret mission for Milo.

But first Henry had another confession to make: he had to confess his love for her and he was hoping that she had the same feelings for him. She would understand this crazy mess. She could forgive him and then they could be together – forever. Henry was sure of that, but he could not find the words and his silence was making Helen more furious.

"Little bastard," Henry finally said. "I should have killed him myself. But no, I didn't do it. So he's dead and there's nothing more to say about it. We've got more important things to talk about."

"You're right – McCarthy has subpoenas out for both of us. And that's fine with me because I'm going to do it this time. When I go into that courtroom tomorrow, I'm going to blast that fat bastard right between the eyes – and this time you're not going to stop me!"

"Helen, Helen – wait a minute! For something that big, you can't decide this on your own! Moscow has to be consulted. And think about it, if the Party wanted to eliminate Joe McCarthy, they would have done it a long time ago. So please, just relax."

"Ha!" Helen shouted, throwing up her hands. "What is it with you? Always waiting, more hesitation, more delays! When do you ever DO anything?!"

Henry put on his best tough-guy smirk as he tried to pull her close, but Helen turned away.

"You've got to listen to me," Henry said soothingly. "Let me tell you what happened there tonight because we don't need to worry about McCarthy anymore. The man is unstable. Think about it: What United States senator would question the loyalty of the country's top generals? And I saw it firsthand tonight. The man is a screwball! At first I thought he was just playing along with this Commietown nonsense – him being the Supreme Commissar and all – because he's calling me 'comrade' and he's whispering to me 'I'm with you, you are with me.' And then the strangest thing of all: He looks me straight in the eye and asks me if I have a duck. A duck! I'm telling you, Helen, the man has gone off the deep end!"

Helen grabbed Henry by the arm. "What do you mean 'a duck'?"

Henry laughed, "That's what he said. He asked me if I have a duck. Then he says HE'S got a duck. Now how do you like that?"

"Vladimir, that's incredible! Do you know what that means? Joe McCarthy isn't crazy – he was giving you the password! Joe McCarthy is a Communist!"

"Because he has a duck?"

"No – it's one of the codes I learned at Camp Unity!" Helen paused and then she smiled at Henry. Suspicions began to fill her mind. "I'm surprised *you* didn't know that."

"Of course, I knew that," Henry blustered. "It's just, well … it was just such a shock to hear it coming from McCarthy is all. I mean, how can that be – Joe McCarthy, a Soviet agent?"

Still smiling, Helen would not answer him. Instead, she walked up to Henry and wrapped her arms around him. "And tonight you saved his life!" she gushed. "The Party will be very pleased with you, Vladimir."

"Oh, I don't think McCarthy was in any real danger, do you?"

"Well, if it wasn't Milo then Martha might have killed him. The way she was talking in the car, she obviously has abandoned the Party. She kept telling me that I have to open my eyes – me and Rosie both – we have to open our eyes and see that it's all been a lie. Maybe she's the crazy one."

Helen pulled Henry close and laid her head on his chest. "Tell me, Vladimir? Has it been a lie?"

Struggling to breathe, Henry could feel his heart against the warmth of her body.

"I don't know what Martha could be talking about," he sighed.

Helen looked up at Henry. He looked exhausted. She put her hand to Vladimir's cheek and his knees grew weak. Moving her hands across Henry's face, Helen paused for a moment, trying to decide whether she should continue down to his throat.

"It's late. You look so tired," she said.

"You're right. I am." He put his head down and, before he realized it, it was resting against Helen's shoulder. Then his eyes grew wide as Helen kissed him. With one hand on his belt, Helen moved Henry back into her bedroom, pressing him down onto the bed and peeling off his clothes. His pants ended up on the bedside table, covering the gun that Helen would steal later that night. As Henry lay naked on the bed, Helen turned off the lights.

"I don't know what to do," he pleaded. Helen put a finger to his lips.

"Hush, Comrade," she whispered. "I do."

"It's only a paper moon.
Hanging over a cardboard sea
But it wouldn't be make believe
If you'd believe in me."

"IT'S ONLY A PAPER MOON" ✳ *Lyrics by Yip Harburg and Billy Rose*

CHAPTER FIFTY-NINE

NOTHING BUT A FRAUD

The sun on that winter morning was unexpectedly brilliant, the kind of improbable day that made anything seem possible.

The Soviet flag, a remnant of Commietown, was still flying over the federal courthouse. Its red banner with the white hammer and sickle were set against the azure sky as three birds – perhaps frightened homing pigeons or possibly turkey vultures – circled overhead. Henry looked up at it all and wondered how he ever got to such a strange and lovely place.

And how did I find a gal as swell as Helen Gamble? Henry asked himself. So beautiful and smart and willing to forgive. He was sure that she would forgive him – eventually anyway. The night before had been a beautiful start.

Henry sighed again. He had been sighing all morning, so thoroughly in love with Helen that, notwithstanding her commitment to the Communist Party, Henry could close his eyes and instantly see their future together, happy forever as man and wife. Henry would even visit her in prison if that's what it would take to prove his love.

When Helen finally arrived at the courthouse, Henry came bounding down the sidewalk to greet her. But his winning smile and his hands flapping 'hello' only reminded Helen of the mistakes she had made the night before. The first was choosing to make love to this ridiculous man. Whatever he was – a traitor, a double agent, or just some incompetent fool – she should have killed him in his sleep. That was her second mistake. She wanted to do it, but for some reason she could not pull the trigger. It seemed too cruel, like shooting a lost dog.

Henry was so clearly in love with her and Helen was so thoroughly disinterested in him that these polar opposites only seemed to pull them closer together. Quickly, Helen considered her options.

She had read in magazines about the difficulties women have in breaking off relationships. The best approach, they advised, was always the most direct. This was no time for subtlety and Helen could feel Henry's gun inside her blouse, pressed between her breasts. Perhaps it wasn't too late to get rid of him right then and there. Even with all the police and spectators waiting for the start of McCarthy's hearing, just one well-placed shot and she would be done with him. Better yet, if Henry truly was a traitor or a secret American agent, the Party would certainly be impressed by her bravery and decisiveness.

Helen was reaching for the pistol when Henry shouted, "Hello there, you!" If he had a ring in his pocket, Henry would have proposed to her on the spot because anything seemed possible on a day as beautiful as this one. As he moved toward her, Henry was expecting an embrace after their romantic night together, but Helen withdrew from him again. She crossed her arms and scowled at Henry, wondering how he could be so oblivious.

"You were up so early this morning. I thought – "

"Why are you still here?" Helen snapped.

"I thought I would make us breakfast this morning, but then you left before I could – "

"Didn't you hear me? Look around here, will you? There are cops all over the place and they are after you, Vladimir! They think you killed

Klingman, remember? Do-you-un-der-stand-what-I-am-say-ing-to-you? Now go away – I can't be seen with you!"

But the police were the last thing on Henry's mind. Before he could face Joe McCarthy's inquisition, he had to get things straight with Helen. He needed to tell her the truth about his life as former CIA Agent Henry Brownale. She needed to know this – and, of course, to forgive him – because Henry needed more nights with Helen.

"Listen, before we go in there, I have something important to tell you."

"Not now, I said! What don't you understand? If the cops see us together, they'll think I had something to do with Klingman's murder!" Helen spun away from him, nearly throwing the gun out of her blouse. She pushed the gun back into place as Henry grabbed her arm.

"Helen, wait. I love you."

They both knew it was true and yet they could not help but look at each other in surprise as Henry's voice carried across the courtyard. It echoed, just once, against the walls of the courthouse and then disappeared. Exhaling in disgust, Helen stormed off toward the Flag of the Unknown Soldier leaving Henry alone and confused.

Like everything else in Schenectady, the Flag of the Unknown Soldier was not what it seemed. There was nothing "unknown" about the Unknown Soldier. He had always been known. It was just that the community wanted to forget Gustave Fleuhkleumpklen, the Schenectady man who single-handedly killed more than 200 Germans during World War I.

Fleuhkleumpklen never wanted a monument in his honor and he certainly wanted no part of any celebration. He told everyone that war was cowardly and wrong and that he wanted them to know how sorry he was for killing all those Germans. Fleuhkleumpklen's pacifism greatly upset the city's leaders and they were determined to keep the monument in spite of Fleuhkleumpklen's wishes. His name was eventually chiseled off the memorial and neatly replaced with 'Unknown Soldier.' No one could pronounce Fleuhkleumpklen anyway.

Helen took a seat by the monument and waved at Henry to turn around and go inside. But the courthouse was the last place Henry wanted to be, with all the news cameras and reporters and, of course, Joe McCarthy waiting for him. He turned back toward Helen, but she was too busy throwing stones at the birds pecking near her feet.

Henry slowly climbed the courthouse stairs, one eye still focused on Helen, hoping she would turn and look his way. The birds knew better than Henry and they flew away before Helen could throw any more stones at them. Finally, Henry gave up and went inside, pressing himself through the thick crowd and past the stocky, young priest who was standing alone outside the courtroom.

Father Peter Lamonte was wearing his long, formal vestments, which drew curious looks from the people nearby. A few of them smiled, but no one approached the imposing priest.

It came naturally to him now, the training Father Lamonte received at the FBI's training academy at Lake Unity. Hidden up his sleeve was a long-barreled revolver. He would need two hands to control the powerful weapon, but the gun held only one bullet. There would be no time for a second shot. In this cavernous, marble hallway, the gun's explosive discharge would cause just enough chaos for Father Lamonte to escape. He wasn't expecting trouble – after all, he was a priest – but he took precautions nonetheless. His cloak, like the stole around his neck, was bulletproof and, inside his pocket, was a bottle of holy water and a set of brass knuckles.

Henry walked cautiously into the courtroom, taking a seat near the back of the gallery. The same fearful reluctance was shared by McCarthy's chief investigator, Duck Robertson, and the rest of McCarthy's team. They had conducted dozens of hearings over the years, but never had they seen anything like this: their star witness had been murdered and now the prime suspect was about to testify! After fruitless years of searching, they had finally caught an actual Communist spy. McCarthy's men were totally unprepared for this. They tried to look busy with small talk and theatrical pantomiming, straightening papers and arranging briefcases, rummaging through file folders that were only there for show – anything to hide the fact that they had no idea what they were going to do. They never had.

None of them could express the helplessness they were feeling as they looked at the enormous bank of television cameras and news photographers and the gallery filling up with politicians, union members, and G.E. executives. In their gut was the realization that none of this mattered. All of their half-baked "investigations," interrogating printing clerks, Foreign Service librarians, and left-wing book clubs had been a colossal waste of time. They had been hounding housewives and grilling meaningless bureaucrats without once uncovering anything of significance, much less a single, prosecutable crime. Four years of playing cat and mouse and all they had to show for it was this big piece of cheese, Senator Joseph R. McCarthy.

Until now. Until Nick Lansing, aka Vladimir, the murderous spy.

McCarthy's team tried to understand the gravity of what they had uncovered in this sleepy Upstate city. But the sun was shining outside and this gave them hope that everything would go right that day.

Question: What should we do about the Soviet spy system in America?
Answer: Since American Communists are so necessary to the Soviet spy rings, we must concentrate on exposing every one of them, wherever they may be found.

100 THINGS YOU SHOULD KNOW ABOUT COMMUNISM IN THE USA
PUBLISHED BY THE HOUSE UN-AMERICAN ACTIVITIES COMMITTEE

CHAPTER SIXTY

SORRY PAL

Henry's night with Helen had been one of the greatest moments of his life. How many moments, he was not exactly sure. (Not enough, he guessed, based on the way Helen was acting this morning.) Somehow, he had gotten through it and now he wanted more.

Henry did not have a lot of experience with this sort of thing. None of his previous "experiences" with women had lasted very long or, perhaps, long enough. Henry knew this going in, so to speak. It was Helen who was the revelation. She was more beautiful than he could have imagined and he had been imagining Helen for a very long time.

As Helen undressed him – roughly tearing away at his shirt and his pants – Henry realized that some sort of distraction would be necessary if he was going to be the kind of man Henry wanted to be that night. Joe McCarthy seemed to be an obvious choice. Bringing Joe along would keep Henry's mind off Helen, while every other part of him was all over her.

So Henry, naked and afraid, shut his eyes tightly and thought long and hard about Joe McCarthy and the hearing taking place the next day, testifying before a United States Senator, and knowing that he had no clue about what he was going to say. How could Henry explain that an ex-CIA agent had gotten himself entangled in the same Communist conspiracy that he was supposed to be exposing? Thinking of an explanation was going to take some time and time was exactly what Henry needed as he made love to Helen.

Just a little more time, Henry prayed, as he anxiously moved around Helen's bed and over her tender body; longingly, achingly, awkwardly kissing and fawning over her, constantly watching for any kind of signal about what he should be doing and where he should be doing it and, throughout this libidinous ordeal, Henry was trying to keep Joe McCarthy foremost in his thoughts, rehearsing the lines that he would say in front of all those television cameras and newspaper reporters, until it occurred to Henry that thinking about Senate testimony or baseball or almost anything else is virtually impossible when so much else is going on: all that rubbing and grabbing and breathing and moaning and reaching for this and holding that, over here and over there … yes, there! Nearly –

There.

And so the Earth moved that night and with it came another day. Now Henry was truly out of time. Sitting alone in the courtroom was nearly as excruciating as lying in Helen's bed. He was feeling just as naked and unprepared. Making love to Helen had been unexpected, of course, but testifying in front of McCarthy was even more absurd.

Here was the son of the late, great Congressman Conrad Brownale, the scion once in line for the Presidency of the United States, now accused of spying for the Soviets! How could he hope to make McCarthy understand when even Henry could not believe it?

Milo! It had to be Milo. Milo could explain this mess. He promised he would. But where was he?

Henry craned his neck above the crowd, but it was difficult to find such a little man in a crowd this large. Everyone was jammed elbow to elbow until they were spilling out of the courtroom gallery, filling the hallways and lining the courthouse stairs. Every few feet stood a Schenectady cop. At Volk's instruction, they were to keep "Nick Lansing" in their sights until Senator McCarthy had thoroughly grilled him. Whatever was left of Nick Lansing would be put under arrest.

The crowd started to notice Henry as he searched the courtroom for Milo. They gawked and pointed until Henry could hear their whispered accusations:

"That's the one – he's the spy!"

"They say he's a murderer!"

"He killed the Lindbergh baby!"

Trapped in this make-believe conspiracy, Henry suddenly remembered that old song from the radio, "It Could Only Happen in Schenectady." Nothing about that song was any good. It certainly didn't end well.

Suddenly, McCarthy's one-eyed investigator, Duck Robertson, was standing over him. The hearing was about to begin.

Robertson led Henry to the front of the courtroom and before Henry could sit down, Robertson handed him a note. "Don't worry," it read. "Wait for my signal. I still have my duck. – J. McCarthy."

Henry's mouth fell open. Maybe it *is* true! What if Helen is right and Joe McCarthy is actually working for the Reds? Could McCarthy help him escape this nightmare? If pretending to be a Russian agent could set him free, then Henry was willing to play along for a little while longer.

Helen would know what to do, Henry decided. He had to talk to Helen!

Henry scanned the courtroom again, but his eyes immediately locked onto the steel-jawed glare of Wotan Volk. Volk smiled stiffly from the back of the courtroom, weighing Henry like a slab of meat in Schicksal's butcher shop window. Next to Volk stood Frankie Pepper, smiling eagerly as he thought about the promised merger of Local 1389 and the IUEW. On the other side of Volk was Walter Thurston, that FBI flatfoot. Thurston smiled meekly at Henry, putting his hands up as if to say, "Sorry pal, what can I do?"

Bastard, Henry snarled.

Duck Robertson cleared his throat and the courtroom grew still for Senator McCarthy's grand entrance. This time, McCarthy came in from the hallway connected by a side door in the courtroom. (The district judge had locked his office door directly behind the bench. He was not going to let McCarthy steal any more of his liquor.) Still, McCarthy was able to find one of the judge's robes along with a gavel that was much stronger than the one he had broken in his first visit to Schenectady. He was ready this time.

"Ladies and gentlemen," McCarthy began, "I'm afraid I have shocking news this morning. Our star witness, Arthur Lindbergh, has been murdered. Based on very convincing evidence gathered by the Schenectady Police Department, Mr. Lindbergh's death appears to be the work of the Soviet Secret Service!"

The audience gasped as news photographers, leaping like gazelles, jumped from their seats as McCarthy held up photos of the crime scene. There were pictures of grim-faced detectives standing over Klingman's body, his tiny arms and legs spread out like a bloody snow angel. McCarthy struck his gavel, returning order to the courtroom.

"Clearly, this cowardly and barbaric act was meant to keep Mr. Lindbergh from testifying here today. He would have told us about the ongoing conspiracy behind the walls of General Electric, a plot by the International Communist Conspiracy to steal high-security building passes, floor plans, and, ultimately, top-secret weapons from G.E.!"

McCarthy leaned over the bench. "In other words people: KA-BOOM!" He lifted his hands off the bench, pantomiming the mushroom cloud of a nuclear bomb. The spectators turned in horror to one another. This time, McCarthy let the murmuring continue.

Outside the courthouse, Helen was still sitting alone under the Flag of the Unknown Soldier. She smiled a little as she looked up at the Soviet flag. It reminded her of Camp Unity and the people she had met there – Anna Tilson most of all.

"Helen?" Martha Milwaukee, overdressed and overbearing, was

standing over Helen. "Were you day dreaming, Helen? Not very vigilant of you, comrade."

"Not very funny," Helen said under her breath. "What are you doing here, Martha?"

"I came down here because Milo is going to be making a big announcement this morning. And what about you? I thought Senator McCarthy wanted to talk with you."

"I'm actually looking forward to meeting him. I am not afraid like some people."

"I don't understand."

"No kidding, Martha. You never did."

Martha forced a smile. "So where is that young man I saw you talking to?"

"That idiot? He went inside."

"Honestly Helen, when will you learn? All men are idiots. It's our job to set them straight."

"You're always so helpful, aren't you Martha? Always setting people straight. Why the hell did I ever listen to you?"

"Listen to me? You didn't hear a single thing I said last night!"

"No, I heard every stupid word of it: How the Communists are monsters and Communism is a nightmare. Fine, Martha, that's your opinion. But did you ever think to say, 'Thank you, Helen?' How about a thank you for saving your neck last night or thanking me for running around town the past three years, carrying out all of your ridiculous plans!"

"We all have made sacrifices."

"Ha – you can say that again! I paid for mine in an alley off James Street."

"Honestly Helen, make sense! What are you talking about?"

"I mean all of your stupid ideas, Martha: The bowling, the beer, the TV shows – all of the fluff and nonsense that you pushed me into – none of it was for the Revolution! It was all about you, wasn't it? I learned the importance of vigilance at Camp Unity and then – because of you! – I had to learn it all over again. Petrov beat it into me good this time and it was all because of you and your counter-revolutionary bullshit!"

"Beat you? Petrov beat you? When did this happen? Why didn't you tell me?"

Helen looked hard at Martha and for a few seconds she wouldn't speak. "That's funny, Martha. Somehow, I thought you knew."

Martha tried not to show it, but she knew, of course. She had made the phone call to Petrov and now Martha could not hide her shame.

Helen looked down at her hands, surprised that they were shaking. "Yes, I got the message loud and clear, thanks to you and Comrade Petrov. For months now, I have been living in absolute terror, afraid that he was going to come back here and I would not be ready to show him what I have accomplished, that I have learned my lesson – that I am vigilant now! The funny thing is, why was I the only one who suffered? How vigilant were you, Martha? And what about Milo? This was all his idea, wasn't it? Of course, it's always better to be the boss instead of the worker, isn't that right, you Capitalist stooge?"

Martha stepped toward Helen. "I'm nobody's stooge – not anymore. And neither is Milo. He has been trying to do what's right – you know that – and I'm sorry that things have gotten so out of hand. It's what I was trying to warn you about last night. You have to listen to me. Yes, there is great danger, but we have more choices than you realize. We know the truth now! Just wait and see. Milo will make it right today, I promise you."

"Make it right? What are you saying?"

"Local 1389 is moving into the IUEW."

"Frankie Pepper's union? Milo is closing the Local? You can't be serious!"

"No he's *saving* the Local, don't you see?"

Helen turned her face away from Martha. It was another gut-wrenching betrayal by the Milwaukees! Rage swelled inside of Helen until the lessons of Camp Unity came back to her: disguise your feelings from your enemies. Helen turned around and with innocence and faux wonder reflecting in her eyes, she smiled at Martha as if everything was forgiven.

"Of course," she said, "I see it now. It had to come to an end." Helen held out her arms and embraced Martha – until her arms suddenly dropped to her side. She lifted her head toward the courthouse, listening intently. Then Martha heard it too.

Shouts and screams were coming from inside the courthouse, terrifying noises that grew louder as people fled down the courthouse stairs and the police tried to push their way in. Loudest of all was the blast of a single gunshot and for a brief moment everything went quiet before the pandemonium continued into the streets and down State Street hill.

All on a midwinter morning too beautiful to be believed.

"How can we account for our present situation unless we believe that men high in this Government are concerting to deliver us to disaster? This must be the product of a great conspiracy, a conspiracy on a scale so immense as to dwarf any previous such venture in the history of man. A conspiracy of infamy so black that, when it is finally exposed, its principals shall be forever deserving of the maledictions of all honest men. Who constitutes the highest circles of this conspiracy? About that we cannot be sure."

SENATOR MCCARTHY *guessing again, in a speech before the Senate*

CHAPTER SIXTY-ONE

EARLIER IN THE COURTROOM

" – and so, on behalf of the Senate Subcommittee on Permanent Investigations, I wish to express our condolences to the entire Lindbergh family. Will everyone please join us in a moment of silence?"

In the Senate, it is called a filibuster. But in the federal courthouse on that February morning, as the gallery, the cops, and the news reporters baked under white-hot camera lights, Joe McCarthy gave an opening address that stretched for nearly twenty minutes. He catalogued every complaint and all the suspicious activity that he had investigated, chewed on, and spit out since the day he claimed to have a list of 205 Communists working in the State Department. McCarthy's list of "accomplishments and victories" was long and monotonous, punctuated every few seconds with McCarthy raising his head toward the courtroom door and his eyes searching the crowd. McCarthy then asked for another moment of silence to honor Arthur Klingman. This time the prayer went on for thirty seconds and then a minute – and then for another minute – as McCarthy continued to check the door, check the clock, and then check the crowd again.

Finally, McCarthy could not wait any longer. Reluctantly, the Senator called for the first witness.

"Nick Lansing," announced Duck Robertson. It took a moment for Henry to realize that his name had been called and that everyone in the courtroom was looking at him. Suddenly, he felt a gigantic hand grab the back of his collar and lift him off his chair. He turned to see Wotan Volk's belly pressed against his face as the massive detective pushed Henry toward the witness table.

"Let's hurry this up," Volk said, loud enough for McCarthy to hear. The crowd stepped aside as Volk strode back to his place in the rear of the courtroom. He scanned the line of cops standing at attention, all of them waiting for Volk's signal to arrest "Nick Lansing."

"Inspector Volk?"

Volk recognized the voice. It was George Schidell, General Electric's Chief of Security, but Volk would not look down at Schidell. He kept his eyes locked on Henry Brownale seated at the witness table.

"Uh … Chief Inspector?" Schidell asked again. "Chief Inspector – please! Mr. Reedy needs to speak with you."

Volk swiveled his head toward the door. There was Philip Reedy, the General Electric CEO, standing by the courtroom entrance and alongside him was Milo Milwaukee. Why they were together, Volk did not know and he did not have time to find out. Volk's gaze swiveled back to Henry.

Volk said quietly, "You see that witness up there, Schidell? That is the man responsible for the murder that took place on company property the other night. Mr. Reedy should be very pleased that we caught this guy, don't you think?"

"Yes, but Mr. Reedy …"

"So why are you still bothering me, Schidell, when I am about to make an arrest?"

"That is what I've been trying to tell you! That man up there is not the one you're looking for!"

Volk turned away from Henry and smiled down at Schidell. "Schidell – listen to me. You're a security guard. A well-paid security guard, but still, you're just a security guard. Leave the police work to me, all right?"

"Chief Inspector, you are wrong and that's what Mr. Reedy wants to tell you! That man is not a Russian spy, he's actually – "

Volk squared his shoulders as he bent over Schidell. "Are you gonna keep tellin' me how to do my job, Schidell? Of course not. So why don't you go away now and tell Mr. Reedy – " The words suddenly caught in the detective's throat. Volk turned to the front of the courtroom. Instantly, he knew something was wrong.

Surveying the courtroom, Volk took in the missing pieces: McCarthy – gone, Nick Lansing – gone.

"What the – ? Where did – ? Where are they? *WHERE IS HE?*" Volk shouted frantically, hoisting spectators out of his way as he lumbered down the aisle. "Goddammit – where did they go? WHERE ARE THEY?"

The Schenectady patrolmen looked stunned. They all assumed that Volk had been watching as McCarthy got up from the bench and pointed his gavel toward Philip Reedy and Milo Milwaukee, directing them to meet him outside the courtroom. McCarthy then signaled for Nick Lansing to follow him out the door. Had Volk missed that too?

The crowd drew back in panic as the giant detective flipped over chairs and tossed the witness table over the railing. In their fright, none of the spectators would notice the slight Russian accent that suddenly appeared in the voice of Wotan Volk.

The detective feverishly pulled on the door to the judge's chamber, but it was tightly bolted from the inside, protecting the judge's liquor cabinet. Volk pounded on the door with both fists until Duck Robertson grabbed Volk by the arm to steer him toward the side exit.

"What did you *DO?*" Volk screamed as he heaved Robertson to the floor. Volk was lost, spinning in circles, as he pulled a gun from beneath his trench coat.

"Don't shoot!" Robertson shrieked in a voice that leaped above high C. Spectators, reporters, and even the police stampeded for the doors, falling over chairs and climbing out windows as Volk pointed the gun in all directions. In the crush of bodies, Father Lamonte calmly followed the mob out into the hallway. He made no attempt to stop the fistfights and wrestling matches between the rival unions, the cops, and the courthouse security. Instead, the priest took a position on a small, ornamental staircase. He set his feet on the smooth, marble stairs and carefully drew the gun from out of his sleeve. Standing above the crowd, Lamonte had an unobstructed view of his target at the far end of the hallway.

There, on the opposite staircase, stood a befuddled Joe McCarthy huddled between Philip Reedy and Milo Milwaukee. Milo was trying to be heard above the chaos echoing in the hallway, shouting at McCarthy that "Nick Lansing" was actually a former agent of the CIA. But McCarthy was too frightened to listen as he tried to hide between two Corinthian columns. Through Father Lamonte's gunsight, McCarthy looked like a Roman sitting duck.

Loosening his collar, the priest took in a deep breath as his eyes narrowed on the target: a birthmark just below McCarthy's hairline. The priest silently recited one Hail Mary as he wrapped his finger around the trigger and waited for McCarthy to stop fidgeting. McCarthy's men, meanwhile, were desperately fighting their way through the crowd. Clawing his way behind them was Henry Brownale, straining to reach Milo's outstretched hand.

"Henry!" Milo shouted. "Tell him! Tell the Senator – !" Henry lifted himself over the clutch of bodies, his feet and knees riding on top of backs, shoulders, and heads, until he was eyeball to eyeball with Joe McCarthy. Henry tried to gather the words to explain what he was doing there – not just on top of this mob, but why he had been posing as a Russian spy, trying to do what his father had instructed him to do but then he fell in love again – with another Communist, wouldn't you know? – and that's when things got really complicated, Senator –

Father Lamonte squeezed the trigger.

The gunshot exploded through the courthouse, sending everyone diving for the floor. When they opened their eyes again, the white Corinthian columns were splattered in red and a delicate mist of blood and bone was sprayed across Joe McCarthy's face and down the judge's robe. Henry saw this, too, before everything seemed to turn upside down. The ceiling suddenly rotated into view as the chandeliers and wall portraits disappeared below. Henry's head bounced against the floor, his lifeless body sliding through the pool of blood that was spilling out of his skull. There wasn't time to feel any pain. There was no need to worry about what he should do next. Finally, Henry Brownale had come to rest.

At the other end of the hall, Father Lamonte stashed the gun inside a trash can before smoothing his cleric's robe. He walked briskly to the car waiting for him in back of the courthouse. Special Agent Walter Thurston was at the wheel.

"Did you get him?" Thurston asked, gunning the engine.

The priest took out a cigarette and shook his head.

"We are all imperfect creatures."

"What the hell does that mean?"

"It means I missed."

"Christ," Thurston muttered. "The boss is not going to be happy."

Lamonte rolled down the window, letting the cigarette smoke escape into the breeze. Squinting into the sun, Lamonte sighed, "God's will be done."

"As an American, I am shocked at the way Republicans and Democrats alike are playing directly into the Communist design of 'confuse, divide, and conquer.' As an American, I don't want a Democratic Administration 'white wash' or 'cover up' any more than I want a Republican smear or witch hunt … They are equally dangerous to you and me and to our country. As an American, I want to see our nation recapture the strength and unity it once had when we fought the enemy instead of ourselves."

"DECLARATION OF CONSCIENCE" BY REPUBLICAN SENATOR MARGARET CHASE SMITH

read before the United States Senate on June 1, 1950

CHAPTER SIXTY-TWO

THE BIG ONE

Milo put his shoulder under McCarthy's arm and helped him down to the floor. They stepped over Henry's body, slipping along the wet marble and the bloody shoe prints spread across the floor. Wotan Volk and Philip Reedy were waiting for them by the courthouse door. In his daze, McCarthy looked skeptically down at Milo.

"Who are you?"

"We met last night, Senator. I'm Milo Milwaukee."

"You think so? You look different."

"McCarthy – eyes front!" Reedy barked as he grabbed hold of McCarthy's robe. "Now pay attention – this is what you're going to do. You're going to take off this stupid robe and you're going to follow Milo here outside. Then you're going to stand next to him while he makes his announcement to the press. Have you got that? And you'll keep your mouth shut, do you hear me? No speeches, no nothing! You just stand there and, by God, don't you screw this up!"

McCarthy tried to nod his head, but his eyes could only search the air, spinning like a Whirl-a-Bed.

"Sure thing. Whatever you say."

With panic in her voice, Martha raced up the courthouse stairs, shouting, "Milo! Where's Milo!" For the first time in their tumultuous marriage, Martha and Milo met each other halfway – and eye to eye – as they embraced in the middle of the staircase. She lifted him off his feet and called his name with every kiss she planted on his face. "Oh, Milo, Milo, Milo, Milo, Milo!"

When she put him down, Milo wiped the lipstick off his cheeks and adjusted his pointy hair. The crowd parted ahead of them as Milo took Martha's hand, leading her toward the crowd of reporters gathered at the Flag of the Unknown Soldier. The sun had melted away the snow and a breeze unfurled an enormous American flag flying above the Little Giant. Behind him stood Joseph McCarthy, Philip Reedy, Mayor Mudlick, and several members of Local 1389. Some of the men looked nervously at McCarthy, wondering why he was standing next to their boss, and McCarthy, still in a daze, smiled back at the union men, happy to see news cameras – and not guns – pointed his way. In the back of this scrum, Frankie Pepper was jumping up and down, struggling to get in front of the cameras. Milo's men locked their arms to keep Pepper back.

"I have an announcement to make," Milo said solemnly. "As we all know, thousands of Americans have given their lives in the two world wars of this century. Thousands more have been lost in the conflict to save South Korea. But no matter when and no matter where our soldiers have died, all of them were fighting to protect our way of life and to keep us safe here at home. This week, sadly, we have learned that we are still not safe – not even here in Schenectady."

Milo looked over to the courthouse as Henry's body was being carried down the stairs. His eyes moved down the sidewalk where Helen was standing next to Martha. The Morale Coordinator – his cheerleader for the union – was smiling at him, but she did not look happy. The fury in her eyes made Milo pause for a moment before he returned to his speech.

"I say to you today that this bloodshed cannot continue. A new chapter must begin and it will begin today with the members of Local 1389. Our union must confront an inescapable question – can our Local stay together or will it be torn apart and break this city along with it? As the elected leader of Local 1389, it is my responsibility to protect the interests of my members. I have the same responsibility to this city. We need a new beginning and an acknowledgment that there are real dangers facing our union, our city, and our nation."

A messenger walked up to the group and nodded to Philip Reedy.

"They're ready," Reedy whispered to Milo.

"Local 1389 is made up of loyal, hard-working Americans," Milo told the reporters. "Skilled laborers who make this country great. Many are war veterans who fought and suffered for their country – all of them patriots. For too long, their loyalty has been questioned by people who have mistaken unionism for Communism. We are unionists first, just as we are Americans first. Starting today and, for every day hereafter, no one will question their patriotism again! I want everyone to follow me now – down to the plant. It's time for our workers to be heard!"

The reporters were shouting questions at Milo as the Little Giant pulled a hat over his pointy hair. With a snap of his hand, he led the crowd down the hill to Milwaukee Hall. Frankie Pepper reached out his hand to Milo, yelling "Milo! Milo, wait!" Milo grabbed it roughly, pulling Frankie into an awkward embrace.

"I got a call from the police chief, Frankie. He says a patrolman spotted you and me out together last night – searching for Joe McCarthy! Imagine my surprise!"

"That's crazy. You and me?"

"But we both know you were drivin' around with that little gunsel from Scarpino's gang, weren't you Frankie?"

"Look Milo, I can explain!"

"Too late, Frankie. What's important now is your cooperation because something big is about to happen and if you don't go along, Mr. Reedy and I won't be able to help you fix this problem with the Schenectady cops. Do you understand what I'm saying? Now here's your ride, Frankie."

Pepper turned in surprise to see his union car pulling up beside them. Inside were Pepper's secretary, Darlene, and Maury, his accountant. Frankie stumbled toward the car, but Milo waved it on ahead.

"Think about it, Frankie!" Milo called over his shoulder as everyone else raced to keep up with Milo's parade. The sunshine was pouring over their faces as, one by one, the press men turned to one another and smiled in surprise: the scent of fried bacon came floating up the hill. Martha smelled it too as she took Milo by the arm and the two of them marched together down State Street hill.

"Senator McCarthy!" shouted Helen, straining to break through the pack. "Senator – do you have a duck?"

McCarthy stopped in the middle of the street. He turned to see a beautiful, young woman far back in the crowd. More astonishing were the words she was calling out to him.

"A duck?" McCarthy replied. He called to his bodyguards, "Let her through! Let that woman pass!" Helen walked up to McCarthy, close enough to whisper, "Yes, I have a duck. Do you?"

McCarthy smiled in wide-eyed wonder. "I have a duck too!" McCarthy pulled her aside until they were alone on the sidewalk.

"Comrade," he said urgently, "I have been waiting so long for this. I was so afraid the Party was going to leave me here – leave me behind! They promised to keep me safe if there was ever a time when, you know, they were going to drop the Big One and now you're here!"

Helen put her hands to her face as she started to cry.

"Please don't cry, my dear. Please don't cry. Is it because of that young man – the one that was shot? Did you know him?"

Helen nodded her head as she pressed her face against McCarthy's shoulder.

"He was not with us," she cried softly. "He was an imposter, but he loved me, I guess."

"Comrade, hush. We must be brave."

"I will be," Helen said. She wiped away her tears and looked straight into McCarthy's eyes. "I can be brave. I will do it right now – but I need your help."

Up ahead, Milo was turning the corner onto Erie Boulevard, a street as wide as a football field, and, as he came into view, a thunderous roar came from 40,000 General Electric workers filling the entire street, from Milwaukee Hall to the front gates of the factory. At Milo's request, Philip Reedy had ceased operations in the plant. Workers from every shift had hurried downtown and now every face was turned toward Milo as he strode up the stairs of the union hall.

Milo stopped at the front door, taking in a deep breath as he looked up at the plaque bearing his name. He turned to face the G.E. workers as McCarthy and the others crowded in behind him. Martha stood over Milo's left shoulder and Helen was on his right. Martha looked curiously over at Helen, who was smiling and waving to the crowd. Why should Helen be hogging the spotlight with Milo and me? Martha asked herself. She was about to say something when Milo raised his hands and the enormous crowd went still.

"My union brothers and sisters," Milo said into the microphone. "We have come together for a moment of great importance for Local 1389." Gesturing to the people behind him, Milo acknowledged the "trust and support of my family and friends – including some new friends." McCarthy meekly waved as boos rippled through the crowd. As Milo turned farther to his right, he was surprised to see Helen Gamble standing between him and Joe McCarthy. Milo hesitated for a moment as Helen scowled back at him. Milo quickly turned the other way and he smiled to see Martha standing there. She gave him a reassuring pat on the shoulder. Joe McCarthy, meanwhile, was urgently pulling on Helen's arm.

"Comrade – comrade!" he whispered. "This is bad, isn't it? The Party won't like this, will they?"

"Shhhh," Helen replied angrily.

At the microphone, his voice echoing through the loudspeakers, Milo proclaimed, "Local 1389 was built with your muscle and your sweat. Together on this day, we stand once more to dedicate our lives to building a new and better future for our union, our city, and our country!" As the crowd cheered, McCarthy continued to plead with Helen.

"Comrade, we have got to do something! I don't want to die!" Helen pushed McCarthy's hand off of her. "I'm so afraid of what they're going to do!"

"Members of Local 1389 – " Milo shouted as McCarthy kept blathering to Helen, tugging on her sleeve, pleading for an answer.

"It's the Big One, isn't it? Are they going to drop the Big One?"

"A union is meant to protect its members from outside forces, corporate, political, and all others. This has become nearly impossible when we are forced to choose between our rights as American citizens with our rights as unionized craftsmen and laborers. For these reasons, I am proposing today that Local 1389 move into the International Union of Electrical Workers. Those in favor – "

Helen turned to McCarthy, a gun in her hand. "It happens right now," she said. Helen raised the gun in the air until it reached a spot behind Milo's right ear.

" – please signify by saying 'aye!'"

"AYE!" roared the 40,000 as Helen pulled the trigger.

No one seemed to notice the gunshot or the fact that Milo's snappy fedora was now floating alone at the top of the stairs. Milo had disappeared beneath it, his knees buckling as he fell into a heap at the bottom of the stairs.

EPILOGUE

No one in Schenectady could ever forget 1954.

America's Red Scare had fallen over the city like a poisonous cloud and then, just as quickly, it had floated away. It was also the end for Joe McCarthy.

Four years after his speech in Wheeling, West Virginia, McCarthy would be exposed as a fraud in front of a nationwide television audience. His investigation into the U.S. Army ended abruptly when J. Edgar Hoover provided crucial evidence against his former protégé, leading the Senate to officially censure McCarthy. In just three more years, Tailgunner Joe was dead, his liver shriveled from years of heavy drinking.

Near the end, McCarthy would ask anyone he encountered whether they had a duck and would they please take him to Moscow before somebody dropped the Big One. No one ever had a duck and no one heard the disgraced senator crying himself to sleep at night.

The murders in Schenectady ensured that no one would know the truth about Wotan Volk. Other Russian spies were not so fortunate. A number of them were discovered over the years. One of them, Harold "Kim" Philby, was a young scholar at Cambridge University where he and four other students were recruited by the Soviet spy service. For years, Philby was a Russian mole inside the British Secret Service – nearly becoming the director of MI6 – before his spy ring was discovered and Philby absconded to a hero's welcome in Russia.

Communist espionage would continue. In less than a decade, a luckless Marxist named Lee Harvey Oswald would take a job in the Texas Book Depository and, with one lucky shot, Oswald would change history.

Other unions in America would steadily break free from the Communists. It didn't change the politicians. Both Republicans and Democrats courted votes by railing against the Red Menace. Congress even voted to outlaw the Communist Party in 1954. It didn't matter much by then: the American Communist Party had evaporated to just a few thousand members. Finally, J. Edgar Hoover stopped writing checks to keep the Party alive.

Hoover's great enemy, the CIA, continued to fumble its way around the world. In the summer of 1954, the Agency staged a successful if improvised coup in Iran, overthrowing the country's religious leaders in favor of the Shah. The agency would be less successful when it tried to manipulate the leadership of Vietnam, the French colony few Americans had ever known.

The consumer boom and prosperity that followed World War II was in high gear by the mid-1950s. General Electric executives reaped a huge financial windfall in 1954 when they shared bonuses worth $10 million. That was also the year Ronald Reagan visited Schenectady, his first stop in a new career as the television spokesman for G.E.

Television was by then the dominant entertainment medium in the country. Thousands of television sets were sold that year and by Christmas millions of kids would find a coonskin cap under the tree, just like the one worn by Davey Crockett on TV.

That was still ten months away. Spring would arrive soon and with it came the first pitch of the new Little League baseball season. Michael Milwaukee would rejoin the team and by the end of that summer, Schenectady would win the Little League World Series. When he got back home, Michael got his first kiss from Sandra Pepper.

For Helen Gamble, it would be a last kiss that she would remember – the last time she held her baby boy in the infirmary of the Mid-Hudson Correctional Facility for Women. The little boy she named Vladimir could not be raised in a women's prison. He would be given to a good home, they told Helen. Their tone was kind and solicitous as if they were trying to convince Helen to make the right decision, as if she had any choice at all.

Civil rights moved forward in 1954 as the Supreme Court ruled against segregation and the convenient lie that public schools could be "separate but equal." It would be another three years before President Eisenhower would bring in the National Guard to escort nine Black students into an all-white high school in Little Rock, Arkansas.

Then the world changed again: on July 19th, a skinny kid from Memphis recorded his first hit record. Elvis Presley sang, "That's All Right" and the song became a huge hit. Martha, of course, hated rock and roll and she tried her best to keep Michael from listening to it.

Loud music, loud guns – Martha's nerves were shot.

Milo had put her through a lot in those last years: him pretending to be a Red and plotting with Helen to foment a phony Communist Revolution. Of course every marriage has its ups and downs. Husbands and wives drive each other crazy and there were so many times when Martha wanted to give Milo a swift kick in the pants.

Years later, Martha would realize that she and Milo should have talked more. At least, they could have been more honest with each other. But there was no time for words or regrets on the stairs of Milwaukee Hall that fateful morning. There wasn't time to shout "Watch out" or "I love you" once Helen pulled out that gun. There was only enough time for Martha to step forward and take charge as she always wanted to do.

And didn't Milo deserve a little help considering all that he had done and all that he was going to do? After all their years together, didn't Martha deserve that – and Michael too?

So when Martha saw the gun moving toward her husband's pointy head – when there was only enough time for her to step forward and give Milo a swift kick in the pants – that's exactly what she did on that brilliant February morning, sending Milo tumbling down the stairs – safe from Helen's bullet – as 40,000 workers cheered their new day.

The End